He removed the stones one by one, dropped the kindling into the pit, dropped the stones on top and lit the fire. When the rocks glowed, he removed his boots, and when he walked across the red-hot stones, Venus felt a visceral convulsion.

She knew she was next.

She had heard of fire walkers. She had heard they met secretly in the mountains, often in the national forests, to hold their scorching rituals, to test their faith in the power of prayer, or simply, in the strength of human will.

Gerald stood on the opposite side of the glowing stones. With one arm, he beckoned her. "Come across," he said.

She could barely make out his facial features. He repeated his command. "Come across." So this was how he tested loyalty.

He waited, but Venus could feel his growing impatience. She leaned down, slowly removed her boots, her socks. Reminding herself that others had done this and survived, she leapt onto the stones.

———————— ————————

SKYE KATHLEEN MOODY

K FALLS

W RLDWIDE®

TORONTO • NEW YORK • LONDON
AMSTERDAM • PARIS • SYDNEY • HAMBURG
STOCKHOLM • ATHENS • TOKYO • MILAN
MADRID • WARSAW • BUDAPEST • AUCKLAND

K FALLS

A Worldwide Mystery/July 2002

First published by St. Martin's Press, Incorporated.

ISBN 0-373-26426-7

Printed in U.S.A.

Acknowledgments

Thanks
to Matthew Speten, fellow explorer and river runner,
to DM for fire walking,
to Tony Outhwaite for insight and encouragement,
and to the late Edward Abbey,
whose novel *The Monkey Wrench Gang*
got it right.
As always, thanks to GBS, a true friend.

In Memory of

Peter John Giles and Russell Brisendine
and for all the victims and families who survived
the November 3, 1999, Northlake Shipyard tragedy.

Grandfather
Look at our brokenness.
We know that in all creation
Only the human family
Has strayed from the sacred way.
We know that we are the ones
Who are divided
And we are the ones
Who must come back together
To walk in the sacred way
Grandfather
Sacred one,
Teach us love, compassion, honor
That we may heal the earth
And heal each other.

—Ojibway prayer

PROLOGUE

EVERY RIVER HAS A headwater, a place of birth. High in the Canadian Rockies, the Columbia River is constantly aborning. Up there, encircled by ice-clad alpine peaks, lies a diminutive lake, sparkling cold, deep, and freshwater blue. For eons, this modest lagoon, named Columbia Lake, has birthed a mighty river flow that travels a remarkable 1,210 miles on a serpentine ramble to the ocean at the border of Washington and Oregon. From its pristine Canadian headwaters, the Columbia grows in size and power, flowing due north for 198 miles, headed straight for the Arctic Ocean, its raging waters carving sheer cliffs through the granite Selkirks. But when the river reaches the head of the Selkirks, it turns west, hugging the mountains' curve in an abrupt hairpin turn that takes it sharply southward again, where it flows down-continent, crossing the Canadian border and entering the United States in the Lower Okanogans in eastern Washington State. From there, the Columbia travels 688 more miles before turning west toward the Pacific. On the way, the river barrels over numerous natural waterfalls, its icy blue waters tossing up crisp freshwater spray and the whitest foam rapids any human has ever tried to conquer. Gouging through natural coulees, it carves through sandstone bluffs, forges a deep channel in the arid desert scablands, and, nearing the ocean, sculpts out a deep granite gorge, deeper even, than the Grand Canyon.

Until the arrival of the first white settlers on the Columbia, explorers, salmon fishermen, and loggers, before what they called "civilization" came to the Columbia, the river teemed with marine life, with salmon, steelhead trout, eagles, with beaver and river otters, whose fur made fine cloaks for the native people who settled near its banks. For thousands of years, the river had lived in harmony with the lands it visited and had provided abundant gifts to those who took only what they needed, and took with respect, knowing that the river and each of its inhabitants, like all the creatures of the land and sky, had souls. The river abounded with riches, but it also claimed lives as the new settlers first used the raging waterway for fishing, then to float logs from the massive timber harvests, then as irrigation, and, finally, for hydro-electric power. In the short space of two hundred years, the fishing, logging, and agricultural industries sucked the river's natural estuaries dry, diverted the flow. When in springtime, the farmers' fields lay strewn with millions of silver corpses of salmon that had lost their way home in the irrigation diversions, putrid, decaying corpses, the farmers marveled over the way their fields shone bright silver beneath the sun. The salmon's silver skin reflected so brightly that it blinded the farmers, who cursed the damage to their fields. After ''civilization'' discovered the Columbia River, change came rapidly at the hands of people who had forgotten that Nature has a soul.

ONE

THE BEAVERS INHABITING Turtle Creek Basin had jury-rigged a cedar-stick dam across the flow, creating a still pond that the big man hadn't counted on. He had to step high to avoid being splinter-pricked in the caboose, and when he finally had navigated the beaver dam, he then had to wade the shallow pond it had created to get where he was going—a dam bigger than any damn troop of beavers had ever dreamed of, if beavers dream. His galoshes slogging through the pond exactly matched in rhythm and cadence the thumping sound of Bobby Beaver's flat tail. The big man peered through stingy moonlight and eventually spied Bobby, hunched over a cedar stump whose flesh he had gnawed into a pencil-point peak, whose trunk had been felled for the sake of the little beaver industry. Humph, thought the big man tromping the pond. You wanna see a dam? Follow me, Bobby Beaver, and I'll show you what fer.

Over the bald, dry ridge lay an attenuated coulee that the big man had to cross to reach his destination three miles distant. A moldy yellow moon with a toothless, gaping sneer shed thin light across the barren mountaintops and poured down along the coulee's granite walls onto the flat valley floor, where, eons past, raging glacier melt had carved a zigzag pattern that made the big man think of an Indian rug. He lifted his mud-soaked boots out of the pond, tightened the straps of his bulging backpack, and climbed a knobby knoll, where he stood on the brink of the rise, his black shadow throwing a light-starved void across the coulee. And he thought of Darla.

A man about to commit an especially heinous crime ought to stay focused on the present moment, but all the big guy could think about was Darla. She lived in Astoria, below the great winding steel bridge that soared up and over the mouth of the Columbia River, connecting Oregon to Washington. Darla worked at Astoria First National Bank, where he had discovered her one prodigious day at her little desk beside the bank's safe. She had bachelor button eyes and hair the shade of cedar bark. She loved a good margarita and loved to fool around. She had perfect breasts, passable waist and hips, a magnificent fanny, a GED diploma, and enough experience to use them all to her advantage and his supreme satisfaction. He couldn't wait to see Darla, have a good long do, and pay a brief visit to her bank vault. He'd do it, too, and he'd do something even more exceptional over Easter vacation.

Good Friday. Forty-four days from today. Today was Ash Wednesday, and the big guy could honestly say that he missed the familiar ritual of the priest smudging the black ashes on his forehead. From his Patagonia vest, he fished out a crumpled pack of Big Chiefs, lit one up, smoked, allowing the ash to build up, and carefully tapped the ashes off into the palm of his hand. When they had cooled, he stood on that rise overlooking the coulee and, with the middle finger of his right hand dipped into the ashes, he intoned, "From ash you came, to ash you shall return," then reached up and smudged a fat blotch on his forehead. He wasn't a religious man, just fixated on burnt ashes and other remnants of fire. Releasing a coil of rope from his hip belt, he wrapped one end around Bobby Beaver's stump and rappelled down the coulee wall.

Hours later, the resplendent moon now barely visible, he had traversed the coulee's dry creek-bed floor and had pick-axed his way up the far wall. Now he stood on the opposite

ridge and looked back from whence he had come. If he
squinted, he could almost make out the silhouette of Bob
Beaver up on that other ridge; then the moon slipped behind
the mountain and the shadows succumbed to blackness. He
turned and faced the low rim of concrete bulkhead on the
western edge of Rocky Reach Dam, where its concrete wall
choked off the Columbia River at a narrows, half a mile
across.

It was early March, a mild, windless night, perfect for shenanigans. A man does what he must to assuage his conscience, to rationalize his motives, and now the big guy allowed all the bitter gall churning in his stale gut to rise to
the occasion. A gush of yellow anger hottened his throat and
spurred him on. He set down his backpack and began un-
loading the explosives. Because he was seasoned in the art
and science of anarchy, and because he had assiduously studied the contours of Rocky Reach Dam, including its pair of
fish ladders and hatchery ponds, he thought he knew just
where and how to place the dynamite and plastic explosives
in order to achieve the desired effect. He worked for nearly
two hours, careful to avoid detection by the power company's
security force. He was still young enough to possess agile
legs, and yet old enough to have finely honed his intuitive
senses. He could smell danger a mile away, and now he felt
confident that he and his tiny-big packages had so far gone
undetected. As he worked, he could hear the swoosh of the
river below the dam's concrete wall, where, after it spilled
over in tightly controlled measure, the water pooled around
great granite boulders, regaining its natural manic rhythm.
Downriver, it was again choked by Rock Island Dam, then
Wanapum, Priest Rapids, McNary, and John Day dams, The
Dalles, and Bonneville dams, until finally the Columbia's
once-wild, free-raging waters flowed passively under the Astoria Bridge. From Astoria, the river swirled gently past the
lighthouse at Cape Disappointment. Gagged and harnessed
by its concrete shackles, it just whimpered out to the raging

sea. Not what Nature had intended, but what evildoing tech-
nocrats had devised. The big guy would fix all that, given
time, wherewithal, and a pinch of weed to heighten the whole
experience.

By the time he had finished priming the dam's west-side
fish ladder, the moon had completely abandoned eastern
Washington. The glabrous mountains and parched coulees lay
in wretched darkness, waiting on the next pass of the sun.
The big man checked one last time and found everything in
order, everything just as it should be, everything going according to plan. One last time, he checked the remote timing
devices, then scrambled over the ridge and down into the
coulee, where in the darkness waited his getaway vehicle. He
had parked the old Jeep behind a clump of scrubby trees
alongside the dried-up, diverted riverbed. He had a hiding
place underneath the trees, where he had dug a hole, and now
he placed the backpack down in the hole and covered it over
with a plastic tarp that he kept in the Jeep. He covered that
over with rocky soil, then covered the soil with a camouflage
of dried-up tree leaves. He dragged a snatch of tumbleweed
across his footprints, eradicating them, and climbed in behind
the Jeep's steering wheel. He lay the remote-control device
on the passenger seat, removed his muddy boots, slipped on
a pair of sneakers, lit up a joint, blew out smoke, and pondered the dark sky. When the weed had burned down to his
stained fingertips, he crumbled it on the Jeep's banged-up
door and flicked the skimpy butt into the darkness before he
reached over and pressed the button on the remote control.

The explosion lit the sky bright as a morning sun ball and
the noise made him think of volcanic force. Damn, he was
good. He turned the key in the Jeep's ignition, revved the
engine, and, just as the sky turned crimson and smoke, roared
off down the coulee in the opposite direction of Rocky Reach
Dam.

When he reached Astoria, Darla was sitting up in bed
watching CNN.

"Didja see the news, honey?" Darla asked the big man. He said no, he hadn't seen the news.

"Well, apparently some terrorists blew up Rocky Reach Dam. Ka-blewee. It made havoc. God, what will they do next?"

He didn't bother asking Darla whom she meant by "they."

Darla said, "And just this morning, they announced that President Benson's coming to campaign on the Columbia River. Cripes, can you picture if that bomb had gone off on the president of the United States?"

He said nothing, just grunted. He peeled off his shoes and trousers, went into the bathroom, then came back and crawled up beside Darla in bed. She was munching a Dunkin' Donut and nursing a Red Hook. She couldn't take her blue-button eyes off the television screen, and who could blame her? Havoc reigned up along the Columbia River. Chaos and mayhem prevailed. Rocky Reach Dam had burst its seam and dumped a couple billion gallons of freshwater that flooded the riverbanks, the overspill making mash of Wenatchee's apple orchards and floating three corpses to the surface: one was a cougar, one was a deer, and one was Bobby Beaver's Uncle Fred.

Darla glanced over at the big man. "Why, honey," she remarked upon noticing the smudge on his forehead, "looks like you've been to church." She laughed, then kissed him, her deft hand crossing the Rubicon on the first grope.

Often when asleep, Darla would mumble incoherent phrases in her own private language, with her own made-up words. On this night, beside the big guy, a dreaming Darla spoke words he understood, each one clearly enunciated. "If you're my mother," Darla mumbled into her pillow, "why don't I look like you?"

The big guy opened his eyes and stared at sleeping Darla. She looked so pure and innocent. Wrapping his strong fingers around the soft white skin of her neck, he stroked her throat, gently, wondering what it would feel like to strangle her. She didn't flinch in her sleep, but mumbled something about swans, then lapsed into her private language.

The big man watched the moon drift across the window shade and thought about where he had been, and where he was going. Reaching up, he felt his forehead. A trace of ashes remained. He sighed, shut his eyes, and felt himself skate across the thin membrane between awareness and repose.

TWO

A WEEK LATER, on a dank, spiritless morning, Darla woke up in bed and saw that the big guy was gone. Cursing men in general, she placed her feet against the hardwood floor and stood up. "Yowser," she said aloud. "It's effing cold."

Darla's spaniel heard her mistress's sultry voice, shook in place at the living room heat register, stood on all fours, and padded into the bedroom to see what "Yowser" was all about. By now, Darla was in the bathroom, and when the spaniel finally located her, Darla purred, "C'mere, Pussy, you effing creep."

Pussy, the spaniel, comprehended the gentle tone of Darla's voice and skittered into the bathroom, bent on love. Darla stroked Pussy's spotted coat, all the while staring out the bathroom window at the morning light.

There wasn't a sky in the clouds.

"Oh hell," Darla complained to Pussy. "Another Pacific Northwest morning."

She had her shower and instant oatmeal, her thyroid tablets and herbal tea. She let Pussy out for a stroll through the rhododendrons, then locked the spaniel in the house and drove away in her classic 1978 Thunderbird, powder blue, with white leather upholstery and a white canvas convertible top. It was 7:35, and Darla always arrived at work before eight o'clock, when Mr. Owens, the branch manager of Astoria First National Bank, stopped by on his way to breakfast, just to see which employees cared enough to be early birds. Darla had worked at Astoria First National for only six months, hadn't yet completed her one-year probation period. She arrived early everyday to show she was up to snuff. Rounding the corner of Lewis and Clark streets, Darla noticed that the block of Clark on which the bank was located had been cordoned off with that yellow plastic tape she'd seen at crime scenes on television. Police cars, emergency aid vehicles, ambulances, and fire trucks choked off Clark Street, flashing red and amber lights. Darla slowed the T-bird to a crawl behind a Volvo and craned her neck to see what fer.

A helicopter clamored overhead, and when Darla poked her head out the window, she honestly felt the churning air. She couldn't see everything, but she saw enough to know that the bank was the point of interest, uniformed officers and firefighters rushing to and fro, and then she saw the gaping hole in the bank's old brick wall, the wall with the freshly painted salmon mural. The hole in the wall poked out of a salmon's belly, and Darla strained to see inside the bank, her first thoughts being related to the left-hand top drawer of her desk, which contained a small cosmetics bag, which contained a tiny pill box in which resided a small collection of ecstasy. Her guilty fears were somewhat diminished when she saw that whatever had blasted the hole in the bank wall had also obliterated most of the bank's interior, including the area beside the safe, where Darla usually sat at her desk. Possibly the blast had obliterated Darla's desk, the left-hand drawer, the cosmetics bag, and the pillbox therein. Darla chewed her lip.

A television news reporter was kind enough to pause at Darla's window and describe the situation. "Bomb went off inside the bank this morning just before daylight. Blew out the wall there." He pointed. "Blew into the safe. Bank robbers."

"Holy bananas," said Darla, and she whistled, all the while sweating over the ecstasy. "What's it look like inside?"

"Chaos. And in case you're interested, no one was killed."

The reporter went away, leaving Darla to brood over the ecstasy. She turned on the car radio and tuned in to KAST-AM. Sure enough, the local station was broadcasting the story. Darla fine-tuned and bent her ear down to the speaker so she could hear over the din.

A security guard had been slightly injured. Darla's boss, Mr. Owens, and Darla's pal, Leelee Thuc Dien Phu, had witnessed the blast from the Chick's Nest Café, across Clark Street from the bank. They were sharing a predawn repast, following a hot night of adultery (the media didn't report this, but Darla knew about Leelee and Mr. Owens), and, seated at the front window, they saw the whole thing. There were other witnesses, though not many at 5:00 a.m., when the bomb blew. KAST wasn't permitted to interview Mr. Owens until the police finished with him, but Leelee Thuc Dien Phu went on radio to describe the shocking event.

"Just like Mount Saint Helens," Leelee told listeners. "Only smaller, and there was no ash, but I vomited anyway, just out of fright." Typical Leelee.

Bank operations were temporarily moved to a mobile unit parked in the Safeway lot. Bank customers were already flooding the phone lines, demanding to know if their safe-deposit boxes and hard-earned cash had blown up, and if so, what then? Darla could almost hear Mr. Owens's hands wringing.

No use hanging at the scene just to gawk. Darla wasn't a gawker. She had better things to do with her time. Darla maneuvered out of line and drove home. Pussy was puzzled, even slightly irritated, to see her mistress come home early. Darla removed her panty hose, her black polyester business suit, and her white Dacron blouse. She slid into a pair of men's pajama bottoms, pulled a T-shirt over her two friends, grabbed a Red Hook, and reclined on the bed to watch television's version of the event. She could hardly wait to tell the big guy. Speak of the devil, here he comes now.

But the big guy didn't want to talk. He wanted something else. Darla had no problem with that, but Pussy grew snarly when the big guy dragged her out of the bedroom and shut the door. Pussy could hear Darla's moans and cries and knew full well that her mistress was having a ball, but Pussy wasn't, so she howled and yowled, until the big guy came out of the bedroom, grabbed her by the scruff, and tossed her outdoors, where a mean mist fell over the yard, scotching Pussy's flower garden plans. She stayed up on the porch, where, through the bolted door, she could hear Darla's ecstatic whinnies. After awhile, the big guy appeared on the porch. He made a swipe at Pussy, but Pussy shrank back, and he missed. The big man cursed at Pussy and strode deliberately down the garden path. Pussy watched him climb into his van and drive away. When the van had disappeared, Pussy began scratching at the front door and whimpering. Eventually, Darla opened the door and let the soggy spaniel inside. Then Darla bathed and napped while Pussy licked her paws.

When he returned that night, a looming shadow in the doorway, the full moon backlighting his broad chest, haloing his head, his bulk threw a dark shadow across the candlelit room. Darla, in place on the love seat, made a come-hither circle with her big toe. He stepped inside, shutting the cold moon out, and bolted the door. He set his boots where he usually did, beside the front door, and approached the temptress.

The only things she had on were toenail polish and a ruby rhinestone necklace that showed off her soft white neck but, unfortunately, drew attention to her one flaw, a receding chin. She rotated the talented toe, and he walked over and stared down at her. He was hungry and still chilled from the night air, but he could see what Darla wanted so desperately, so he gave it to her, not so much out of generosity as out of expediency. When she finally settled down, they shared a joint and a Tab. Darla showered, and now she wore a towel wrap and a terry-cloth turban. He was rolling a second joint when Darla flicked on the eleven o'clock news and through the waning candlelight came images of the Astoria First National Bank building, the destroyed salmon mural, and the tumult of earlier that day. Darla, curled on the love seat, wiggled her toes at the screen.

"There I am, see? Behind that Volvo. See? There I am."

He lit the joint, inhaled, then passed it on to Darla, but she waved it away.

"I have to work tomorrow," she said. "At least I think I do."

He persisted. "It'll help you sleep."

Darla shook her pretty head. "I don't need it. I can fall asleep anywhere, anytime. You'll learn that about me, when you get to know me better. When I'm stressed? I automatically drop to sleep. Even in the middle of havoc. I'm just that way. When Mount Saint Helens blew? I slept through the whole thing and woke up with ash all over my face and everything. Even way up in Kettle Falls, we got ash. We really did, honest."

They watched the news report of the bank blast, or at least he did. He was pretty sure Darla had lapsed into one of her trances. He glanced over and saw her hands resting on her knees, fingers and thumbs kissing. Maybe she didn't care that her workplace had gotten blown to smithereens. Maybe she didn't care about anything much, or much about anything. He smoked and listened to the broadcast. When it ended— telling him nothing he didn't already know—he clicked off the tube and went into Darla's bedroom and lay down on her bed. In less than a minute, he was asleep. He slept so soundly that he didn't notice Darla crawl into bed beside him, or hear her whisper, "I hope they catch those bastards." In the living room, Pussy slept fitfully, bothered by a field mouse playing in the wall.

WHEN DARLA AWOKE, the big guy was gone, his satchel missing from the front hall. Darla knew that meant the big guy was going away for a while—on another one of his business trips. Darla was still unsure what he did for a living, but she assumed from all the secrecy and avoidance of the subject that he was in the pot-smuggling business. Darla's vivid imagination had conjured a picture of the big guy meeting a rogue band of Canadian reefer rats at the Astoria docks near the mouth of the Columbia River, where they off-loaded fish carcasses stuffed with potent BC weed. She saw him making his purchases, then heading upriver in the van, along the lower river road, peddling his wares at each little river town. She imagined that he stopped at Bonneville and The Dalles and that he sold pot to the power company employees who ran the dams all along the Columbia River. He'd move upriver, one dam town to the next, keeping the entire hydroelectric power system supplied with reefer. These power guys would make steady customers—anything to distract them from the tedium of dam work and river life.

Darla knew about a particular brand of upriver tedium, having been raised from the age of seven up at Kettle Falls, Washington, at the top of the state, where the Columbia flows out of Canada, where the vintners grow grapes to make icewine. You don't live fifteen years in a backwater without grasping the definition of tedium. Darla had experienced enough tedium for a whole village before she escaped Kettle Falls and headed southwest to Astoria. She loved the ocean breezes but despised the rain, so it was love-hate right off the bat between Darla and Astoria. Almost immediately, she landed a job interview at Astoria First. They had fingerprinted her, analyzed her urine, and checked her references umpteen times before they hired her on at the bank. They were shocked to learn she held Mensa membership, which Darla never bragged about but only listed in the job application under the category "Hobbies and Organization Memberships." Darla smoked pot, but seldom, and she never moved beyond reefer to the hard drugs. The ecstasy in her cosmetics bag in the desk drawer at the bank? It wasn't hers. It belonged to the big guy, and she never should have offered to stash it for him.

Until this fateful incident, Darla had possessed a kind of luck, or kismet, that a lot of girls back in K Falls had envied. Kismet happens when your destitute single mom lands a big fish like Albert Denny, the cattle rancher who owned more property than anyone else in eastern Washington, and Darla's mom, Sue Ann, and Darla herself being his only heirs. Darla got what she wanted, and she never had to work too hard for it. But life with Sue Ann and Albert didn't much suit Darla, didn't match her notion of how life ought to shake out for a pretty girl with adventure in her heart and romance constantly on her mind. So Darla had fled the backwater and come to Astoria, Oregon, where there were fewer Bible-thumpers and aging survivalists, where the bars served liquor seven days a week past midnight.

When she'd arrived in Astoria six months ago, she had fallen into this awesome Victorian cottage rental. Soon after that, she got hired on at Astoria First, and then her stepfather surprised her with the classic T-bird for a "new job" present. Soon after settling in, she adopted Pussy from the pound. After meeting Leelee Thuc Dien Phu at the bank and understanding from Leelee what it meant to have a college degree, Darla had enrolled in the community college, where she studied yoga and Pilates for college credit. All this in the first six months of her Astorian adventure. Under Leelee's maternal influence, she had vowed to graduate from college, and at Leelee's urging, she had just embarked upon a soul-searching self-actualization regime, guided by a lavishly illustrated edition of the *Kama Sutra*. But when the big guy came into her life, things just went topsy-turvy. A certain type of man can do that to the Darlas of the world.

One day at the bank, the big guy had walked up to Darla's desk and inquired about changing foreign currency. By foreign, he meant Canadian. He was large and rugged and reminded her of a lumberjack. He wore army fatigues and a Patagonia parka. He had a solid build, like he worked out with free weights, and he had short hair the shade of rich earth, and no beard or mustache. She wasn't used to clean-shaven men and decided that he must not be a lumberjack after all. He had soft brown eyes that seemed perpetually out of focus, so she had trouble reading them, but when he spoke, lordy, how she tingled in all the right spots. Not the words, but something in his tone and manner turned Darla on. She must have conveyed this sexual energy, because after she made the exchange from Canadian to U.S. currency, the man asked her out.

She met him after work at a lounge. She had two double margaritas and he had a Tab; then she took him home. She had never taken a guy home on the first date. But something about the big guy made him irresistible. Sexually, he was insatiable, and that intrigued her, since she was fascinated by people's various obsessions (her darkest secret). She'd known him now for six weeks, had given him a key to her place, and had never questioned him about what he did or didn't do for a living. He had wherewithal, which was more than she could say for most of the guys around Astoria, and he wasn't any kind of moocher. He didn't wish to discuss his past or present, or to speculate on the future, even on their future together. About the future, he'd only say, "It's coming, and it's going to hurt." Something about the way he said it bothered her, but she dared not ask him to elaborate. He had a temper; it had flared at Pussy a few times, and Darla didn't want it flaring at her. He didn't, in fact, talk much at all, except to criticize the government and authority in general whenever the subjects arose. He believed that all politicians were pawns of the CIA, and he believed in government conspiracies, corporate conspiracies, and CIA vaccine conspiracies against the common man. She decided he was an anarchist and let it go at that. After all, the crux of their relationship, the central focus, was the sex, and that was superb. Being pragmatic, Darla accepted sexual attraction in lieu of romance, but secretly she hoped that romance would develop. Meanwhile, she endured his comings and goings, his mysterious history, his silences, and his antigovernment ravings.

Once every few days, he'd show up and they would spend a night or two together. They never went out, just stayed at home, watched television, ate microwave food, and bunked. He was usually gone when she woke up in the morning. She found it odd that he never told her his name, but even odder that she hadn't the nerve to ask him. She just called him "honey" and "Big Guy" and let it go at that.

Darla made herbal tea and climbed back into bed. Pussy wanted up, but Darla said, "No, you stay down. You don't belong in this bed." Pussy sulked on the hardwood floor as Darla made a phone call to work. She got a tape recording that instructed all Astoria First National employees to meet at 9:00 a.m. that morning at the Chick's Nest Café.

When she arrived, a police officer checked her photo ID, then let her go inside, where she joined a dozen other bank employees at a big table in the private lunchroom in back. Mr. Owens, the bank manager, seated backward astride a folding chair, checked his watch as she walked in at 9:00 a.m. on the nose. She found a seat beside Leelee and sat down. Someone passed her a plate of bear claws and someone else poured her coffee. She felt like a celebrity.

Mr. Owens told the bank employees that the bank's safe had been blown open and its contents stolen. Not everything, just the cash that was stashed there, like cash always was one night each week, waiting for the morning armored truck detail. Someone apparently knew exactly which day that week that the cash would be stashed in the safe overnight. Someone knew exactly which predawn to hit the bank. Mr. Owens said that the investigation was ongoing, that so far no suspects had been apprehended and nothing had been found to identify the robber or robbers, except a tiny pillbox containing a small amount of ecstasy. They were checking the pillbox for fingerprints. The police strongly suspected this was an inside job.

Darla sat frozen to her chair, her heart pounding. She tried to recall if she had placed the pillbox in her cosmetics bag or if the big guy had put it there. Whose fingerprints were on it?

Leelee bristled audibly and said with indignation, "Mr. Owens, I hope that you are not implying that one of us robbed the bank."

Mr. Owens removed his eyeglasses and wiped them with a table napkin. After a thoughtful pause, he said, "Not I, Leelee. The police. Remember, I am just as much under suspicion as any of you."

Another bank employee piped up, "What about this pillbox? What connection is that to the blast?"

Mr. Owens tilted his head sideways. "I'm not sure," he said. "But apparently the police believe that the pillbox belonged to one of the culprits. Probably because it contained an illegal substance, and, as we all know, none of us keeps illegal substances at his or her desk." He gazed soulfully around the table.

Leelee said, "How dare the police suspect us!" Others concurred, and Mr. Owens had to raise his voice to quiet them.

"We'll get to the bottom of this, I assure you," he said. "Meanwhile, each one of us will be individually interviewed by Detective Brown, who has set up a temporary office here in the Chick's Nest. Before you leave here today, you must give a full and complete statement as to your whereabouts over the last forty-eight hours. You'll be asked to provide witnesses and other proof to back up your statements."

Someone said, "When do we go back to work?"

A general rustling around the table, and then Mr. Owens said, "We guess it will take about two weeks to put the bank back in working order. Meanwhile, we'll operate a small mobile unit in the Safeway lot. Therefore, we won't be needing the full staff. Ms. Thuc Dien Phu and I will operate the mobile unit with the assistance of security guards. The rest of you will have two weeks off...."

"But...," several voices cried in unison, and Darla heard the groans and bitterness brewing. Then Mr. Owens raised his hand for silence and added, "With pay, of course. Think of it as a paid vacation. Now, let's all give our statements and then you lucky devils get the hell out of here and have some fun. Leelee and I will take care of everything."

After fervent applause, each employee gave his and her statement. While she waited her turn, Darla ate two bear claws and worried. When her time came, she made a huffy entrance into Detective Brown's imposing presence, hoping to intimidate. She knew nothing, she said, batting her blue-button eyes. She had been at work or with her boyfriend during the past forty-eight hours, and her boyfriend could vouch for her whereabouts, and she was pretty sure her neighbors watched her come and go. In spite of her trembling, Detective Brown seemed convinced and let her go home. On the way out of the Chick's Nest, Darla saw Mr. Owens and Leelee standing together near the coffee tray. She went over and said, "Mr. Owens, I need to speak with you. In private."

They stepped outdoors, into the damp winds coming off the ocean. Darla's hair blew in her face and Mr. Owens reached up, helpfully pushing it out of her eyes.

Darla said, "Mr. Owens, that pillbox?"

"Yes, Ms. Denny?"

"That pillbox, was it brown leather embossed like crocodile skin?"

Mr. Owens's eyes widened. "Why, I think it was, Ms. Denny." He leaned in close. "Do you know something about it?"

Darla shivered and fought with her hair. "Maybe. Maybe, but, well, I'm not sure."

"You're not sure," repeated Mr. Owens.

"That is, I can't actually recall, like, what the actual pillbox I'm thinking about actually looked like. I…I need sometime to think it over."

Mr. Owens studied Darla's face. He might have thought she was just playing for attention, or he might have thought Darla knew something she wasn't willing to share immediately. She was very afraid he would march her back inside to Detective Brown. But Mr. Owens did no such thing. He just patted her on the shoulder and said, "You do that, Ms. Denny. And then you come to me. Directly to me. Do you understand?"

Darla said yes, she did, and fled.

THREE

DARLA HAD NO PLACE to go and nothing to do. She wished the big guy was around. She wished he had taken her with him wherever he'd gone. She was mad as hell at him for putting that pillbox into her cosmetics bag. Or had she put it there for him? She just couldn't recall. Feeling despondent and resentful, she drove home to her little Victorian cottage, vowing to chastise him, but her mood instantly brightened when she saw the big guy's van parked out front. She rushed inside, tearing off her clothes as she went, ignoring Pussy's pleas, and dived into the big guy's burly arms. "Do me," she said breathlessly. And he did.

They left Astoria that afternoon, heading east along Highway 30, the lower river road on the Columbia's Oregon side. "I'm going to make an anarchist out of you," he told her as they drove east through Clatskanie, then south toward Scappoose. She didn't bother asking what he meant by that, because she knew he'd explain in his own good time. But she knew he meant business, because he had made her leave Pussy at the kennel and pack everything she'd need for ten days on the road.

The thin winter sunlight began to fade and the river turned from blue to ocher to gunmetal. By the time they reached Portland, darkness had engulfed the river and its banks and the city's lights seemed suspended over the river, like celestial bodies. They pulled into a cheesy motel's parking lot, and he instructed her to go inside and register under the names Tom and Linda Justice. He handed her a credit card with the name Tom Justice embossed on it, and a phony picture ID with the name Linda Justice on it, and, to her astonishment, the picture was of her. He wrote down the license plate number, the van's make and model. She gathered up all this information, steeled her nerves, and went inside the motel's office. Minutes later, she emerged, wearing a jubilant grin and waving a room key. He brought in dinner from Pizza Hut, which they ate in bed while watching television. That night, she was turned on more than ever, danger's perfume stirring her into an amatory frenzy that served him fine.

WHEN MORNING BROKE and Darla awoke in a strange bed, she had to blink a couple times and focus on her surroundings before she remembered where she was. Her first thought was of Pussy, then the big guy. But she was alone. A clock on the television set said 7:03 a.m. in bold red digital numbers.

Where had the big guy gone? When—and why—had he left her alone in this strange room? She didn't have to wonder for long, because as she stepped out of the shower and into her Capris, he came into the room, loaded down with breakfast and newspapers. When she took the coffee from him, his hand felt chilled to the bone, as if he'd been outdoors for a long time.

"What time did you get up, honey?" she asked, trying to sound casual.

"Never mind," he replied with the usual curtness.

She ate voraciously and he read voraciously. By now, she knew he was keenly interested in current events, in particular the Rocky Reach Dam bombing and the search for the bombers. She turned this over in her mind and for a fleeting moment considered what she'd do if he was involved in something like that; then he glanced over at her with those soft brown eyes and she assured herself that he would never do such a terrible thing. And then it came to her that even if he was a terrorist, say one of those British Columbia Algerian jihad soldiers, she would probably stay with him. What had locked her on was the big guy's enigmatic scent of danger, as compelling as if somewhere inside Darla dwelt his dark twin.

The big guy folded the newspapers and spread a map of Washington State across the unmade bed. She sat across from him, trying to follow his studious gaze. She saw the Columbia River flowing from the top of the map in the Canadian Rockies, first northward, then sharply in a U-turn southward into eastern Washington and farther south to the Washington-Oregon border, where it flowed due west, meeting the Pacific Ocean at Astoria and Cape Disappointment. She saw The Dalles on the map, on the Oregon side of the river, and north of The Dalles, across the wide river, Klickitat County, Washington. She wondered what kind of people would live in Klickitat County and what they did for a living. Then the big guy put a finger on the map, as if to hold his place, looked up at her, and said, "It's time you learned to make a bomb."

They made it in the motel room, on a wide shelf beneath a window. The venetian blinds, only half-shut, leaked pale sunlight across the pipes and nails and plastic explosives. Hypnotized by fear or love—she couldn't tell which—she watched her own gloved hands guided by his, and saw them construct a small deadly package.

The lead pipe had been sealed on one end with a threaded cap. She saw her hands drop three-inch industrial nails, razor blades, and threadlike wires into the other end, around patches of plastic that reminded her of Silly Putty. He showed her how to thread the wires through a hole in another cap, this cap placed on the open end, screwed on, and now he showed her how to twist the threaded wires to make a fuze. When this was done, they made another, then another, working all day and into the night, all the while his gloved hands guiding hers. When they finished the bombs, he showed her how to construct blasting caps. Only once during these long, tedious hours did she dare to ask him a question.

"Honey," she said, "are we going to blow up a dam?"

He didn't answer right away. When finally the words came, his tone of voice was severe. "Now that you know, if you try to leave me, I'll have to kill you. And don't open your mouth again unless I tell you to. Understand?"

She said, "Yes, honey," and experienced the naked shame of coerced submission.

When they went to bed that night, he didn't want anything to do with her, maybe saving his energy, conserving power. That was okay with Darla. She lay in the dark, surrounded by pipe bombs and blasting caps, boxes of plastic explosives and timing devices. She lay very still, afraid to move, fearing the slightest stir would kick off an explosion. She lay in bed wondering what it was about the big guy that made her pride go haywire. She couldn't stand up to him, or didn't want to, but she wasn't usually so submissive. Not to anyone, even to her mom. Why did the big stranger hold so much power over her?

Darla lay very still. Employing all the techniques suggested by her community college visualization instructor, she tried mentally conjuring her father. She had never actually met her real father, never even knew his name. Darla's mom would say only that Darla's father had been a "sorry son of a bitch," leaving it at that. Over the years, Darla had formed a mental picture of her father, what she imagined he looked like, his personality, his voice, his mannerisms. Since Sue Ann (Darla's mom) was intellectually challenged (Darla's opinion), Darla strongly suspected that she'd inherited her own intellectual prowess through her father's genes. And also, Darla bore no physical resemblance to Sue Ann. Darla's physical attributes, her rich copper-toned hair, cornflower blue eyes, even the receding chin, must have come from her father's genes. Darla believed that she was a cross-gender clone of this stranger, and she often pictured him in her mind. But tonight, lying in bed beside the big guy, surrounded by the accoutrements of a revolution she didn't understand,

Darla had trouble conjuring a picture of her father. She tried a few more times, failed, and gave up, deciding that God was protecting her father from seeing his daughter surrounded by bombs.

She glanced over at the big guy. His eyes were shut, his breath calm and even. Darla rolled over on her side and turned herself into a swan.

WHEN SHE WOKE, it was still dark outside. The clock read 3:07 a.m. The big guy was shaking her, telling her to get up, get dressed, and make it snappy. Meanwhile, he moved the bombs from the room to the van, using her suitcase. She went to the motel desk and paid with cash. She gave him the receipt. He sneered at this; then he told her to rip it up and eat it, which she did.

They drove east along Highway 30, through Portland, Troutdale, into the Columbia Gorge, and past Bonneville Dam. When they reached The Dalles, just before the dam, he turned left onto a bridge, crossing over the river into scrubby beige southwest Washington. In the dawning light, Darla saw the dam's broad concrete face, its spillway running full force, the water making wet clouds that reflected rainbows. She saw the massive power turbines, and she saw the fish ladder. She saw salmon leaping against the dam's waterfalls, struggling to get past the concrete behemoth, determined, in their procreative frenzy, to reach their spawning grounds before their ripeness burst. Darla was imagining how they felt, when she noticed a fish counter perched above the ladder.

"What a sweet job," she said. "Counting salmon."

The big man glared at her. "What did I say about talking?"

As the pastel sun rose up over the high cliffs of the Columbia Gorge, they drove on in silence, thinking their separate thoughts. They drove along the Washington side of the river, northeast. She didn't know where the big guy was headed, but she guessed it was to the dam at John Day. She was surprised when he passed John Day and kept heading north. A few vehicles passed them, going in the other direction, and once a logging truck roared up behind them at the foot of a hill, but he gunned the engine and left the logger behind in the dust. Alongside the highway, a few purple wildflowers sprouted from the dry soil, and she wondered what they were called. She had the urge to pull off the road and pick the flowers, to hold them up to him and say, "See, honey? Aren't they purty things?" But she knew he wouldn't pull over, and she guessed he wasn't fond of wildflowers.

Darla had never received flowers. Even at her junior prom, the year before she dropped out of school, Darla was the only girl without a corsage pinned to her dress or clipped to her wrist. The other girls had pretended not to notice, but she saw them laughing behind her back. Darla never lived down that humiliation. Shortly after the prom fiasco, she dropped out of K Falls High School and never looked back. Still, she harbored a secret dream of a lover who would lavish her with great bouquets of blowsy roses, who would spread sweet jasmine petals across her bed and make love to her on top of them, crushing out the perfume. She longed for that day to arrive, and until the big guy came along, she had counted on it. Now she wasn't so sure about flowers and sweet fragrance mixing in with her love life. Anyway, she wasn't sure this was love she felt for the big guy. Maybe lust plus some weird transfixion. His mystery still intrigued her, but she now realized that she had begun to fear him.

The sun lay cold against a leaden sky. Darla had been dozing until the van hit a bump and she jerked awake. The big guy was pulling off the highway. She saw a sign to Crow Butte State Park. The park was closed for the winter, but he drove through the entrance anyway, skirting the iron gates. The campgrounds were deserted. He parked the van in a grove of tall evergreens and turned off the ignition. Darla hoped he wasn't planning on camping out, but she dared not inquire. The big guy had fallen into a palpable funk that oozed a threatening energy she dared not stir.

In the van's rear, he rummaged and organized. Besides the bombs, there was a lot of junk in the rear of the van, stuff she wasn't particularly interested in seeing. Instead of offering to help him, she went for a walk. She wanted to smoke some weed but was afraid to near the bombs.

The air felt cold, crisp, and dry. The vegetation had changed from the lush Doug fir forests of the Washington coastline to the blended firs and pines in the Puget Trough, and now ponderosa pine took over and the ground was bone beige and parched. Soon, if they continued driving east, they would enter the desert, but she had a hunch that they were headed north through the coulees, following the Columbia upriver. That would take them—where? To the high prairies. If they traveled long enough and far enough upriver, eventually they would reach Kettle Falls. The idea made her snicker out loud. What would the backwater babes of K Falls think when they saw Darla Denny back in town with this handsome big guy on her arm?

She was mulling this over when she noticed a sign posted on a camper's bulletin board. Darla went over and read the notice. There was a telephone number printed in large, bold black letters, an 800 number for the U.S. Fish and Wildlife Service's poacher hot line. Darla wasn't sure why she memorized the number, but she did. She was reading the fine print on the sign when the big guy appeared on the trail, startling her.

"Don't do that again," he said, an angry expression distorting his face.

"Do what, hon?" She was honestly confused.

"Don't you ever leave my sight. Unless I give you permission. Because I will have to kill you. Have you got that straight?"

Darla said yes, she had, and now she really felt scared.

The next morning, he took her to a cheap motel and instructed her to wait there for him. She did, for three days and nights, watching television the whole time.

THE BIG MAN DROVE his van onto the road that crossed the spillway on Grand Coulee Dam. He wore a hardhat and white overalls, and beside him in the passenger seat was a yellow lunch pail. When he stopped to show his photo ID at the employee entrance, the security guard said, "Hey, dude," then checked his ID and waved him inside. He parked the van in the western parking lot, grabbed the lunch pail, and went inside the dam. He rode the elevator down four stories to the bottom of the dam, got out, and walked through the tunnels in the concrete structure until he reached his assigned workplace. No one noticed anything out of the ordinary at the dam that day. No one noticed the big man's hands deftly planting plastic explosives on the rear of the dam's interior security cameras. After all, those big hands were meant to fondle the security cameras, to check them periodically, and to repair them when necessary.

THAT NIGHT, the big man stood at the rim of Banks Lake, gazing across the flooded coulee at distant lights. Through the cold, crystalline air he could see the brightly illuminated towns of Grand Coulee, Electric City, and Coulee Dam. He could see the rim of lights across Grand Coulee Dam's spillway. He could see the lights tracing silhouettes of giant electrical towers. They twinkled like so many fallen stars on the horizon. But right now, he could not appreciate the nocturnal beauty of electrified towns. The big man had trouble on his mind, big trouble, the only kind that counted.

The Rocky Reach Dam blast hadn't gone as planned. His careful placement of the explosives should have caused total destruction. But already, the dam was back in operation. Something about his placement of the explosives, or the type of bomb he had used, wasn't right.

Inhaling the fresh evening air, the big man felt a familiar

twitch at his back. His shoulder blades began moving in a familiar slow rhythm, back and forth, back and forth. He stood alone on the bank of the flooded coulee, and it was a good thing, because when a man yearns to become an eagle he doesn't want witnesses.

The big man lit a joint, inhaled, and reveled in the sensation in his shoulder blades. After a while, the moon rose and washed across the parched mountains. He heard a lonesome howl, the unmistakable war cry of another of Earth's anarchists. Coyote.

BACK WHEN the Colville tribes first lived among these coulees, when Coyote was a person, there was no Columbia River. Up here in the mountains was a beautiful lake. A string of mountains lay between the ocean and the beautiful lake. Coyote realized that he could bring salmon from the ocean to the Colville people who lived beside the lake. He made a big hole in the mountains and through this hole, the lake waters drained down to the ocean and formed a wide river. The salmon in the ocean found this freshwater river and swam up it. From then on, the Colville tribes had plenty of salmon for food.

ONCE MORE, the lone coyote howled. As the moon sank behind the mountains and the stars winked out, the big man dug a pit, built a fire, and dropped stones into the red-hot flames. Removing his boots and socks, he renewed his vow to avenge the river, and when a night owl hooted through the silence, he took this as a sign.

FOUR

The National Academy of Sciences has named Hanford
Nuclear Reservation a "national sacrifice zone," the
largest of twenty-seven land sites in the United States
too contaminated for human access, now or ever, stating,
"Complete elimination of unacceptable risks to humans
and the environment will not be achieved, now or in the
foreseeable future."

THE FISH COUNTER sat on a concrete bench above the fish
ladder at the edge of Priest Rapids Dam. A chill wind from
the west blew upriver as chinook salmon struggled against
the dam's roaring waterfall, great hunchbacked, leaping scim-
itars stapling the sky to the river. Some wild, some hatchery-
bred; some would make it through the dam's fish ladder and
others would fall back and die. The counter's thumb tapped
a small handheld ticker once for each big silver banana fighting its way home. Overhead, the somber skies revealed nothing of a noontime sun except a pale, diffused light that north-
erners recognize as a spring's day. Within the dam's raging
crystalline waters, a few dozen adult chinook leapt upward,
desperately aiming to breach the crest on the upside of the
dam, where they would rest briefly before continuing upriver,
only to encounter another concrete obstacle, and then another,
and yet another, until their journey home resembled a
salmon's worst nightmare. Those who failed to locate the fish
ladder fell back to struggle again, or get hooked or netted by

keen-eyed poachers who lurked on the riverbanks in spite of laws against out-of-season fishing. Those lucky chinooks who made it back home to the creek and eddies of their births celebrated their arrival in an orgy of egg and sperm dispersal, then flopped over and died.

On this particular spring day, Good Friday, beneath this putty sky, enveloped in relentless bitter winds, the fish counter broke no records for sighting returning chinooks. The lonely job demanded a keen, quick eye and supreme patience; otherwise, it asked little of the gray cells.

Fish number forty-five, into the ladder. Over the top. *Click.*

The fish counter focused his eyes on the leaping salmon, but his mind traveled to another place and time and his lusty thoughts were not of fish but of a certain female of his species whom he had yet to conquer. The salmon had their challenges, and Louie Song had his.

She stood facing the fireplace, gripping the mantel, taut and still, awaiting his attentions. He stood behind her, contemplating her appeal, and nursing a Jameson neat, the better to appreciate her qualities. He could see nothing of her facial expression, but the clever lady displayed enough personality in her backside to hold his interest. She was tall, even taller in stiletto heels. Her pale thighs beckoned above poison green silk stockings held up by a matching garter belt. Her inky hair fell long and straight down her back, but he could still see her...

Fish number forty-six, into the ladder. *Click.*

Song tried hard to concentrate, but this speculation thwarted his best intentions. In truth, his fantasies bore no resemblance to actual circumstances; namely, the female in the fireplace fantasy was in reality a total stranger to Song, a woman whom he had never actually seen undressed except in his daydreams. He knew her only as a frequent flyer on the north elevators in the Bumbershoot Building. The woman, young, nubile, and fair of face, always got off at the twenty-sixth floor. Going down, she usually exited at the parking garage level, though sometimes she got off at the lobby level and rode the south elevators to some mysterious destination. Song had never followed her out of the north elevator, and thus far their encounters had taken place entirely within that cold steel box, usually crowded with other passengers.

What he speculated upon as he sat on the fish ladder at Priest Rapids Dam, a few miles down river from Hanford Reach, was whether or not Miss Delicious recognized her own seductive powers. Song couldn't decide if she had meant to entice him last week, on the morning she wore the poison ivy stockings, her garters pressing torrid patterns into her tight-fitting gray flannel skirt, or by the way she glanced at him through careless bangs, or the way her tongue seemed to savor her own full lips. He couldn't decide if she had noticed his appreciative glances. Usually, Song wore one-way Revos indoors and out, but for her, he made an exception. Whenever Miss Delicious got on his elevator, Song removed the Revos, the better to study her curves and grace. Now, on the fish ladder, Song thought back to the last time he and Miss Delicious had ridden the same elevator, yesterday morning, and he could almost swear that on this most recent ride, she had returned his craving glances with a similar ardent glint aimed in his direction. Consigned now to this cold bench overlooking Priest Rapids Dam, where it constricted the Columbia River, the last concrete dam before the river's only remaining free-running stretch of fifty-two miles, Song tried attending to Miss Delicious in his mind. But his heinie was freezing and his sinuses dripped, ruining the torrid tableau. He went back to counting leaping salmon.

Forty-seven, over the top. *Click.* Forty-eight, into the ladder. *Click.*

All this misery, from frozen heinie to interrupted elevator fantasies, had been visited upon Song's life just because some jerk in the federal bureaucracy saw a need to punish him for being so cool. That's how he saw it, anyway, and he was pretty sure he had it right.

In the first place, a U.S. Fish and Wildlife agent had no business working "on loan" for the National Marine Fisheries Service, never mind that both agencies fed from the same government trough, that their species maintenance and protection duties often overlapped. What didn't overlap in the federal government? Nonetheless, a special agent ought not to be wasting his time as a fish counter. Louie Song was an ecocop, trained in the fine art of tracking and capturing big-game poachers. Big game did not include fish. Fish and game are separate entities. Song's art and craft had nothing to do with randy piscine, certainly not with counting them. He was too savvy, too high-zest to be a fish counter. But there was more to the story of Louie Song, fish counter, for the fish counter persona mostly represented a disguise. Song's principal duty was looking out for mad bombers, anarchistic eco-terrorists who might see a target in Priest Rapids Dam. Personally, Song wouldn't have chosen this particular disguise— fish counter—and anyway, most of the salmon were trucked around the dam, but his superiors called the shots, so here he sat, when all along he would rather have been in Seattle.

Why the Emerald City? Not just the vision in the north elevator. In fact, Song had lately been trying to clean up his mental carousings, curb his wanton yearnings, unite his divided body and soul. No small quest for Seattle's most eligible Asian-American playboy. But there was more. Besides the elevator vision, Oz was home to the rare human subspecies, *Eco pacificii northwestii,* or the politically correct Pacific Northwesterner, a native species found only west of the Cascade Mountains. Its vivid red and swollen nostrils, arrogant sniff, and acerbic tongue distinguish the phenomenon. When threatened, it presents a bright facade, but otherwise, it exhibits a laconic, even depressed nature. Lately, the native species had been cross-pollinating with an Oregon visitor, *E. eugenicus oregonus,* many of which were flocking like locusts to the shores of Puget Sound to make mayhem. The cross-pollination had proved inflammably anarchistic. Ore-

gonus bore superficial similarities to *P. northwestii,* yet the
two differed in one important aspect: Their politically correct
behaviors almost inevitably clashed. Lately, Song had been
researching this new sub-subspecies phenomenon, and he had
found rich specimens in the Seattle vicinity. He had, in fact,
discovered that a new form of seeping anarchy was lately
infiltrating the Seattle City Council, even the mayor's office,
where real estate development moguls, a secretive, closeted
breed, ran amuck. Song felt close, very close, to uncovering
a major philosophical truth about Oz and its many layers of
anarchy. This ambitious research project combined with increasingly vivid "Miss Delicious" fantasies, and a sincere
desire to expunge the more lurid visions, greatly distracted
his sensitive brain cells, so it came as no surprise to him
when he noticed that several salmon had nearly escaped his
ticker count.

Forty-nine, fifty, fifty-one. Over the top. *Click, click, click.*

He'd been counting fish since 6:00 a.m. Now it was noon,
and the ticker had clicked off a measly fifty-one salmon, half
of which, he guessed, were hatchery-bred, not wild. The
hatchery fish had little tags wired onto their snouts, but the
fish counter couldn't see them, and so they got counted along
with the wild, untainted stock, thereby throwing the eyeball
count. Did anyone really care about accuracy? He pondered
this as he sat on his perch above the Priest Rapids Dam fish
ladder on the west side of the Columbia River. Looking
across the great gorge, Song could see the dry central ranges
of Hanford Nuclear Facility fading southeast, carved through
by a fifty-two-mile stretch of river called the Hanford Reach.
When his shift ended at two o'clock, Song thought he just
might toodle across the dam into Hanford Reach and check
out the golden hawk population on Dry Ridge, see if they
had mutated yet from nuclear pollution. Song snickered at
the thought of hawks with fish's fins and squirrel tails, discarded the plan, and was inventing a new one in his mind,

when something—not a fish—distracted him. A gleam of light glanced off a flat plane, catching his eye.

He wasn't supposed to take his eyes off the dam, but the gleaming persisted, until he could bear it no longer. He turned his gaze away from the dam and toward the gleaming light. Did it come up off the river? Or did it come from the riverbank? He stood and walked over to the apex of the fish ladder, where he might have a better view. Below, the dammed river plunged straight downward, then swirling out of the waterfall's foaming remnants, it formed Priest Rapids Lake before moving on to the ocean. Song had a pair of binoculars looped around his neck and now he raised them, turned, and surveyed the upriver side. No boats in sight. He scoured the length of the river as far as he could see, then guided the binoculars to scan the scrubby banks. Blink. A gleam blinded him through the lens. He lowered the binoculars and watched. Now he could see with his naked eye a small but vibrant light coming from upriver, from inside the dry bushes very near river's edge. He raised the binoculars once again, but just as he pinpointed the spot, the gleaming ceased.

Little mysteries abound in such picaresque countryside. Out here in the scablands, where humans rarely trod, fairies and gremlins scale the high cliffs, and harbor their secrets along swollen riverbanks, up in the crowns of ponderosa pines. Out here in this eastern Washington scrubland, an exotic noise or unexplained flickering light was not uncommon, and so for the time being, Song dismissed the glinting curiosity and went back to counting fish.

Fifty-two. Fifty-three. Fifty-four, and so on.

When his replacement reported for duty at two o'clock, Song gladly relinquished the handheld counter and the cold bench. The whiskered man—presumably, a genuine fish counter—yawned and scratched and told Song to get the hell out of there, that it was his watch now. Song took the stairs to the employee parking lot, climbed on his Harley, and rode

east along the lower river road until he came to a small gravel
trail leading into Hanford Reach. A sign at the trailhead told
visitors not to trespass, but Song had credentials, and even if
he hadn't, he wouldn't have stopped for a sign. He followed
the trail along broadly sloping cliffs overlooking the river.
The land in here was stark and barren and, to the untrained
eye, uninteresting. Song knew the Reach; he had trained as
a wildlife agent in this high-prairie scrub. He knew the sta-
tistics by heart; more than two hundred avian species and
twenty-two mammal species inhabited the scablands, and in
here, the last free-flowing stretch of the Columbia supported
forty-four species of fish. An angler's paradise, but Song
didn't fish. Eventually, the trail led him to a clump of dry
brush at the edge of a high sandstone bluff.

When he looked down into the gorge, Song saw the Columbia's deep, swollen rapids. As the howling wind roared
through this sandstone tunnel, this yawning crack in the
Earth, Song noticed a lone kayaker riding the river's crest.
Down there in the river, the kayaker wasn't trespassing. But
camping was banned in the Reach, and unless the kayaker
had enough strength to paddle twenty-five miles in one day
to reach the only public access road, he'd be stuck overnight
in the Reach. The kayaker's crimson jacket billowed in the
wind. Song watched until the crimson sail disappeared around
a bend. Then he headed back down river to the dam. From
the southern edge of the dam, he could just barely make out
the bench above the fish ladder. But what's this? No fish
counter. Song lifted his binoculars, aimed at the dam, and
slowly surveyed the structure and then the surrounding area.
In the employee parking lot beside the dam, he spied a lone
figure standing beside a van. The fish counter? From this
distance, Song couldn't be certain. The man wore a stupid
grin that almost split his face in half and he was laughing
into a cell phone. This indulgence continued for several
minutes before he got off the cell phone and tucked the device into his pocket. Now he was rolling a joint, and now he

was lighting it, and now he inhaled. Song lowered his binoculars and frowned. Something did not bode well for the first chinook run of the season.

Song held no grudge against slackers. He, too, had made social phone calls during work hours; in fact, he had occasionally lapsed in more serious aspects while on the job. But this was war. A band of anarchists, or maybe international terrorists, had gone haywire down at Rocky Reach Dam. So far, at least six different underground organizations had claimed responsibility for the attack, adding to the confusion. Maybe it was only a matter of time before the bombers targeted the Priest Rapids Dam. What Song didn't know for another instant was that time had run out.

When the bomb went off, Song saw the initial explosion and felt it under his feet. As he ran for cover, the convulsion jarred the scrubby cliff top, ripping it apart from its sheer sandstone walls. The ground below him shivered and gave way. With all his strength, Song leapt forward, his arms outstretched toward the crumbling bluff, his whole being grasping at air, at hope in a vacuum. At the instant he leapt, he had a vision of a woman. Not Miss Delicious. This was another woman, the babe he called "the Firecracker." In the vision, the Firecracker, dressed in her usual black leather costume, was straddling his Harley, her arms outstretched, beckoning him. But she wasn't looking at him. She had thrown her head back and was laughing at the sky. She didn't belong there, on his Harley, but he reached out for her anyway, a last desperate grasp at life. Then a second explosion sent tons of rubble soaring skyward. Sandstone boulders rained down into the gorge, where the floodwaters rode a raging cataract into Priest Rapids Lake.

The explosion had created a gaping hole in one side of the concrete dam, causing a destructive flood, but no major structural damage. One body surfaced, and it was human, and nobody knew who it was or where it had come from, though speculation favored the fish counter.

FIVE

> PIT tags: Passive induced transponder tags are mechanically inserted into hatchery smolt. A computerized counter at the Ballard Locks, and at most other major smolting outlets, reads these tags. PIT tags allow humans to track the number of smolt leaving the hatcheries on the way to the ocean.

SPECIAL AGENT Venus Diamond, intrepid champion of endangered species, archenemy of black-hearted, money-grubbing big-game poachers, thorn in the fleshy side of the International Safari Club, sat at her desk pondering the quid pro quo du jour.

Had the Pacific Northwest traded its guileless soul for affluence and prosperity?

The small blond Firecracker put her lips to a latte vente and let her tongue explore the froth. She sipped absentmindedly, preoccupied with the prickly question. Such philosophical mulling ought to wait until a brain had registered copious caffeine infusions, and yet, the sticky wicket had jumped out of nowhere into her morning ruminations, spoiling everything. Why should a borderline, trivial, media-hyped query prey so relentlessly on her? Early risers are prone to this phenomenon, this deep Aristotelian vein throbbing through dawn's early light, portending no good and pretending intellectual and spiritual significance.

Had the Pacific Northwest traded its soul like a second-

string baseball card for cold cash? Did that mean that polluted
marine sanctuaries, savaged, piebald timberland, and self-
replicating concrete sidewalks groaning with the weight of
money-sucking opportunists constitute a loss of soul? That
expunged public spaces, blocked city views, and eyesore ar-
chitecture constitute a loss of soul? That smug, narcissistic
dilettantes sparring over garden walls for rights to the rho-
dodendron bush that preceded them both by decades consti-
tutes loss of soul? That carpetbagging, cheapskate chiselers
disguised as futon salesmen and city planners might secretly
be stripping the region of its soul? Did a native have a right
to ask these questions? Did natives still enjoy any rights at
all? Did the very definition of *native* assume a different
meaning when the word was uttered by an influxer? If you'd
seen a spotted owl and/or eaten at Dick's, did that automatically qualify you as a native? Did the concept of native rights
mean anything at all? What the heck was a native, anyway?

These and other recondite wounds festered in the small
woman's brain until she discarded such trivia for more im-
mediate job-related matters. If Louie Song had blown up in
the Priest Rapids Dam explosion, why hadn't more tangible
evidence surfaced? Why had the search for Song been called
off just because they found his binoculars in rubble near the
fish ladder? Why was Song's Harley missing? Why was she
the only one who couldn't accept that Song had plunged off
the dam into the swollen river and drowned? Why couldn't
she get off the subject, for crying out loud? She had to stop
obsessing over Song. Life goes on. Life has to go on. It was
Friday morning, after all. Let's get our priorities straight, she
told herself, something Song would have said if he were
around to comment. She briefly revisited the Pacific Northwest soul question, but the prickly subject no longer capti-
vated her imagination. The weekend…ah, there was a welcome subject.

She had completely abandoned the quid pro quo du jour
and Louie Song and was contemplating a seriously ho-hum
weekend, when a Federal Express agent, evidently nursing a

fresh grudge against someone or something, burst into her cubicle and lobbed a pungent package that landed with a crash perilously near her latte. The delivery person fled, leaving Agent Diamond gagging, and pondering perhaps the day's most important question of all. From what quarter came this whiffy antinosegay?

Truly, Agent Diamond had craved a respite from the fray, these proximate two weekend off-duty days with nothing to achieve but a lolling ennui. Now this smelly intrusion conveyed the distinct odor of lackluster-weekend sabotage. Oily. Scaly. Rotting. Pinching her nostrils, she jerked the denizen tail-first out of the FedEx carton, held it aloft, and surveyed it.

A chinook salmon of medium weight and girth. Approximately twelve pounds. Eyeballs dull and dry, deporting that creepy dead-fish stare. Only, this particular pair of fish eyes looked more human than piscine. A fish with human eyes? Hello, Hanford? Have you lost a resident?

A rip in the rayed tail fin suggested the fish had once snagged a hook or inherited a flaw, but she was no ichthyologist, and the rip might simply be a rip. The fish might have snagged its tail fin on a floating branch, or, pushing the envelope, another fish might have bitten its tail.

Do fish bite one another?

According to scribble on the FedEx label, the putrid parcel had slid down the undiscriminating throat of a FedEx chute at Colville, Washington. Colville? That eastern Washington backwater? In that virtual ghost town, the sender could easily drop a pungent package down a FedEx flume without being observed. In which case, man or woman, adult or child, pink, green, or purple alien, whoever had sent the dead fish to Agent Diamond might as well have come from Pluto, because no one could identify him, or her. Or it.

By *it,* Agent Diamond meant to imply that anyone who would conjure such a nefarious scheme, not to mention execute it, must be at least half hippogriff. No human being with a modicum of respect for its species would mail to a fellow human being—overnight service notwithstanding—a decaying fish corpse. Therefore, an alien brute with a short grip on etiquette and zilch respect for postal regulations must have mailed it. Or else a sadistic salmon hater who had surpassed him-, her-, or itself. Alternatively, it might have been dispatched by one of those legendary ghouls haunting the Pacific Northwest's backwoods, leaving a Bigfoot print and terrorizing innocent human beings, not to mention more savvy animal species. Certainly the sender of this abomination possessed a twisted sense of humor, and apparently a shy side. Why else would the creep have used Venus's name and home address for the "Return to Sender" lines and charged the send to her personal FedEx account number?

She sipped her skinny vente and stared at the fish. The creep must hold a grudge against someone. Against her? Why? Surely Special Agent Diamond enjoyed a sterling reputation as a paragon of geniality, amigo to all but the most evil-bent poachers of rare and endangered species. Who could possibly hold a grudge against the affable, if not entirely charismatic, Special Agent Venus Diamond?

A former boyfriend perhaps? Impossible. There weren't any, at least not in the Pacific Northwest. There was Reuben in Singapore, but they hadn't exactly been lovers, and anyhow, according to their history, Reuben would have been on the receiving end of such malice, though, in truth, she felt none. So it wasn't a disgruntled beau's revenge. Considering the poachers she had snared in the dark act, few still drew breath, and most of them languished in Asian prisons. Her American foes had all fallen in action. Yet someone in the general vicinity of Oz apparently hated her enough to have lobbed this decaying fish.

Aha. Now she had it. Why hadn't she thought of this first? Of course, her husband's secret mistress had lobbed the rotting fish. They would deny it, both Richard and the hussy. Who was she anyway? Another ecosavior like Richard? An old flame? Surely not what's-her-name—oh, yes, Jeannie, the unlovely ex. No, Jeannie wouldn't send fish; she'd fire bullets. So who was the tart? Actually, all Venus knew was envirohubby had been behaving strangely lately, as if he'd caught a premature case of the seven-year itch—five years prematurely. A mistress was strongly suspect. But why would a jealous mistress send her lover's wife a dead salmon?

Wasting no time, Agent Diamond took steps to uncover the culprit. First, the Firecracker sought the advice of an expert, but when C. Paganelli, M.D., answered the phone, the Norwegian doc with the Italian handle sounded like a lemon in labor.

"Who bit you?" Venus asked, flicking the fish's raggedy fin. Claudia mumbled something Nordic. "Come again?"

"I said, 'Goddamn it to hell,'" Claudia snapped. Even snapping, Paganelli's voice came off soft and refined, soothingly sweet, like warm milk from a van Eyck teat.

"Why say that?" Venus pushed the fish away.

"I'm late for a flight to Maui," the Norwegian sun ray said. "Then *you* have to call. If this has anything at all to do with the Columbia River bombings, I am completely unavailable until a week from today at the earliest."

Venus explained about the dead salmon.

Claudia said, "I'm a physician. I don't know about fish. Why don't you show it to a fish biologist?"

"You're an expert on criminal evidence. In my limited circle, you were the logical choice. By the way, do you have any Dutch in you?"

"First off, no crime has been committed. Unless mailing dead fish is against the law, but I once sent a fresh and very dead Copper River sockeye salmon packed in dry ice from Kodiak to Denver, and nobody called it a crime. It's probably a gift, Venus. A gift that went wrong. What do they say? 'Never look a gift fish in the mouth.'" She paused, then added, "Maybe a little Dutch."

"What were you doing in Kodiak?"

"None of your damn business." The mother's milk soured.

"Can you help me?"

"In a word, aloha."

Interior's regional bureau occupied the forty-third floor of the Bumbershoot Building in downtown Oz. Being so high up, the feds enjoyed gluttonous wraparound vistas, a gull's-eye perspective of the Emerald City. Perched on the southern horizon, the big spumoni, Mount Rainier, periodically threatened to spew lava, and to the west, idyllic, verdant islands rose from the itinerant mists over Puget Sound. When the fog wasn't too thick or the rain pelting, the view encompassed Elliott Bay's colorful maritime chaos, including thirty-six red cargo cranes genuflecting to progress, but only in those halcyon Seattle-sunbreak moments. Surrounding all this majesty, the snowy sawtooth Cascades and Olympics encircled the burgeoning city like a shark's open jaw coddling a mouthful of flotsam just before a major swallow. Oh yes, spectacular peekaboo vistas, if you ranked an office with windows. Few did, and they jealously defended their territory.

Venus's office in the Fish and Wildlife section was a small cubicle off a pedestrian corridor, situated somewhere in the vast Nowhereland between Reception and the Mr. Coffee machine. Nothing fancy, just three blank walls and an open space into the corridor, which made a laughingstock of privacy.

"You want to complain about your office?" her boss, Oly Olson, had snapped the one time she had requested that a fourth wall with a door be added to her space. "Who the hell do you think you are? Sally Ride? Just because you were astronaut-for-a-day on that space flight last June doesn't earn you the right to a private office." Olson had shaken a finger in her face and tacked on: "I'll tell you what will earn you a private office. Just one thing will get you a private office. You go out and track down and capture the Unknown, and then maybe we'll talk about a private office."

"But the Unknown is just a figment," she had complained to Olson back then. "A figment of the bored, bucolic imagination. Like Bigfoot. It isn't real."

Olson had scoffed. "Ha, so say you. Try telling that to

half the population of Washington State, and Oregon, too, and British Columbia, for that matter. And while you're at it, explain to these eastern Washington cowboys just exactly who sucked the blood from the jugular veins of their prized heifers. As long as unexplained phenomena occur, the Unknown will exist, at least in rural folks' minds, and we'll be deluged with complaints that we're harboring half-human, half-elk monsters on our wildlife preserves."

"But I'm just trying to say that it isn't real...."

Olson had turned his back to her, having swiveled the chair at his desk to face his own splendid wraparound views. What did he care if she didn't have a fourth wall and a door, let alone a window on the world?

She had never raised the sticky subject again, though she silently fumed and plotted ways to enclose her semipublic work space. And this May morning, as a soporific pall stymied even the keenest eye, she might have gloated over Olson's wasted windows were it not for the stinking parcel on her desk. Had anyone else in the office noticed the reek from her cubicle? God, how mortifying. She pondered what to do, and soon she was rewarded with a bright idea: True, the package was addressed to her, but—possibly from a sadistic impulse—she wanted to share it with the boss.

Drawing soft white cotton evidence gloves over her hands, taking care not to smudge the evidence, she gripped the package's outer wrapping by one corner. In the other gloved hand, she pinched the fish's tail between her thumb and index finger, held this behind her back, and, thus arranged, padded along the corridor to Olson's office, her Doc Martens barely audible against the industrial carpet. Did anyone notice the odor accompanying her short journey? Possibly Eric Sweetwater, for when she passed his cubicle, she heard him gag. Other than that, no major events occurred between her cubicle and the boss's lair.

SIX

Fact: A 1996 study indicated that the caffeine content of Puget Sound rises eightfold between 8:00 a.m. and 8:30 a.m. each morning. The origin of the caffeine in Puget Sound is the sewer system. Caffeine does not break down, but passes virtually unchanged through the human body. Little is known about the effects of caffeine on fish and wildlife, although presently scientists believe that the caffeine contamination in Puget Sound likely has a "minimal effect" on marine wildlife inhabiting Puget Sound. Since the 1996 study, the number of coffee shops, drive-in coffee stands, and coffee carts in the Puget Sound region has nearly doubled.

TURTLE EYES glanced up when Venus entered the room. Had Olson binged last night? She wouldn't be surprised. Everyone at Fish and Wildlife had been behaving irresponsibly since the Priest River Dam explosion, since Song disappeared in a blast of rock and water. Olson might have turned to his old pal for comfort. Anything to expunge the memories of Revos Man. Then Olson sneezed, and she wondered if he hadn't binged after all, but had simply snared a bad cold.

"Gesundheit."

"What do you want?" Gruff, congested, surly. Olson's charisma could wallow in a stuffed thimble.

"FedEx just delivered this." Ceremoniously, for she possessed a theatrical gene, she set the FedEx box on Olson's desk, directly under his nose. The boss sniffed; his nostrils twitched.

He said, "Did you shower this morning?"

"Yes, sir."

She flashed her most disarming smile, but Olson wasn't charmed. He read the return address on the FedEx label. "What did you send yourself via FedEx and how does it concern me?"

She started to explain. "Someone used my name. I didn't—"

Olson interrupted. "Another crackpot. These gray winters breed them."

Another sneeze. Another "Gesundheit."

"Maybe a crackpot," Venus said. "But why did the giver go to all this trouble? This box contained a twelve-pound, uh, object. And my birthday was last month, though some people forgot." Hint, hint.

Olson swatted a pesky invisible insect. "Crackpots are unpredictable. So what weighed twelve pounds?"

She stepped forward. Her sea-nymph eyes engaged his red whites and blues. "This." With flair, she slapped down the ex-animate fish. Olson got one good whiff, then gagged.

"Pee-uw," he said. "Get that thing out of here. What kind of joke is this anyway?"

"Check out the eyes. It's got human eyes."

Olson inspected the fish, never actually touching the slippery piscine, only prodding and poking at it with a letter opener. After awhile, he shoved the corpus delecti across the desk.

"Maybe you have time to fritter away, but I'm a busy man and under too much stress. Already we have posttorpor bears running rampant through eastern Washington towns looking for food and water. We have elk attacking VW Bugs, and the roadkill isn't pretty. We have job descriptions, and in case you've misplaced yours, I can provide you a copy. Now, what kind of a jerky prank is this?''

Venus shrugged. She didn't know.

The boss's eyelids fluttered. His body sagged. Speaking of dead fish...

He might be back on the sauce, she thought. Then he said, ''Federal agencies get dozens of these petty harassments every week. Just cranks who haven't anything better to do with their lives. If we took them all seriously, we'd never get any work accomplished.''

''This one smells genuine,'' she said.

He glanced up. ''Genuine what?''

''Genuine trouble.''

''I'll tell you what's genuine trouble. You are genuine trouble. Now, get that fish out of here before I puke.''

She went away with the fish, leaving Olson clutching his head and muttering darkly. When she came back, she said, ''I realize that you're very busy, sir, but I'd appreciate the opportunity to talk this over.''

Olson squinted up at her, as if making his eyes smaller could reduce her size, her significance, and the amount of frustration she chronically visited upon his life. He waited for her to say something, and eventually she did.

''It's a chinook salmon.''

''How the hell do you know that?'' he asked, irritated.

''I'm no fish expert, but a native knows these things. It's *O. tshawytscha*. See? You can tell by the dark spotting on its back and tail. And the black lower lip.''

''Fish don't have lips.''

''Yes they do.''

''No they don't.''

''Jaw, then. The lower jaw is black.''

Olson shrugged. ''So it's a chinook. So what?''

''I think it came from the Columbia River.'' She was insistent. ''Because, if you will just take a gander at this small rip in the tail, it seems to have been tagged at one time. The tag must have been ripped off. It might have come from a hatchery. It might be one of those test specimens out of Hanford Reach. Then again, it might be a wild salmon. And, too, it might have come from Puget Sound.''

Olson gripped his head. It wanted to pop off. He had to hold it securely on his neck or risk losing his mind, literally. She did this to him frequently. "They don't tag their tail fins. But for the sake of argument, say it did come out of the Columbia. What's the big deal?''

She said, "You may recall that my current assignment, until you ordered me back into the office to perform more mundane tasks, was tracking the Columbia River bombers. Maybe that's why this little love token was sent to me. Maybe they're trying to kill us off one by one, first Song, then—''

"Dozens of law-enforcement officers are on the case, from the Fisheries Service to the ATF to the FBI to the goddamn Canadian Mounties. From our office, besides you, Sparks and Dottie are on that same assignment. Have they been similarly gifted?''

"I haven't checked with them, sir. But since you loaned out Sparks and Dottie to the Fisheries Service, Dottie's been reassigned to the salmon-count artifice. She's working the Snake River, with a crew up at Ice Harbor Dam. And Sparks is down at Astoria, counting fish and anarchists.'' Bread and roses. Loaves and fishes. Guns and butter. "I should be out there with them. Except you made me come back into the office to help you plan Song's memorial service. Then you decided to put it off because, as you put it so succinctly, Louie hated rituals, wildlife is running amuck, and we saviors of the wild kingdom have no time for pithy sentiment. So here I am, when I really ought to be up—''

"Your point, Diamond?''

"So I haven't yet checked with either of them.''

Olson pawed around his desk for Alka-Seltzer. "Screwball.''

Venus pushed on. "At any rate, I think it's worth delving into."

Olson murmured unintelligibly.

"Pardon me, sir?"

"I hate your goddamn 'pardon-mes' and 'sirs.' Why can't you just say 'whaa-at?' like us blue-collar Ballard folks? Why do you have to call me 'sir' when everyone else is content to use my last name? Why do you have to flaunt your Magnolia Bluff heredity? Why can't you be like the rest of us?"

The blond firecracker bit her fuze. "I can't help the way I was raised. Or where. Or the old money, for that matter. Sir."

"Well, you can goddamn help the way you act now." Olson's beefy hands gripped the desk and a pungent memory of rotting fish flesh wafted upward. "You're a goddamn upper-class snob who expects every moment of every workday to embody high drama, and all you ever do around this office is attract trouble. Now, *please,* for the love of Pete"—he clutched his throbbing temples—"get lost. I need to finish this bear-attack report."

"If people would quit encroaching on their territory—"

"Cool it."

Special Agent Diamond was small, with delicate bones. Her Fish and Wildlife uniform hung loosely from her frame because she had recently lost several pounds due to personal problems. Private matters. Nothing she couldn't handle outside the office. Special Agent Diamond never allowed private troubles to interfere with her work obligations. Unlike Song, Diamond harbored few fantasies about her professional colleagues, and she had never met a prospective partner in the north elevator. She had seen Miss Delicious a time or two, but her circuitry wasn't wired that way. True, she had admired the poison green stockings, had been somewhat awestruck over the garters pressing through Miss Delicious's gray flannel skirt. But this wasn't Venus's orientation, alas, so Miss Delicious got nowhere when she winked at her. No, she wasn't preoccupied with such trivial minutiae, and, given a choice, Agent Diamond would rather be focusing on her personal crisis. But ever since the Priest Rapids Dam bombing, since Song had gone down into the gorge like so much dry rubble, no federal agent had enjoyed the luxury of personal crises, never mind straying eco-hubbies.

"Maybe it's not important," she said to Olson. "Maybe it's, like you say, just a crackpot trying to waste our time. Still, the Fragrant One was addressed to me, and I'd like your permission to delve into it."

Olson whimpered, "Why?" Still ferreting out the elusive Alka-Seltzer.

"Maybe it's the Columbia River bombers. Or maybe someone's trying to warn us that he, or she, or someone else, is going to commit a crime. I can't be anymore specific than that. I'd like to spend a few hours checking it out."

The boss squared his shoulders. When facing off with Special Agent Diamond, he had found that his best strategy was to puff out his enormous chest and be quite firm. "Permission granted," he intoned softly. She was halfway out the door, wearing a satisfied smirk, when he lobbed his premeditated malicious postscript: "On your own time, Diamond. Not the government's."

She turned around. "Once upon a time," she said, "you promised me an office with walls if I could solve the mystery of the Unknown. Now you're telling me that tracking down a potential lead to the Columbia River bombers is an off-duty kind of activity. What's the difference between the two, besides that one is real and the other's a figment?"

Olson had unearthed the Alka-Seltzer. Dissolving two tablets in a glass of Aquafina, focusing on the fizz, he said, "You're awfully naïve, Diamond. If you think you can trick me, you're sadly off-base."

"By the way," she said casually, "whom are you voting for in November?"

"None of your damn business...*whom*'"

She ignored the mock, flicked a stray fish scale off her sleeve. "They say President Benson is planning a visit to his native state, to kick off his reelection campaign."

Olson grunted. "Barry Benson's native state is mental."

"Ah. So you're voting for the lady candidate?" she asked, fishing.

"I like Jenny Pickforth."

Venus held out an empty palm. "Benson's the pro-environment candidate."

"Benson's a frigging hypocrite. Don't preach Benson to me."

Time to drop politics. She leaned against the door. "What say I solve the mystery of the dead chinook—on my own time—and it directly contributes to capturing the bombers, to bringing justice for Louie, you'll then give me walls?" She decided to milk it. "And windows?"

Olson glugged down the frothing elixir in one smooth swallow.

"Sure, Diamond," he said, wiping his mouth. "It's a deal. I want those anarchist bastards. Hell, we all want to get our hands on them."

"One thing puzzles me," she said, relishing her small victory.

"Just one?" Very grouchy.

"If, as we surmise, the bombers are truly environmentalists, wouldn't they be educated about the dams and their effect on salmon? Wouldn't they know that the dams on the Columbia River are more crucial for energy production than the dams on the Snake? The big fuss is all about breaching the Snake River dams, the less important dams. Why didn't they just go after the Snake River dams?"

"Oh my God." Olson gripped his egg-shaped head. "I am not a mind reader. I don't know what the bastards are thinking. How the hell would I know? Now, go away, and for chrissake, get rid of that putrid fish. I can still smell it."

AN HOUR LATER, her phone rang. She jumped out of a reverie, answered. Hiroshi, the office receptionist, said, "There's a girl on the phone who wants to speak to someone about the dam bombings."

"Better put her through to Olson."

Hiroshi said, "She insists on speaking to a female agent. So should I give her to you?"

"Go ahead." Venus added, "And put a tracer on the call."

At first, the young voice stammered and hesitated. Venus listened as much for veracity as for details.

When she was finally able to speak, the girl said, "I think I know who blew up those dams."

Venus said, "First give me your name and location."

"I can't. I mean, this has to be a totally anonymous call." Hesitation, then: "Kettle Falls, Washington. That's all I'm going to tell you."

Kettle Falls was in northeastern Washington, on the Columbia River, near the border with Canada.

Venus said, "All right. Give me your information."

The girl's voice trembled. "He's, like, my boyfriend. He'll kill me if he finds out I made this call."

"What's his name?"

"I…I don't know."

Venus made a face. "You don't know your boyfriend's name?"

"That's right."

"How long have you known him?"

"Couple months. I…I've been afraid to ask him."

"Tell me what you know about him. Describe him."

"He's a big guy. Clean-cut. A really sexy dude."

"Be more specific. Ancestry, eye color, hair, that sort of thing."

"He's white. I mean, I guess you'd say Anglo. Really awesome brown eyes. He's got short brown hair. No beard or anything, not even a mustache. He's maybe thirty, at the most. He's very fastidious. You should see his fingernails. And he never removes his socks, not even when…'' Her voice trailed off.

"Any scars or birthmarks?"

"Not that I've noticed."

"Is he armed?"

The girl hesitated. "You mean does he have a gun?"

"Right."

"I…I'm not sure. He always carries this satchel. Whenever he comes to visit me, he brings it. But he doesn't sleep with it or anything. Maybe there's a gun inside. I've never seen one, though."

"What kind of vehicle does he drive?"

"A van. It's, like, a real van. Not an SUV. It's dark brown."

"License number?"

"He…he keeps, like, changing the plates. One day they say Alabama and the next day California. I can't tell what's real or not real."

"What about the van? Make and model?"

"I…I'm not sure. I can't tell the difference between cars and vans. They all look the same to me."

"Is it new? Old?"

"It's pretty new. Totally clean inside. And it smells like a new car. I mean, van. I think it's American-made."

Venus said, "Where is he now?"

"The big guy?"

"Yes. Where is he right now?"

"I don't know. He comes and goes. What made me suspect him is, he's been gone both times those dams were hit. And, well, I've seen the bombs. The bombs he makes."

The girl still refused to give her name. Venus said, "Take down my private cell phone number." The girl said she could memorize it and then repeated it back to Venus. "Can you get his vehicle make, model, and registration number and call that into me?"

"If he comes back. I could try. It might take awhile. He watches me pretty closely when we're together. I'll try."

"Why are turning him in?"

The girl hesitated longer this time. "I really like him. But he scares me. I have to go now."

The girl hung up. Hiroshi came back on. "It's a south-central Washington area code. The number belongs to a public phone booth."

So the girl had lied when she said, "Kettle Falls, Washington."

Venus said, "Find out the exact location of that phone booth."

"I'm trying," said Hiroshi. "It might take awhile."

"We can't wait that long," Venus told Hiroshi.

She hung up and went to tell the boss about the mystery girl.

SEVEN

How fish are followed: Washington State law requires that hatchery salmon be easily distinguished from wild salmon. The way humans identify fish is by tagging them. In the salmon-tagging process, a three-inch hatchery fingerling's adipose fin, located on the rear quadrant of the fish's spine, is snipped off. Wild salmon possess an adipose fin; hatchery salmon have theirs removed. Until recently, this snipping was performed by human hands. Today, hatchery fingerlings are mass-fed into the high-tech marking and tagging system (MATS), where, in addition to the adipose fin removal, the machinery punches holes through the cartilage above the mouth and clips on a wire with an identification tag. With infrared beams and digital cameras, the MATS system can measure by assembly line and process approximately 2 million salmon fingerlings per week.

VENUS LIVED IN a beach mansion at Alki Point, a space too big and grand for one person. She lived there alone because her life partner had flown the nest to perform environmental heroics in West Africa. If she was lucky, ecohubby might deign to visit on furlough in June. Meanwhile, she lived without pets or companions of any kind, and some observers, Song included, had speculated that she preferred the solitude. Song had detested her husband, firmly believing that she should never have married Richard Winters, and from day one, he'd predicted a doomed union. Unknown to her, Song had waited, somewhat opportunistically, for the big split. Sooner or later, the Firecracker would cool on the hubby, and then Song could make his move. This had been Song's secret plan, so secret that even Song had not consciously known about it. But Song had numerous secret plans, several of which he didn't know about, and not all of them had ever perfectly meshed.

Venus slipped the dead salmon into a plastic freezer bag and popped it into a massive deep freeze that hummed sonorously against one garage wall. Back inside, she helped herself to a Dalwhinnie on the rocks. One heavy-handed shot nicely disengaged her petite limbic system, permitting the subconscious freedom of expression. Wasting no time, she wriggled into her Speedo, plucked a large fluffy towel from the linen closet, and slipped outdoors by way of the beachfront terrace.

The Taj fronted on Alki Beach. Clad only in the Speedo and a pair of rubber beach socks, she stepped into the frigid evening air, crossing the nippy sand to Puget Sound's unkempt tide line. At dusk, sooty buffalo clouds herded across a creosote horizon, spurred on by a snappy wind, and the sound's choppy surface reflected a leaden quality, like mercury. The tide, on its way out, deposited wee drops of indolent spittle that glistened along the taupe sand. She chased two perfectly innocent gulls off a pale driftwood log, placed her towel neatly across the log's length, secured it with two large rocks, walked across the narrow beach, and tramped bravely into the water. Once she reached hip height, she plunged headlong into the icy water.

She was a native, ya sure, you betcha. Only a native survives a winter swim in Puget Sound without a wet suit. You take a Californian, or one of these oysterphobic midwesterners and put 'er down at Puget Sound's tide line and you'll hear one heck of a yowling. They can't take it, like they can't take the rain after a few years. If you weren't born here, you won't last a decade before the Pacific Northwest sucks the calcium from your damp bones and rusts out your aching ligaments, before your flesh evolves to mold. You'll wish you'd been born with fins and flippers, gills and scales, and dream of hot desert sands and perpetual Taos sunshine. It's all in the genes, and if you ain't got 'em, you won't survive. Tyee Sahale, the Creator of all things, had made the Pacific Northwest for fish, for great clawing crabs, for octopi and orca, black bears and bald eagles, for slugs and moss and mushrooms and giant dripping Doug firs, and any other waterlogged species that thrives on incessant effluvial product. Take it or get the hell out, and most natives wished most influxers would. Most, not all.

Venus did the breaststroke parallel to the beach as far as Alki Point lighthouse, where in the shallows she encountered several salmon, apparently seeking nourishment on their journey to the river's mouth at Three Tree Point. When she left the water to rest on the beach, she saw a salmon leap out of the water near the shore, its fiery red skin a sign of ripeness, of sexual urgency, and she thought its golden eye was focused on her. She wondered if the fish would make it upriver to their spawning grounds. She wondered if fish really did have souls.

LONG AGO, before salmon became an industry, the Indians believed that everything had a soul. Rocks, soil, plants, trees, mountains, rivers, and even salmon had souls. When an Indian set his weir and took salmon from the river, he treated the fish with respect. First, he would kill the fish quickly and painlessly. Then he would clean it, cook it, and return the bones to the river, where he believed they would regenerate, grow a new fish. Before eating the salmon, he would give thanks to the fish, ask for its blessing.

The Indians believed that salmon were supernatural beings that dwelled in five houses underneath the river. The houses represented the species: chinook, sockeye, pink, chum, and

coho. Like the land animals the Indians killed for food, the
salmon allowed man to kill it and consume its flesh. The
killing was ceremonial and not final. The killing was
salmon's gift to man, a ritual of union, and the eating of
salmon was a commingling of flesh. But the salmon never
really died, for when its bones were returned to the river, its
soul returned to its house beneath the river, and there it re-
incarnated.

Each season, the tribes held a First Salmon Ceremony.
When the first salmon of each season was pulled from the
river, a great ceremony accompanied its killing and prepa-
ration. At a festive potlatch, the salmon was shared among
all members of the tribe, so that all might partake of the first
salmon's soul, the first salmon's blessing, the goodness of the
fish. The Indians made a weir from reeds and bone, and they
built the weir across the river. But, according to custom, each
weir could be used for only ten days and nights, and then it
had to be destroyed. If the tribe wanted more fish, they would
have to construct another weir, and this took time. Meanwhile, the salmon continued running upriver to spawn. In this
way, the natural economy provided enough fish to fill the
five salmon houses and to feed the land creatures.

Sometimes, the Indians would use hooks or spears, and
sometimes they would cast nets made of reeds and branches
into the rivers and oceans and gather great numbers of
salmon. But they kept only what they could use. What was
not consumed was dried to provide food for the barren times,
when the salmon weren't running. This respectful relationship
existed between man and salmon until capturing salmon became an industry and lost its spiritual significance. Because
industry lacks a soul, the salmon was treated as soulless, its
bones were not returned to the rivers, and the nets and weirs
stayed long in the water. Thus, the salmon did not regenerate
and its numbers dwindled, some subspecies became extinct,
and some rivers lost all their salmon forever. In the oceans,
salmon were hauled into nets by the millions. Great floating

fish processors put the salmon flesh into cans and shipped the product to a hungry world market. No thought was given to depletion. Or to the salmon's soul.

DAYLIGHT WAS fast fading. Venus waded into the icy water and did a breaststroke on the return, all the while allowing her subconscious to perform its mysterious exercise, wherein the brain probed intuition and eventually the two gave birth to an idea. By the time she had reached the sandy beach in front of the Taj, her skin was mottled purple. She sprinted back to the house, ignoring the hectoring gulls. What did they know about hypothermia?

The Water Pik's pulsating feature shot scalding liquid needles onto her numbed skin. She couldn't feel the heat, just the sharp stabs of spray. When she'd had enough, she toweled off, dressed, fished a nonseafood snack from the fridge, and sat down to think.

Why would anyone mail anyone else a dead fish? Some unspoken message? A metaphor of some kind? Dead fish equals…Rhymes with…Looks like… And what about this girl's anonymous phone call? Just a cuckoo bird, or was she for real? She seemed genuine. A little off, maybe. She didn't even know her boyfriend's name. Maybe a tad eccentric; still, she seemed authentic. And scared. Definitely scared.

The phone rang. Venus snatched it up and said, "Agent Diamond," like she was at work, her tone a trifle rottweiler. Luckily, it wasn't envirohubby; he'd have taken the gruffness personally.

"Gut me," barked a muffled voice of indeterminate gender before clicking off.

She tried the sharp knife that the hubby used to filet fish, but the salmon, already half-frozen, resisted, so she popped it into the microwave until the fish scales sizzled and popped. Awkwardly, for she was no chef, she filleted the fish, and, pulling the two sides apart, exposed the guts, the intact roe.

The salmon must have been heading upstream to spawn

when it was caught, before it had a chance to unload its eggs. Picking through the decaying flesh, she found a tiny plastic bag, maybe an official fish tag. Or it might be a ruse. Using a loupe, she saw that the tag bore a number. And a name: "Fish #4554PS. Ella" was printed on the plastic in black marker.

OLSON HAD DEFINITELY been straddling the bottle. She could tell by his slurred consonants, and by the tinkle of ice against glass. No one could binge like Olson. She said, "Salmon Ella."

He said, "You eat something bad?"

She explained. "The initials on the tag might stand for Puget Sound. The number may be a sign of a hatchery fish, tagged as a fingerling. The name Ella is a mystery. Also, I remembered that hatchery salmon don't have adipose fins because they've been snipped off. And there's a ring that has been inserted through the mouth, with this tag on it. I gather this fish swallowed its tag, or else someone stuffed it down its throat just to make me work harder. Anyway, Salmon Ella is definitely a hatchery specimen."

More ice-to-glass clinks, then: "Hell, Venus, you know crackpots love to invent fraudulent decoys."

"Maybe the bombers sent this...." She paused a beat and said, "Or maybe the anonymous girl. Maybe I'm the next casualty. After Louie."

Over the line, she could hear the wind blowing in off Shilshole Bay in Olson's Ballard neighborhood. Then Olson said, "That's the last frigging time I loan my agents out to another federal agency." He grunted, ice tinkled, and then more silence.

Venus said, "Any word on the phone booth trace?"

"I was just going to tell you. Why do you always have to preempt me?"

She said, "I wasn't trying to—"

Olson cut her off. "Phone booth near Crow Butte State

Park, several miles downriver from McNary Dam. I sent an agent up from The Dalles to check it out. Phone booth's at a Washington Visitors' Center. Agent brushed for fingerprints. Nada. But he found a plastic bag on the floor of the phone booth. Bag came from Astoria Pet World. Nothing inside. Just a crumpled-up bag.''

''Astoria,'' she said. ''Did we ever determine if that Astoria bank bombing is related to the dam explosions?''

''ATF's checking explosives tracings from all three. We should know something in a few days.''

Venus said, ''Think he's targeting McNary for the next hit?''

Olson said, ''Or John Day. Anyway, no one gets within a mile of those dams without our agents knowing about it. He'll never succeed.''

''I think I'll head down there.''

''The hell you will. We've got people down there. You don't need to go down there.''

''I spoke to her, sir. I stand a better chance of identifying her.''

''Never mind. You're not going down there. You'll just get into trouble. Besides, I need you in the office. And remember, this is the Army Corps of Engineers and the Fisheries Service's baby, not ours. We're just minor players here. We follow orders on this one.''

''But it was our agent who got blown up....''

''I'm telling you for the last time, Diamond.''

''But...''

''I'm going to check on Sparks and Dottie. I'll get back to you.''

She said, ''Why won't you put me back in the field?'' But he had hung up.

WHILE SHE WAITED for Olson to call back, she went on-line to her favorite browser, typed, ''Salmon Ella,'' and hit the predictable circuitous jackpot: 48,271 references to the bacterial infection. She tried, "Salmon AND Ella." Nothing.

The phone rang. Venus leaned over, checked the caller ID. Her sister Echo's phone number appeared on the display. She let the answering service pick up the call, and finished surfing for Salmon Ella.

An hour later, Olson still hadn't called back. She dialed his number. Busy. She dialed again. Still busy. She dialed Echo's number. The sibling snatched up the phone on the first ring.

Echo lived in Manhattan, where she wrote poetry and lived off her trust fund. She owned a three-bedroom condo on Washington Square where, in a slack season, she received sixteen active male suitors, give or take, per week. She possessed a Chanel wardrobe that put Blaine Trump to shame. She was sleek and long-legged, oddly fastidious to the point of being squeamish, and was a nymphomaniac, but only in the shower. She had Dresden blue eyes and a sulky mouth that men longed to bite, and did, often. Echo spent most days in bed, writing poetry, or in the shower, cavorting with her various partners. She had installed a condom dispenser in her powder room and a video cam in her bedroom. The condom dispenser was self-explanatory. The video cam was used primarily to record the poet's compositions even as they spilled raw from her talented lips. For Echo had as much literary acumen as she had sexual prowess.

"I've been named a MacArthur Fellow," Echo gushed over the line.

Venus checked her Swatch. "What time is it there?"

"What difference does it make?" Echo snapped. "I've just been declared a literary genius."

"Great," she said half-sincerely. "Now what will you do?"

"That's exactly why I called. Venus, I have decided that my next chapbook will be comprised of poems about the endangered salmon of the Pacific Northwest. Somewhat coincidentally, Mother has just today informed me that you are currently counting fish on the Columbia. How fascinating for you. So with this in mind, I plan to arrive in Seattle this coming Monday, and from that day forward, I shall follow you around on your assignments, all the while drinking in the untamed atmosphere of the species's sexual adventures as it struggles against all odds up the once-mighty Columbia River. Don't worry, I shan't get under your feet.''

"But—"

"Never mind. I am committed. You'll be famous, Venus, when I have finished with you.''

"Echo, please don't do this...."

"Bye-bye, darling. See you in three days.''

On the next try, she got through to Olson. "I've been on the phone for the past hour,'' Olson said, "and I couldn't locate Sparks or Dottie. Until I called up to the fisheries office at Priest Rapids. Turns out, both of them had the same idea to visit the Reach and scour the area for signs of Song. That is in direct violation of my orders. They are being disciplined as we speak.''

"Nothing too harsh, I gather.''

"I'm fed up with my agents' lack of respect.''

A FREAK STORM blew off Puget Sound carrying hard rain and vacillating winds that rattled the Taj's windowpanes. Venus had just nodded off, when the phone rang. The voice was husky, and the r's thick when it slurred, "Roll on, Columbia, roll on.''

"Who's that?'' she muttered groggily. "Woody Guthrie?''

The caller rasped, "Stay out of Kettle Falls,'' and hung up.

She didn't go back to sleep immediately, but lay across the sheets, twiddling her toes, missing envirohubby more than she cared to, and worrying over his potential marital infidelity. This was a no-brainer compared to Song's mysterious fate.

Richard Winters, the same man who had looked her straight in the eye and vowed "till death us do part," had already cheated at least once. Why? She knew he still loved her. Still, lately he seemed changed, preoccupied, and introspective. Maybe it was just a personality quirk she had missed before now. She had decided to give him his space, not to pry. But she knew he had cheated.

He had denied it, of course. Had Richard wanted to keep his cheating a secret, he shouldn't have kept a silky souvenir from the tryst. Venus had discovered the damaging evidence with the aid of a cocky seabird one remarkably warm winter morning.

Picture a clear blue Pacific Northwest dawn, lemon-pink sunrise over Mount Rainier, bracing salt air robustly wafting off Puget Sound, tiny fishing vessels skimming the horizon. Venus was standing half-naked, or half-dressed—she couldn't remember which—gazing out at the lovely dawn, wishing that her husband would come home from his crusades.

She flung open the French doors and inhaled some tangy, energizing salt air. Since she hadn't recently enjoyed the stimulation of a husband in residence, at least she could resort to the sensory tease of a salt-air tonic. She inhaled, swooned, exhaled, and then turned her back to finish dressing.

Flap, flap.

What was that sound? Turning to face the open window, she beheld the uninvited visitor. A gull—*Laurus glaucescens,* to be precise—had stepped through the French doors and now, with no sense of propriety, waddled across the bedroom carpet and into Richard's California Closet.

Pursuing the invader, she heard the bird thrashing around in the closet. When it eventually emerged from a shelf of Richard's sweaters, Venus immediately noticed the gull held between its mandibles something purple and lacy. What's this? Why, a skimpy purple thong bikini, the likes of which had never inhabited Venus's lingerie drawer. Clamped in the gull's bill.

True, she wore enticing lingerie; in fact, she was a sworn-for-life string-bikini addict. These purple thong panties, however, had never graced her derriere, and, she strongly suspected, neither did they belong to Richard.

How, then, did these exotics come to rest among her husband's suits and ties?

She had the bird cornered in the depths of the closet. Moving in, she made a quick decision to try to save the evidence. But the gull didn't want to give up the panties. Flapping featherless arms, Venus failed to intimidate the wary but worldly-wise gull. She moved slowly to the right. The gull sidestepped to the left, its pink legs trembling only slightly.

"Grrr," she said in her angriest voice, meaning it.

The gull blinked its red eyes but otherwise stood motionless, the sleazy purple thong draping down its mandibles like Manchu's mustache, its dusky wings fluttering only slightly. Standoff.

She moved in slowly, with resolve. The motionless gull watched her creeping closer, closer. As she reached out to grab the thong, all she grasped was salty air, and the gull flapped over her head, flew from the closet, across the bedroom, and through the French doors. It sailed north over Puget Sound, thong panties clamped tightly in its bill.

He'd give the Ballard boys something to talk about.

Richard, of course, had denied any knowledge of the mysterious panties. They had discussed the purple thong incident via telephone, since Richard was already in Ivory Coast when the gull-burglar incident occurred. "The gull must have brought them in," he had suggested lamely.

Sure, sure. And how was Ivory Coast treating ecohubby? "Oh, just a lot of hard work and no play," he had complained.

Sure, sure.

She knew he was lying. Whenever he lied, a frog bothered his throat and he'd constantly clear it. She hadn't figured out who had worn the purple thong thing in her husband's company. That was still a mystery. But she was increasingly certain that envirohubby had strayed, and maybe more than once. The gull incident was just the most recent, and blatant, clue.

Now she needed a diversion, something else to fret about. Grieving for Song seemed ever so much more manageable than dissecting her troubled marriage.

Had Louie died instantly? Had Mystery Girl actually slept with a man whose name she didn't know? Had M.G. actually seen the bombs, or just thought she had? Why would Dottie and Sparks violate Olson's orders?

Do salmon really have souls?

She slept restlessly between hideous dreams.

EIGHT

ONE MORNING BEFORE DAWN, the big guy woke Darla and told her it was time to decamp. Darla didn't argue, even though she vehemently disagreed. Predawn ramblings were not her idea of a good time, and she would have told the big guy so had he not had such a gruff edge to his voice.

Darla scrambled into her clothes and popped a Penguin. She was hooked on the tiny white mint-flavored caffeine tablets that lent her mornings a whole new zest. She had discovered Penguins on a shopping spree, while passing time at a mall. Spending money always tired her out. Exhausted from store hopping, she had ducked into an SBC coffee shop and ordered a double-shot skinny latte grande. The Penguins were prominently displayed in their distinctive black-and-white tins beside the cash register. Darla, a pinniped lover, couldn't resist the little penguin on the tin. She bought one and, on the way back to the motel, popped her first Penguin tablet. Euphoria.

Hooked. When the big guy rousted her this predawn morning, a groggy Darla popped two Penguins and soon fully awoke. As they drove along the Columbia River on the Washington side, the big guy concentrated on his driving. Darla kept popping Penguins, feeling more and more awake. After awhile, she got up the nerve to say, "You never told me your name."

He scowled but concentrated on his driving. A long silence ensued, then he said, "You can call me Gerald."

"Okay...Gerald." Darla giggled. "I would never have

guessed that was your name. I thought it would be, like, Rick or something. You don't look like a Gerald to me. You don't even act like a Gerald—I mean, what I think a Gerald should act like…."

"Shut up," Gerald said in a quiet but firm voice.

Darla tried to still her tongue, but the Penguins had loosened it beyond her control. She read aloud every road sign they passed, including the signs warning of deer crossings and the little milepost markers.

She read the billboards as they climbed over Horse Heaven Hills on the outskirts of Kennewick, and she read the signs in West Richland that told her they were just eleven miles south of Hanford Reservation. Gerald let her ramble because he couldn't shut her up, unless he stopped driving and smacked her good, but Gerald had discipline. This was no time to let go. He needed Darla, so he didn't try to silence her ramblings, but he did take the Penguins tin away from her, and when they stopped for breakfast in Grandview, he wouldn't allow her to order coffee.

"What happened to the river, Gerald?"

"We left it forty miles back."

Darla tuned in the local public radio station. The NPR news broadcast held little interest for her until the local version came on and the anchor said, "President Barry Benson's campaign appearance in eastern Washington, scheduled for three months from today, may be canceled if authorities fail to identify and capture the Columbia River bombers, who remain at large and may strike again."

Darla glanced across the truck cab. Gerald's brow was furrowed, his jaw tight and pulsing. Darla said, "Gerald, by any chance are you planning to assassinate President Benson?"

The big guy glanced over at Darla and the look on his face sent little rivers of ice along her spine. "Someday you'll thank me for this," he said. And Darla dared not question him further.

She had figured out that the van was an American make and had written down the make and model. He continued swapping license plates, so she gave up trying to keep track of those. A couple of times, she tried to locate the van's serial number. She thought she remembered that it would be on the front dash, visible through the windshield. But each time she had approached the van, he'd called her away before she had time to locate the number. She'd try again, but he was watching her more closely, so she'd have to be very careful, very discreet.

Where the river flowed north-south through Hanford Reservation, the highway turned into dry land rolling westward. Only authorized personnel were permitted on Hanford, and Gerald had no desire to enter the Reach, no suicidal tendency to explore a radioactive waste site. They drove through Yakima, on the perimeter of the U.S. Military Reservation. Darla exclaimed over the parched landscape and allowed how it made her feel estranged from nature. At Ellensburg, he turned onto a short section of Interstate 90, heading east to where the highway reunited with the river above Hanford Reach. Like the salmon that were lucky enough to make it this far, he followed the river upstream. He didn't drive as far as Vantage. Instead, he crossed the river bridge and turned south toward Wanapum Dam. But a park ranger's truck sat idling at the gate, so he got out of there fast and drove zigzagging along country roads, and didn't stop again until they came to Rock Island Dam. Above the dam, the river narrowed and its choked flow seeped into broad banks, fertile river-fed earth nourishing budding apple orchards.

"Oh God," cried Darla, gesturing at the neat rows of trees, "the blossoms look like Japanese clouds." Then, chattered out, she lay her head on the doorjamb and instantly fell into a trancelike sleep.

Gerald drove on through orchard country, through Wenatchee, still mopping up from the Rocky Reach Dam bombing, and he didn't stop until he saw the sign for Wells Dam and Fish Hatchery. He drove down the hatchery road and pulled into the visitors' parking lot. He shook Darla awake.

"Let's go for a walk," he said. Darla moaned, so he gave her a Penguin, and she perked up instantly.

The hatchery was deserted and the visitors' center had been locked up tight. A sign on the door told them that due to recent events at the Rocky Reach and Priest Rapids dams, all dam and hatchery tours along the Columbia River had been suspended. "What now?" Darla asked.

"Just hold on to your britches," he said.

An hour later, they sat in a cheap fishing cabin on the shore of Lake Chelan, where the lake met Chelan Dam east of town. The cabin was one of several in a wooded lot. Gerald had sent Darla to the manager's office to check in, and she felt him watching her back as the old woman at the desk gave her a key and towels. The cabin had hot running water and space heaters, so Darla didn't complain about the cheesy drapes and furnishings. This was not the Chelan Darla knew from childhood.

Darla's stepdad owned a high-end Chelan angler's resort. In her teens, she had visited Lake Chelan every summer, and she still harbored fond memories of fancy resort life, of lakeside campfires and cute Chelan High boys feeding her toasted marshmallows and feeling her up. One particular Chelan High dude stuck out in her mind even today: Nathan Bernstein.

Nathan was a senior at Chelan High when she met him at the lake one August morning. Only a few hardy souls ever braved the cold morning air to go down to the lake for a dip. Darla, bravest of them all, had been working on a tan, so she had arrived early at the shore. Wearing only her yellow bikini and a pair of flip-flops, she had lathered baby oil over her skin, the better to fry it golden brown, and had pulled her hair back up in a high ponytail that swayed when she moved.

Nathan Bernstein was fly-fishing for trout, but he had good eyesight, so when he caught a glimpse of Darla on the floating raft, he packed in the fishing scheme and rowed over to the raft. But once he had reached the raft, now sucked into her alluring aura, Nathan suddenly remembered that he was painfully shy and didn't know what to do next. He needn't have fretted, because Darla knew what to do.

Crooking her talented baby-oiled big toe, Darla had lured Nathan Bernstein onto the raft. He had scrambled up beside her, his youthful chest so skinny that Darla could see his heart pounding. Still, he was cute, and Darla had flirted shamelessly with him, until finally he asked her for a date. They went out that night to the Rock 'N Bowl, then smoked a joint and made out. Nathan taught Darla how to roll joints and how to get the most from smoking them. Darla taught Nathan a thing or two about French kissing. They were fooling around on the lawn in front of the big lakeshore resort, a teenagers' gathering place popularly known as "Penetration Point." Nathan hadn't wanted to go all the way, he said, because he didn't have any protection.

When Darla whipped out a condom, Nathan blushed and said he still didn't want to, and Darla had insisted on knowing why. Finally, Nathan confessed that he was a virgin, so Darla offered to deflower him. But Nathan refused and fled, leaving a very aroused Darla alone in the moonlight. Worse, several other couples at Penetration Point had witnessed Nathan deserting Darla—actually fleeing in a dead-heat run, if you want the technicals—and the next day it was the talk of Chelan. Darla had been humiliated. She had never forgotten Nathan, and she had never forgiven him.

Gerald had gone out: Rummaging through the battered nightstand's drawer, Darla found a hardly thumbed Gideon's Bible and, underneath that, a tattered phone book. The Chelan white pages listed one Bernstein—"N. Bernstein, M.D.," both office and residence numbers.

Gerald apparently hadn't noticed that she had a cell phone. She kept it hidden in a plastic bag that contained her dirty laundry, where she was sure he'd never go. Now she fished the cell phone out of the bag and dialed N. Bernstein's residence.

A woman's voice answered. Youngish-sounding, but crabby. And she had a whine.

Darla said, "Is this the residence of Nathan Bernstein?"

The woman said yes, it was.

Darla said, "Is Nathan available to come to the phone?"

"Who is this?" the woman demanded suspiciously.

"An old friend," Darla said soothingly. "My, uh, husband and I were passing through Chelan, and I wanted to say hello to Nathan. I haven't seen him since high school."

The woman said to wait a minute and went to get Nathan. When he came on the line, his voice sounded wary.

Darla said, "Is this Nathan Bernstein?"

"Yes, this is Dr. Bernstein," he replied cautiously.

Darla said, "This is Darla Denny, Nathan."

After a long silence, Nathan said, "Darla who?"

"Darla Denny. Remember? Senior year? Penetration Point?"

"I...I'm...I'm sorry, miss, I don't recall your name."

"You son of a bitch," Darla shouted hotly. "You have no idea what you missed." She hung up, feeling as if she had just shed a tremendous emotional burden, as if in one fell swoop she had vindicated all the injustices visited upon her childhood. There'd been a few.

Gerald had been gone half an hour. Where? Outside the cabin, dusk turned to darkness, a fierce wind howled, and a throcking sound on the cabin's roof made Darla nervous. Peering out the window, she saw silhouetted against moonlight a whitebark pine's gnarly arms attacking the cabin's shingle roof. Her eyes followed the tree's trunk and then she saw the van. It was parked in the assigned spot, and no sign of Gerald.

Wherever he went, he must have gone on foot. At last, a chance to locate the van's serial number, but she had to hurry. He might return any minute now.

Darla slipped out into the darkness. The parched winds blew cold as she approached the driver's side of the van. She shivered as she stood on tiptoe, peering into the windshield. Darkness hid the interior. She remembered that Gerald kept several flashlights in the van, but the van was locked. She ran inside the cabin, rummaged for matches, but with no luck. Hurry, hurry. He might come back soon.

She ran through the whistling wind to the manager's office. She rang the bell, but no one came, so she leaned hard on the bell. Finally, the old woman came to the door and peered through the glass.

Darla shouted, "I need a flashlight."

The old woman unlocked the door and let Darla in, Darla fumbling with excuses for needing the flashlight. The old woman listened, and when she'd had enough, she labored across the room and rummaged through a plastic bin. While she rummaged, she chewed on something. Maybe her gums. Darla fidgeted nervously. He might come back any minute now. Why couldn't the old bag hurry up? When the old woman finally located a flashlight, Darla snatched it and ran. The old woman cursed at her back, locked up, and drew the window shade.

Darla raced across the parking lot, a wind-whipped Medusa gasping for breath. Looming trees swayed across their own shadows and the fickle moon danced among the groaning branches. Darla ran faster. Her foot struck something and she stumbled and fell. The flashlight flew from her hand. In the darkness, she groped the cold ground and finally located it half-buried in a clod of dry earth. Snatching up the flashlight, she scrambled to her feet and ran to the van. Aiming the flashlight at the front windshield, she switched it on. Nothing happened. She shook the flashlight, then took it apart and put it back together. Finally, it flickered meager life. She aimed the thin beam at the windshield and found what she wanted.

On the dash, on the driver's side, was a metal strip and on

the strip was a number. Serial #859423029-847868400. In segments of three, Darla memorized the numbers. When she turned around, she saw his shadow first; then he stepped forward and she saw his face. How long had Gerald been standing under the tree? Had he seen her check the serial number?

Thinking fast, Darla cried, "Oh God, thank God you're here, honey."

Gerald came forward. Darla ran to him, playing frightened to the hilt. He did not embrace her, just stood and waited for her explanation.

"Oh honey, there was a terrible noise. I looked out and saw this man trying to get into the van." She dry-sobbed for effect. "He was, like, jimmying the lock. So I hollered out the door of the cabin and he ran away. Oh honey, I was terrified."

When he finally spoke, his voice held no trace of emotion, but a broad edge of suspicion cut through the electric wind. He said, "Whose flashlight?"

"I...I borrowed it. From the office." She pointed.

Moonlight glittered in Gerald's dark eyes, reflecting suspicion, but he said nothing, and the subject was never raised again.

THAT NIGHT, as Darla lay sleeping in a lumpy bed in the cold, drafty cabin, Gerald went out. Darla woke up when she heard the van's engine turn over. She listened as Gerald drove off; then she lay back in bed and took emotional inventory.

Darla had developed a personalized chakra checklist. Whenever she felt strong emotion, she consulted her chakras. Where did the emotion settle? Now Darla checked her chakra barometer vis-à-vis Gerald. When she thought of Gerald, what area of her anatomy was involved? (Besides the erotic zones, which in Darla were always active and participatory.)

Gerald. Thud in the pit of her manipura.

Gerald. Light squeeze in the anahata.

Gerald. Fluttering, fluttering...fluctuation, involving the sahasrara and the svadhisthana; crown to genitals. Dear, dear, dear.

The fourth and final time Darla thought his name and pic-tured him, some hardweight bypassed the anahata and plunged to her gut, whereupon, she instantly recognized fear. So it wasn't love after all.

He had threatened to kill her if she was uncooperative, if she tried to leave him. Since the bomb-making day, Darla had genuinely feared him, but now she recognized that she was also growing closer to him, even dependent. She tossed restlessly in bed.

He was gone now and she was alone. Should she take advantage of his absence and escape before it was too late? Or, was it too late already? Maybe not. Maybe she could phone her stepfather in Kettle Falls, ask him to come rescue her. But that might take too long. Besides, she didn't want to involve her parents, place them in danger. Maybe Nathan Bernstein would come get her, if she talked nice. But then, Gerald would never give up until he hunted her down and killed her. She already knew too much about him. She prob-ably knew more about Gerald than anyone else knew about him, and that wasn't saying much. Better not leave him, not yet anyway. Besides, now that she noticed, a hint of com-passion had leaked from her solar plexus into her heart chakra. Maybe with a little love, Darla could change Gerald, turn him around. Yes, that was it. A little love and under-standing could do wonders.

That phone call to the federal agent, maybe that had been a terrible mistake.

ON THE FOURTH DAY of waiting for Gerald, Darla turned surly. How dare he leave her alone so long? Maybe he had a wife somewhere, maybe even kids. Like Nathan Bernstein. Why else wouldn't he take her along on his secret missions? And why did he apparently trust her enough to leave her alone? Maybe she was being watched, or even followed, by

82 K FALLS

Gerald's accomplices. Maybe another woman. Darla's mind spun and it was all she could do to keep from falling asleep, her instant cure for everything.

After another brief but resolute chakra consult, she fished the cell phone out of her laundry bag and made the phone call. This time, she got the Fish and Wildlife agent's message service. Darla hated recording her own voice, but she figured, Here goes.

"This is a message for Agent Diamond," she said to the impersonal machine. "That number you wanted? It's 859423029847868400. It's a Dodge Sportsman, this year's model." On an impulse, she added, "My parents live in Kettle Falls. My stepdad's name is Albert Denny, and my mom's name is Sue Ann. Sue Ann Denny. Tell them I'm fine. Tell them not to worry." She hung up, feeling as if she'd already said too much, hating her impulsive nature, and remembering that she hadn't given her parents' phone number. Should she call back? Should she get them involved? Already, Darla regretted making the phone call. Overcome with anxiety, she fell into bed and immediately dropped off to sleep.

On the fifth day of waiting for the big guy to return, Darla tried turning herself into a swan, which she normally could do without much effort, but this time, in this shabby cabin at Lake Chelan, she failed. When Gerald finally returned late that evening, she ran to him with open arms. And when he said, "We're going to blow up Grand Coulee Dam," she didn't argue.

NINE

Icewine, or *eiswein*, is a late-harvest wine made from grapes that are harvested while frozen and pressed while still frozen. It is usually made from Reisling and Vidal grapes, though three varieties of vinifera grapes may be used, the grapes are left on the vine until the first frost, then they must be harvested frozen before 10 AM and immediately pressed. During these processes, the temperature may not exceed −8 degrees Celsius. At this temperature, the frozen grapes are as hard as marbles. When pressed, the water is driven out as shards of ice, which leaves a highly concentrated juice, very high in natural acids, sugars and aromatics. A finished icewine must have a Brix of 35 degrees or higher, and a residual sugar of 125g/litre, a minimum Brix of 32 degrees in the fermentation tank. The alcohol must derive exclusively from the natural sugars of the grapes. Icewine harvests must start after 15 November, and most icewine vintners are members of the Vintners Quality Alliance, an organization that monitors the quality of icewine product.—Vintner Quality Alliance, Ontario

SUE ANN DENNY had cranked up the barbecue and left Albert to supervise the briquettes while she paid off the poacher who handed her two ten-pound chinooks then drove off in an "Ella's Fish Market" truck. It was Sunday afternoon, the weather, already acting like summer, brought hot, arid breezes. Overhead, a sizzling orange disk dangled from an electric blue sky. Albert Denny blew on the barbecue's hot charcoal lumps. He always wore sunglasses outdoors, and when he glanced up at the sky through UV filters, he could have sworn he saw little devils leaping off the sun. Little devils with little pitchforks. Albert averted his eyes and said to himself, "So that's what we're not supposed to see."

Denny, forty-nine, local Republican party leader, deacon of Kettle Falls First Methodist Church, firmly believed in devils. He'd actually seen them on the battlefield in Vietnam. They scampered among the dead soldiers, and Albert would never forget the sound they made. So they occupied the sun, too. Somehow, that didn't surprise Albert. Not much surprised him anymore, with the exception of his wife's occasional peccadilloes, always thinly disguised as playful shenanigans, although Albert knew better. But, hey, who was complaining? Not Albert Denny. Not the wealthiest man in Okanogan County. If you counted riches by cash holdings and investments, Albert Denny was the wealthiest man east of the Cascade Range and west of…well, maybe Missoula. He owned the most successful icewine vineyards in North America, two thousand acres of apple orchards near Wenatchee, a fishing resort on Lake Roosevelt and another one on Lake Chelan. He owned a couple thousand head of steer and a dairy ranch over near Spokane. He had never gambled on Microsoft, but he had managed his own spectacular portfolio, and a serious collection of preembargo Sierra Leone diamonds. In short, Albert Denny was a shrewd businessman with no financial worries. In fact, Albert Denny had no worries at all, unless you counted recent developments. Darla shouldn't have left home so huffy and rude. When he thought about it, which was often, Albert figured his stepdaughter must have tired of Sue Ann's criticizing her about every little thing. That explained Darla's leaving home so abruptly, just when Albert was ready to bring her into the business.

Sue Ann and Albert hadn't heard from Darla in over six

weeks. Sue Ann wasn't at all concerned about Darla's sudden silence, but Albert was, and he had contacted Darla's friend Leelee Thuc Dien Phu, who worked with Darla at the bank in Astoria. Leelee told Albert that Darla had gone off with some dude she had gone whacko over. Leelee had never met Darla's boyfriend, but she said Darla talked about him all the time. Mostly about how good he was in bed. After this dude came into her life, Darla had quit her nighttime classes. Then after the bank robbery, Darla had locked up her rental house and put Pussy in the kennel. Leelee was car-sitting the T-bird and didn't mind at all. Albert was sick with worry, but he didn't tell Sue Ann what Leelee had told him, because that would just get Sue Ann riled up. He could just hear her now: That little two-bit whore has finally gotten herself into some kind of mess. I've always predicted this, Albert.... And so forth. So Albert kept his fears about Darla to himself, but every time the phone rang, his heart leapt hopefully.

Darla had always been a respectful daughter, except in her heart, where (as Albert had so keenly observed) she harbored many black thoughts about Sue Ann. Sue Ann scoffed derisively at her daughter's romantic ideas, and they never discussed men, money, or sex. When Darla had moved out of the family home and taken the manicurist's job in Kettle Falls, Sue Ann had been mortified. All Sue Ann's friends were having their nails done by Darla. What was a vintner's wife to do? Sue Ann knew exactly what to do; she made Darla's life miserable, until finally Darla moved on one day, dragging her bag of cheap rags to Astoria, where nobody knew Sue Ann Denny, where nobody could gossip about Sue Ann Denny's daughter turning out so weird.

Aside from the Sue Ann versus Darla situation, Albert Denny had no regrets, and abundant blessings. For Albert, life wore a platinum lining. Now if only he could bring Sue Ann around from her salmon-saving hysteria, everything would be, as they say, copacetic.

WHEN SUE ANN brought the salmon, filleted and dressed, out to the air-conditioned terrace, Albert had the grill ready. She deftly slid the raw fish onto the grill. It sizzled and popped. Sue Ann had a knack for barbecued salmon, a talent written into her genetic code. As Albert watched his wife set the picnic table—his job was watching the salmon—he observed that even at fifty three, Sue Ann still had a swell figure. An inch or two thicker around the middle, "boomer's bulge," but the hips were nice and slim and so were the legs. She kept herself up, dressed fashionably, listened to the right kind of music (Kenny G), and accompanied him to church on Sundays. For all these fine attributes, Albert was grateful. There were a few snags. About a year ago, Sue Ann had lost all interest in connubial bliss. Albert had tried talking about menopause, but Sue Ann refused. If only she'd take some female Viagra, Albert thought, she'd be the perfect spouse. But Albert wasn't a man to dwell on "if only"; he was a pragmatist and found practical solutions to life's little frustrations.

Besides, in spite of her aversion to sex, Sue Ann was no slacker, no mere trophy wife. She had her own interests, including a few that Albert didn't approve of, like her volunteer work with Fritz Fowler's river radicals. Albert and Sue Ann sat on opposing sides of the dam-breaching issue, the same place they sat on virtually every political, social, philosophical, and religious issue. Still, Albert loved Sue Ann, and he was proud of her accomplishments. While other wealthy men's wives lolled and primped and wasted hard-earned resources at fancy health spas in exotic locales, Sue Ann was content to stay at home with Albert, who hated spending frivolously and hated flying even more. And Sue Ann had her own little business going on the side, too, and that kept her occupied when Albert had to work late or run down to the ranch.

Sue Ann owned and operated Sue Ann's Truffle Locators, Inc. Sue Ann leased her trained potbellied pigs with the tal-

ented snouts to Austrian truffle collectors, and her business
flourished. Albert had only one criticism of how Sue Ann
conducted her little operation; she was constantly on the
phone with her clients, checking on her pigs' condition. Were
they feeding the pigs enough fresh fruit and vitamins and
veggies? Were they keeping the pigs in clean and sanitary
conditions when they weren't sniffing out truffles? Were they
talking to the swine, stroking them, feeding them little turnipy
treats to reward them?

Sue Ann treated her potbellied pigs better than she had
ever treated her daughter, and this slightly irritated Albert,
but being a loving husband, he refrained from criticizing.
Then, too, people who knew Albert Denny often remarked
on his affable, laid-back personality, his nonjudgmental spirit.
Albert wasn't easily aroused to anger, and his employees and
his clients appreciated that. He often wondered if Sue Ann
fully appreciated his supreme affability, his forgiving nature.
For example, just last month, when Albert caught Sue Ann
pilfering funds from the winery's bank account, using them
for God knows what—probably lingerie and furniture (her
two weaknesses)—he had forgiven her indiscretion and even
had increased her personal spending allowance. Albert was
that kind of fellow, and he guessed that no matter what Sue
Ann did next, he'd probably forgive her and forget. Albert
prided himself in being a model husband.

The icewine vineyard stretched for miles along the Columbia River, north of the Colville Indian Reservation, nearly to
the Canadian border. The Denny house, a sprawling ranch-
style showplace on a landscaped slope, overlooked horizontal
rows of grapevines and lushly planted terraces. Directly
across the highway, the Columbia River, flowing out of Canada, curved sharply beside the road, and made another hairpin
turn south toward Grand Coulee Dam. Sue Ann often spotted
bald eagles along the riverbanks, and sometimes she saw
bears. When the bears came to fish in the river, Sue Ann
would scream for Albert to come and chase them away.

"I don't want those bears in my vineyards," she would tell Albert, and Albert would inevitably reply, "Sue Ann, bears don't get into vineyards. Bears like to fish for salmon, and if there's salmon near, why, the bears won't touch a grape."

But Sue Ann would insist. "I want those bears chased off." So Albert would get in Sue Ann's Lexus and drive down along the highway, honking the horn to drive the bears away. Albert hated it, but what could he do? Sue Ann would make his life miserable if he didn't. Better to maintain the peace.

Albert was turning the salmon on the grill when he heard Sue Ann screaming from her rose garden. Albert dropped the spatula and ran into the rose garden, where he found Sue Ann hunched over and vomiting. Albert averted his eyes. When she had finished, he said, "What is it, cookie?"

Sue Ann pointed toward the base of a Miss Betty Gamble high pink. "There," she cried. Albert looked where his wife indicated and saw the slug.

"Slugs have no business east of the Cascades," Albert declared flatly.

"Get rid of him, Albert. Now."

The slug incident had barely subsided when Albert heard a pleasant purring sound. Glancing up from the barbecue, he saw a jazzy Aston Martin convertible, top down, slinking up the winding vineyard road toward the house. Being a gentleman, he immediately went to greet the stranger.

Agent Venus Diamond apologized for interrupting a Sunday salmon barbecue, but Albert said, "Never mind, strangers are always welcome," and shook hands cordially. When Sue Ann looked out the kitchen window across the terrace and saw her husband standing in the driveway, leaning into an Aston Martin, very nearly lip-to-mustache with a petite blond floozy, she nearly went ballistic. Before going out to face the competition, Sue Ann adjusted her panty girdle, smoothed her slinky Donna Karan dress, and stepped into a pair of high-heeled mules that made her look tall and almost thin. She swept her freshly tinted raven hair up into a sexy French twist, secured it with a clip, and checked her makeup. On the way out, she congratulated herself for being twice as good-looking as this blond intruder, and when Albert brought the stranger forth onto the terrace and introduced her as some kind of federal agent, Sue Ann managed a forced smile. Still, she could not entirely conceal her pique. Nobody came calling on Sue Ann Denny without telephoning first.

When Venus showed the Dennys her badge, Sue Ann and Albert exchanged glances, but otherwise showed no sign of curiosity. Albert said affably, "You'll have some salmon, won't you?"

"It's fresh, wild Columbia chinook," Sue Ann put in proudly. "None of this hatchery-bred fish."

"No thanks," said Venus. "I don't eat endangered species."

Sue Ann flushed and Albert stared; then a keenly intuitive Albert crowed, "Well, hey, why not just sit down here and enjoy a glass of icewine?" He pulled out a chair and Venus sat down. Albert went for the wine bottle.

"Thanks anyway," said Venus. "I don't drink when I'm driving."

Ever the cheerleader, Albert shifted his affability into full stride. "Hey, well, that's a sweet little Aston Martin you drive. I drive a Jaguar myself. Brand new. Blood red. I'll show it to you sometime. Well, hey, the icewine business is good. The local economy's booming. How about some juice? Sue Ann, honey, get the young lady a glass of fresh-squeezed OJ. You do drink orange juice, don't you? Heh-heh. All these housing tracts coming up around here, bad as I hate to see them mess up the landscape, they've made us rich. They buy our beef; they buy our vino. Yes siree, business is grand."

"We aren't rich, Albert," Sue Ann cautioned her husband, who was divulging far too much to a perfect stranger. Sue Ann speared a piece of salmon. "Just comfortable." She popped the salmon into her mouth and chewed with her eyes closed, ecstatic. "God, it's like butter, Albert."

"Melts in your mouth," offered Albert. "Sure you won't try some?" He held out the fish platter to Venus. The salmon fillets lay flesh side up, garnished with capers and little lemon wedges.

Venus shook her head. Maybe they didn't understand English. She waved the platter away. Albert shrugged. Sue Ann rolled her eyes and said drolly, "Some people carry environmental correctness to extremes."

Albert, trying to deflect his wife's impolite comment, said, "Like you, Sue Ann. You and Fritz." He explained to his guest, "Sue Ann's active in this crackpot organization that thinks salmon deserve a better life than humans. Damn bunch of bleeding heart liberals."

"Shut up, Albert." Sue Ann wasn't kidding. Albert shut up and finished his dinner in silence. Sue Ann, meanwhile, blathered on about Albert's inability to comprehend the intricacies of salmon preservation.

"If you support species preservation," Venus asked Sue Ann, "why do you buy fresh wild salmon when the season's closed?"

Sue Ann didn't like the question, but she had an answer ready. "It was a gift. Wasn't it, Albert? It was a gift from a neighbor who fishes along the river. I could hardly let it go to waste." She glared at Albert, who kept his eyes downcast, ashamed of his wife's lies. "Isn't that right, Albert?"

The conversation lagged. Agent Diamond drank her orange juice. Albert, who despised lapses in dinner table banter, tried futilely to think of something clever to say, then the visitor came to his rescue. Venus said, "You're both from this area?"

Albert said proudly, "I'm a native. Sue Ann's from Seattle. How we met was, Sue Ann was visiting Grand Coulee Dam. This was what? Fifteen years ago?"

"Sixteen."

"Right. Sue Ann was a tourist. I generally avoid them, especially the Seattle variety. We eastern Washington folk aren't too fond of the webfoots. No insult intended. A bunch of snot-nosed, do-good liberal hypocrites, if you ask me. Especially Seattleites. They like progress as long as it doesn't raise their electric bill. Then they turn crybaby. But like I was saying, Sue Ann was different. We met at a café near the dam, where all the tourists hang out. I was just divorced and horny as all getout, and Sue Ann was sitting by herself near the entrance, looking so fresh and purty. Our eyes met and, hell, we just locked on each other. Got hitched a week later."

"A month later," said Sue Ann, correcting him. She began clearing off the table. On the way to the kitchen, she said, "Maria's off tonight. We give all the help Sundays off."

"Sue Ann's daughter was a flower girl at our wedding. Nothing fancy, but we wanted the girl to feel included. Sue Ann's four years older than me, but hell—"

"Albert!" came Sue Ann's voice from the kitchen, forceful.

When Sue Ann came back onto the terrace, Venus said, "Your daughter contacted me."

The Dennys exchanged a glance; then Sue Ann said, "Daughter?"

"You have a daughter named Darla, don't you?"

Sue Ann stammered, "I have a daughter...by...a former union. She's a grown-up and she's...well, flown the nest. She is a bright-enough girl, but she has no common sense. Absolutely none."

Albert set down his coffee cup and said, "Is Darla in trouble?"

Before Venus could reply, Sue Ann said, "Albert, I wish to speak to you in private."

WHILE THE DENNYS huddled, Venus scoped out the lush gardens terracing downhill toward the vineyard. The blazing sun penetrated her clothing and her skin felt dry as a desert corpse. She found meager shade beneath an ancient silver linden tree and was enjoying the nice view when a western tanager landed on a nearby flowering quince. Venus watched him fluff his brash yellow chest feathers, then dip and bob and trill a springtime song. No one came. The bird put oomph into its song. Still no prospects. The lonely tanager groomed moodily, then bobbed once and took off. In its wake came a fluttering swallowtail butterfly, an eastern Washington variety Venus hadn't seen before. Fascinated, she followed the swallowtail down the terraces and into the vineyard, where the butterfly disappeared among the lush vines. She was heading back uphill through a row of grapevines when she had an impulse to look at the ground. What prompted her to look down at the earth?

At her feet, carved into the dry earth, she saw the two words: "Salmon Ella." She blinked and knelt down to inspect the scrawl, but when she looked a second time, the ground was smooth. The eastern Washington heat must be getting the best of her. Maybe these locals could take the sizzle, but not this water baby. She was relieved to hear Albert Denny call from the upper terrace, beckoning her back into the air conditioning.

When she sat down again at the table, Albert cleared his throat and said, "If our daughter is in some kind of trouble, we want to know about it. No beating around the bush." Albert pressed his lips together.

Venus told them about Darla's two phone calls. When she had finished, Albert said, "This is a hoax. Darla would never be involved in such a thing. She's incapable of breaking the law. She's a good girl."

Sue Ann trembled, daubing at her dry eyes. "Darla has always embarrassed me."

"Give us some time to find her," Albert pleaded. "We'll prove she's innocent. We just need some time to find her."

"I didn't come here to threaten you. I think your daughter

may be in danger. We expect more bombings. Any information you can provide may help save her life.''

Sue Ann's eyes pooled tears and her pouty lips quivered. Albert rushed to his wife's side and embraced her, stroking her hair as if comforting a wounded cat. Maybe she was. A cat. Wounded. Her head nestled into the crook of Albert's neck, and now, finally, she wept, and Venus saw real tears. At least they were wet.

"There now, babe," whispered Albert, handing Sue Ann a crisp handkerchief. "It's okay. You don't have to say anything. It's going to be okay."

Eventually, Sue Ann wiped her mottled face and mewled, "I'm sure you think I'm a just a big sissy. It's just that my daughter has been such a burden. I have tried so hard to keep her out of trouble. This could all be so embarrassing for Albert."

"Oh, pancake, honestly," Albert said to his wife.

Venus glanced across the terrace. The tanager was back, perched once again on the quince. It looked around, as if it had forgotten something. Maybe its suitcase. It didn't sing this time, and from the gardens came only the distant murmuring of a fountain on the lawns. Venus said, "A lot of hoax leads have come in. These calls from your daughter are the only leads that ring true."

"What about the van?" Albert asked. "Did you trace it?"

"The plates and serial number are phony. We've circulated a vehicle description."

Sue Ann moaned, wiping her tear-stained face.

In the quince, the tanager made little thrashing sounds. Venus watched until the bird sailed away, and then stillness came over the garden, and she said to the Dennys, "You'll have to be more forthcoming. You aren't giving me enough information."

Albert stared at her. "I'm telling you, we don't know anything about this person. My stepdaughter never mentioned him. What else can I say? And what's more, if anyone is guilty of these bombings, it's Fritz Fowler. Everyone suspects Fowler and the Dambusters.''

Sue Ann said, ''Oh, Albert, leave it alone. Poor Fritz, just this morning, he found his cat poisoned. I wouldn't be surprised if some redneck—''

''Tell me more about Fritz Fowler.''

Albert and Sue Ann exchanged glances; then Albert said, ''Fowler runs the Dambusters Fund. He's always in the news, talking about breaching the dams, opening up the Columbia and Snake rivers so the salmon can get back to their spawning grounds. I've never met him personally.'' He looked at his wife and added, ''But Sue Ann knows him.''

He said it like an accusation. Sue Ann shrugged and said, ''Fritz and I are both active dam opponents. I've done some volunteer work for his organization.''

''Dambusters? Isn't that a pretty provocative name?''

Sue Ann said, ''Maybe. Maybe now, with what's happened at Rocky Reach and Priest Rapids. At the time Fritz named the organization, it was just a sort of play on our intentions. Maybe we should have called ourselves the 'Dambreachers.'''

In the kitchen, a telephone rang. Sue Ann went to answer it. Soon, a great wailing emanated from the kitchen. Albert excused himself from the table and rushed into the kitchen. A brief pause in the wailing, then Albert came back, weepy Sue Ann in tow. This time, the tears were genuine.

''My baby,'' Sue Ann said, sobbing. ''My Julia.''

''You have another daughter?''

''No,'' explained Albert. ''Her baby potbellied pig. One of her Austrian truffle clients had leased Julia. Julia apparently accidentally swallowed a poison mushroom. She might die.''

After Sue Ann had regained her composure, Venus said, ''I'm sorry to change the subject, but I need to talk to Fritz Fowler. Where can I find him?''

Sue Ann seemed hesitant, but Albert said, ''He has an

office on Main Street. When he comes to K Falls, he's usually in his office or across the street at Prospector's. That's a saloon. But he moves up and down the river. He's not up here all the time.''

"Has he got a cell phone?''

"His phone number is unlisted,'' Sue Ann said. "He won't even share it with me.'' Her eyes glittered flatly.

Venus took out a small notebook and jotted down Fritz's name. "Where does he live?''

Sue Ann said, "Nowhere, I guess. He's always on the road. He goes from one end of the river to the other, trying to convince people to support removal of the dams.''

Albert, trying to be helpful, added, "When he comes to K Falls, he stays overnight at the Grand View Inn. He's got a fat expense account all right. Dambusters is financed by a bunch of webfooted lobbyists that suck money out of unsuspecting taxpayers. Sorry, Sue Ann, but that's just how I feel. Damn hypocrites use up all the hydroelectricity, then get all weepy over salmon. Like the president. Damn Democrat, using salmon as a campaign stunt, to win over the Seattle voters. Hell, it's all a gimmick. Campaign hyperbole. I don't care if Benson is a Washington native. He's from Seattle and he stinks.''

"Albert, please.''

Venus said, "So Fowler found his cat dead at the Grand View Inn?''

Sue Ann flushed deeply. Albert, looking slightly puzzled, said, "That's what Fowler said. Right there at the Grand View. Right, Sue Ann?''

WHEN VENUS LEFT the Dennys', Albert was standing on the terrace beside the barbecue grill. Sue Ann had disappeared into the house. Venus pointed her Aston Martin south and drove along Highway 395 until she reached a side road bordering the Dennys' vineyard. She pulled off onto the side road, turned off the Aston's headlights, rolled in behind a clump of vine cuttings, where she could watch the highway without being seen, and turned off the ignition. Less than five minutes dragged by before a blood red Jaguar passed on the highway.

Albert Denny drove south, in the direction of Kettle Falls. Venus followed at a discreet distance. Denny drove fast, erratically, swerving onto the road's shoulder, overcompensating for the curves. The highway ran straight through the middle of Kettle Falls. Denny didn't stop; he kept driving southeast until the highway crossed Palmers, then kept going until he came to Colville.

TEN

Driving a vehicle that does not contain a litterbag is illegal in Washington State.

ON THE EDGE of Colville was a shopping mall, a dreary clump of bargain stores anchored by a Hartell's Drugstore. Albert Denny drove into the parking lot. Venus pulled into a nearby spot and watched.

So far, Denny hadn't noticed his tail. Leaving the engine idling, he stepped out of the snazzy Jag, walked around to the passenger side, opened the door, and removed a package. Tucking it under his arm, he crossed the parking lot, walked past a liquor store, paused at a seafood market to poke at the display of fresh fish, then moved on to the Hartell's, where he went inside. While he was gone, Venus conducted a close-up reconnaissance of the Jag and its contents.

Fine beige leather interior. Burled walnut detailing. Above the dash, a silk cord hanging from the rearview mirror dangled a pewter object, a talismanic grape cluster. The glove compartment doubled as a litterbag for several DoveBar ice cream wrappers; it also contained a pair of ostrich-skin driving gloves, the Jag's operating manual, insurance and registration papers, all in the name of Albert Denny. There was a small flashlight, a tube of lipstick in a shade called Bite Me, and a birthday card not addressed to Albert.

The birthday card was mailed from Astoria, addressed to Sue Ann. The date on the postmark was ten days earlier. The card reminded Sue Ann that though youth had fled, she nevertheless retained her sex appeal. It was signed in flowery cursive: "Love, Fritz."

Maybe Albert had intercepted the card. Maybe he was holding it as evidence. Blackmail? There was nothing else in the glove compartment except dead air. Venus went back to the Aston and waited. Eventually, Albert sashayed out of the drugstore, minus the package, gnawing on a DoveBar. He slid into the Jag and revved the engine. It purred like a newborn kitten. He pointed the Jag north. Maybe going home.

THE CLERK AT the photo counter inside Hartell's had a frizzy gray halo and a senior citizen hair-across-the-ass attitude. "Don't come in here trying to intimidate me with your badge," she snapped at Venus. "I may be old and hoary and have crow's-feet, but I'm no dunce. It's against the law to allow anyone to inspect anyone else's mail, even if it's only Federal Express and not the real post office. What do you think I am? An old coot with hay for brains?"

The old coot wore a red apron over an oxford-cloth shirt, navy-and-red-striped necktie, charcoal gray trousers, and a frosty glare. Maybe a uniform. To soften her up, Venus bought a disposable camera and a pack of emery boards. The clerk thrust the articles into a tissue-thin plastic sack and shoved them across the counter. So far, she hadn't defrosted.

Venus said, "I've always wondered why the town of Kettle Falls is called that." The clerk glared at Venus's outstretched empty palm. "Can you explain that?"

"Any idiot knows the answer to that," snapped the clerk. "That town is situated at the headwaters of Kettle Falls. Therefore, the town has adopted the name."

"I didn't notice any waterfalls. Where are the falls?"

The old coot sucked in her cheeks and sniggered. "Underneath the damn reservoir."

"Gotcha." Venus started to leave, but halfway down the aisle, she remembered something. She went back to the counter. The clerk was reading a small red leather-bound book. Psalms. Or Falun Gong. Or maybe salmon recipes. Venus said, "Excuse me. Again." The clerk glanced up, saw the pest. Sighing, she shut the little red book. Venus said, "Out of curiosity, where exactly are the falls?"

The clerk had had enough. "Young woman, if you knew your Washington State history, you would know they are underneath Lake Roosevelt." She dipped back into the captivating red book, and after the young woman with the intriguing green eyes had gone away, she muttered, "Sheesh."

On the way past the FedEx bin, Venus paused, but the coot was eyeballing her. Somewhere in the warped ethers of Venus's intuition, a rasping voice taunted, Mabel, Mabel, set the table.

Outside, Venus paused at the fish stand. From a bed of shaved ice, six fresh chinook salmon stared up at her with distinctly humanoid eyeballs. Above the fish, a sign read PUGET SOUND SALMON. EASTERN WASHINGTON'S REVENGE. Above that, another sign identified the market as Ella's.

Inside the market, teenage trouble lounged behind a high glass display case, twirling a pistol in one hand while the fingers of the other pulled thoughtfully at an imaginary goatee. Venus showed him empty palms. The kid put the gun away and shuffled over to the counter. If he moved any slower, he'd turn to salt.

"Is Ella around?" Venus asked.

"Not anymore." His voice had miles to go before qualifying as manly. He grinned and said, "She's dead."

"Where do you get your salmon?"

The kid jerked his head, indicating the outside display. "Read the sign."

"That sign says your salmon come out of Puget Sound."

"Bingo."

The kid had the attention span of a gnat. He shuffled in place, his arms dangling at his sides, hands in constant motion, the fingers wiggling like a junkie with the heebie-jeebies. He said, "What can I do ya fer?"

She showed him the tag, told him she had found it in the salmon's gut. He studied it, then nodded.

"Must have swallowed the tag," he said. "Or else some-one shoved it down its throat." He laughed in an adolescent falsetto. "Yeah, we mark 'em by lot. To prove we're legal. That's one of ours all right." He studied the number again. "Can't say who bought it, though. How the hell can I remember every customer?"

"I'm looking for a man," she said. "Big guy. Brown hair, brown eyes. Clean-shaven. Driving a brown van. He might have come in here recently and purchased one of your Puget Sound salmon. Sound familiar?"

The kid rolled his eyes into the back of his head but couldn't lock onto his memory bank. "Uh, don't recall no-body like that. Maybe he came in here. Maybe not."

"What about the van? Does that sound familiar?"

The kid picked his teeth. Maybe searching for inspiration. Finally, he shook his head. "Naw."

"You got a license for that handgun?"

The kid leered. "What're you? A cop or somethin'?"

She showed him her badge.

He said, "Cool, man." He showed her ID that claimed he was twenty-one and a permit to carry a concealed weapon, explaining, "We been hit up here by robbers lately. Take our fish and our cash, too."

She gave him her business card, told him to phone if he noticed anything unusual, if he saw the van. When she left, he eyeballed her backside, and when she got into the Aston Martin and revved the engine, the kid drooled into his imaginary goatee. If he was twenty-one, she was Cleopatra.

THE INNKEEPER AT the Grand View Inn didn't like Venus's looks, but after flashing a credit card, Venus saw twenty-eight strong white teeth set in a florid oral cavern, bright red, healthy gums, the kind of mouth grown in towns that fluoridate the water. Nice teeth, but the overall effect came off as too disingenuous for her tastes. She leaned across the desk and said, "Do any of your guest rooms have kitchenettes?"

"One or two. Dishwashers, garbage disposals, microwaves. Nothing gourmet."

"How about pets? Do you allow pets?"

"No pets. You got a pet?" The innkeeper frowned suspiciously.

"No pet," she replied soothingly. "Has Fowler checked in yet today?"

The innkeeper had a broad face, pale and apparently insensate, from which gazed a pair of blank-slate eyes that studied her credit card. Solemnly, he said, "You one of Fowler's cohorts?"

"Just heard of him. You know, the story about him finding his cat poisoned, here at the Grand View?"

The blank-slate eyes narrowed. Something wasn't sitting right. He said, "Fowler doesn't stay here anymore."

"Blackballed?"

The innkeeper nodded. "Who needs that kind of trouble? Now, have you got any more questions before I get back to my work?" He handed over a room key.

"As a matter of fact, I do have another question or two. For starters, what do folks call you besides 'innkeeper'?"

"Grimm. Trevor Grimm. Just Grimm to you."

"And I was wondering, do you know the Denny family?"

"Everyone knows the Dennys. I mean, who they are. They're not real cozy with the hoi polloi. I mean, Albert's a local, and he used to be real congenial, but ever since he married that fourth wife or whatever number she is, Albert's turned pretty stuck-up. Or maybe it's just that he's afraid of her." Grimm shook his head. "She's sick, that woman. She's from Seattle."

"What about the daughter? Do you know the daughter?"

"You mean her daughter? Darla? Albert doesn't have any

kids." Grimm shook his head. "Never met the girl. Just heard about her."

"What about her? What have you heard?"

Grimm stared at empty space. "That she's a looker. That she has a large IQ. That she can't manage to lasso a man or make something of herself. That she moved down to Astoria to escape her mom's talons. She has 'em, too. Talons. Can't say I blame the daughter. But, hey, I'm no gossip."

VENUS HAD PAID for a room with windows overlooking the river, or reservoir, officially known as Lake Roosevelt, a one hundred fifty-one mile widening of the river up above Grand Coulee Dam. She got the room, and the windows, but no view. Outside the window of room 112 at the Grand View Inn, a dense fog, reeking of seawater, had swallowed up the river, smothering all promise of the grand view. How could seawater fog find its way over the Cascade Range into the hinterlands?

MORNING BROKE clear and bright, without a trace of the salty fog. A crisp breeze wafted through the open window when Venus looked out, and now she beheld the grand view from the Grand View Inn. A cow pasture, a hamburger joint, and a drive-through latte stand. She was in the parking lot, packing up the Aston Martin, when Grimm's voice barked out her name. "You got a phone call in here," he yelled. "Says it's urgent."

Venus went back inside the Grand View Inn, picked up the phone. Lurking behind the desk, Grimm blatantly eavesdropped. Chafing laughter came over the line. Venus held the phone away from her ear, and then the voice said, "I know where you are, day and night. Stay out of K Falls, or I'll give you a fright."

"Cute," she replied, "but not scary enough." She handed the receiver back to Grimm, who set it gently in its cradle.

"Trouble?" Grimm inquired too casually.

"Crank call."

A zebra-striped cat with no tail padded out of the back office and up to Grimm. Grimm leaned over, picked up the furry creature, and stroked it. "Lots of my guests get crank phone calls." He set the cat down and went back to sorting receipts. The cat hissed at Venus, but she lunged at it and it skittered away and ran upstairs.

"That your cat or Fowler's?"

"Mine."

"Oh, that's right. Fowler's cat died."

Grimm didn't say anything.

Venus said, "Salmonella, I believe."

Grimm didn't blink. "Cats don't get salmonella. Only humans."

Venus leaned on the counter and said, "How did the town of Kettle Falls get its name?"

Grimm said, "Not sure. Maybe it was named for the Kettle tribe of Indians. I mean, Native Americans."

"Why were they called Kettle?"

Grimm scratched his neck thoughtfully. "Now there's a good question, miss, I mean, miz. Folks around here have always called 'em the Kettle People. I learned all about 'em back when I first moved over here, but I reckon it didn't sink in." He brightened. "I can tell you who would know."

"Who's that?"

"Miss Fobia. Local historian. She's pushing eighty now, but Miss Fobia's got a hell of a memory, and she's a native. I mean, a white native. The Fobia, she knows everything. She knows all about how the coulees were formed, about the different Indian tribes that settled along the river. I mean, Native Americans. She knows about the pioneers, the Okanogan ice-grape growers, and the big cattle ranchers, just everything. She's the expert on Kettle Falls and Columbia River lore. I betcha Miss Fobia knows how the Kettles got their name."

"Where can I find this Fobia person?"

Grimm thought for a minute. "It's Sunday," he said finally. "That means Miss Fobia is manning—I mean womaning—the desk over at the Kettle Falls Historical Society office. You can catch her there until about five o'clock. That's when she locks up and goes home." Grimm gestured. "Back up on the north side of the bridge. Can't miss it. It's a yaller cottage with a cedar-shake fence."

"Yaller?" Venus squinted.

"Yep. Yaller as a Carolina hound."

"Oh," said Venus. "You mean yellow."

"That's what I said. Do I have to spell it for you?" he asked caustically.

"No thanks. I know how to spell it." She thought of another question. "By the way, where are you from originally?"

Grimm showed all the healthy teeth again. "Oz," he said. "But I left before the Californians invaded."

She was halfway through the door when Grimm called out, "Y-a-l-l-e-r."

THE YALLER COTTAGE sat on a narrow shoulder of the narrow highway that snaked alongside the Columbia. A sign on the cottage door commanded all who entered to remove their shoes first. Venus pulled off her Doc Martens and set them on the porch stairs. In the tiny foyer, a row of white cotton slippers shouted, Put me on. She did, then padded across the foyer's creaking floor. Only one door led off the foyer, so she knocked on it. After a brief silence, an imperious voice crowed, "Come in." Venus turned the knob and went inside.

Miss Fobia didn't glance up from her needlework, but Venus could see enough to know she had a Mabel face, a Mabel scowl, that she had on a pair of turquoise reading glasses, and that she was the same old coot from Hartell's.

"Ms. Fobia?"

"*Miss* Mabel Fobia." One gnarled hand clenched into a

fist whose knuckles rapped impatiently on the desk. Her other hand clutched the needlework. "So it's you again," said the coot in her familiar tease.

But something was melting inside Miss Mabel Fobia, for when the petite visitor smiled, Mabel actually felt her own internal crust defrost. A slight tremor erupted in the older woman's chest. She felt fluttery, thin of breath, and sensed a lot of inner turmoil. This young woman might be dim-witted and rude, but, well, candidly speaking, the girl had lovely green eyes. Mabel liked green-eyed girls. Mabel liked girls in general, but especially green-eyed girls.

The Fobia set aside her needlework. "You want to know how the Kettle People got their name? I don't have all day, so sit down in that chair over there and listen to me. There will be no interruptions during my presentation, do you understand?"

Venus sat down. Mabel leaned across the desk and inspected the dimwit's feet. "Very good," she said. "At least you can follow directions."

"Why the white slippers?"

"Can't get this old wide-plank cedar anymore. You'd be amazed at how a bunch of clumsy tourists can abrade the finish."

Mabel made a short jaunty journey across her office to a bookcase. Straining upward, she plucked a book off a lofty shelf, and in doing so, the lacy edge of a red slip peeked below her skirt. Evidently, the coot wasn't as prudish as her exterior suggested. She shouldered the thick volume back to her desk, brusquely assembled herself, and made a woodpecker sound in her throat.

"Now then," she began, "it's time for a history lesson. This is a book of local legends, written down many years ago by my great-grandfather Elias Fobia. People used to know these legends by heart, thanks to my ancestor. But you young people have all been victims of inferior educations, and so have not been exposed to these important legends. I can't tell you how this pains me...." She flipped the pages of the book, stopped, read silently to herself for a moment, and then began reading aloud. Sharp consonants rolled off the old coot's razor-edged tongue as the story of Kettle Falls unfolded.

ELEVEN

MANY EONS AGO, a tribe of native people settled near the edge of a mighty waterfall on the Columbia River. Back then, the river had no name, and the waterfall had no name. The people noticed that the "In-Tee-Tee-Huh," or salmon, were abundant in this river, that salmon loved this waterfall, so they decided to settle on the riverbank beside it. Back then, there was enough salmon to go around. The Indians called it "holy fish" and "sacred food." The rocks below the waterfall all became hollowed out from the force of the falls, and resembled the natives' cooking pots, or kettles. Eventually, the tribe living beside the waterfall came to be known as the Kettle People, and where they fished was called Kettle Falls.

The men of the tribe made weirs and nets and placed them out over Kettle Falls to catch salmon. Everyone in the tribe shared whatever fish were caught. What remained after feasting, the people preserved for the seasons when salmon didn't come. In bountiful seasons, they traded preserved salmon for dry goods from the Spokane People and Plains tribes. The Kettles grew prosperous from salmon. By then, the great Chief Kin-Ka-Now-Kla was leading the Kettles. Kin-Ka-Now-Kla was a respected leader and he made sure that every tribal member had enough salmon to eat. But the white man's government ran Kin-Ka-Now-Kla's people, and the other river tribes, off the river, moving them to a reservation, combining the Kettles with other tribes, who spoke other languages. This conglomeration of tribes came to be known as the Colville Confederation of Tribes.

Once the natives were evacuated from the riverbanks, the white man's leaders had the idea that they owned the river and its water and fish. They diverted the river, flooding the biggest of the coulees, or ravines, and several of the smaller coulees, destroying the tribal villages along the riverbanks. When the ''Grand Coulee'' had filled up with water, they named it Banks Lake, though it was just a reservoir. Then they dammed the river up above that reservoir, flooding that land, and they named the upper reservoir Roosevelt Lake, as if it weren't just a widened stretch of flooded river. When they backed up the waters to make these reservoirs, the waters covered Kettle Falls, the Indians' sacred salmon-fishing grounds.

The original town of Kettle Falls, established by natives, disappeared under the floodwaters. Then the white people built themselves a town on the east side of the upper reservoir and they named *it* Kettle Falls. They stole the town's name from the Indian village they had flooded and from the waterfall they had drowned.

MABEL FOBIA paused in her story, then said, ''Have you ever heard of a waterfall drowning?''

''I'll have to admit—''

''Kettle Falls lies beneath this reservoir, this so-called Roosevelt Lake.''

Fobia had long ago departed from the text and was ad-libbing. ''If they ever opened up the river, and the river ran naturally again, why, I imagine the falls would reappear. But that's not likely to occur, not in my lifetime anyway. Now, here's a curious anecdote: There are some folks who insist they can hear the falls, even today, even though the falls lie under forty feet of water. I call it poppycock.'' Fobia dabbed a handkerchief under her nose.

''Well, pretty soon after the dams were built all along the river, the salmon stopped coming in such great numbers. They could breach the natural waterfalls, but not these massive concrete structures. They fell back and died before having a chance to spawn. This destroyed the livelihood of the native tribes, and gradually, as the salmons' numbers diminished, the tribes' numbers dwindled down to only a few people who could not defend themselves against the white man.

"So that is how Kettle Falls got its name, and the falls live on in legend as the best salmon-fishing waterfall along the entire stretch of the Columbia River, the place where Kin-Ka-Now-Kla, the great salmon chief, fed his people until the white man destroyed the Columbia River and drowned Kettle Falls."

Fobia glanced up at her audience.

Venus said, "Was your ancestor—the one who recorded this book of legends—a member of the Kettle tribe?"

Fobia laughed sharply. "Of course not. I haven't a drop of Indian blood in my veins. These people couldn't write things down back then. All they had were oral histories, the stories they passed down by talking them. Elias Fobia, my great-grandfather, was one of the earliest white settlers around here, and he was educated. Elias Fobia, from Scotland. Elias Fobia wrote down these stories he heard from the Indians. If he hadn't, they might have been lost forever."

Venus said, "So…Miss Fobia…where do you stand on the issue?"

"What issue?" Suspicious.

"The destruction of the Columbia River."

"Who called it destruction? I didn't." Mabel slammed the book shut. "This is legend, not some factual journal. You wanted to know how the Kettles got their name. I am the local historian. It is my duty to provide this information to tourists, whether or not I like them. I have just related a legend. The facts of the matter are something entirely different, in my educated opinion."

"In other words, you're a dam enthusiast."

Fobia's voice grew shrill. "Call me whatever you wish. I have always, and always shall, support the existence of Grand

Coulee Dam.'' She sniffed. "After all, my father was one of the dam's chief architects.''

Somehow, that made sense. Still, something wasn't right. Venus said, "The dam was constructed in your father's time. When did your great-grandfather compile these legends?''

Mabel stared. Nothing was going right today. From the foyer came sounds of newly slippered guests. More tourists to hound her. She sucked her teeth and scowled, contemplating how to murder them. Tourists shouldn't visit until summer. Maybe never. She laid the book beside her neglected needlework on the desk. "It was a long time ago,'' she said. "Doesn't matter anymore. Now, I'm busy here. Why don't you just go down to the Elias Fobia Cabin at Roosevelt Lake? That's what they call the reservoir. Roosevelt Lake. Now, there's history worth knowing. Anyone can tell you how to find it.''

Venus stood at the door. From the other side came tourist sounds and knocking. Venus said, "Why should I do that?''

"What?'' Mabel almost shouted.

Venus opened the door. A busload of Japanese tourists poured in, chattering in their native tongue. Mabel regarded them bitterly.

On the way out, Venus said, "Maybe that old legend was a kind of foretelling.''

Mabel had had enough. Over the tourists' heads, she cried, "You might be a perky green-eyed blonde, a little bit cute, but you're a damned fool. I can see that I'd be wasting my precious time trying to educate you.''

At that moment, the tourists mobbed Mabel Fobia and she forgot all about the perky green-eyed girl.

On the front porch, Venus pawed through several pairs of Nikes until she uncovered her Doc Martens, which she put on. Then she cranked up the Aston and pointed it at the town of Kettle Falls. In Kettle Falls, she turned left onto a narrow paved road, following signs to Roosevelt Lake.

TWELVE

LIQUID HAZE rolled down the broad valley where the river flowed between two mountain ranges. The haze vaporized off the river's cool surface, and immured the shore. Venus pulled off the highway, walked to the top of a ridge, and looked down into the throttled waters. Coulee Dam, a hundred miles to the south, had backed up the mighty Columbia, clotting its rage in a still-water reservoir called Roosevelt Lake. According to Mabel Fobia, deep beneath these waters lay the rocky chasm that had formed Kettle Falls, sacred to the Kettle People, a fount of life that spewed up mighty chinook by the millions, which nourished and blessed native tribes for eons. Venus imagined the thundering crash of waterfall and the fishers tossing nets across the chasm. But the haze lay thick and low, and in reality, she saw nothing. She vaulted a fence to a footpath leading through a woods to the shore, following signs that pointed to the former site of Kettle Falls, where the rapids once raged.

Now she didn't see the river, but the signs pointed the way through a thinly wooded pine grove. In the still, damp air, she heard her footsteps crunch on the pine needle carpet. Eventually, the winding path led to a small split-log cabin, boarded up tight. A plaque on the front door identified it as the Elias Fobia Cabin, home of the first Scottish missionary in Kettle Falls. Mabel's ancestor.

The cabin's door, made of hand-hewn wood planks, had been bolted shut. Peering through a narrow gap in the planks, Venus saw only blackness. She moved on, following little arrow signs to the shore, and when finally she stood at the place that once marked the headwaters of Kettle Falls, she knew instantly that the legend told around town was true. Kettle Falls, the sacred salmon-fishing site for countless generations of Indians, might now lie beneath forty feet of dammed-up river beneath this man-made reservoir, but the waterfall hadn't died.

Venus could hear the falls.

But wait. Was that shouting? Was she imagining it, or did she really hear a raving voice? Squinting through the haze, she saw a figure moving toward her, an eerie yellow thing whose footfall sounded like thunder. The thing wove and bobbed through the dense mist. When it emerged from the haze, she saw a grizzled old man.

He wore a yellow rain slicker. In one hand, he carried a bucket; in the other, a spear. Venus watched him approach. The geezer hadn't noticed her. He was talking to himself as he climbed up the riverbank.

"Damnation, that was a close call, buddy. Yep, it sure was. Damnation, don't you try that ever again, you hear me? Damnation…whew! Talk about a close call."

He stopped abruptly in front of Venus. He had been tall once but now was bent with age; his face was ghoulish white, his hair pale as the fog, and tattered. But his eyes glinted like dancing fire, clear and flame blue. Venus had startled him. He set down his pail, stood his spear on end, and bellowed, "What in tarnation brings you out here?"

Venus shrugged. "Checking out the falls."

The old man grunted and scratched his ear. "Seems foolish, don'tcha think? Trying to see the falls through this here fog?"

Through this here lake was what Venus thought he meant to say.

The old man picked up his bucket. "Well then," he said gruffly, "come on and let's get off this river before one of us falls in."

The geezer snorted and headed up the trail. Venus followed him, and when they reached the road's shoulder, where her car was parked, the old man stared at the Aston Martin.

"Damnation," he said, and whistled. "This is some roadster."

Venus got in, gunned the engine. The Aston purred.

The old man said, "How about a lift, then?"

"Where you headed?"

The geezer climbed into the passenger seat, carefully balancing spear and bucket. "Take me to K Falls. That's where I live."

Venus pumped the gas, swung around, and headed north, back to K Falls. The old man was a little shaky, so she took it slowly along the highway. Speeding cars honked and their drivers lobbed obscenities at them, but she didn't care, and neither, apparently, did the geezer. He sat beside Venus, bellowing, "Damnation, this puppy rides smooth. Da-a-a-m-m-m-nation."

He directed her to a weathered wood house no bigger than a garden shed, half a block off Main Street, in the heart of K Falls. On a patch of overgrown lawn lay a tangled pile of fishnets. In the driveway, an ancient Airstream sat like a magic bullet, twice the size of the hut where the old man lived. A sign on the Airstream read FOR RENT.

The old guy kept three languid basset hounds on a lumpy daybed inside the hut, and the cremains of his mother rested in a jar on the fireplace mantel. When he dropped the bucket on the living room floor, the hounds waddled over and sniffed it. One dead fish lay inside the bucket, and the hounds averted their discriminating noses and waddled back to their daybed. Venus tossed her black leather jacket on a tattered armchair and followed the old man into the kitchenette.

From a pot on the stove, the geezer served up plates of corned beef hash. He boiled some old coffee grounds and uncovered a jar of Cremora on the littered Formica breakfast table. When he shoveled the hash into his mouth, his tongue hung out and he chewed with his mouth open, the tongue tilted downward like a coal chute, so that half the food fell back onto his plate, or the Formica. It was a wonder anything got swallowed. Venus noticed the tremors in his arm as he raised the fork to his mouth. In all this time, she hadn't noticed the Parkinson's. The old guy had enough control over his tremors that he could hide it much of the time, but his time was running out, and he knew it better than anyone did.

"Go on," he said after a long silence had passed. "Ask me how old I am."

"How old are you?"

The old man chuckled and his eyes glinted like two sapphires. He wiped corned beef hash off his mouth. "Ninety-six today."

"Hell you are."

"Hell I am." He smacked his lips and they curved into a satisfied grin. He leaned back, tilting the chair precariously. "Yes sirree, ninety-six and goin' strong," he said. "You wanna know my secret?"

Venus swallowed a mouthful of thick coffee. "Tell me."

"Just this. You go down to the river everyday, and you holler at it. You tell that no-good river that it won't never swallow you down, won't never claim your life, no sirree. See, you blink once, and wham! The river takes you down. But you go down, stand in those rapids, and you defy that force. Then you live another day longer, and the river respects you."

Venus said, "That's it?"

The old guy nodded and clicked his tongue, a sign that prophesy was forming on his lips. Staring at his visitor, his cold blue eyes burning two holes in Venus's soul, he whispered, "Beavers comin' atcha." Then he rose slowly to his feet. "Come back," he said abruptly, leading her to the front door. "Right now, me and the boys here"—he gestured at the bassets—"we have our naptime. Come back again and I'll show you how to holler at the river."

"Thanks," she said. "Maybe I'll do that."

"Oh, you'll do it," he called after her. "You'll do it for sure, young lady. You're just like me. I can tell. A river shouter."

THE SHOUTER LIVED on Harmony Lane, second lot from the corner of Main Street, in Kettle Falls. The lot next door, at the corner of Harmony and Main, was vacant except for heaps of discarded garbage and a LAND FOR SALE sign. The lot was overgrown with weeds, a haven for crows. Waiting at the intersection for the town's only stoplight to change, Venus watched the crows scavenge through trash. She counted fifteen crows in the lot; then the light changed and she turned left onto Main Street and headed south toward the highway to Seattle.

She had gone two blocks along Main Street when she spotted the Harley parked slantwise to the high curb. She would have recognized that bike anywhere. It had once belonged to her. Standing in the street, beside the bike, cheap aviators shading his eyes, a very alive Louie Song was smoking a Gauloise with one hand and petting the Harley with the other.

Venus pulled up and said, "Could you please try harder to resemble a tourist?"

THIRTEEN

BEHIND THE bargain-basement aviators, Song's exotic eyes fairly smoldered.

Venus parked the Aston, then went over to where Song stood beside the Harley. She said, "Fancy meeting you here."

She petted the bike nostalgically. Song had tricked her out of the bike. Maybe not tricked, but opportunistically acquired it from her in one of her rare love-blind moments, on the eve of her wedding day. She had regretted it ever since, and Song refused to sell it back to her. She stroked the Harley longingly, recalling better days. So it had survived the blast, and, by the way, so, apparently, had Song.

Song watched her, he pursed his lips making a kissing sound she didn't understand.

She said, "What brings you to K Falls?"

He waved the Gauloise. "Looking for Fowler."

She stared at him. "How did you know about Fowler?"

He blew smoke, flicked ashes into the street. "Little bird told me."

A woman passing on the sidewalk spotted Song and gaped. He was that handsome, that alluring.

Venus said, "So spill, dead man."

Song popped the Harley's stow bin, leaned down, fished out a Federal Express box, and showed it to her. "You'll get a bang out of this," he said straight-faced.

She didn't have to open the box to know what was inside. She did, though, just for the thrill of it. One dead salmon.

No tag this time, just the fish, with the familiar crazed eyes. She looked at Song, tried to see through his mirrored aviators. Where were his nice Revos? All she could see was her own frustrated expression.

She said, "So you're Woody Guthrie."

"Roll on, Columbia." He grinned. His fingers made air riffs on an invisible guitar; then he said, "I was just on my way to mail it. Since you're here, I can deliver it in person."

"I bet you buy your fish at Ella's."

"How'd you guess?" he said, faking surprise.

"So did the fish swallow the tag or did you stuff it down its throat?"

"You figure that out."

They were standing on the sidewalk, the occasional pedestrian looping around them. An ancient couple labored toward them, pushing identical walkers. She waited until the old folks had rolled passed, then snarled, "Wipe that smirk off and dish. Why mail a dead fish and make stupid muffled phone calls?"

He shrugged. "Worked, didn't it?"

She reached up, touched his cheek. "Where'd you get that phony scar?"

"You can tell?" He was crushed.

"Give me five minutes with my makeup kit and I'll make it look so real, you'll want plastic surgery."

Song said, "Turn around."

"Why?"

"Just turn around." He guided her shoulder. Now instead of facing the street, she faced a redbrick building, three stories high, with a Victorian-era facade and a cornerstone that identified it as the Omak Building. He led her over to a small directory near the entrance. The tenants were listed in no special order: "Kermit's Tattoo Parlor, Second Floor. Lady Lisa, Certified Public Masseuse, Third Floor. Dambusters: Give Fish a Chance, Ground Floor."

Song made her wear his sunglasses and a sailor cap he

kept in the Harley's stow bin. Steering her by the elbow, he led her across the street, heading straight for a tavern called Prospector's Saloon. On the way, Venus's foot struck the curb. She fell to the ground, writhing in pain.

Song helped her up. "You okay?"

She tried standing. She could stand, but the injured foot hurt. "I think I broke my toe."

Song took her arm. "Naw. Probably just a minor sprain."

Prospector's Saloon had double swinging doors. Prospector was Sumo-shaped and surly, and right now he had his hands full, lording over a poker game at a table in the rear, but his snaky eyes didn't miss their entrance. The bartender on duty said her name was Tiffie, and that wasn't all she wanted to share with Song. She wore her phony flaxen hair in a beehive, and her sylph's figure undulated in a skintight outfit that might as well have been tattooed on. She had already figured out a sultry voice, how to make it lilt across the hand-carved antique mahogany bar. "Bet I could help you," Tiffie purred, eyeing Song salaciously.

Song dropped some bills on the table. "Jameson, neat. The lady will have a Beck's. The nonalcoholic version."

Tiffie didn't bother checking out the lady. She instantly produced a bottle of Jameson and a double shot glass. She poured the Jameson. She might as well have handed him the bottle. She put the Jameson down, leaned her elbows on the counter, and cupped her dimpled chin in her hands. "Where'd you come from?" she purred at Song. "Persia? Or heaven?"

Song, accustomed to female adulation, sipped the whiskey and said, "Oklahoma. Tulsa."

"Cowboyland doesn't deserve you," said Tiffie, batting her Maybellines. "You better stay here in K Falls. With me."

Song smoldered, encouraging the cheap flirt.

Tiffie said, "You Chinese?"

"Part."

"Which part?"

"Left side's Chinese; right side's European-American."

"I can handle that." Tiffie caressed her hips.

Soon the two had descended into sleazy cocktail banter. Venus slipped off the bar stool, slid behind the counter, and found the icebox. She plucked a Beck's low alcohol content beer from the case, slid back around the bar, and drank straight from the bottle. After a few minutes of sheer boredom, while Song continued to seduce the local coquette, Venus abandoned the flirt scene and toured the saloon, Prospector's snake eyes watching her every move.

Near the rest rooms, a bulletin board had been tacked to the wall. She idly perused the notices. Straining through the mirrored aviators, she managed to decipher several outdated garage sale notices, numerous flyers plugging sundry church events, a few apartment vacancies, baby-sitters' propositions, and "Services for Hire," some highly suspect. Nothing pulled her chain, although she carefully scrutinized an ad for "Kermit's Tattoo Parlor. Pain guaranteed. See Kermit. Second floor, Omak Building."

Finally bored with flirting, Song slipped away from the bar, much to Tiffie's chagrin. He stole over to the bulletin board, sneaked up behind the Firecracker, and made a growling noise. She didn't turn around, didn't even flinch. Steady as ever. Maybe she had the nerves to play his new game. He ushered her outdoors.

They stood on the sidewalk outside the saloon, Tiffie watching them through the window.

Venus said, "Spill, Scarface."

"I'd heard about Fowler in Seattle. I asked Olson to let me go undercover with the Dambusters. Olson said no deal."

She started to say something. He held a hand up to her mouth and continued.

"So when the dam blew, I saw my chance to go undercover. I've been tracking Fowler along the river, but so far, no sightings. When I heard he had an office in K Falls, I came up to check him out. As you can see, the office is shut down tight. I've been up here three weeks, and the Dambusters office hasn't been open once during all that time. No sign of Fowler anywhere. I hear he's an anomaly."

She said, "Why the hell didn't you tell us? Why lead us all down this primrose path, making us believe you exploded into tiny particles? That makes me mad as hell."

"Yeah, well."

"Is that all you can say, 'Yeah, well'?" He placed his hands on her shoulders. She shrugged them off.

"Listen," he said, "before you go off on a tantrum. This was the only way."

She started pacing. Inside Prospector's, Tiffie, swabbing the counter, glanced out the window, and noticed her cowboy and the chick. Tiffie curled her lip at Venus. Song led Venus down the sidewalk, out of Tiffie's sight.

Venus said, "I demand to know why you left me, of all people, out of this undercover scheme."

He shrugged. "I figured I could go it alone. Besides, what with all your personal problems—"

"That's absolutely, totally ridiculous. I never allow my personal life—"

Song raised a hand. "I didn't say you do." He shifted uncomfortably. "Aw, c'mon, Venus…. Anyway, I finally realized that I need your help."

That calmed her down, somewhat soothed her bruised ego.

Song said, "I had to find a way to involve you without Olson suspecting. So I sent you the dead fish, hoping to spark your curiosity, attract your attention."

"Why the hell didn't you just phone?"

"Too risky."

"Be more specific—about you, I mean."

"Just before the explosion, the fish counter disappeared off the dam. I saw a dude in the parking lot, on a cell phone, a couple hundred yards off the dam, too far away to tell if it was the fish counter. I think he detonated the explosives. The fish counter might be our man. Just in case, so he wouldn't recognize me, I shaved off my sideburns and goatee.''

"Thank God for small favors.''

"After the dam exploded, I saw my chance. I no longer existed. So I created a new identity and started tracking this Fritz Fowler. He's an elusive SOB. He snakes in and out of these river towns, and whenever he stops, his supporters hide him. Like they fear for his life.''

"He might be our man.''

Song said, "How about it? You game for an undercover gig?''

While she thought it over, she said, "So what's your new persona non grata?''

"Juneau Jones, demolitions expert.''

"Juneau? Jones?''

"With fake ID, you can't be picky.''

The couple pushing identical walkers reappeared on the sidewalk, huffing and puffing. Song and Venus made room for the old-timers to pass. Both seniors wore Nikes. The woman had on a fake-fur coat and cat-eye sunglasses with rhinestone studs. The man wheezed, and Venus could hear his drowning lungs complain. When they had passed, Venus said, "I should have known you didn't blow up. But you might have sent me a message of some kind. You could have at least let me know the Harley was okay. And I dropped one hell of a bundle on a memorial bouquet, too. When Olson postponed the services, the damn wreath had already been delivered.'' She bit her lip. "I refuse to buy you another one when the real time comes.''

"Olson postponed my memorial service?'' Now Song's ego smarted.

"Work issues took priority. Species miffed over territorial encroachment. So said Olson.'' She wriggled her foot. "I think I broke a toe.''

In the fading daylight, Main Street's sidewalks were fast rolling up. Song climbed on the Harley and headed for the highway. In the Aston, Venus followed the Harley along Highway 20 through the North Cascades. They stopped once in Concrete for gas and chow, then drove on through the night, arriving in Seattle before midnight. At the Taj on Alki Point, they iced the FedEx package in the garage freezer unit. It might still be edible. They went inside and while she iced the injured toe, she brought him up-to-date on the brown van and the strange Darla. Then they played Scrabble, which Song won with the word *xyztus*. When he yawned and got up to leave, she handed him his jacket. He put it on, then impulsively wrapped his arms around her. She pushed him away.

"Easy, dead man," she said, keeping it friendly. "I'm still married."

Song loosened his grasp, smacked his forehead. "Oh yeah, I forgot. Tell me again—when was the last time you saw your old man?"

She opened the door. "Go away."

"I have nowhere to go. I'm dead, remember?"

She stood in the doorway trying to decide if she felt angry or sexually aroused. Something had triggered an adrenaline rush. She let him stay, but in the guest room.

WHEN THE PHONE RANG shortly after dawn, she was in bed with two French schoolboys. Both boys wore capes, and dear spit curls poked out from the little berets on their heads. They wore sturdy boots that came halfway up their calves and carried baskets that presumably held schoolbooks. Both sported similar devilish grins. Venus loved them both, and loved what they did to her. But the phone pealed again, insisting. She reached for the receiver. Ecohubby, calling from Ivory Coast, had innuendo in his voice and someone—maybe Venus—on his mind. Cradling Richard's apologetic equivocations in the crook of her neck, she gently draped the schoolboys across her naked breasts, where they rested in the heave of her quickening breath. Bittersweet fellows, they were the closest thing to French breakfast.

Richard cooed on. She sincerely cared more for him than she did for the French schoolboys, but the truth was, right now, she wanted the boys. Richard said, "I feel that I'm interrupting something."

He waited until she had noshed both chocolate-coated biscuits and washed them down with stale Dalwhinnie. The schoolboys traveled south toward her stomach, but the sugar rush shot straight to her brain, evoking euphoria. Even if she'd wanted to, she felt incapable of hostility.

"Missed you, too," she purred. "When will you come home?"

Ecohubby stammered. Funny. He'd never stammered before.

"We have trouble here, babe. Big political mess. I'll need to hang on here for another five or six weeks. Maybe longer."

"Hang on to what?"

"What do you mean by that?"

She brushed biscuit crumbs off her lap. A dab of dark chocolate had melted in her shallow cleavage. She rubbed it in and said, "Oh, nothing. I was just wondering what you're doing for a good time when you're not out saving Ivory Coast's forests. Surely you can't be pulling twenty-four/seven in the bush."

Silence. Then: "Maybe you think I'm having a vacation down here."

"You must do something for fun. And to be brutally frank, Richard, I cannot imagine you going this long—what's it been now, two months?—without sex. So why don't you just be perfectly candid with me? Get it out in the open. You know, straight from the heart. I am your wife, after all. I deserve a little honesty from my husband. That gull didn't bring those purple panties into your closet." She despised the complaining tone of her own voice, the paranoia lacing her accusation.

Richard's sigh made static over the phone line. Then came the dreaded, ominous stillness. Involuntarily, she couldn't breathe.

"All right," he said finally. "Maybe it's time for brutal frankness."

Her stomach churned. She could breathe again, but her heart had nose-dived. She said, "Go ahead."

"I've been…involved with someone. Intimately."

Her world echoed.

He fumbled on. "I mean…what I mean, well…I've been involved with someone but…"

"Who is she?" As if it mattered. She sat up in bed.

"The wife of a forestry official here. I'm not proud of myself."

"The wife of an Ivory Coast forestry official?"

"Correct."

"Wait a minute," she said. "You're not by any stretch speaking of that café au lait beauty we met at the international forestry conference in Banff last year?"

"The same. I'm sorry to tell you like this, over the phone. I wanted to wait until I came home."

"Is that so?" She sat on the edge of the bed. Outside the window, the rising sun battled dawn's wool blanket, losing. "This isn't even a joke, is it?"

"I wish it were. I'm sorry, babe."

"Are you in love with her?"

"It's not like that."

"Maybe you can explain what it is like."

"I'm struggling for the right words," he said finally. "They just won't come."

"I'll bet." Venus stared at the gray dawn light. The predictable thick fog rolling in off Puget Sound obscured the beach at Alki Point, but at intervals she saw the bleep of light from Alki's lighthouse and felt a strange comfort in the beam's reliability. More reliable than the sun, or moon, or stars. Once every three seconds, it penetrated the haze, the fog, or the darkness. Count on it.

"Are you there?"

She heard her own voice say, "She's visited you here? In Seattle?"

"Couple times. You know, Venus, this wouldn't have happened if you weren't so married to your job."

"What does a 'couple times' mean? Once, twice, forty times?"

"Babe," he said. "I'm worried about you."

"Really?" She slid off the bed, her bare feet smacking the cold wood floor, and began pacing. "I'll tell you what, Mr. Envirohero. Don't bother worrying. Just don't bother about anything. Just don't."

"This would never have happened if you weren't such a workaholic," he complained again.

"Look who's talking, buster."

"I'm coming home," he said urgently.

"Maybe you are," she countered hotly. "But not to me."

"Babe, we need to talk this out," he said, his voice desperate now. "I promise you it's nothing serious—between Magda and me, I mean. It's just sex...."

"Magda?" she yelled. "What kind of a name is that for a black African?"

"Her mother is English. That is, Caucasian," he murmured almost apologetically.

"Well that explains it," she retorted sarcastically.

"Sweetheart, you asked for honesty. Listen. Venus. Are you listening?"

"Mmm."

"My darling, I love you more than anyone in the world, which is why I'm being so brutally frank. Anyway, I'm now realizing that I've made a terrible mistake."

"Just now you're realizing that?"

"I should never have told you about this over the phone. I'm coming home right away. We need to talk this out."

"The hell we do. You need to talk, Richard? Talk to Magda." She clicked off the line and threw the phone across the room. The fog crept over the beach, shrouding the house. She stood at the window, staring out at thick nothingness. Thick nothingness staring at thick nothingness. All dense energy, without light or hope. She watched the first drops of rain skitter down the windowpane. Behind her, from a remote corner, the telephone rang. She ignored it. Her stomach churned. The Alki light blinked through the fog. She felt two hands rest softly on her shoulders. She turned and faced the dead man and he saw her tears. Song pulled her close and let her weep. She said, "Now I'm dead, too."

FOURTEEN

TSAGIGLA'AL, Watcher of the River, heard that one hundred cedar waxwings were found dead up near Omak, their purple-stained beaks indicating the cause of death was an overdose of fermented privet berries. Alcohol poisoning. Some careless privet bush owner had neglected to rake up the fermenting fallen fruit. The River Watcher vowed to avenge the birds, and on the first day of June, a flock of inebriated wax-wings attacked privet bush owner Mitzi Carlysle as the elderly woman left the Omak Safeway. Mrs. Carlysle suffered pecks and feather burns and was hospitalized for heart palpitations. "Birds are filthy," Mrs. Carlysle proclaimed.

When Tsagigla'al learned that Indians from the Colville Reservation were poaching elk at Fort Spokane, he sent the Inchelum beavers down to gnaw down the Colville's sweat lodge. When the lodge fell into the river, Jack Foxes Moon, a tribal elder declared, "I've lost all respect for beavers." Then Tsagigla'al saw a crew of humans on the riverbanks at Hanford Reach, and he saw them pumping nuclear waste into the river, so he sent a strong army of black bears. The bears attacked the polluters, killing all of them. "Humans are filthy," the River Watcher proclaimed. When a boatfull of fly fishermen poached wild chinook salmon on Roosevelt Lake, Tsagigla'al infused the dead fishes' corpses with *E. coli* bacteria and the fishermen fell ill and died, and the Watcher saw that this was as it should be. When a real estate developer in Electric City took a sacred salmon-spawning pool, created a landfill, and covered it over with condominiums, the

Watcher sent bands of cougar to stalk the condo dwellers. And all the river dwellers of the human species began to fear for their safety and well-being. And Tsagigla'al rested for a day before his next assault.

Days later, havoc reigned at Wenatchee when apple growers discovered a locust infestation in their orchards. When a population of black bears invaded the holding ponds at the Pasco Hatchery one night while the humans slept, they devoured the hatchery's prize experimental salmon fingerlings, causing havoc for the fish biologists.

A paranoia spread. Perhaps these were not isolated incidents, but conscious acts of sabotage carried out by a rebellious animal kingdom tired of the human species encroaching on the river wilderness. While the authorities wrung their helpless hands, the news media made light of the "animal incidents," amusing viewers with news snippets of rogue wildlife invading human territory. But the people along the Columbia River weren't laughing. The river people knew that something had gone terribly wrong.

DARLA HAD fallen asleep. She wasn't sure how long she'd been asleep, but when Gerald pulled the blue van onto a gravel road, the bumping woke her. She stretched and blinked her eyes. It was night, but Gerald was driving with just parking lights on. In the dimness, she could barely make out a narrow strip of gravel road wending through scrubby chaparral. She dared not ask where they were headed.

The day before, he had gone away in the brown van and come back a few hours later in this older-model blue van. He had transferred everything into the blue van. She had asked him about the switch, and once again he warned her about asking questions, so she dropped the subject, but she couldn't help feeling a tiny bit afraid.

As they followed the gravel road, she tried making small talk, but Gerald wasn't in the mood. For a long time, the van lurched and rolled, until finally the gravel road ended and

Gerald turned into the scrub brush and onto a dirt path. The path led uphill, and Darla saw a high ridge ahead of them and, above the horizon, a broad expanse of glittering, star-studded sky. When they reached the top of the ridge, Gerald parked the van, unloaded the bombs, and told her to wait for him. He disappeared into the dark.

Darla stood at the edge of the ridge and looked down. Three hundred feet below her, at the base of a dry coulee, the earth was swallowed up in blackness. No sign of life anywhere on the horizon. The glittering sky was all she could see. She studied the cloudy path of the Milky Way and imagined her swan self gliding along it. She sat down to wait. Maybe Gerald would be gone a long time. Maybe there was time to turn into a swan. But she had hardly started when Gerald came back and told her to gather up kindling for a fire.

While she gathered broken scrub brush, Gerald gathered fist-sized rocks. She watched as he dug a pit, placed kindling in the bottom, piled the rocks on top, then more kindling on top of the rocks. He lit the kindling and the fire flared up, illuminating the place where they stood. Darla could see Gerald's face, expressionless except for the dancing glint in his eyes. In a few minutes, the fire burned down and the rocks glowed. Gerald crouched down and removed his boots and his socks. Darla dared not ask him why.

When he stood up, he looked at her and said, "Take off your shoes."

"But honey—"

"Take them off."

She did as he said. He took her hand. He led her toward the glowing stones. His hand gripped hers so hard, she cried out in pain. He ignored her and stepped forward, taking her with him. At the edge of the glowing stones, he let go of her hand and she gaped in horror as he placed first one foot, then both on the hot stones and walked across the fire. When he stepped out of the fire on the other side, he looked across the glowing embers at her. She knew it was her turn.

"I can't," she pleaded.

"Come to me, Darla."

"I can't, Gerald. I'm afraid." She was weeping now.

Gerald said, "There are those who think they know but don't. There are those who don't know, and know they don't know. There are those who know but don't know that they know. And there are those who know that they know."

Darla wept. "I just can't do it."

"Come to me across the fire."

Darla summoned all the courage she could, but still she was afraid.

"You must come across the fire. If you love me, it won't hurt. It's now or never."

At that moment, Darla sank into the jaws of the Stockholm syndrome and convinced herself that she loved her captor. She stepped onto the hot stones and screamed.

VENUS AND SONG had assumed the identities of Mr. and Mrs. Juneau Jones and had set up housekeeping in a mobile home on the outskirts of Kettle Falls. Mrs. Jones, a petite redhead with bobbed hair and hazel eyes (tinted contact lenses), wore baggy cotton dresses and walked with a pronounced limp. Mr. Jones—Juneau—had a bad scar on his cheek, like one from a knife fight, and always wore the same cheap pair of aviator sunglasses. Juneau was undeniably part Asian, but that wasn't unusual up near the vineyards, where illegal Asian immigrants hid out from the law and got work picking grapes. Word went around that Juneau was a demolitions man, but he never seemed to have work.

Juneau Jones and his wife, Kay Lynn, lived in an old Airstream silver bullet. They drove a shabby Buick station wagon. They had no children or pets. They were a quiet couple and kept to themselves. In the first weeks of their residency, Kay Lynn Jones was seen frequently at the local shopping mall, pawing through the sale bins, and Juneau could be found in the local bars, most frequently in Prospector's Saloon, flirting with that Tiffie tart. The Joneses seemed like any other normal Kettle Falls couple.

The Airstream had a built-in cherry-wood dinette with battered chartreuse cushions. When they had rented the trailer from the Shouter, he had insisted on charging them only a dollar a day, but he made them promise not to spill a drop of anything on the chartreuse cushions. As they sat inside the Airstream one cool evening, Venus said to Song, "Remember the Astoria bank blast?"

"What's that got to do with anything?"

"Olson had Paganelli run a check on the explosives. The color codes in the powders matched dynamite used in both the Rocky Reach and Priest Rapids blasts. And guess what? The Astoria blast turned up powder from the same batch of dynamite."

Song lit a cigarette and watched her through the smoke. He said, "So Olson knows you lied about going to Africa to rescue your marriage?"

"No way. I swore Paganelli to secrecy. It's too early to tell the chief. He's far too skeptical. He'd go ballistic, then fire us both."

"Hell, that's a fait accompli."

She ignored that and said, "After the bank blast, the cops found a small pillbox in the rubble. The pillbox contained two hits of ecstasy. The bank manager said the pillbox might belong to Darla Denny, but he couldn't be certain. There were fingerprints on the pillbox. One set. They match fingerprints in Darla's employee file. Still, there's no other evidence, nothing else to link her to drugs, or to any illegal activity. The bank manager suggested she might have a boyfriend with a drug habit. But she's who she claims to be, the Dennys' daughter, and until this, she was clean as a whistle.

"According to her bank employee records, she was born in Spokane, but then soon after her birth, her mother moved with her to Seattle. They stayed in Seattle until she was about seven years old; then her mother married Albert Denny and they moved in with him here in K Falls.''

Song said, "How much have you told the parents?"

"Other than informing them that their daughter contacted me, zilch."

Song studied her through the cigarette haze. "Why's that?"

"Why zilch? Because I don't trust them."

"Why?"

She thought it over, then said, "Not sure. He's respectable enough. Maybe too respectable. And he's loaded. Besides the icewine vineyard up here at K Falls, he's a big rancher. Owns half of Spokane County's ranch lands. And he's politically powerful this side of the Cascades."

"How powerful?"

She shrugged. "Chairman of the Eastern Washington Republican party."

Song snickered and reached for the Usher's, the cheap scotch being a reluctant concession to Juneau Jones's persona. "Can't be worth much leading the local Republicans. He a white supremacist?"

She didn't know. "No overt signs of racist tendencies. He's a staunch churchgoing Methodist with an unblemished record, including service with valor in Nam. He's clean as a whistle."

Song squinted. "What about the mother?"

"Not much on her. No police record that we could trace. Seems fairly standard-issue trophy wife. She raises truffle-sniffing potbellied pigs."

"Get out."

Venus raised her right hand. Song poured the Usher's into a plastic cup.

Venus said, "And we also know Mrs. Denny is active in the Dambusters."

Song sipped the Usher's, made a sour face. "Tell me again about her involvement."

"According to her husband, Sue Ann recently spoke out publicly, on a local radio station, in favor of breaching the dams to save the wild salmon runs. Her husband says some narrow-minded eastern Washington folk took it the wrong way, accused Sue Ann of being an ecoterrorist because she supported breaching the dams. And there's been a lot of paranoia about ecoterrorism, a lot of rumors floating around."

Song said, "Ecoterrorism is almost an oxymoron."

Venus said, "Well then, ecotage. Now, here's another puzzle. The body that surfaced after the Priest Dam bombing? You and I both know that wasn't the fish counter's body. The so-called fish counter was standing in the parking lot fondling a cell-phone detonator...."

Song held up a hand, "Conjecture."

"You saw it, Song. Conjecture, yes, but I've asked Paganelli to get ahold of that autopsy report. Identify him. So far, no missing persons reports have turned up—nobody's looking for their uncle Fred. We know the body was a male. That's about all we know. We need to close that chapter."

Song eyed the cheap bottle of Scotch and said, "We need to change Juneau's drinking habits."

BY MID-MAY, the territorial wars between human invaders and wilder species had gained full force. Olson gathered what was left of his crack team of agents and moved east of the Cascades, a logical move in the face of events. The trouble with wildlife had provoked Olson to the snapping point. The hunt for territorial invaders of the nonhuman species now escalated into war.

The team headquartered at a dingy Days Inn in Colville. Over breakfast, Olson convened a strategy meeting. Olson arrived first with Sweetwater. Then Sparks, Olson's most laconic agent, drifted in. Sparks had been working the Columbia's mouth during the fish count and he'd driven all night, since he got a call to meet the team upriver at Colville. Dottie Nichols was the last of Olson's crack team to show up. Dottie had been up on the Snake, counting fish and watching for ecoterrorists. She was still recovering from a turbulent breakup with Song when he disappeared. She wasn't coping well, and Olson had thought about taking her off the case, but he needed every agent. When they assembled over breakfast at 6:00 a.m., Olson noticed that tall, lanky Sparks was bleary-eyed, and when he slid into the booth beside Olson, the chief felt a chill dampness waft off Sparks's jacket.

"You look like hell," Olson said accusingly.

Sparks pretended not to hear, ordered a double espresso and full breakfast, including rashers dripping in grease. "Where's the Firecracker?" he asked Olson.

"Gone to Africa."

"Hubby?"

Olson nodded.

Sparks guffawed into his bacon. "Figures."

"I disagree. I say it's out of character."

Across the table, Eric Sweetwater splayed out Section 118 in the *Washington Gazetteer* while Dottie peered over his rugged shoulder. Olson, sober and alert this morning, announced the game plan. "We're looking for a band of black bears that, according to the locals, have been menacing the Colville shopping mall. Eric and I will take the chopper up. Dottie, I want you on the river, up near Kettle Falls. Cover every inch of riverbank, and I mean scour it. Sparks, you do the town, ask around Colville. Find out if anyone's actually seen these bears."

Sparks raised his hand. "I'm much better in the wild. Maybe Dot and I should switch—"

"I know what I'm doing," Olson snapped. "Now, pay attention, because as far as we know, these bears could strike again if we don't kick our collective ass into gear."

Sparks sipped his hot java, making little slurping sounds that annoyed Olson. Olson continued: "The manager of a

fish market in the mall reported two adults and one cub re-
treating at dawn, when he came on his shift. He said they
scampered off into the woods just west of town. I sent a local
patrol out there. Nada. So here's the plan." On the map,
Olson's beefy finger traced the Columbia River's banks.

"Sweetwater and I will head northeast, as far as the border,
then down south to Grand Coulee. I want to check out an
incident down there. Dam techs called in a bear sighting half
an hour ago. We'll turn around at the dam, circle back, and
meet you here this evening."

Sparks said, "Shoot to kill?"

"What do you think?" Olson sucked his teeth.

"I'll find those bastards," Sparks said.

"They're bears," Dottie said to Sparks. "They aren't
poachers."

"They're naughty bears."

Olson glanced out the window and saw daylight. "We're
lucky," he said. "Weather's bright and clear. Forecast is for
a clear, dry day."

"I just have one question," said Dottie. "Why are we
wasting our time on these bear sightings when we could be
tracking a serial bomber who could strike again at any moment?"

Olson's eyes flickered. Irritably, he said, "Do what I tell
you and don't question my decisions. And remember, you
work for Fish and Wildlife, not fisheries, not the ATF. They
have their jobs, we have ours, and right now, ours is tracking
pesty bears."

"So let's go," said Sweetwater. Sweetwater was tall,
graceful, and when he stood up and stretched, a passing wait-
ress swooned, hoping to land in his arms, but Sweetwater
didn't notice because his eyes had caught a news broadcast
on the television propped over the bar.

"How about that," Sweetwater remarked to no one in particular.

Olson slid out of the booth, followed Sweetwater to the cashier. "How about what?"

Sweetwater jerked a thumb at the tube. "Bank robbery over at Kettle Falls Savings and Loan. Blew a hole in the wall. They got away with the dough."

Olson humphed.

"Anyone blown up?" asked Sparks, always macabre.

Sweetwater said, "Nobody killed. Nobody injured. They're calling it 'an expert job.'"

When they were alone, Sparks said to Olson, "He's dead. I feel it in my bones. Blown to smithereens. Or else he drowned. All I know is, he wouldn't break contact with us."

Olson said, "So why didn't his body show up? If he was still on that ladder with his replacement? Anyway, why would Song still be counting salmon? His shift was over."

"Phuh," Sparks said. "Who was with him?"

"Far as I know, just his replacement. Fellow whose body surfaced. It came up short. They never found the head or the legs."

"That would be the fish counter?"

"Who else?"

Sparks shrugged. "They do DNA?"

"On the fish counter?" Olson made a face. "Why the hell would they do that?"

Sparks shrugged. "Hell, why not? Routine, I'd say."

Olson rubbed his bald head. It itched. Something in the air in eastern Washington, some pollen his scalp couldn't tolerate. He said, "It was the body of the fish counter."

Sparks shrugged, said, "If you say so. Personally, I'd ask Paganelli to scan the autopsy report. Just in case somebody missed something." He leered at Olson, then walked away, leaving the boss to curse spring allergens.

FIFTEEN

"NITROGLYCERIN IS the explosive ingredient in many bombs. The nitro forms gaseous air pockets that are ignited when the gunpowder in the blasting cap goes off. Clay added to the nitro makes dynamite, a more stable form of explosive. Dynamite is still used for large demolition projects, such as blowing out cliffs to make traffic tunnels, or blowing up riverbanks to widen them, or to divert the flow. The way rock is mined is that holes are drilled, loaded with explosives, and detonated from a safe distance with remote-control devices. Ammonium nitrate and fuel oil, ANFO, costs around thirty cents a pound. Today, smaller bombs made of plastic explosives can cause much destruction. Still, dynamite is favored for many large projects."

Darla glanced at Gerald for his approval. The big guy winked at her across the front seat of the van as they drove north along the river.

Darla's feet were encased in heavy woolen socks so that she wouldn't be tempted to look at them oozing infectious green pus. He had told her that the best way to heal third-degree burns was to keep them open to the air, allow healing to occur from the inside. The infection had caused a fever, and the infected blood made red streaks that ran from her feet up her legs, toward her heart. Every few hours, they pulled into a rest stop and he would bathe her forehead with cool water from the drinking fountain. Then he would remove the woolen socks and drain the green pus, and she would cry in pain as he cleansed the wounds. But his hands were gentle and he held her when she cried, whispering softly that she would heal soon. He told her the next time wouldn't hurt so much. His compassion overwhelmed her, even more than the pain.

Why had she made those stupid phone calls to the Fish and Wildlife Service? How could she have been so disloyal? He had been good to her, kind and gentle, except when he lost his temper, but that wasn't often. No one had ever treated Darla so gently; no one had ever loved her so much. How could she have turned against him?

"I knew your name wasn't really Tom Justice," Darla said, snuggling up to him as best she could while keeping her feet immobile. Even so, they throbbed painfully. "But I never would have guessed Gerald. It's hard to say. Gerald."

The big guy shrugged. "I told you to call me whatever you want."

Darla searched her mind, then decided. "You're my Mr. Big Guy."

"What about liquid explosives?"

Darla recited from memory. "Liquid explosives are safer and easier to store. Liquid explosives are pumped into holes drilled in, say, rock. Can I have a Penguin now?"

The big guy gave Darla a Penguin. She sucked and watched the scenery. At Tonasket, they turned east and drove through Okanogan National Forest. Around dinnertime, they stopped in Republic and found a cheap motel. Gerald slipped a pair of rubber galoshes over the woolen socks on her infected feet. They walked slowly, each step causing her to wince in pain.

They ate spaghetti in a café and watched a gang of local skinheads gather outside in the street. The skinheads followed them when they left the café, and one whistled at Darla. The big guy ignored the whistle and kept walking, steering Darla by the arm toward the motel. The skinheads kept close behind them along Republic's main street, calling out challenges, but the big guy wasn't having any. Darla said, "Gosh, honey, I'd be scared, except I'm with you."

When they had sex that night, it felt like love to Darla, and when she climaxed, her fever broke and the red streaks on her legs began to fade.

Early the next morning, they set out from Republic, driving east past the survivalists' enclaves and crossing Kettle Creek at Sherman Pass. Darla's feet had started to heal and the infection had left her body. "Yowser," she said, "we're really, really close to my parents' house."

The big guy nodded, like he already knew that.

Darla said, "Honey, would you like to meet my folks?"

He reached over and patted her hand, and by the way he smiled, Darla knew that the man she loved wanted to meet her family.

They practiced their story. Darla and Gerald had met at the bank in Astoria. Gerald was a loan officer, and since the bank robbery, both of them had been on paid leave. Gerald was originally from Cedar Rapids, Iowa, and all his family was dead. Gerald had a master's degree from the University of Iowa. Mathematics. So if he seemed introspective and reticent, it was because he was a math nerd. He was just a dude, a nice dude with a big heart who loved the Dennys' daughter. Darla figured her folks would be ecstatic when she and Gerald sprung a surprise visit upon them. As long as she kept quiet about the bombs.

When the young couple arrived, Sue Ann was at the pet spa, supervising her truffle-sniffers' health-glo treatment. Albert was up at the wine cellar, consulting his vintner. Darla and Gerald sat on the front porch swing and waited for them to come home.

"Remember," Darla said, "Albert's my stepfather. My mom has never told me who my real father was."

Gerald examined his fingertips, said nothing.

"Are you scared?" Darla asked.

Gerald shook his head.

"Well, I'm petrified," confessed Darla. "Not because I don't think they'll like you."

"Then why?" Gerald asked her.

"I'm afraid my mom will insult me in front of you. She always does that to me. She insults me in front of the guys I date."

Gerald said, "Don't worry about it."

"You won't side with her?" Darla cracked her knuckles nervously.

Gerald said, "Stop making that noise. I don't like it."

Darla sat on her hands to keep from cracking her knuckles. It was late afternoon, a nippy breeze rippling the river's surface, waving the tree branches. Suddenly, Darla pointed. "In that tree. A bald eagle. See it?" Gerald looked where Darla pointed and saw the bald eagle, and at that moment something touched the big guy's soul and it stirred.

"Yes," he said to Darla. "I see him."

"They used to hunt them for their feathers and their claws."

"They still do, Darla."

Darla said, "Eagles mate for life. Did you know that?"

"Mmm. How are your feet?"

She stuck out her legs, studied her feet, now encased in her own shoes. "They won't know," she said.

"They wouldn't understand."

"My mom's one of that group they call the Dambusters." Darla laughed nervously. "If she only knew…"

Gerald shot her a hard glance. Darla flushed and said, "I'm cool, really I am. Don't worry, honey."

WHEN SUE ANN came home with her potbellies all soft and glowing and smelling of citrus oils, she appeared shocked to see Darla and the young man on her front porch. How dare her daughter arrive without notice? Then Sue Ann recalled that she was supposed to be relieved to see Darla, and then Gerald smiled at her, and all her hostility melted like so much butter on a hot griddle. God, he's an attractive creature, Sue Ann thought, and she invited them inside.

Darla lied convincingly. Those calls to the Fish and Wildlife Service? That was her friend Leelee who had called up with the phony information. Trying to get even with Gerald because Gerald had dropped her for Darla. Sue Ann and Albert seemed to accept her explanation.

That night, the young couple slept in Darla's old bedroom, in Darla's old bed, beneath the pink comforter, on the lace-trimmed sheets. Albert and Gerald had gotten along handsomely at dinner, and, predictably, Sue Ann had flirted shamelessly with Gerald, intentionally insulting Darla numerous times during the meal, just to impress Gerald with her power. Darla was mortified, but Gerald seemed oblivious to Sue Ann's mean snipes. Frankly, Darla was just relieved that at least Sue Ann hadn't brought up the subject of the Dambusters. Darla feared she might spill the beans through some involuntary twitch or phrase, or that her mother or stepfather would read a guilty conscience in her evasive eyes. But luckily, Sue Ann had no intention of bringing up the Dambusters and salmon. Salmon had no place in Sue Ann's flirting repertoire. Darla had noticed that whenever Sue Ann vamped men, her chronic whine metamorphosed into throaty, sensuous murmurings, accompanied by a lot of leg crossing and chest puffing. Sue Ann had twice as much chest as Darla, and she flaunted it during that first dinner with Gerald, and Darla thought Gerald was altogether too nice to Sue Ann.

Albert didn't seem to notice his wife's flirtations. But then, Albert never seemed to notice when Sue Ann flirted with other men. In fact, lately, Albert never seemed to notice much about Sue Ann, except the whining and the fact that she could cook a salmon better than anyone in eastern Washington could. Maybe it was Albert's lackadaisical attitude toward his wife that caused her to seek out other men's approval. That's what Darla guessed, but she never said it aloud.

Darla and Gerald settled in at the Dennys'. Albert was

elated to have Darla back safe and sound, and he immediately
offered both Darla and Gerald jobs in the business. To his
delight, the young couple agreed to try it out. Darla was
placed in the office beside Albert's, while Gerald was ap-
prenticed to Jean Paul, Albert's faithful vintner. Darla's feet
gradually healed, and she was surprised to notice that the
more they healed, the prouder she felt for fire walking.
Though she no longer remembered the excruciating pain, she
still recalled the euphoric high she'd felt after her fire walk.

Each evening after dinner, Darla, at the piano, regaled Albert with her flawless Kenny G tunes. A new vitality charged
life in the Denny household, and Albert went around sporting
his old exuberance, revived by the zesty presence of youth.

AS THE WEEKS PASSED and the young couple grew accustomed to the vineyard routine, Darla realized that she had
forgotten all about Astoria First National Bank, all about her
awesome Victorian cottage, her belongings, and, oh golly,
Pussy in the kennel. Darla made a few telephone calls, officially quit her bank job, bribed Leelee to clear out the Victorian and ship her belongings to K Falls, and gave Pussy up
for adoption. Leelee didn't have the stomach to leave Pussy
at the mercy of the pet brokers, so she adopted Pussy herself.
Darla was delighted with how kismet had so kindly stepped
in. Pussy had a good home. Gerald and Albert had become
fast friends. Now Gerald seemed more outgoing and less tem-
peramental. Even Sue Ann appeared pleased with the ar-
rangement.

Just one thing bothered Darla. On several occasions, she
had awakened in the middle of the night, to find Gerald missing from their bed. Each time, she had gotten up and searched
the house, but she found no trace of Gerald. Each time, she
would go out to the garage and discover that Gerald's van
was missing. Each time, she would peek in at her parents'
bedroom door and discover that Albert lay alone in bed. Darla
wasn't sure what to make of this dual disappearance of Ger-

ald and Sue Ann, but she dared not raise the subject with either of them, fearing Gerald's wrath and Sue Ann's stinging scorn. Still, Darla wondered, and she did not sleep well at night.

One idyllic summer morning, as the sun rose over the river and kissed the ripening vineyards, nourishing the young fruit, Darla was working in her office, when Gerald came in unexpectedly. He said, "Look at me, Darla." Darla looked at Gerald.

He said, "It's time."

Darla just nodded, because she understood what he meant. He meant, "It's time to blow up Grand Coulee Dam." Inside, she was terrified, not sure if she wanted to go along with Gerald's antics. But this was neither the time nor place to discuss such matters. Darla vowed to raise the subject with Gerald later on, when they could be alone. She returned to her paperwork and Gerald went back to his wine casks.

When evening came, as Sue Ann fed a salmon loaf into the oven, Darla suggested to Gerald that they take a walk through the vineyards. Sue Ann watched from the kitchen window, saw the young couple strolling hand in hand between the rows of the ripening fruit, saw that they were speaking intently to each other, maybe arguing. Sue Ann watched, and she smiled. Maybe now Gerald would understand what she meant about Darla being a goody-goody. When the salmon loaf was done, Sue Ann went out onto the terrace and rang the cowbell. Its clang scared some crows out of the vineyards, but it didn't bring back Darla and Gerald. Why weren't they answering the dinner bell? Sue Ann and Albert ate their salmon loaf in charged silence, and then Albert retired in front of the television set while Sue Ann gathered her dark thoughts, a cell phone, and a Martha Stewart basket, and slipped outdoors to the pig shed.

AT EIGHT O'CLOCK, Mabel Fobia finished her shift at Hartell's. The evening air felt warm and gentle to Mabel, so instead of heading straight home, she decided to take a leisurely drive over to the Elias Fobia Cabin and there pay her respects. When she pulled onto the trail approaching the cabin, she saw the Shouter coming up from the riverbank. Mabel tapped on her horn. The Shouter had been raving to the winds, but he heard the honk and he looked and saw Mabel's car. He came over, taking his own time. Mabel rolled down the window. "Catch anything?"

"Hell no," said the Shouter, climbing into the passenger seat. "What's fer supper?"

"Who invited you to supper, you old geezer?"

The Shouter laughed, if you could call it that. Mabel thought of it as a bark. "Hell and damnation, Mabel," he said, "when did I ever need an invitation?" He reached over and caressed Mabel's knee. She jerked her leg away.

"Not so fast, lover boy," she said, turning the car around. "You just hold on to your horses till we get home." Then Mabel made a beeline for town.

Jean Paul, Albert Denny's Alsatian vintner, a middle-aged man of few English words, was walking the vines when he saw Mabel Fobia's car drive past the Denny estate. Jean Paul did a double take because he thought he saw the Shouter riding in the passenger seat of Miss Fobia's car. That seemed odd to Jean Paul and he scratched his head. He honestly couldn't think of two people more unlike each other than Mabel Fobia and the Shouter. After he thought it over, Jean Paul decided that Mabel probably was just giving the old maniac a ride home. They did both live on Harmony Lane, after all, and that made them neighbors. Nothing odd about offering a neighbor a lift home. Jean Paul had done the same once or twice on a good mood day.

SIXTEEN

Skamonah Shawnawwah, a venerated woman among the Wishram People who lived near The Dalles, told this tale about a bridge over the Columbia River: "The spirits of the mountains used to quarrel with the spirit of the river. During one of their battles, the mountain spirits raised a great barrier of rock across the river, blocking its descent. But the river spirit, drawing on its great power, attacked the barrier and clawed a subterranean passage through it. The river poured through the tunnel, but the roof remained as a bridge over which people were able to cross the river dry-shod. While it stood, the people called it the Tamanawas Bridge, the Bridge of the Gods."—David M. Buerge, *Columbia Gorge* (Sasquatch Books, 1992)

IN THE OLD DAYS, millions of salmon fingerlings hatched in gravel pools and riffles in the streams and eddies that poured into the Columbia River. Some salmon eggs were stolen from their redds, or nests, by sculpin and mergansers, but those that survived to become fingerlings fed on the dead corpses of their own ancestors. Thus strengthened, the young fingerling made their way downriver to the ocean, where those that survived the arduous journey matured, feeding on abundant marine vegetation. But there were dangers in the ocean, great sharks and whales and other denizens that loved to eat salmon. Those that survived the ocean's many dangers eventually swam back to the Columbia's mouth, and there at the mouth, they fed until their sleek bodies reached maximum strength. Then, during the spring melt, when high in the Cascade Range, the rivers overflowed fresh snowmelt and rushed into the Columbia, it was time for the last great journey. Fattened from the ocean's nutrients, adult salmon began swimming against the Columbia's currents in a determined quest to return to their birthplaces, the streams and eddies of the upper Columbia and Snake rivers.

If they survived the trip, the fertile salmon spawned, arching their backs in an ecstatic ritual of dispersal as the female laid her eggs and the male simultaneously fertilized them with his sperm. Then, exhausted from the journey and spawning, they flopped over and died in the exact location in the river where, years earlier, they had hatched from redd.

After Lewis and Clark drew attention to the Columbia River, the settlers came in droves. They traded with the Indians who fished the river, but the new settlers didn't understand the meaning of salmon, the significance of salmon, the sacredness of salmon. Just as the new settlers believed that the bear was put in the forest for man to kill for its fur, and the eagle was put in the sky to make good target practice and clawed talismans, they thought the salmon had been put into the rivers solely to benefit humans, to satisfy their appetites. The new settlers never understood the link between a salmon's soul and his own soul, never understood that the river had a soul, just like the Earth and all its creatures. Still, the salmon came in great numbers. Then the white man's leaders got an idea about hydropower, and irrigation, and before long, they had devised a plan to corral the mighty river's force and appropriate it for their purposes.

Electricity.

Grand Coulee Dam was constructed from three thousand tons of concrete that formed a massive bulkhead, backing up the waters, causing a great flood. When the man-made deluge came, and for decades, afterward, parts of the Colville Reservation would have no drinking water or telephone service. The Indians call this intentional destruction of their sacred lands "the Flood," and today when they speak of "before the Flood" and "after the Flood," every river dweller knows what the Indians mean.

West of the concrete behemoth, the river briefly resumed its natural rolling pace, its swift waters tumbling over huge granite boulders on its way some hundred miles southwest to the Pacific Ocean. But between Grand Coulee Dam and the Pacific Ocean, nine smaller dams interrupted the river's natural rage to the sea. All these dams provided cheap, clean electrical power for the Pacific Northwest's burgeoning population. All these dams provided jobs for local people, irrigation for the eastern Washington farms and orchards, and a safe passage for barging their products downriver. All these dams represented incredible feats of man's victory over nature. And all these dams blocked the wild chinook salmon on their journeys to the ocean and back upriver. As the decades rolled by, fewer salmon returned to spawn.

ON HAT SUNDAY MORNING, the First Methodist Church of Kettle Falls welcomed worshipers with a special service. Albert Denny led the choir in a heartfelt "Glory Coming By the River," and then stepped up to the pulpit to read from the Bible. In the front pew, Mabel Fobia stood clutching her white gloves and wondered if her new Hat Sunday bonnet was blocking anyone's view. Behind Mabel, Sue Ann aimed a disposable camera at Albert, but Mabel's damn bonnet kept blocking her shot. She tapped Mabel on the shoulder, and when the old coot turned around, Sue Ann pointed at the camera. Mabel adjusted her bonnet and smiled. Oh God, thought Sue Ann. She thinks I want to snap her picture. Sue Ann gestured for Mabel to move aside, but Mabel smiled and posed for a picture. Sue Ann gave up and snapped Mabel's picture, then aimed the camera at Albert in the pulpit, but when she pressed the camera's button, it was out of film. By now, Mabel had turned around, and Sue Ann cursed at her back.

In the pulpit, Albert finished his Bible reading and the Reverend Fred Beveridge took over, flitting to the pulpit like a moth to flame. Albert swung around the Communion railing, smiled affably at Mabel Fobia, and slipped into the pew beside Sue Ann. The congregation, arrayed in their Hat Sunday best, seated themselves and prepared to hear the Reverend Fred's latest sermon.

Reverend Fred complimented the ladies on their pretty headgear and reminded the men to fill the collection baskets. His Hat Sunday sermon, carefully written and rehearsed, was about miracles, heavily interspersing biblical quotations. Reverend Beveridge cleared his throat and began his sermon, but when he embarked upon the sermon, a strange thing happened. The sermon he had intended to let flow from his tongue remained on the paper resting on the lectern. Instead, what burst forth from the Reverend Beveridge arrived as prophecy does: through, but not of, his body. His vocal chords, a mere vehicle, had been hijacked by some unknown force, and the Reverend Beveridge had no control over what now spilled from his own wondering lips.

"Everything has a life force," began the force speaking through Reverend Beveridge's body. "The birds have a life force; the fish have a life force. The trees and flowers have a life force. Even inanimate objects, even rocks and mountains and coulees, have life force. And it is all the same life force, just in different forms. Though we are different in our physical forms, we are all connected, we are all one, and each of us has our own unique perfection built in."

Albert leaned over and whispered in Sue Ann's ear, "What the hell is he talking about?" Sue Ann placed a finger to her lips. Albert shook his head. Maybe he was mishearing Reverend Beveridge. On the other side of Albert, Darla and Gerald sat side by side, Darla, hatless, in a new turquoise suit and white mules, Gerald in a neatly ironed shirt and khakis.

Darla thought Gerald's thighs were too thick to wear khakis, and she had told him so, but Gerald had worn them anyway.

"Every living thing possesses a soul," Reverend Beveridge went on. "The birds possess a collective bird soul. Fish have their collective soul. Fowl have theirs. Even the rocks possess a collective soul. Then there are humans, the most unique life-form on the planet. Humans possess a dual soul."

Albert could only shake his head and wonder what had gotten into the Reverend Beveridge's morning tonic. He glanced over at Sue Ann. Her eyes were riveted on Reverend Beveridge and she wore what Albert could only describe as a self-satisfied smile.

He poked her, but she did not respond. Darla glanced over and noticed the same thing about Sue Ann, as if her mother were having telepathic sex with the Reverend Beveridge. That's what it looked like to Darla.

"The beauty of the human species is its duality of soul," Reverend Beveridge went on. "We have a collective soul, like the other life-forms. But we also, each and everyone of us, possess an individual soul, which is guided by free will."

Albert looked around. He saw friends and he saw strangers in the congregation. All of them seemed to share his perplexity. All of them seemed to wonder collectively if the Reverend Beveridge had perhaps lost his marbles. Even Mabel Fobia seemed disturbed by the strange sounds emitting from the preacher's runaway lips. The only person apparently unfazed was Sue Ann.

"When we harm a stone," cried Reverend Beveridge against his will, "we harm all stones. When we chop down a tree," he continued, accelerating his delivery, "we injure all trees. When we pollute the rivers, the oceans weep toxins. Until we understand and accept responsibility for encroaching on other species's territory, for being at the top of the food chain…"

Poor Reverend Beveridge could not stay his wayward tongue. Try as he might, words he'd never composed flowed from his lips as smoothly and sincerely as a mountain brook, leaving behind the aftertaste of red velvet cake, so that the preacher's experience was not altogether unpleasant. When the sermon about the collective soul of different life forces finally came to an end, the congregation stirred and audible sighs of relief filled the church. The collection baskets came back only half as full as usual that Hat Sunday morning, and later, outside the church, as he greeted his congregation, Reverend Beveridge would confess that some scurrilous devil had apparently gotten hold of his tongue and wagged it against his will.

Mabel Fobia refused to shake the preacher's hand and could only remark, "So much for free will, Reverend," before huffing off to the parking lot. She wasn't sticking around for coffee and doughnuts, not this Hat Sunday morning. Not with this heretic.

Sue Ann, on the other hand, embraced Reverend Beveridge warmly. "I've always admired your penetrating intellect," she whispered into his ear, and the man in Reverend Beveridge felt her breath where it wasn't intended. "A splendid sermon. Simply splendid."

Sue Ann waited in the parking lot, in the silver Lexus with Gerald, while Albert and Darla sampled the church doughnuts.

In the back seat, Gerald sat lost in his private thoughts. His demolitions training might not be sophisticated enough to fissure these concrete behemoths. He had tried at Rocky Reach and Priest Rapids dams, and both times he had failed to achieve the desired effect. Yet he knew that these concrete dams could be fissured so that they would leak slowly at first, allowing time for deep fissures to develop before the dam crumbled and sent havoc raging downriver to the ocean. The fissure on Grand Coulee Dam should part slowly, gradually, like the legs of a woman resisting ecstasy, finally opening to receive the fruit of the sea into the womb of creation, to spawn, to mate, to die. That is how he envisioned the breach,

SKYE KATHLEEN MOODY   151

and the very idea sent carnal yearnings through his talented but disciplined body.

He knew it could be done. Had to be done. Had to. With the proper placement of the proper explosives, in the proper combination and quantity, it could be done.

He needed an expert in the field. Where could he find one?

In the front seat, Sue Ann turned down the visor and checked her reflection in the mirror. She could see Gerald's reflection, too, and their eyes met. Sue Ann blinked first.

"What did you think?" she asked him. "I mean, about Reverend Beveridge's sermon."

Gerald said, "Wasn't listening."

"Got your mind on something else?"

"Maybe."

"On Darla?"

"Nope."

"What then?"

Gerald said, "Something a slug once told me."

Sue Ann made a face. "What did the slug say?"

Gerald whispered into Sue Ann's ear.

Sue Ann applied lipstick to her mouth and kept her thoughts to herself.

SEVENTEEN

SONG SAW THE GIRL before she saw him. She stood out of the hot sun, huddling beneath the overhang on the sidewalk outside Prospector's Saloon. She had on a billowy dress that reminded him of lingerie. When he walked toward her, she stared warily, but he wiggled his fingers at her and she relaxed, as if the enemy wouldn't know how to wiggle its fingers. She was pretty and she wore her soul on the outside. Her hair, like sun-drenched copper, fell across her shoulders, framing her face. Her skin was equally sun-kissed and bronze, her sweet lips red as flame, and her eyes a shade of blue Song had never seen before. The one flaw in this pretty picture was a receding chin. Otherwise, Song found her extremely attractive. But the soul that she exposed so innocently to the world was suffering deeply, probably more deeply than she herself realized. Song could feel it, though, and he cautioned himself to beware.

She reached out with a tentative hand and said, "Juneau Jones?"

Song nodded.

The girl said, "If you really are Juneau Jones, then show me the message we sent you."

Song produced a scrap of a paper. She read it, then put the note in her mouth, chewed, and swallowed. He steered her inside Prospector's, ignoring Tiffie's come-hithers, to a table by the window. He noticed she had a spectacular figure, which almost, but not quite, canceled out the receding chin. He could see her internal beauty, and he could see her spectacular body. Still, he couldn't get past the chin. Maybe when she wasn't all agitated and jumpy like she was now, maybe then her chin jutted out more. Song lit a Marlboro. She was talking to him. What was she saying?

Something about meeting a friend of hers. He had heard about Juneau Jones. Word gets around when a bank wall is blown out with expert precision. Her friend had heard that Juneau Jones had blasted out that K Falls Savings and Loan wall. People who knew about these things said Juneau was a demolitions expert. Would Juneau agree to meet her friend? He had a proposition for Juneau, a very lucrative offer. Then she began crying. If Juneau didn't come with her, her friend would get angry, and when he got angry, she feared him.

Song watched as the girl who called herself Carla brushed hair from her near-perfect face, blew her swollen nose into a crumpled tissue, and alternately wept and smiled. She was a mess, and somehow Song didn't buy her story, but what the hell, he'd play along for a while, until she gave him what he wanted.

Darla said, "Sometimes I turn into a swan. My feathers are snow white and fluffy; my beak is blazing gold. My neck is as long as my arm is now, and very gracefully curved. When I become a swan, my soul unites with all other swans. I become a part of them. But I can only become a swan when I'm in a calm frame of mind." She looked dolefully up at Juneau. "Right now, I can't become a swan. I tried very hard a few minutes ago, and I just couldn't." Song made a regretful little noise. Darla brushed her hair out of her face. "I have message for you."

Song read the note Darla handed him. "If you're interested in making a lot of money in a very short period of time, in a high-risk operation, then tell the girl."

Darla was gazing at the television over the bar, directly above Tiffie's platinum beehive. Song looked up just as the news anchor said, "During the past twenty-four hours, no births or deaths have been reported in all of Washington

State. If this becomes a trend, the region will soon be severely overpopulated with geriatric citizens...."

Darla said, "I can't figure out if, like, in this life, I've burned off a lot of karma or created a lot of karma."

Song said, "Take me to him, Carla," and she did.

VENUS, AKA Kay Lynn Jones, peered through the Airstream's window and saw Song coming home. It was about time. She was starving, and she didn't know how to cook. She was still nursing a broken baby toe, and her limp had become second nature. She limped over to the table and began placing silverware, having noted with satisfaction that Song was carrying a box from the China Doll Café and a brown bag that might coddle a six-pack. They sat at the tiny counter, eating kung pao noodles and swilling Red Hook. Outside, a blue van sat idling near the trailer park's entrance, its occupants watching the Airstream. When Song spoke, his voice was a whisper. "I'll be going out tonight. With Gerald and the girl. They took the bait."

Venus said softly, "I want to go along."

Song shook his head. "This next step, I have to go alone. I'll have to convince him to include you. I might be gone for a while, so don't worry."

"I told you, I'm not sending another memorial wreath."

Song made a face, said, "Lucky I boned up on detonation devices."

She said, "We need to win over Darla, gain her trust."

"She's going by the name Carla." Song put on his jacket. "She likes me. Maybe I can win her over."

"Good luck, Romeo."

She patted his chest. "Be back by dawn, or else I'm coming after you."

"Now you do sound like a nagging housewife."

"Careful, or I'll throw a lamp."

At ten o'clock, the lights went out in the Airstream. Moments later, a lone figure stepped outside the trailer and walked softly to the van. A door opened and Song hopped up inside. Gerald hit the gas and headed southeast out of K Falls.

When they reached Colville, Gerald took back roads through the dry scrub, then drove southwest toward Fort Spokane, but instead of going that far, he veered off the road at Gifford and drove overland across a high prairie, then followed a gravel path back toward the river. The moon was full and bright and Song could have seen where they were headed, except that Gerald had instructed Darla to place a blindfold around his eyes, and Song hadn't resisted. He knew this night would be a test of his demolitions know-how, and his courage. When Gerald finally stopped the van and turned off the engine, Darla removed the blindfold. Song had to blink his eyes a few times before he could see.

Song could see the river now. They were standing on the side of a cliff, and the river was about fifty feet below. Gerald handed Song a pair of boots three sizes too large and a backpack weighted down with supplies. He handed Darla two paddles big enough to push a small boat through water. The three set out across the scablands, moonlight their only guide. The cold air nipped at Song's ears and his feet ached in the uncomfortable boots, his toes cramping to keep in balance.

Darla had tucked her hair up underneath a knit woolen cap and looked like a boy, but Song could see where her breasts curved out, and he could see the familiar receding chin, so he was sure it was the girl who called herself Carla. Carrying a backpack, Gerald led the way through the dry scrub. Every hundred yards or so, Gerald would stop, make them brush out their foot tracks. They walked silently, according to Gerald's instructions, until Gerald stopped at the cliff's edge and pointed. Song looked down and saw the river, still about fifty feet below. Gerald said, "We'll go down the cliff."

Darla was terrified, but Gerald coaxed her down and Song brought up the rear. The way Song handled the sheer drop impressed Gerald. When they reached the riverbank, Gerald handed him a water-filled canteen and he drank thirstily. Darla disappeared behind a boulder. Both he and Gerald could hear her humming to herself. When she came back, she said, "Honey, are we going into that cold water?"

Gerald's answer came in the form of an inflatable boat. When they'd blown it up with the little battery-powered pump, they set it in an eddy in the river, climbed aboard, and pushed away from the cliff. An hour later, the river cut through a deep canyon, but the moon, still high overhead, poured into the crevice, lighting their downriver journey. The river water, choked by the dam below, lay placid and smooth along this stretch.

"Keep an eye out for Indians," Gerald warned. "We're passing the reservation."

No Indians appeared on the cliff tops overhead, only a coyote that howled at the silver moon. They kept close to the riverbank. Darla held on to the raft for dear life as Gerald and Song steered it around great boulders and snags of gnarled tree limbs that had swept offshore.

"We won't go all the way," Gerald said, and Darla felt somewhat comforted, for she knew that ahead of them just a few miles was the crest of Grand Coulee Dam. So this wasn't a suicide mission Gerald had planned. Darla relaxed then and said, "Wheeee, this is a hoot."

As the cliffs receded and the riverbank widened, the lights of Electric City came into view. Gerald brought the boat to shore on the upper riverbank in the Coulee Dam National Recreation Area. While Song deflated the boat, Gerald unloaded camping gear and Darla helped him set up the tents. Gerald told Darla to watch the tents, handed Song the backpack, and said, "Follow me."

The two men followed the riverbank until they came to a sharp bend. Gerald stopped walking, pointed to a cluster of boulders, and told Song to stay put and wait for him. Gerald disappeared into the boulders.

Song stood on the riverbank, looking up at a dazzling starlit sky. He thought he saw a satellite blip across the Big Dipper, or maybe it was a UFO. He could hear the river's gentle swooshing and once or twice he heard a coyote. Otherwise, the night air was silent and still. Occasionally, he heard muffled voices coming from the boulders, and once he heard shouting, but still too muffled to understand. All he could make out was the tone of the voices. And he was pretty sure that one of the voices was a woman's. Then the shouting stopped and Song heard only the natural, wild sounds of the night. After awhile, Gerald came out of the cave. Song saw that he was carrying a large canvas bag that he hadn't taken inside with him. Gerald came to the river's edge and set the bag down. He reached into the bag, rummaged, fished out a smaller bag, and handed this to Song.

"Make me a bomb, Juneau Jones," he commanded. "Out of these materials."

Song sorted the materials on the ground: dynamite sticks, a lead pipe, two screw caps, nails, razor blades, gunpowder, latex gloves. There were a few items Song didn't recognize. So this would be the first test, a deadly one, constructing an antipersonnel bomb, a bomb meant not just to maim but to kill.

Gerald sat back against a boulder, lit a joint, and watched Juneau work as the full moon shed light on Juneau's steady hands. He worked for an hour or more, Gerald never taking his eyes off him. He constructed the bomb carefully, and when he finished, he walked away from it and let Gerald examine his work. Gerald did, then said, "You made one mistake."

"What's that?" Song felt sweat on his brow.

"You left a signature." Gerald pointed to the fuze Song had threaded through the hole in one of the end caps. "The way you knotted that fuze—that's distinctive."

Song thought fast. "I leave a signature only once," he said. "As a diversion. Throws 'em off."

Gerald stared at Song as if wondering if he could trust

him. Song lit a Marlboro, smoked it while Gerald deliberated. After awhile, Gerald said, "Now disassemble it." Song did, and when he had finished packing the materials into the backpack, Gerald handed him a drawing of Grand Coulee Dam and told him to describe how he would forge a slow-leaking fissure in the five-hundred-fifty-foot-high concrete wall.

Song showed him how, and Gerald saw that Juneau Jones knew his stuff.

"This is war," said the big man. "Are you willing to die if necessary to save this river?"

Song didn't answer right away. No use appearing masochistic. Finally, he said, "How much do you pay?"

Gerald grinned, flashing his bright teeth. "You goddamn mercenary," he said, and told Song how much he would pay. Song resisted the urge to whistle, but the amount impressed him.

"Another thing," Gerald added, "this is my show. Don't ever forget that. If I say something gets done according to my plan, don't contradict me. Don't try to take over. If you do, you're a dead man."

They hiked back to the campsite, where Darla sat lotus by a kerosene heater, her hands cupped in her lap, her eyes rolled upward, the whites glowing. They slept under the cold, bright moon, even in slumber aware of the coyotes' yowl, and the swishing of the river, and the occasional plunk of a salmon leaping toward home.

EIGHTEEN

AT DAWN, Song woke to discover the man named Gerald missing from his tent. Song dug into the backpack Gerald had given him the previous night, fished out a carton of caffeinated beverage, and walked to the riverbank, where the girl calling herself Carla was brushing her teeth with her fingers. "God, I hate camping out," Darla complained. "I like my facilities."

Song asked where Gerald had gone. Darla said, "Oh, I never know. He just goes where and when he pleases and never bothers to inform me. It's been this way ever since I've known him." And in a moment of candor, she told him the truth about how she'd met Gerald. At first, she did not mention the fire walking, fearing he'd think she was weird.

Song crouched down beside the girl, the better to hear her story over the river sounds. When she had finished, he said, "So Carla's not your real name?"

The girl shrugged and said, "Is Juneau Jones your real name?"

It was Song's turn to shrug. The girl smiled and made a zipping motion across her mouth. Song said, "Are you afraid of him?"

The girl shook her head vigorously, and he admired how her long hair with its copper highlights fell across her shoulders and into her eyes. He wanted to reach up and gently push a lock of her pretty hair out of her pretty eyes, but then he remembered the chin, and that scotched the idea. She was sexy, though, Song had to admit.

She glanced up at him, smiled, and said, "Are you?"

"Am I what?"

"Afraid of him."

Song laughed. "Naw. Gerald's a puppy."

Darla shook her head, more vehemently this time. "Oh, he's no puppy dog, no way. Gerald is, like, the most dangerous, most inscrutable person I have ever met in my life." She leaned in close and said, "Say, I'll bet your lady friend is one, too."

Song frowned. "Kay Lynn? She's my wife."

"And I bet she fire-walks, too. That limp tells it all. Am I right?"

Song, at a loss for words, placed a finger to his lips.

"I thought so," said Darla smugly. "She's weak, so she burns."

Song said, "So, have you met a lot of dangerous and inscrutable people?"

Darla plucked a small pebble from the riverbank and tossed it into the water. To her surprise, the pebble skipped three times. "I've met a few. There was this guy I knew in high school; his name was Darthan Dixon. He was a bad, bad dude. He made his enemies eat live mice, and if they refused, he'd tie them up and let a bunch of rats loose on them. He was bad. Then there's this dude down in Astoria. He's the brother of my best friend, Leelee. His name is Phuc. I know what it sounds like, but that's really his name, I swear to God. Phuc belongs to a Vietnamese gang, and they've actually shot some people. Other dudes, from other gangs. But no, Gerald is the most dangerous dude I've ever met."

Song said, "That turn you on? The scent of danger?"

Darla seemed to think it over. "Maybe," she said. "But that in itself wouldn't be enough. Gerald cares about important issues. Like saving the river. I know he seems almost cruel sometimes, but he's a sweetheart, really. He'd never do anything to hurt me. I mean, like, as long as I don't, like, get in his way."

"What do you know about him? About his past."

She shrugged. "He never talks about it. And it's for sure I'm not going to bring it up. He got all riled up just when I asked him his name. He doesn't like people prying into his past. I think he's a victim of child abuse. When we have sex? He always wants me to hold him afterward and stroke his head. Like a little boy in his mama's arms. I kind of feel sorry for him sometimes. But, yeah, I guess what, like, really turns me on about Gerald is he's sooooo enigmatic. He keeps me guessing. I like a dude to do that."

Song nodded. He understood this last comment perfectly, this attraction to mystery. All his life, women had flocked to Song, begging to be ravished by a man they perceived as sexy but also mysterious, and possibly dangerous, if you crossed him. Song understood the Darlas of the world, and he pitied this girl, but he didn't say so.

Gerald had put Song in charge of the Penguins, and now he gave the girl two and they walked back to their campsite. Gerald still hadn't returned. Darla had brought along a deck of cards, and they played blackjack, because that was the only card game Song knew. When they got tired of blackjack, she taught him how to do cartwheels. Darla had learned to do cartwheels from none other than Nathan Bernstein, that fateful evening on Lake Chelan. Now, finally, she realized that she had gotten something out of the fleeting relationship. At least she could do cartwheels. But Juneau wasn't very good, and they laughed when he almost fell into the river. That was a mistake, their laughing, because Gerald appeared suddenly and heard them.

"I told you to be quiet," Gerald said menacingly. "Have you got that straight?"

Darla said meekly. "Yes, Gerald."

Song made eye contact with Gerald, and the big guy saw Juneau Jones's exotic dark eyes flicker slightly, maybe defiantly. Like Juneau didn't respect him. Like Juneau might want to be the leader of this little army. Gerald made a mental note to watch Juneau more closely, to observe his body language. He needed Juneau, true, but if the dude presented any challenge to Gerald's authority, he'd have to take steps. Gerald knew how to handle mutiny before it got out of hand.

"I've surveyed and measured," Gerald announced over a lunch of energy bars and canned Tab. "We'll need two houseboats. That means we'll need another remote cell-phone detonator, and more explosives. This will be a tough baby to break open."

Song said, "How about we do it from an airplane? Fly over and drop the explosives? Hell, just drop a bomb."

Gerald said, "Don't joke. And don't tell me how to do my work. Maybe I can use your technical know-how, but I know what will get us caught and what won't. I'm in charge here. Have you got that straight, Jones?"

Song said yes, he did, and put some humility into his voice.

When darkness fell, they retraced their path along the riverbank, up over the cliff, across the scablands. Hours later, Gerald and Darla dropped Song off at the trailer park. As he climbed out of the van, Gerald said, "Be ready."

Song nodded. "How will I know which day?"

"You won't until I tell you. And it won't be tomorrow. Or the next day. And you better tell that little wife of yours that you're going away for a couple weeks. Give her a credible story. Don't let her suspect anything."

Through the darkness, the lights inside the Airstream glowed softly. Song glanced at the trailer, then caught Gerald's eye. "Kay Lynn's a pro," he said. "How do you think I got into that bank safe in K Falls?"

Gerald stared. "Your old lady went in with you?"

Song nodded solemnly. "She opened the safe. She's one hell of a partner. Trustworthy, too. Rock-solid."

Gerald considered. Could he trust Juneau? He could use another able body. He said, "She limps. Your old lady has a bum pin. She could never keep up."

Thinking fast, Song said, "She broke her toe. It's healing.

She can outrun me. And she can climb. She rappels; she can drive spikes. She does it all.''

"That a fact?" Gerald was interested.

"You come over some evening, you and Carla. Meet Kay Lynn. Check her out. You'll be impressed, I guarantee."

Gerald thought this over. Darla personally didn't like the idea of another female joining the trio. She was happy the way things were now, herself and two good-looking dudes. She didn't want the competition. But then she remembered how Kay Lynn looked, so scrawny, and she had that limp. Darla decided Juneau's wife wouldn't be any competition at all. Darla said, "Gerald, honey, why don't we just meet her? See what she's like?" Then Darla whispered something into Gerald's ear.

Gerald said, "All right. But not at your place. I don't want to be seen at your place. We'll meet in the woods at K Falls. Where the falls used to be. There's a cabin near the riverbank. It's an old split-wood cabin, all boarded up. There's a plaque on the front door that says ELIJAH FOBIA HISTORIC CABIN."

"It's Elias," Song said. "I know the cabin."

Gerald seemed suspicious, or impressed—Song wasn't certain which. He studied Song's poker face for a while, then said finally, "All right. Tomorrow night. In the woods. There's a trail beside the cabin that dips back into the woods. Park your car back in there where it can't be seen. Circle around the trail and come back in on foot. Go around to the backside of the cabin, the side that faces the river. Wait there."

"What time?"

"Nine o'clock. Don't be late. If you're late, I'll be gone. You'll never see me again. Then one day, you'll wake up dead. Got that?"

Song nodded and walked toward the Airstream.

In the van's cab, Darla pressed her folded hands to her breast. "Honey, you are, like, just soooo awesome." Gerald rewarded her that night in her childhood bed, beneath the pink comforter. She made so much noise that Sue Ann sat up in her bed and turned on the light, waking Albert.

"What's this all about, Sue Ann?" Albert asked grumpily.

"I hear noises."

Albert listened. "Hell, that's just Gerald and Darla."

"No, it's not," snapped Sue Ann. "It's something else."

"How can you say that? It's obviously the kids having fun."

Sue Ann slipped out of bed and pulled her bathrobe over her skimpy nightie. "I'm going to find out."

"Hey," cried Albert, "you can't do that. You can't just walk in on the kids while they're doing it."

"The hell I can't. She's my daughter, isn't she? She's in my house, isn't she?"

Before Albert could say more, Sue Ann had left the room. Albert held his head. In a few minutes, he heard Sue Ann scream at Darla, and he heard Darla screaming back. Then silence. Eventually, Sue Ann came back to bed, her breath smelling of whiskey.

Sue Ann reached over and adjusted the bedside lamp so that it illuminated another part of the room and not the bed. "Albert," she said. He didn't answer. "Albert," she said more insistently.

"Hmm?" Albert replied sleepily.

"Make love to me. Right now."

In spite of his drowsiness, Albert sat straight up in bed and stared at Sue Ann. "Why, what's got into you, hon?" he remarked. "We haven't made love in…well, I guess it's still…yes, in months."

"Do me, Albert," Sue Ann commanded.

"But Sue Ann—"

"I said, 'Do me.'"

Albert did.

Sue Ann, always a polite lover, cried, "Oh please, yes, oh yes, please. Do that. Yes, yes, oh yes, *puh-leeze.*"

Albert would say, "There you go," and then Sue Ann

would say, "Oh please, yes. That's right, yes, please, oh yes." Then Albert would say again, "There you go." This went on for as long as Sue Ann could sustain her energy, which was quite a long time. And the more Albert pleased her, the louder Sue Ann's cries grew, until Albert was exhausted and could do no more. Falling spent onto the sweat-drenched sheets, Albert nevertheless slept fitfully the remainder of the night. Sue Ann slept deeply, satisfied that Darla and Gerald had heard, if not everything, the most important parts.

LUDMILLA, queen of the beavers, came up out of the river and stood on the bank, looking up at the moon. It always seemed to be up there just when Ludmilla needed its light. She surveyed the ground around her feet. Bone-dry earth, void of branches and other useful objects. But what's this? Ludmilla pressed her face to the ground to get a closer look. Something like string, with a knot in it. Hey, you take what you can find. Beggars can't be choosers. The string would add strength to Ludmilla's dam.

Reaching far out into the river and curving back again to shore, the Ludmilla family dam formed a deep and broad barrier that controlled the spill of spring overrun from Stranger Creek into the Columbia River. Here, for generations, the Stranger Creek salmon had come to spawn, to lay and fertilize their eggs. Here, the eggs had hatched, and the fingerlings had fed on rich nutrients trapped by the dam. It was the beavers' job to keep the dam supported, maintain the dam's structural integrity. This had been Ludmilla's job ever since she could remember. "Strengthen the dam, strengthen the dam," her parents had constantly carped, and she soon learned why. If the dam burst, all of the beavers' hard work would have been for naught: The water would flow free, and the salmon—beaver food—would have no place to spawn. At an early age, Ludmilla learned that her raison d'être was maintaining the dam.

Ludmilla grasped the string and was heading back down to the river when she heard the message. *Thump. Thump, thump.* Ludmilla recognized the signal of the beavers of Inchelum. Something was happening on the river, and the beavers of Inchelum wanted every river dweller to know about it. In the past, Ludmilla had paid little attention to the Inchelum tribe, but lately she had personally witnessed a number of disturbing incidents on the river, and now she paid attention whenever the Inchelum beavers sent their messages.

A poacher at Gifford had reeled in a rare Stranger Creek salmon, a female ripe with eggs. The angler had used a QuickFish lure with a fresh sardine impaled on it to snag the fish. The fish checked in at record weight and girth, and the angler had won a prize from his sportsmen's club. Meanwhile, waiting for the female in their birth eddy, a lone male salmon thrashed frantically in the riffles. Where was she? It was time. Where was she?

When she failed to return, to meet him at their spawning grounds, the male expired, having failed to live out his destiny. His fresh red corpse was snatched up by a poacher, and cooked over an outdoor grill. The beavers of Inchelum had witnessed the capturing of the female and the death of the male, perhaps the final and irreversible extinction of the Stranger Creek salmon.

Ludmilla slid into the river and swam back to her dam, where she wove the string into a portion of the structure that needed strengthening. It would never do for the dam to burst, because hope springs eternal, even for beavers.

NINETEEN

Global warming and the growing human population have combined to increase the use of electrical power, much of it coming from the hydroelectric dams on the Columbia River. During high-energy-demand, hot summers, in order to supply Californians with the power to run their air conditioners, the Columbia River dams must force more water through their turbines and less water over the spillways. This forces more young salmon through the turbines, killing, maiming, bruising, and causing deadly infections in young fish making their arduous downriver journey to the ocean.

IN A HOUSE full of sinners, breakfast can be tortuous. Albert and Gerald tried making small talk, but the two women kept snapping at each other like a couple of old carps. When Sue Ann asked for the marmalade, Darla lobbed it across the table, the jar narrowly missing her mother's most arthritic elbow. When Darla asked Gerald to pass the kippered salmon, Sue Ann grabbed the platter and scraped all the kippers onto her own plate. "Poof," sniped Sue Ann maliciously. "No more kippers." When Albert tried reading the sports section, Sue Ann crabbed irritably, "This is a family, isn't it? Why can't we talk to one another at the breakfast table, instead of hiding behind the newspaper? Anyway, there's nothing to read in that piece of garbage."

Albert took exception. "The Orioles are leading the league. Say, Gerald, do you follow baseball?"

Gerald started to answer, but Darla cut in. "Mother, if Daddy wants to read the newspaper at breakfast, then I think that should be allowed. After all, Daddy works, and you don't do anything but loll around all day eating bonbons and playing with your stupid potbellied pigs."

"I do not eat bonbons," Sue Ann exclaimed. "I have never eaten a bonbon in my life. I don't even know what a bonbon looks like. Albert, what is a bonbon?" Sue Ann batted her eyelashes at her husband.

Albert said grimly, "Girls, I do wish you would be more courteous to each other. It's seven-thirty in the morning, after all. And I didn't sleep last night, for reasons I prefer not to delve into at the moment."

"Albert, you have no idea what went on last night—" Sue Ann began.

"And I don't want to know," Albert yelled. "Now, for Chrissake, shut your trap, or I'll stuff it with my fist. And that goes for you, too, Darla."

Even as he exploded, Albert burned with shame over his hot-tempered outburst. But looking on the bright side, from then on, Sue Ann and Darla kept quiet while the men discussed baseball.

Gerald was a Mariners fan. That got Albert's blood circulating, and by the time he set out to the vineyard office, he felt, if not rested, energized. Gerald had an infectious energy, a way of injecting some verve into an otherwise-vapid household. This morning, Albert felt grateful for Gerald's arrival in the Denny household, and he vowed to tell Gerald how he felt. Before going to his office, Albert detoured, climbing the hill to the vintner's office. Albert's vintner, Jean Paul, barely spoke English, but he knew his icewine. Jean Paul was tasting a new vintage when Albert walked in. "Try this, *mon ami*," Jean Paul murmured, holding out the goblet. Albert sniffed, sipped, rolled the wine around his mouth, spit, paused, and then smiled. "Fine, Jean Paul, fine," he said. "Has Gerald come up yet?"

"Gerald, he is in the casks," said Jean Paul, wishing for more attention than Albert cared to display at the moment. Jean Paul sighed and watched Albert walk away, admiring Albert's backside. When the boss was out of hearing range, Jean Paul said, "Still, he is sexy."

Albert found Gerald checking valves on the casks. He stood at a distance for a few minutes, watching Gerald work. The young man had a real knack for vintning, and for the first time, it occurred to Albert that Gerald would make a fine chief vintner—that is, if anything ever happened to Jean Paul, God forbid. But the idea sparked a more serious question in Albert's mind.

What were Gerald's intentions regarding his stepdaughter? Did Gerald intend to marry Darla, or just go on living in— what Albert personally considered—sin? Albert would never presume to interfere in anyone else's personal affairs, not even Darla's, when it came right down to sex and so forth. Albert had gone so long without a woman that he had actually forgotten what it felt like, until Darla had returned home with Gerald. Through Darla and Gerald, Albert had enjoyed vicarious erotic pleasures, and he had begun experiencing a reawakening of his own special needs. Albert had become preoccupied with how to fulfill his needs more directly. On several occasions, he had tried romancing Sue Ann, but she had just scoffed at his gestures. Albert had ruminated over the idea of straying. He hadn't done it yet, only thought about it. Then, last night, Sue Ann said she had to have him. What was that all about? he wondered.

As he watched Gerald checking the vat valves, Albert noticed the young man's youthful build, the glistening biceps, the full head of hair, and the boyish face. Well, boyish compared to Albert's sagging jowls. And Albert felt a pang of envy, a wish to exchange places with Gerald. The idea instantly shamed him. Albert stepped forward and called out to

Gerald, his guilty conscience causing his voice to overexude geniality. But Gerald apparently did not notice Albert's festering mental wounds, and when Albert slapped Gerald on the back and complimented his good work, Gerald smiled up at the old man and said, "Thanks, dude," making Albert feel young again.

AT FIVE O'CLOCK that evening, Sue Ann received an emergency telephone call from Austria. Her Julia had died. Sue Ann descended into hysterics. Albert, with the aid of Gerald, was able to pry Sue Ann off the telephone and drag her to the couch. During the next half hour, Sue Ann insulted Jean Paul when he arrived at the main house with a nice bottle of wine, and then she whirled around and fired the cook. Later, Sue Ann served a dinner of cold cuts and bread. If she suffered, the world suffered with her.

Darla played piano for Albert; then the family tuned in a nature program on TV about the mating practices of porcupines. When Gerald yawned, Darla excused herself, saying she was going to bed. Gerald followed her out of the living room. Albert was dozing in his leather armchair. Sue Ann sniggered and said to Darla, "Go on, you little pervert. Drag the poor man off to your sleazy lair to perform his slave duties." When Sue Ann shot a hostile glance at Gerald, he leaned down, kissed her cheek, and said, "Good night, Mom." Emphasis on "Mom."

When Gerald and Darla had left the room, Sue Ann found herself alone with Albert and the incredible mating porcupines. Cursing under her breath, she opened a small sterling silver box on the coffee table, took out a cigarette, and smoked for the first time in six years. That little box had been sitting there waiting for just such a moment. Sue Ann hacked, the room spun, and then she felt better.

WHEN VENUS AND Song arrived at the wooded spot, they parked the Buick far back in the brush, where it could not

be seen from the main trail leading to Kettle Falls. Venus
carried a small penlight she held pointed down toward the
ground to guide her way as she limped along the rugged path
behind Song. The clearing where the Elias Fobia Cabin stood
was shrouded in darkness, and Song and Venus moved cautiously, quietly. At the cabin's rear, on the river side, the door
was bolted from the inside. Song knocked. From inside a
voice said, "Blindfold her."

Venus heard the door bolt slide. The door opened a crack
and a hand appeared, clutching a bandanna. Song took the
bandanna and wrapped it around Venus's head, covering her
eyes. Then the door opened wider and Song helped Venus
up into the cabin's dark interior.

"Leave the blindfold on," Gerald instructed from the darkness. "I don't want her seeing me yet." Song helped Venus
sit down on the cold wood floor. Venus felt pine needles and
grit on the floor, and she detected the odor of weed. So the
man named Gerald smoked pot. Why hadn't Song mentioned
that? Maybe he forgot. The weed aspect made sense to Venus, but when the joint was passed to her, she declined,
pleading an asthmatic condition.

"She's asthmatic, too?" said Gerald angrily. "That's all I
need. An asthmatic with a bum foot."

"It only acts up when she smokes. The asthma. Otherwise,
she's fine," said Song, thinking fast.

"Well, I don't need any invalids," grumbled Gerald. "She
better not be a prima donna."

Song laughed. "Hell, Kay Lynn could wrestle a man your
size and pin him down before he knew what happened."

"Is that right?" Gerald grinned. Song's eyes had become
accustomed to the dark, and now he saw Gerald's white teeth.
Gerald was seated on the hearth, before a stone fireplace.
Then Song saw Carla seated on the floor beside Gerald. Gerald said, "So let's test her right now." He stood.

Venus, still blindfolded, struggled to her feet.

"She keeps the blindfold on," said Gerald. "She can find me by my voice and—"

Before Gerald could finish his sentence, Venus had flipped him over onto the floor.

"Ooof," said Gerald, holding his head.

Carla caught her breath and whispered, "Yowser!"

Song grinned.

Gerald said, "Take that thing off her eyes."

Song removed the blindfold. Venus blinked her eyes a few times until she could see. When Gerald's face came into focus, she saw a rugged-looking man towering over her. He wore a dark woolen knit cap pulled down low over his forehead and ears. He had nondescript features, except for the teeth. Big, bright, nice teeth. The kind of teeth you'd see in a town with fluoridated water.

Gerald said, "Sit down." She sat on the floor. Gerald said, "Now tell me who you are."

"Kay Lynn Jones. Juneau's wife."

Song started to say something, but Gerald silenced him. "You keep quiet while I interrogate the lady. Now…Kay Lynn…where do you stand politically?"

"You mean am I a Republican or a Democrat or a Green?" Venus joked.

"I don't like sarcasm," he replied sternly.

Venus said, "If you want to know how I feel about politics, you'll have to be more specific. You want to know what I think about Arab terrorists? Chinese Communists? Israeli commandos? You need to be more specific."

"Dambusters."

"You're a member of that group?" Venus sounded surprised.

"Negative. Tell me what you think about the Dambusters."

Venus paused to think, then said, "Don't know much about them, really. I've heard of them; everyone has. They're environmentalists. They want to save salmon by breaching the dams along the Columbia and Snake rivers. They have some big court battle going with the government. That's about all I know.''

"Where do you stand?"

"On salmon?"

"On dambusting."

Venus sniffed. "I think the wild salmon should be saved. They should open up the dams' earthen sides, let the salmon get through. They should breach the dams. But legally."

Silence, then Gerald said, "You ever break the law, Kay Lynn?"

"You mean other than robbing the Kettle Falls Savings and Loan?" she asked glibly.

"I'm talking about violence."

"If you mean where people or animals are intentionally injured or killed, I'm against it," Venus stated firmly. "What about government property? Are you opposed to destroying government property?"

Venus saw Song wink at her. She said, "Maybe not."

Gerald said, "Think you'd ever change your mind? About violence?"

"You mean," said Venus, "could I justify violence, in certain instances, against people or animals?"

"Right."

Venus seemed to take a long time before she responded. From Song's perspective, she was taking too long, but Gerald waited patiently for her to answer his question. Everything depended on her answer. Everything.

Venus said, "Generally speaking, I'm against violence."

Gerald frowned. "Okay," he said, standing up. "That's all for tonight. You two leave first. I'll be in touch in a couple days."

On the way out of the dark cabin, Venus passed Carla. "Hi," she said, and the young woman replied dully, "Yeah."

When they got into the Buick, Song said, "You may have blown this deal, you know."

"My nonviolence stance?"

Song said yes, the nonviolence posturing.

"Doesn't pay to be too eager," Venus replied.

"What bothers me is the girl. She's ditzy, but very bright. And she's soulful and intuitive. I don't get it."

"Maybe you're falling in love with her."

Song laughed, more to himself than aloud.

They drove home in silence. When they reached the entrance to the trailer park, Song braked and turned the car around, aiming it toward the bridge that crossed the river. He said, "I could use a quick trip to Oz. How about you?"

"Not on your life, Juneau Jones," snapped Venus. "Not while we're under a microscope."

"Hell, we could make it down and back in two days' time. We're cool for two days. You game?"

"We're being watched."

Song laughed, until Venus nodded toward the rearview mirror. He glanced across her, into the mirror. A silver Lexus sat idling on the shoulder of the highway. Inside, a woman sat behind the wheel, smoking a cigarette, making no pretense. She was watching them and she didn't care if they knew it.

"Oops," said Song, reversing gears.

At the door to the Airstream, Song grabbed Venus and kissed her long and hard. When he let her go, Venus said, "Was that for the benefit of the lady in the Lexus?"

"Nope," said Song, and he went to bed.

Venus tried reading *The Anarchist's Cookbook*, but she couldn't concentrate. She went on-line and checked her E-mail. There was one message, from the sibling Echo:

"What kind of sister are you, anyway? I have been sitting here at Mother's house, waiting for weeks. Mother told me that you went to Africa to be with Richard. I know damn well that this isn't the case, as I contacted Richard and he told me everything. I mean, everything. I always knew that cad was wrong for you. Now, I came all the way from New York to accompany you on the job, to honor you with a chapbook dedicated to you and salmon. The least you could do is phone or send an E-mail. I'm your sister. Call me immediately. Regards, Echo. P.S. In case you are at all interested, here is my first chapbook entry:

Man on shore casts fly to wind
Water ripples, salmon swim
Man tempts fish, With dazzling fly
In an instant wink of eye

All is changed, all is lost
Struggle useless, salmon tossed
Man on shore reels him in
Blind to future drained by sin

He the victor with two feet
Takes the salmon home to eat
Never thinking past the taste
What he's spoiled by his waste

River, O River, take him down
Snatch the angler, let him drown
Return the salmon to their redds
Restore your holy flowing beds.
Amen.

"Holy flowing beds?" Venus deleted the message, and went to bed. From where she slept on the forward bunk, she could hear Song's soft breathing in the rear of the trailer. She could still feel Song's kiss, where his lips had pressed against hers. She was reliving the scene, when she heard an engine turn over. Peering out the window, she saw the silver Lexus drive away.

PULLING INTO THE DRIVE, Sue Ann saw Albert coming out
of the vintner's cottage. Why were Albert and Jean Paul
working so late? Was Albert checking up on the books again
to see if Sue Ann was still pilfering? That wouldn't surprise
Sue Ann.

Albert saw the lights from Sue Ann's car and walked down
the hill to the garage. When she had parked the silver Lexus
in the garage, Albert took Sue Ann's hand and walked with
her into the house. He never asked her where she had been
at this time of night. And she never told him.

TWENTY

Dams destroy young salmon and steelhead in two ways:

1. When excess water flows over the spillways, it becomes supersaturated with nitrogen, which kills young fish.

2. The young fish are sucked into the dams' power turbines.

   Industry's Solution: Spread nets across turbines. Catch young fish, and truck or barge them around the dams.

   Envirosolution: Remove dams, restore rivers, return salmon.

   Ecoterrorist's Solution: Ka-boom

ONE MISTY JUNE MORNING, a fish truck transporting salmon smolt from above Grand Coulee Dam and around the concrete behemoth to the other side was hijacked by a band of elk, which chased the driver into the woods. The truck and the fish inside disappeared and were never found. On the first of July, one of the Inchelum beavers attacked Mrs. Cobb Collins's two Dobermans, pinning the dogs against the side of a barn. So fierce was the beaver that it left the two dogs scarred and bleeding before it escaped into the river and swam away. Mrs. Cobb Collins decried the event, telling all who would listen that she, too, like Jack Foxes Moon, had lost all respect for beavers. On July 2, a male deer broke through the front door of the caretaker's house at Wanapum Dam while caretaker Turner and his wife slept. The couple awoke when they heard water running. Upon investigating, the Turners discovered the deer in the bathroom. It had turned on the bathtub tap, tipped over a jar of bubble bath, climbed into the tub, and was luxuriating.

One week later, a U.S. Fish and Wildlife agent patrolling Hanford Reach was attacked by a horned owl with a five-foot wingspan. The owl's needle-sharp talons left fifteen puncture wounds on the agent's body. Shortly after that, a Fort Spokane National Park ranger leading a tourist group into the parklands was dive-bombed by a juvenile barred owl; it took five tourists to beat off the winged attacker.

Nothing was sacred anymore, neither man nor domesticated beast. Pet owners worried that even their farm animals, their faithful old collies, and their poker-faced marmalade cats would either be viciously attacked or, worse, join the mutiny. Then, on the seventeenth of July, a herd of dairy cows near Wenatchee became the chief suspects in a mysterious attack on a farm family, in which each person's jugular vein had been punctured and the blood sucked out.

Darla read about the increasing animal trouble along the river and wondered about her Pussy. She called down to Leelee in Astoria. Sure enough, Leelee reported that Pussy had escaped her backyard fence and had last been seen taking up with a band of street dogs that had camped down by the river's mouth and were viciously attacking fly fishermen at Tansy Point. No one was safe, at least no one who owned land along the Columbia, or worked its hydroelectric dams, or fished or otherwise recreated there. The last straw came in the form of the Inchelum beavers, joined by reinforcements from Badger Mountain, who dammed up the Aplets and Cotlets fruit orchard irrigation canals.

Was this all a paranoid fiction concocted by the human species to excuse its own attacks against wildlife? No one could be sure.

By the middle of July, the U.S. Fish and Wildlife Service, under the command of its director, Oly Olson, had mustered all its regional forces and formed a dragnet along the Columbia River's banks. For the first time in eastern Washington history, local private enterprise joined the Fish and Wildlife Service and U.S. Marine Fisheries on the same side of an environmental battle. Even the Seattle City Council, that interfering, liberal salmon lobby, in a press release issued from the Emerald City, agreed that something had to be done to rein in the wild kingdom, starting with the bears.

Olson and his colleagues envisioned an arduous summer along the Columbia's banks. Lacking sufficient forces, volunteers from the community were deputized and given permission to kill or maim any wild animal, or any postdomestic creature, posing a threat to humankind's territory. With the summer heat came more trouble.

THE SPRING MELT had washed glacial waters into the Columbia, and the river had risen until now, in mid-July, it nearly overflowed. Along its banks, wildflowers bloomed and the occasional beaver was seen gnawing at pine scrub. One balmy evening, Venus sat inside the Elias Fobia Cabin, listening to Gerald lecture her on the CIA's worldwide vaccination conspiracy. In the distance, she could hear loons crying on the reservoir, and once or twice, she thought she heard a fish jump. *Splosh.*

So far, Venus had proved her mettle, convincing Gerald that Kay Lynn Jones was capable of almost any physical task required of his soldiers. True, the broken toe, still mending, interfered with her rappelling skills, but Gerald was more concerned about what he called her "political naïveté" and "misguided moral training." Gerald worked long hours with her, requiring her to meet him privately at the cabin night after night to discuss the justification for ecotage, for using violence against the enemy. The enemy, in case she was interested, was the human species.

"Once we drive out the humans," Gerald told her, "the ecology will start to recover."

"Drive them out? Or destroy them?" she asked.

Gerald's jaw tightened. "Sometimes killing is the only way."

On these occasions, when Gerald and Venus sparred over ethical details, the big guy always ordered Darla to stay in the van to keep a lookout on the trail leading to the Elias Fobia Cabin. Song, meanwhile, had been sent to the Midwest to purchase two floating catamaran houseboats, several tons of fertilizer, and various other bomb-making materiel. Gerald provided hard cash for the purchases—laundered cash.

Doing her best to maintain Kay Lynn characteristics, Venus was stifling a huge yawn, when suddenly she heard Darla's hoot-owl signal. Someone was coming along the Kettle Falls trail. Gerald heard it, too, doused his joint, and told her to sit very still inside the darkened cabin.

In a few minutes, they heard footsteps crunching along the dirt trail. The footsteps grew louder, and Venus noticed sweat glistening on Gerald's brow.

So he wasn't perfectly cool all the time. Some things, like this sound of unidentified footsteps, made Gerald sweat. Outside the cabin, near the rear door, the footsteps stopped. They listened as the intruder circled the cabin. Then, from a distance, came the sound of a powerboat on the river. Then the boat's engine abruptly died. Then the sound of footsteps outside the cabin resumed, and gradually the sound grew softer, until they could no longer hear anything. Then Darla hooted twice to signal that the coast was clear. By the time they reached the van, Darla was hysterical.

"It was one of those Fish and Wildlife agents," she bawled, groping for the fresh joint Gerald had lit. "I'm pretty sure it was a woman. She had, like, a shotgun, or a rifle—a big gun, anyway. She must have come onto the trail by foot. Maybe parked up on the highway. I didn't even hear her coming at first, and it was a lucky thing I didn't get out to tinkle just when I'd planned to, because she came along just then. I don't think she saw the van, though. She didn't stop walking when she passed the bushes, just kept going toward the cabin. That's when I opened the door and hooted the warning.''

Darla inhaled the dope, exhaling in little bursts, like she'd learned to do from Nathan Bernstein years ago at Lake Chelan. ''Then I heard a powerboat over on the reservoir. Out there.'' Darla pointed toward the river. ''Then the powerboat cut its engine. I looked through the trees and saw a light come off the river. The woman with the gun, the wildlife agent? She saw it, too.''

Gerald said, ''What kind of light?''

''Just a short blink, a kind of white light. Like maybe a flashlight signaling someone. Then it went out and I couldn't see or hear a thing. The wildlife agent went over to the reservoir and looked around. But I guess she didn't see anything, either, because she turned around pretty soon and came back out of there. She went up the trail to the highway. I heard her engine start up; then I heard her drive away.''

Venus said, ''There might be more than one vehicle. Maybe she's still nearby.''

Darla noticed the way Gerald smiled approvingly at Kay Lynn, and she didn't like it much. Darla said, ''Of course, I realized that. But I have an intuition for these things, don't I, Gerald? So I can tell when the coast is clear and when it isn't.''

Gerald led the two women along the trail to the shore. When he felt certain it was safe, he fished a flashlight from his backpack, turned it on, pointing to the ground, and began making a circular motion. Moments later, a single light beam blinked once off the reservoir. Gerald sat down on a boulder and motioned the women to do the same. It was a clear, balmy night, the sky overhead thick with stars, the air still and silent. Venus could have sworn she heard the waterfall, but that might have been her imagination. Then looking out on the blackness of the reservoir's surface, she saw a kayak moving toward shore, and Venus had to smile when she saw who was paddling. Song pulled the kayak up onto the boulders, and from the expression on his face, Gerald was satisfied that Juneau Jones had accomplished his assigned mission.

Gerald said, "Where are they?"

"Up near Roosevelt Marina. Legally buoyed. Look like any other houseboats."

Later that night as Song was headed to the back of the Airstream to go to bed, Venus said, "You okay, Juneau?"

Song looked at Venus and said, "Sure, Kay Lynn. Why?"

"Everything went okay? On the trip?"

Song nodded.

Venus, brushing her dyed red hair, said, "What if Gerald doesn't accept me? What if he thinks I'm too much of a pacifist to convert to his ideas?"

Song placed an arm around her small shoulders. "Then he'll have to kill you, won't he?"

"You don't sound too upset about the possibility."

Song patted her red bob and said, "Now, don't you worry your purty little red head, Kay Lynn." He said it in exaggerated Geraldese.

Venus rolled her eyes and said, "Let's get serious. By the way, did I ever mention that Darla is a member of Mensa?"

Song snapped his fingers. "I knew it. Goddamn it, I knew that girl had a brain. This airhead stuff is just an act."

Venus said, "I don't think so. She may be brilliant. She may have a huge IQ, but I don't think the space case is an intentional facade. I think she's neurotic."

"You mean eccentric?"

"I mean neurotic. She might also have an eccentric streak. But she's neurotic as hell. Just to be sure, I checked with an expert."

"What expert?"

"Dr. Wong, my therapist. I described the girl's behavioral

characteristics. Wong said I was describing all the symptoms of a deeply troubled genius who suffers from starvation of the soul, from a deep-seated emptiness…."

Song smacked his forehead. "Cut me a break, Firecracker. Wong's a walking space case himself. You couldn't pay me to buy his diagnosis."

Venus glanced out the window. In the trailer next to theirs, a light was on. She could see a silhouette through the thin curtain. A man. Eating something. Maybe a bowl of cereal. Maybe he had insomnia.

Song said, "So what else did you dig up in my absence?"

Venus smiled. "You know that silver Lexus that's so fond of tailing us?"

"Yeah."

"It's registered to Sue Ann Denny."

Song opened a beer and guzzled. "The mom?"

"Yeah. The mom." Venus said, "So far, that's all I know about the mother."

Venus stretched. Song's ridiculing of Dr. Wong had touched a sensitive nerve. Right now, Song was not only her work partner; he was her best pal. Replacing Richard. She glanced up at him. He looked tired, his eyes strained from his cross-country trip.

"Go to bed," she said softly. "We can finish this in the morning."

Song went off to bed, wondering if Venus would ever consent to consummating their marriage of convenience. He slept fitfully, dreaming of Miss Delicious and her poison green stockings. Meanwhile, in the Airstream's forward bunk, Venus lay in bed, staring out the window at a star-studded sky.

They had never discussed the magnetism that constantly played their mutual force field. Once she had married eco-hubby, Song had tried putting her out of his fantasies, but he failed time and again, because no woman exits a man's fantasies until he has had her. Still, he had tried, and ultimately he decided to adopt a laissez-faire attitude, not exactly giving up, but not counting on her, either. She, meanwhile, had convinced herself that he was interested in one thing only, adding her to his sexual conquests. She scrupulously avoided his overtures, or at least made light of them, playfully but firmly pushing him away each time he tried. Lately, he had tried less often than before ecohubby came along. The truth was that even before she married ecohubby, both of them had feared a sexual union would instantly transform their mutual attraction into a minefield of emotional turbulence. And they both feared losing face. What if she didn't like how he made love to her? What if he wasn't interested after the first time?

Better to keep it friendly, better to remain "soul mates," as he had lately described their relationship. Working partners and soul mates—what the heck did that mean? No intimacy, no sirree, not between him and the Firecracker. That wouldn't do, nope, not a chance. Still, Song kept fanning the flames.

Richard's peccadilloes would not automatically justify her own. Where was moral fortitude when she needed it most? Oh, here it is, ya sure you betcha. Right here in her empty arms.

THE MORNING E-MAIL brought Venus news from Echo. "Since you are playing hard to get," Echo wrote, "I am sending you the second poem from my salmon chap book herewith:

Spawning smolt
Fingerling fish
Doo-wop, doo-wop
(Snap fingers slowly thrice.)
Spawning smolt
Breaching barriers
Human humps
Concrete caverns
Doo-wop, doo-wop

(Snap fingers slowly thrice.)
O spawning smolt
Fingerling fish
Soul of Salmon
Your bones, my bones
The same bones
Same flesh
Same journey
Doo-wop, doo-wop
(Snap fingers very slowly thrice.)
Come home, wild thing.

After the poem, Echo wrote, "See what creativity you are stifling? Please contact me at once. Regards, Echo."

At breakfast, Venus recited the poem, finger snapping and all, to Song, who listened politely. When she finished, Song said, "'Wild thing'?"

"Doo-wop, doo-wop."

"If I believed in a personal God, I'd promise Him anything never to have to listen to another one of your poems."

"Not mine."

"Who's then?"

"I read it somewhere. Please pass the peanut butter."

Song grabbed the jar of peanut butter, held it away from her. "Kay Lynn, you are not having peanut butter for breakfast. You are going to start eating healthy breakfasts."

"Now that we're married?"

Song grinned. "As your old man, I'm in charge of what you do and say, and when you eat, and what you eat...."

"Cool it, Ju."

Song stared at Venus and said, "Oh my God."

"What's wrong?" She reached up and felt her face. "Do I have some"

Song pointed at her eyes. "Your contact lens. One is missing."

She blinked her eyes. "Which one?"

"Left."

"Is this some kind of joke?" She closed her eyelids and rubbed them gently.

"No joke. You've got one hazel eye and one green."

Venus peered into a small mirror that hung over the table. He was right. One of her hazel-tinted contacts was missing.

"Oh hell, I hate when this happens." She massaged her left eye.

"What? When what happens?"

"I have these extra-deep eye sockets. That's why I don't... usually... wear contacts. They always end up getting lost back in the far reaches."

"You're grossing me out."

"So whenever one gets lost, I have to go to the eye doc. He puts a tinted eyewash in my eye, and that helps locate the lens." She looked in the mirror again. "But since this lens is tinted, it should be pretty easy to find. You'll have to help me."

Song shook his head. "I am not going into your eye. Nope. No way. That just grosses me out. You'll have to find it yourself."

Eventually, she convinced him to help. She lay on the bunk while he peeled back her upper eyelid and shone a Maglite beam into the socket, cursing under his breath the whole time. She tried guiding him. "Way in back. That's where they usually find it. Way back there."

"This is repulsive. I might lose my breakfast."

"You're strong, Ju. Be a man."

"I don't like how you said that, Kay Lynn. Ah, there it is!"

LATER THAT MORNING, they drove into K Falls. Venus dropped Song off in the Buick, watched him sleaze into Prospector's, and then drove over to Colville, to the Hartell's, seeking Mabel Fobia. But Fobia wasn't working that day. Venus drove back to K Falls, acutely aware of the silver

Lexus on her tail. She pretended not to notice and kept driving until she came to the Kettle Falls Historical Society's yaller cottage. The cottage was locked up tight and no Mabel. Venus drove over to the Grand View Inn, the silver tail persisting, parked the Buick, and went inside. Trevor Grimm, his back to the door, said, "Yeah, what can I do fer ya?"

"I'm looking for Fritz Fowler."

Grimm turned around. He saw a girl with a short red bob and hazel eyes. She was wearing a dumpy cotton dress and old balled-up sweater. He studied her closely because something about her bothered him. He then decided it was her nasty clothing and said, "Fowler's persona non grata at my inn. Anyhow, he wouldn't even be here this time of day. He'd be over across from Prospector's at his office. The Dambusters. You tried there?"

Venus shook her head. "That office has been closed for weeks. He never shows up there, never answers the phone."

"Well, hell, I don't know where he is." Grimm turned his back to her, pretended to work.

Venus gave him a few seconds to ponder, then said, "How bad do you want me to go away?"

"Pretty bad. Real pretty bad." Grimm said this with his back still turned. But now, he had figured out what bothered him about her. She had been at the Grand View Inn before, only with different hair, different eyes, and a credit card. He couldn't recall her name, but he could look it up in the records. He started over to the computer.

Venus said, "Just tell me what the deal is with Fowler, and maybe I'll go away for good."

Grimm read the information on the screen, then reached for a small notepad. He wrote something on the pad, tore off the sheet of paper, handed it to Venus. "Here," he said. "Now please go away. Fowler almost ruined my business. I don't want to see him or his friends ever again. So go away."

He said it loudly enough for a couple locals sitting in the restaurant to overhear. He wanted them to overhear. He

needed to expunge Fowler from all connection with the
Grand View Inn. Venus guessed at this and said, "Locals
don't like Fowler, do they?"

"We don't like what Fowler stands for," Grimm said in
an even louder voice. "The folks in eastern Washington depend on the dams for our irrigation. Hell, even the Californians depend on the hydropower. So we don't want the Fowl-
ers of the world coming in here trying to have our dams
breached and wrecking our livelihoods. And if you ask
me"—he was almost yelling now—"that's who's blowing
up these dams. Fritz Fowler. So if you're a friend of his, you
better get out of K Falls, because otherwise, you'll be dead
meat."

"That so?" Venus tucked the unread note into her dress
pocket. "You mean to say there's a local posse out to get
Fowler and company?"

The two eavesdroppers exited the restaurant and sidled
over to help Grimm. Both men had beards and wore boots,
western wear. They towered over Venus. "Honey," said the
heavyset one, "you givin' Mr. Grimm trouble?"

Venus said she didn't intend to make trouble, just wanted
to know how to find Fritz Fowler. The second man, shorter,
with lazy eyelids, said, "What business you got with
Fowler?"

Venus played innocent. "I...I was looking for a job.
Somebody over at Prospector's said Mr. Fowler was looking
for a data-entry person."

The tall stranger bent down and stared directly into Venus's hazel eyes. She hated when people stooped down to
look at her. Why couldn't they be content with looking down
at her? Why did they have to stoop like that, as if to a child?
For that matter, why did people stoop down to children?

The stooping stranger said, "Honey, let me give you some
real solid advice. Fowler and his Dambusters is a rotten group
of radical troublemakers from over the mountains, from over

by Puget Sound. You don't want nothin' to do with them, and anyway, they won't be around here for much longer."

The sloe-eyed man chortled.

Grimm said, "Told you so. Now take a hike, little missy. We got better things to do than talk about Fowler."

She drove all the way to Prospector's with the dedicated silver Lexus tail. At Prospector's, she parked the Buick out front at the curb, then sat in the car and read Grimm's note. Meanwhile, the woman in the Lexus had pulled over behind the Buick. Venus could see her in the rearview mirror. Sue Ann Denny was smoking, blowing the smoke out her open window into the street. When she finished the first cigarette, she lit another off it, then another off the second, and so forth, always tossing the live butts into the street.

"Miss," Grimm had written, "get out of K Falls before Fowler has you killed."

Venus waited half an hour, until Song stumbled out of Prospector's and hit the sidewalk. Tiffie swiveled over to the door and blew him a long kiss. Song blew one back, watched Tiffie swoon, and slid into the passenger seat.

Venus said, "How drunk are you?"

"Hell, Kay Lynn," said Song, slurring. "You even sound like a nagging housewife." He leaned over to peck her cheek, but she swatted at him. Tiffie witnessed this, smirking, then went back inside Prospector's.

They drove across the bridge over the Columbia and took the Highway 395 northward to Laurier, where they crossed into Canada. At the immigration booth, Venus and Song showed their driver's licenses and sailed through. From the other side, Venus watched the silver Lexus turn around and head back down the U.S. highway. Some Americans have no appreciation for the Canadian lifestyle.

THEY DROVE AS FAR AS Cascade, BC, and tucked into a motel room, where Song wanted to make love, not war. She held him off, and called Olson. When he came on the line, she told him the truth, the whole truth, then held the phone at arm's length, the better to suffer the pitch and tenor of Olson's tirade, the gist of which, she later explained to Song, was that in the chief's opinion their irresponsible actions jeopardized the agency's good name, and if they didn't report for duty within twenty-four hours, they were dead meat.

Song said, "I should have told him."

"Like that would've made a difference."

At headquarters, Olson buried his head in his hands and mentally strangled two rebellious federal agents.

TWENTY-ONE

TSAGIGLA'AL, Watcher of the River, loved crow as much as he loved any creature, and so when the ravens of Pasco, those large, hoarse-voiced black crows, accidentally swallowed radioactive sludge leaking from Hanford's waste storage tanks and shortly thereafter hatched mutated broods, chicks with red feathers and no wings, Tsagigla'al wept.

When the ravens tried to feed their aerodynamically challenged chicks, the chicks' beaks glowed, then fell off. Shortly after this incident, the crows of Kennewick also discovered nuclear waste near their personal nesting area. This was the last straw.

Tsagigla'al knew crows were capable of making a great rumpus, and that they rarely keep their promises. Furthermore, crows were notorious rompers, preferring play to work, and particularly enjoyed pecking at newly planted agricultural fields, frustrating the human farming instinct and disrupting agribusiness in general. But humans had gone too far this time, and Tsagigla'al worried for the crows, and so one warm summer evening late in June, Tsagigla'al gathered a murder of crows on the riverbank below Pasco Middle School and instructed them on self-preservation.

Next morning, as dawn peeled away the blackness of night, while the dew still lingered on the flowers and fields of the tricities, Pasco, Kennewick, and the other one, the crows attacked. Performing every bit as gracefully as swans in love, the crows sailed over Sacajawea State Park and bombarded the crowded campsites with hard garbage collected from human trash bins and grocery store Dumpsters. Campers, many of whom were still sleeping when the hard rain fell, scrambled for cover, but to no avail. Each time a camper would run for the public facilities building, a squadron of crows attacked, cawing mercilessly, the bright sun glinting off their sharpened beaks, only emphasizing their menacing potential. Soon, the campers had fled into nearby cornfields, stomping the husks to ruins. Meanwhile, the park rangers, huddled inside their tollbooths, telephoned a higher authority. Could some agency, federal, state, county, whatever, please come to Sacajawea and rescue them from the crow invasion? State troopers were called up, armed with powerful shotguns loaded with crow-killing buckshot. But although the state had sent in its crack-shot troopers, the crows prevailed, dive-bombing in tight formation, leaving foul organic trademarks on the enemy. Buckshot flew but failed to staunch the black-flow pouring out of the sky. Exhausted, drenched in crow excrement, the troopers retreated. The U.S. Fish and Wildlife Service was called in, diverting its agents from another bear attack up at Colville. So diluted were the agency's forces that Director Olson lobbed an E-mail plea to Washington, D.C., requesting reinforcements. But wheels grind slowly in Washington, D.C., and red tape tangles the spokes of progress. Olson received a reply:

"If you guys can't handle a few bear and a bunch of crows, you don't belong in the wildlife industry." It was signed "A Lesser Bureaucrat."

Meanwhile, hundreds of apparently fearless crows gathered along the riverbanks, strutting and pecking, and each time a company of gun-toting humans tried invading the riverbank, the crows formed their thick black cloud and menaced the enemy into fleeing. Up north, along Roosevelt Lake reservoir, the bears of Colville, temporarily freed from pesky Fish and Wildlife troops, enjoyed unfettered access to fly fishermen and anglers. And the bears took only as much salmon out of the river as they needed to survive. And Tsagigla'al watched over the river and its inhabitants. And Tsagigla'al rested for a day.

WHEN SUE ANN WALKED into the Grand View Inn and glanced around the lobby, Trevor Grimm acknowledged her with a single brief nod. Grimm didn't look at her, but he murmured, "All clear."

Sue Ann went upstairs and walked down the pine-paneled corridor to room 217, where she made a fist and performed her special knock. Pretty soon, Fritz Fowler opened the door and let her inside.

Fritz's room was chaos, papers spread over the king-size bed and over the carpet, and half a dozen of Fritz's volunteers splayed out amid the confusion, sorting, folding, stapling, and stamping. The result of their labors was a colorful leaflet, and Fritz shared a copy with Sue Ann. She read the headline: DAMBUSTERS TO BE RECOGNIZED BY PRESIDENT BENSON.

She read the first few lines of the story:

"As has been rumored for several months, President Barry Benson, a Pacific Northwest native, will return to his home state next week to issue a proclamation regarding restoration of rivers and salmon runs in the Pacific Northwest. A long-time advocate of dam breaching, the president is campaigning for reelection against antiriver archconservative Jenny Pickforth...."

Sue Ann stared at Fritz. "But...is this true? He's definitely coming?"

The volunteers chortled. Fritz smiled and led Sue Ann to the desk, where a laptop computer screen displayed Fritz's latest E-mail message from the White House. Sue Ann read the message and cried, "Why, this is just...well, remarkable. I was so sure the president's campaign visit would be canceled. I mean, with the bomb attacks, you'd think they'd be worried about his security."

Fritz shrugged. "Apparently, this is a crucial campaign stop for the president. They've decided to go ahead with it.

They've scheduled his appearance on Hanford Reserve, where they don't have too many security problems"—Fritz spread his hands—"since no one's allowed inside without government clearance."

Sue Ann said, "When?"

"On Thursday."

"Next Thursday?"

Fritz nodded.

Sue Ann said, "But that's my grooming day."

Fritz shrugged. "So change your hair appointment."

Sue Ann said, "Not hair appointment. Next Thursday is my potbellies' grooming day." She chewed her lower lip and sighed. "I'll have to change everything. Life can certainly get complicated, don't you think?"

She sighed again, a bit melodramatically for Fritz's tastes.

"But for an awesome cause," said Fritz to his most loyal follower.

Other than his religious devotion to restoring the river, and his imposing physical stature, Fritz Fowler possessed no particularly remarkable characteristics. He was a large man, about thirty, with short brown hair, soft brown eyes, and no distinctive features. If you saw Fritz riding the monorail in Seattle, for instance, you'd probably never notice him, certainly not pick him out of a crowd and remark, Why, there's a distinguished-looking chap. You probably wouldn't even remember him. Fritz knew he possessed this vapid physicality, and he exploited his inborn talent for blending into crowds, for making himself invisible to the enemy. Then, when the moment dictated, he could transform instantly into a firebrand, a person whose words and facial expressions his audience never forgot.

Fritz had other talents, including the ability to organize perfect strangers, by the hundreds, if not yet thousands, around a political cause. Fritz's singular cause, to which he devoted his waking moments, was river restoration, and for the past year, he had been concentrating on the Columbia

River. When he had opened up his Dambusters office in Kettle Falls, Washington, Sue Ann Denny had been one of his first volunteers. Since then, Fritz's band of river restoration advocates had grown to several hundred, but the bulk of them lived west of the Cascades, around Puget Sound. In eastern Washington, where ranchers and farmers relied on the man-made irrigation systems that interfered with the Columbia and Snake rivers' salmon runs, Fowler claimed few friends and numerous foes. Thus, the Dambusters volunteers now spread out across the floor of his room at the Grand View Inn were all from Seattle, and Sue Ann didn't recognize any of them.

"President Benson is bringing his family along," said Fritz. "This is going to be very big."

Sue Ann said, "Have you told the news media yet?"

"No, no, of course not. I mean, they know he's considering the idea. But the actual date, time, and place—that's Dambusters' secret. We're sworn to secrecy until the day before, until next Wednesday. The Secret Service needs time to do its thing. You know, be sure the coast is clear."

Sue Ann removed her coat, smoothed her hair, and said, "They'll go ballistic. The locals will go ballistic. I shudder to think what Albert will say….Of course, I won't mention this to him."

Fritz led Sue Ann into the bathroom, shut the door, and said, "Did you find out who they are?"

Sue Ann shook her head. "I'm pretty sure they're Canadians. Just white trash. I can't tell what they're up to, if anything. I don't think they know anybody around here. Why are you so interested in the Jones's, Fritz?"

"I had an E-mail from a friend of mine who works at Channel Five. He says some ecoterrorists are moving up the river again. The feds are looking for them. News media is saying it's Islamic jihad soldiers crossing over from Canada. But the feds aren't going for that. The feds still suspect me."

Sue Ann smiled conspiratorially. "And…well, Fritz, you can just nod. Are you or aren't you the—"

"This is no joking matter, Sue Ann. The feds are crawling all over these river towns. I've been down in Astoria and I just drove back up along the river. Everywhere, at all the dams and hatcheries, there are feds. If there's anymore trouble along the river, my friend at Channel Five says, the political tide could turn in the locals' favor. Backlash. It comes down to this, Sue Ann. If there's trouble, we stand to lose our congressional bid to breach the dams. So if you know anything about this…"

Sue Ann laughed. "Fritz, honey, you worry too much about what the media thinks. They're a pack of busybodies, and half the time they are dead wrong. Anyway, so what? So people suspect us. You don't see me getting all flustered, do you?"

Fritz said, "This is serious, Sue Ann. These anarchists are giving all salmon supporters a bad name. We can't have another ecotage incident. If we do, it's certain the president will cancel his visit. Now, we've got everything perfectly timed. President Benson and his family will arrive at Hanford on the day before his party's convention. If his visit here is successful, he's promised to make river restoration one of the party's priorities." Fritz's eyes glittered as he gripped Sue Ann's shoulders. "He'll talk about us, the Dambusters, at the convention, Sue Ann. This is big, I tell you. Right now, all our ducks are in a perfect row. Nothing can go wrong, as long as the anarchists don't strike."

Sue Ann pulled away from him and looked sideways at Fritz, as if crooking her head would allow her to see him in another perspective. "Why are you telling me this?"

In the background, Sue Ann heard the volunteers speaking softly to one another. She was sure they couldn't possibly overhear her conversation with Fritz. Fritz suddenly seized her arm. "We need your help, Sue Ann."

She felt the desperation in his tight grasp. Gently, she peeled his fingers away. "Ask me anything, Fritz. But please, honey, don't wrinkle my new blouse."

"I need you to spread a rumor around K Falls."

"What kind of rumor?"

Fritz bent down and whispered in Sue Ann's ear.

THAT NIGHT, when Sue Ann arrived home, Albert was waiting with a fine bottle of 1997 icewine. Sue Ann, still without proper kitchen help, poached a salmon and served it with asparagus tips and radicchio salad. Gerald and Darla (she still recovering from her tiff with Mom) had gone camping overnight and now arrived home unexpectedly, just in time for dinner. Fortunately, Sue Ann was the kind of cook who overestimated. Darla fussed too much over the poached salmon, by way of sucking up to Sue Ann. She was her heir, after all. Gerald opened the bottle of icewine and poured it into the glasses Albert had chilled. Somewhere between the fish and salad, Sue Ann said, "Channel Five has information that the dam bombings were done by provocateurs."

"Garbage," said Albert. "It's Earth Liberation Front ecoterrorists."

"Channel Five claims they'll prove it was a gang of provocateurs paid by Jenny Pickforth's campaign fund. Pickforth is trying to discredit President Benson, and since he supports breaching the—"

Albert said, "That's malarkey and you know it, Sue Ann."

"I'm just relaying what I heard. You don't have to come off so condescending."

Albert said, "Have I got some news for you."

"Albert, I wish you wouldn't prevaricate. Have you or have you not news for us?"

Albert ignored Sue Ann's rude snipe. "This is an election year," he began, "and you know what that means."

"I don't," said Darla sincerely. "Tell me, Daddy."

"The president of the United States is coming to the river," Albert said, importantly.

Sue Ann dropped her fork, leaned over to fetch it, and said, "Why, Albert, how did you know that?"

Albert smiled. "A little birdie told me."

"What little birdie? Who told you that?"

Sue Ann's voice held an urgent hostility that didn't escape Albert's attention. Tapping his dinner napkin against his own revelatory lips, Albert purred mildly, "Just you never mind now, dear. He's coming, and that's a fact. But that's the bad news."

"What's the good news, then?" Darla asked. "Is he coming here to our house?"

Gerald pretended only mild interest in the discussion, but his ears perked up considerably and his brain shifted into emergency mode. A twitch came to the area between his shoulder blades, the doorway to his soul. He stilled it and listened.

Albert was saying, "Despite Sue Ann's avid support of the Democratic party, I would never allow that sniveling new-world-order peddler into my house. No, when I speak of good news, I am referring to the Republican response to the president's imminent visit."

"Imminent?" Gerald might have sounded too eager for details.

"The president will arrive next Thursday. He'll go to Hanford, where he will declare the entire length of the Columbia River as it flows through the United States a national treasure. Protected habitat. He will ask Congress to approve the Dambusters appeal to breach every dam from Grand Coulee all the way down to Bonneville Dam, including the Snake River dams, thereby unleashing havoc along both rivers and denying states' rights."

Sue Ann said, "I knew that. And it won't unleash havoc, only free the fish."

"In response," continued Albert, "the Republican party of eastern Washington is sponsoring a visit, on the very same day, by Jenny Pickforth."

"Who's that?" asked Darla, wrinkling her nose.

Stunned, Sue Ann clapped a hand over her mouth, muffling a tiny shriek. Gerald put down his fork and reached for his wineglass. Albert belched behind a napkin and said, "Darla, honey, you need to follow current affairs. Jenny Pickforth is the Republican candidate for the presidency in the upcoming election, and she has agreed to appear at Grand Coulee Dam at the same time the president is appearing at Hanford." Albert chortled. "This should be a barrel of fun, huh, Sue Ann?"

"Albert, I don't see anything fun about it. You…you Republicans are trying to sabotage the president's campaign visit, trying to dilute our crowd. I won't have it." Sue Ann slapped her napkin onto the table and fled into the kitchen, where she immediately went to the telephone and dialed the Grand View Inn. Fritz wasn't in, so she left a detailed message with Trevor Grimm, who said, "This could be trouble. Bad trouble."

"Find Fritz," Sue Ann pleaded. "Have him contact me right away."

Sue Ann snatched up her cell phone and huffed out to visit her loyal pigs.

On the surface, the remainder of the evening at the Denny home passed in relative serenity. Albert made a few attempts to cool Sue Ann's scalding affect, but Sue Ann ignored him and concentrated on her stack of mail-order catalogs. She had been looking for a particular type of thigh-busting girdle, and now tried focusing on this quest, but her thoughts churned and each time the telephone rang, she jumped at it. Darla and Gerald had gone out for an evening drive. When they came in at ten o'clock, Fritz still hadn't phoned, and Sue Ann noticed that Darla looked upset.

"I miss my Pussy," Darla said forlornly. "Which is why it looks like I've been crying."

That got Sue Ann weeping over Julia, and it was all Albert and Gerald could do to staunch the tandem flow. That night in bed, Albert reached out for Sue Ann, but she jerked sharply away. "How dare you place your sleazy Republican paws on me," Sue Ann snapped. "How could you be such a salmon hater, Albert Denny?"

Albert couldn't sleep, so he got up, put on his robe, and went out to the garage, where for the fifth time in as many days, he checked the speedometer on Sue Ann's silver Lexus. On the way back into the house, Albert almost tripped over something on the terrace. A closer inspection revealed the object was a large gray slug. Albert ran for the salt.

When the phone rang at 1:00 a.m., Sue Ann grabbed it before Albert. "Oh, it's you," she whispered, and carried the phone into the hall, where she could speak with Fritz without Albert eavesdropping. She didn't notice Gerald standing in an alcove less than three feet from where she stood.

"Fritz, honey, listen up," Sue Ann whispered. "I went into Prospector's this afternoon, and I told that Tiffie Terlock—you know, the bartender?—I told her that I'd heard from a reliable source that the dam bombings had been done by Pickforth provocateurs. She didn't know what that meant, and I had to explain it to her, but eventually she got the picture. And the Prospector was there with his poker pals, and they all heard me, too. So the rumor's out, and I guarantee those bunch of poker gossips will spread it fast."

Fritz, lounging on his bed in the company of two nubile volunteers, smiled. "That's great, Sue Ann," he said. "You do good work."

"But we've got problems," Sue Ann went on. "Huge problems." And she told Fritz about the Pickforth appearance.

TWENTY-TWO

UNTIL HUMANS CAME, beaver and salmon lived to mutual advantage. Beaver built great dams rich in plant nutrients that provided ideal spawning beds. In these idyllic pools, salmon could dig out their redds, lay and fertilize eggs, and the eggs took nutrients from the dammed waters. Thus nourished, the smolt hatched, even as their ancestors' corpses fertilized the protected redds. Salmon gave beaver his body for food, and beaver returned the favor by creating more fine nesting conditions. Even the log dams humans built across the Columbia's arterial streams didn't stop salmon from returning home, or stop beavers from building dams. But trappers came and skinned the beavers, sold their fur, ate their flesh. Loggers came and dropped whole forests, rolling the logs into the Columbia and its arteries until the rivers choked with wood and the salmon had a harder time finding clean nesting grounds. Even so, the salmon still came in great numbers. Then the commercial fishermen came and built their canneries on the riverbanks and cast their nets into the waters, taking millions of salmon each season. Still salmon came home, but in fewer numbers. The species seemed invincible, able to contend with any number of man-made obstacles, able to survive whatever challenges that man placed into the salmons' path. Until concrete was invented; then salmon stopped coming home.

SATURDAY MORNING, as light broke over Roosevelt Lake, the reservoir that covered Kettle Falls lay like a still pond.

Nothing moved but a few gnats skimming the water's surface, and the soft arms of ponderosa pines reaching out to one another. In the woods at Kettle Falls, several deer grazed under the secure watch of the herd's male. Sunlight poured through the trees, dappling the deer's coats, making crazy patterns on the spotted young. A lone hawk rustled somewhere in the pines, a sound the deer recognized as normal, unthreatening. As a young buck grazed, very near its tongue a chrysalis lay underneath a leaf. The creature inside struggled to release itself before the buck consumed leaf and all. The deer's tongue lapped at the leaf as the new butterfly struggled to free itself. From a distance came the soft, distinctive purring of a boat cutting through the reservoir's still waters, but this distant noise didn't frighten the deer. The buck's tongue worked harder at the leaf. The butterfly summoned all of its energy, breaking loose just as the leaf entered the buck's mouth. Free at last, the swallowtail sailed above the water, its maiden flight a perfect dance of arcs and dips riding the tranquil breeze.

The Shouter arrived early at the riverbank, and his footsteps, recognized by the deer, didn't startle the creatures. But the Shouter always made a huge racket when he came to the river, and so the deer moved on to more placid ground. The Shouter climbed to the top of the highest boulder above the drowned waterfall and stood where so many creatures had come before him. Here above the mighty Kettle Falls, for thousands of years, bear had swiped salmon from the falls with their paws, eagles had swooped over the waterfalls and snatched up salmon in their talons, and humankind had tossed nets and raised weirs across the falls, taking salmon. Now the falls lay deep beneath the reservoir, and only the most sensitive beings could hear its mighty roar.

The Shouter paused for breath. As his lips parted, the air stood still, the land trembled slightly, and, even on this warm summer day, the river froze. No ice, just a stillness that defied motion. The Shouter saw that all were prepared for his sermon, and so he delivered his latest, most eloquent soliloquy. What flowed from his lips made no earthly sense to word-speaking creatures. What flowed from his lips was soul utterance, pure degravitated sound waves grasped only by nature's chosen witnesses. Although no human attended his sermon, the Shouter wasn't preaching in vain, for the river listened, beaver listened, deer and eagle, and all the wild creatures of the water and land and air listened whenever the Shouter spoke.

"Damnation," cried the Shouter above the roar of Kettle Falls. He rested for a moment, then yelled, "Pave the Earth, you bastards. Pave the goddamn Earth." Then the Shouter came down off the boulder and traipsed through the woods, muttering to himself. As he passed the old Elias Fobia Cabin, the Shouter felt some strange energy sear through his body. He stopped, letting the strong invisible currents pass through him, and the currents sparked and sizzled and the Shouter's body glowed. Raising his arms to heaven, he hollered, "Blow the whole damn thing to smithereens!"

INSIDE THE CABIN, Venus paused in her political sparring with Gerald to listen to the Shouter. Gerald listened, too, intently, that nervous twitch erupting in his tight jaw. When they were sure he had gone away, Gerald lit a joint and said, "I'm not the hocus-pocus type, but that sounded like justification to me."

Standing near the fireplace, Venus said, "Maybe you misunderstood."

Gerald looked at her, a quizzical expression creasing his brow. Even though it was summer and sweltering, he still wore the knit woolen cap pulled down around his ears.

Venus said, "Maybe the old geezer means the planet."

"He means the dams," said Gerald. But Gerald didn't want to talk about the Shouter. He was all purpose and resolve. Nothing would distract him from the task at hand. Right now, the task at hand was convincing Kay Lynn Jones that violence can be justified, that sometimes violence must be used against the enemy, that this was one of those times. So far, she had resisted his arguments, had refused to adopt his principles. Even though Juneau agreed with Gerald, Kay Lynn held out. Even Darla had tried convincing her that violence was sometimes necessary. So far, they had failed to convince Kay Lynn Jones, but Gerald had not given up. He needed her. He needed her explosives expertise, and he needed her sheer guts. But if I can't convince her today, here and now, Gerald thought silently, I'll have no choice but to kill her. She knows too much. Either she's in or she's dead.

He sucked on the weed. "Meet me here tonight," he said. "Alone. No old man."

ON THE SAME Saturday morning, Reverend Fred Beveridge stood in the produce section of the Kettle Falls Carry Away, a cantaloupe in each hand. When Darla Denny came around the corner, pushing her grocery basket in his direction, Reverend Fred said, "Which is ripest, do you think?"

Darla handled both cantaloupes, then placed the ripest one in the preacher's grocery cart. "You'll have to eat it today, though, Reverend. It's that ripe."

Darla moved on. She was over by the lettuce now, basking in the overhead spray. Reverend Beveridge seized the moment. He went over and took her arm. "Darla," he said, "you remember back in Sunday school, when your mama would leave you at our house all afternoon after class, after all the other children had gone home?"

"Sure," said Darla, holding her face up to the gentle mist. "You and Mrs. Beveridge would let me watch television and play with your pet ferret."

"And remember that sometimes you'd have to spend the night with us? Because your mama didn't come to fetch you until the next day?"

"Oh, yeah, that's right. I remember that. Because, like,

Mom was working on Governor Benson's reelection campaign. That was before he became president."

Revered Beveridge nodded his head. "Yes, yes indeed. Well, Darla, I think it's time that you learned the truth about your mother."

Darla went limp. "Please, Reverend, I already know that my mom was once a professional hooker over in Seattle. I know that I was conceived in the honeymoon suite of the Westin Hotel during a plumbers' and pipe fitters' convention. I know that no one knows who my father was....But that all happened before Mom married Albert. Since then, she's been a moral paragon."

"Ah, but there's where you're wrong," said the preacher. "There's more to your mother than even Albert knows."

Darla turned from the mist and looked Reverend Beveridge straight in the eye. He seemed serious enough, though lately, God only knew what might erupt from this man's untethered lips. Darla said, "What do you mean?"

Reverend Beveridge steered Darla over to the potato section, a cool, dark space filled with bins overflowing with tuberous shapes and forms. "I have to whisper it. And you must promise me, Darla, never to say where you learned this truth." He leaned over to whisper into Darla's ear. Just then, Tiffie Terlock swung her grocery cart around the corner and entered the potato section. Darla and the preacher didn't see Tiffie, but she saw them, and she swore she saw the Reverend Beveridge kissing the ear of Darla Denny.

Oh hey, thought Tiffie, wait till Prospector hears about this.

She got out of there fast, before Reverend Beveridge or Darla saw her spying on them. But she had seen enough to feel quite sure that some special bond had developed between the preacher and the Denny brazen.

Darla listened to what Reverend Beveridge had to say, but she didn't believe a word. Furthermore, the preacher had no right speculating on who Darla's real father was. Anyway, how would he know all about Darla's mother's past?

Sheepishly, Reverend Fred confessed, "I was one of her coconspirators. That was back in the sinful days of my youth. Before I got religion."

"Well, I'll tell you something, Reverend," said Darla angrily. "You don't need religion to have morals. You just need a conscience. Where were your morals back then?"

Other customers wanted potatoes, so the pair moved on, into the seafood section. Darla stared down at a dead fish lying on a bed of shaved ice. The fishes' eyes seemed to watch her, like they were still alive. In that instant, Darla swore off fish for life.

"You've got to believe me," continued the preacher. "It's the God's truth. You can ask my wife if you want. She'll verify everything."

Darla sighed. "All right, Reverend Beveridge," she said. "I believe you. Now, please, just go away and let me finish my shopping."

"Well, thanks for the cantaloupe advice," said the preacher, and he disappeared into the meat section. When he was out of sight, Darla covered her eyes and wept. The seafood attendant came around the counter and put his arm around her. "There, there, Darla," he said. "Is there something I can do?"

Darla wiped tears off her face and shook her head.

"Gosh," said the seafood attendant, "did someone die?"

"No, it's not that."

"Well, what could make you so weepy, then?"

Darla lifted her face and looked at the attendant. It was Danny Dunlop. He'd been two years ahead of her at Kettle Falls High. "Danny," said Darla, "I just found out who my father is."

Danny Dunlop grinned. "Well, hey, that should make you happy, not sad."

"To tell you the truth," said Darla, "it makes me want to puke."

She left him standing beside the dead fish, wondering what she meant.

THAT AFTERNOON, Darla went into the Hartell's Drugstore in Colville and walked directly down the aisle to the photo counter. Mabel Fobia was opening the register, concentrating on her petty cash, so Darla waited until the she was finished sorting and counting, then said, "Miss Fobia, do you remember me?"

Fobia looked up at Darla Denny. "Of course I remember you," she snapped. "What do you think I am, a mummy?"

Darla blushed. "I...I wonder if you could help me."

Fobia shook her head. "I am not a psychiatrist, young lady."

"I...I...I mean help me find some old records."

"What kind of records?"

"Newspaper clippings from, like, twenty-three years ago."

Fobia said, "Why do young people pepper their conversation with extraneous adverbs? Now, as for newspaper records, that's easy enough. You go to the newspaper office and ask for the exact dates of the articles you are researching. They have it all on microfiche. A bright girl like you should know about microfiche."

Darla said, "I do. But the newspaper no longer exists. I...I heard that all the old issues are stored at the Kettle Falls Historical Society."

"Oh, you mean the old *Kettle Falls Crier,*" said Mabel. "Yes, that paper went belly-up about twenty years ago. But, yes, we do keep all the back issues at the society's offices. I could give you the key whenever you would like to do your research."

Darla shifted her feet. "Thanks. That is, well, I could do it alone, but I really want you with me. I think you probably remember a lot of things."

Mabel Fobia knew more about Darla Denny than Darla Denny knew about herself. And now it occurred to Mabel that the girl was finally old enough, and curious enough, to want to know about her origins. Mabel said, "Why do you want me to help you?"

"Because I can't trust very many people in K Falls," Darla replied softly. "I don't trust my parents. I mean my mom and stepdad. I definitely don't trust my boyfriend. I...I really trust you, Miss Fobia. Everybody says you're the smartest person around here. And, you, like, have a kindly manner. Would you help me, please?"

"Oh, all right," snapped Mabel. "I'll go with you to the office and help you look up those files. But you have to promise me that you won't tell anyone who helped you."

"I promise. When can we go?" Darla was smiling now.

"Tomorrow morning. But don't tell a soul about this. Do you understand?"

Darla nodded. She was halfway down the aisle, leaving Hartell's, when she felt an urge to turn around and look back at Miss Fobia. Darla turned and saw a glorious white swan behind the photo counter.

THE PLACID SURFACE of Banks Lake reflected a crescent moon. Just beyond the reflection, in a small outboard cruiser, the big man gazed up at the sky, where he had seen a raptor in flight silhouetted against the moon. The great bird had flown northeast, in the direction of Grand Coulee Dam. The big man felt that familiar twitch between his shoulder blades as he envisioned a golden beak, a smooth white-feathered head, great dark wings, powerful claws, and eyes as cold and bright as starlight. He imagined sailing over the coulees, soaring across the widened river and northward until he came to Grand Coulee Dam.

Circling the dam, the eagle spotted a place to land and swooped silently onto the road above the spillway. Beneath him, water flowed over the dam, three hundred and fifty feet straight down into the spillwater, where it pooled among a confusion of boulders and sandbars, where returning salmon fought in vain to go home.

On either side of the dam, huge steel towers rose, connected by thick cables that the eagle instinctively knew carried deadly jolts of energy. He could see the town lights, and he saw people standing on a nearby cliff, and they were watching the dam. Suddenly, the lights on the dam went out. The eagle froze in the blackness. Then just as suddenly, an explosion of light struck the dam and the sound humans called music blared to life.

The famous Grand Coulee Dam laser light show had commenced. He heard the people applauding, and he heard the astonished wonder in their voices as the multicolored laser lights, dancing to the rhythm of patriotic music, cast narrow beams of red, white, and blue across the face of the spillway. People cheered.

The big man sat on the still waters of Banks Lake and waited until the twitching in his shoulder blades finally ceased, until he could once again reason with man's intellect, until his eagle's wings dissolved. Then he rowed to shore and went to meet Kay Lynn Jones.

He drove her into a deep coulee, across the floor of the canyon, then high up along the opposite ridge, where he parked the van and told her to get out. He instructed her to gather kindling as he prepared the stones. The pit was already dug out and the stones piled inside. He removed the stones one by one, dropped the kindling into the pit, dropped the stones on top, and lighted the fire. When the rocks glowed, he removed his boots, and when he walked across the red-hot stones, Venus felt a visceral convulsion.

She knew she was next.

She had heard of fire walkers. She had heard they met secretly in the mountains, often in the national forests, to hold their scorching rituals, to test their faith in the power of prayer, or, simply, in the strength of human will. Some believed in the power of spirits, their personal gods and goddesses, who would protect them from harm. She had heard about a woman who fire-walked while chanting the name of the goddess Isis. As long as she chanted "Isis," she wasn't burned. Then, so the story went, one night, she was interrupted by another fire walker while summoning the goddess. The fire walker leapt ahead of her into the fire, and when she walked that night, she burned.

Gerald stood on the opposite side of the glowing stones. With one arm, he beckoned her. "Come across," he said.

She could barely make out his facial features. He repeated his command. "Come across." So this was how he tested loyalty.

He waited, but Venus could feel his growing impatience. She leaned down, slowly removed her boots, her socks. Reminding herself that others had done this and survived, she leapt onto the stones.

WHEN SHE CAME TO, he was cradling her in his arms, swabbing her forehead with a cool, wet cloth. She felt his warm breath on her neck. He smelled like gunpowder. She saw his hand reach up and noticed the fingernails were neatly trimmed, fastidiously clean. Pain seared through her body, and she shivered, but she dared not cry. He was armed. He could kill her out here on the edge of this coulee and no one would ever find her. But he didn't. Instead, he carried her back to the van and salved and wrapped her wounds. Then he drove her back to the cabin in the woods. There, he placed her on a blanket on the cold floor. On his cell phone, he contacted Juneau and told him where to find his wife. He leaned down and whispered into her ear, "Thursday." Then he went away, leaving her alone with her agony.

Song had carried her into the Airstream and put her into bed, and they both marveled at her feet. "Minor, first-degree burns," said Song, as he swabbed the swollen red soles. "Hell, you must be a natural mystic." He poured her three fingers of cheap scotch. "Who did you invoke?"

"Saint Blaise," she said, and reached for the hooch.

THAT NIGHT, a raging fire burned the yaller cottage to the ground. Nothing was saved, not even a single news clipping. Local authorities called it arson, and put the blame on some high schoolers drunk on Bud. Mabel told authorities she didn't know how it happened, or why. But Mabel knew how and why, and she even knew who struck the match. And no, Mabel didn't smoke, and she didn't play with matches.

TWENTY-THREE

REVEREND BEVERIDGE'S Sunday-morning sermon sent shivers up Sue Ann's spine and down Albert's. What had taken command of Reverend Beveridge's tongue this time? From the pulpit flowed a baldly lunatic stream-of-consciousness oratory on "Sins of Our Youth."

"Brothers and sisters of Jesus," cried Reverend Beveridge, raising his outstretched arms, "turn back to the days of your youth and examine yourselves. What do you see? Cancers, brothers and sisters, ugly festering growths that tainted your once-pure soul. Now, about half of you seated here in this church today are boomers like me. We, my brothers and sisters, have been the worst sinners of all. Just think back and you cannot help but agree with me when I say that the boomers of the world committed humanity's most heinous sins."

Sue Ann blinked. What had the preacher just said? She listened more closely.

"Let me cite two examples," Reverend Beveridge went on, "from my own wayward youth."

Albert leaned over and whispered to Sue Ann, "This should be good."

Sue Ann scowled.

"As a young man," said Reverend Beveridge, "I was a practising anarchist. Yes, just like those anarchists who today are blowing up our dams. I won't go into details. But this was a sin, and even then I knew that someday God would punish me. Yet I continued sinning, even more grievously, during the postwar era, under the influence of the free-love counterculture, and then even more so under the heady euphoria of the yuppie eighties. Like so many youths of my era, I had abandoned the virtue of self-control and had embarked upon a life of…well, sheer indulgence. Oh, what sins we boomers have committed.''

Reverend Beveridge gripped the lectern. ''The time has come, my brothers and sisters, to confess the greatest, most heinous crime of my youth.''

The congregation stirred restlessly.

Sue Ann said, ''Traitor,'' loudly enough for Albert to overhear.

''I hereby confess to you, my beloved congregation, that during my foolish youth, I participated in the antinuclear protests at Hanford. Not only did I participate in the peaceful protests; I actually committed a criminal act. Yes I did, and I was not alone. Fortunately for me and my coconspirators, the bomb did not go off.'' Reverend Beveridge smiled sheepishly. ''The fuze failed. Heh-heh. Seems my guardian angel was working overtime.''

A buzz rippled through the congregation. Mabel Fobia turned around and stared at Sue Ann. Sue Ann spit out angrily, ''What are you gaping at, you old coot?''

Mabel turned back around.

The Reverend Beveridge clasped his hands together and bowed his head. ''Youth, my lambs, is foolish. Today, as a parent and, yes, even a grandparent, I have come to see and repent the errors of my youthful days. In maturity, I have asked the Lord for forgiveness, and He has truly forgiven me.''

Reverend Beveridge surveyed the squirming congregation. When his eyes fell on Sue Ann, he paused and looked straight at her. ''What about you?'' he asked, and the congregation mistook his question as rhetorical.

''Have you sought forgiveness for the sins of your youth? Have you made amends for the foolish actions you committed during your postadolescent period? Have you? Ah, I think some of you have not.''

Sue Ann squirmed under the preacher's stare. Albert whispered, ''What the hell is he talking about?''

Mabel Fobia turned around again, and Albert thought she sneered at Sue Ann. Albert glared at Fobia. ''Now, what's wrong with her?'' he asked Sue Ann, but Sue Ann wasn't listening. Albert noted a tightening of his wife's jaw, an overall stiffness that bothered him.

From the pulpit, Reverend Beveridge now issued a challenge. ''Those of you who sinned in your youth, who have never asked Jesus for forgiveness, come forward now. Come forward. Come to the front of this church! Let us pray together for forgiveness for the old sins of youth. Come, my fellow sinners, come!''

Soon, the front of the church was packed with aging boomers, many weeping. Albert could not believe his eyes, ''Would you look at that?'' he said to Sue Ann. ''You'd think this was a Pentecostal church. I'm telling you, cookie, we've got to replace this madman.''

Then a curious thing happened. Mabel Fobia stepped out of her pew, came around, grabbed Sue Ann by the arm, and began dragging her toward the front of the church. Sue Ann resisted at first, and Albert said, ''Here now, Mabel. Cut that out.'' Then he saw Sue Ann go limp, and Mabel no longer had to lead her. Sue Ann was moving on her own toward the other weeping boomers. Mabel watched Sue Ann approach the Communion rail, watched as she knelt. Sue Ann wept when the Reverend Beveridge placed his hands on her head and offered her solace.

After the service, Albert refused to go for doughnuts. Sue Ann didn't speak on the drive home. Albert never asked Sue Ann about the sins of her youth. He wouldn't have to, because they would soon be exposed to a stunned congregation.

BY SUNDAY AFTERNOON, word had leaked out. Television and newspapers were reporting rumors of a presidential visit to Hanford Reach. By Sunday evening, the Republicans had retaliated with a press release about Jenny Pickforth's planned appearance at Grand Coulee Dam. Both the hopeful incumbent and the presidential hopeful would appear on the same day—Thursday—at the same hour—2:00 p.m.—on the Columbia River, slightly more than one hundred miles apart (as the crow flies). Both presidential candidates would speak to the river issue, would address the proposal to breach the dams on the Columbia and Snake rivers in order to restore salmon runs, and would state unequivocally their positions on the matter.

No one was more thrilled with the local news coverage than Albert Denny and his Republican pals, including the editor of the *Kettle Falls Gazette* and the owners of the Spokane network affiliates. Sue Ann might not have approved of local coverage of the upcoming events, which mostly smeared the Dambusters and all but called Sue Ann and Fritz ecoterrorists. But she pointed out to Albert, in an unnecessarily triumphant air, as far as Albert was concerned, that west of the Cascades, in Seattle, where real power worked its wonders, the news media was heavily promoting the president's Hanford appearance and playing down the Pickforth plan.

As might be expected, dinnertime in the Denny household quickly degenerated into a hateful ritual, steeped in coy innuendo and reeking of biting sarcasm.

FRITZ WAS FIRED UP and Tiffie got sick of him hanging on the bar, bragging about imminent ecological justice all the while sucking peach schnapps like mom's milk. Finally, in exasperation, Tiffie grabbed Fritz's keys, marched across the street, unlocked the Dambusters office, returned to Prospector's, and said to Fritz, "That's your office, over there. Now get the you-know-what out of here."

Fritz went to work.

Besides the eco hoi polloi, Fritz counted among his supporters numerous news reporters and multimillionaires, including a guilt-ridden society maven, a timber heir, and a sprinkle of Microsoft royalty. Dambusters had money and media, and Fritz felt confident that this visit by President Benson would prove the decisive moment in his career. Swept away by thousands of his constituents cheering him on, the president would certainly declare his support for Fritz and his Dambusters' cause. How could it be otherwise?

On Monday morning, Fritz was sitting at his desk, reflecting on years of struggle finally reaching fruition, when the phone rang. Sue Ann said it was urgent that he meet with her right away. Fritz sighed. Sue Ann had a paranoid streak. Nonetheless, Fritz agreed to meet Sue Ann, and within minutes, she arrived at his door in the Grand View Inn.

"This is serious," Sue Ann said as she swept into the room. "We can't have a Pickforth event. She'll steal all of Barry's thunder."

"You talk like you know the president personally."

Sue Ann smiled. "I do. Personally." Sue Ann felt a craving coming on, but when she lit a cigarette, Fritz made her go out on the balcony to smoke.

"I need to work, Sue Ann. I can't work surrounded by secondhand smoke."

By the time Sue Ann had finished her cigarette, she had an idea. "Fritz, honey," she said when she came back inside, "I'm going to call the White House."

"Oh, sure you are." Fritz laughed and popped a Tic Tac into his mouth. "And who's going to answer the phone?"

"The president, of course."

Fritz listened, as Sue Ann outlined her plan. When she had finished, he said, "Why, Sue Ann Denny, aren't you just the biggest smarty-pants."

ON MONDAY EVENING, Darla and Gerald excused themselves from Sue Ann and Albert's incessant political sniping, saying they were going to spend a few nights hiking Cristina Lake, up across the border in British Columbia. They left the house before dinner, Sue Ann harping at their backs about camping out in the Unknown's territory.

"It's not a superstition, Darla," Sue Ann shouted as the young couple headed for their van. "The Unknown has been sighted by credible witnesses. It exists and it's dangerous. Oh, go on then. Get yourselves killed."

Sue Ann watched Gerald and Darla drive out of the vineyard. She saw the van turn left at the vineyard gate and head north on the highway leading toward the Canadian border. When it was out of sight, she said, "Little tramp." But no one heard her.

At dinner that night Albert brought up Jenny Pickforth again. Sue Ann had heard enough about Jenny Pickforth, and she told Albert so. Albert laughed in Sue Ann's face, sealing his fate. That night, he slept fitfully in the guest room, on a bed that creaked when he tried to comfort himself.

ON TUESDAY, Venus rose before dawn and realized she could walk again. The blisters had healed and the pain was finally tolerable without the soothing benefits of cheap scotch. Even the broken toe felt better. She dressed, then woke Song from a deep sleep. They carried two backpacks and a picnic cooler out to the Buick and loaded them through the tailgate. Venus noticed the neighbor in the next trailer peeping out his window. She waved and limped back into the Airstream. When she had finished packing a bag of groceries, she carried it out to the Buick; then Song hooked up the Airstream and they pulled slowly out of the trailer park, heading north, the trailer snoop noted, toward the Canadian border.

At Island Rock, Song turned back south on a small road that paralleled Onion Creek. There was a campground at Onion Creek. Song checked in and they pulled the Airstream into their assigned campsite.

Once the Airstream was parked, Song and Venus drove

away in the Buick, heading south through Palmers, where they picked up Highway 395. At Addy, they turned off the main highway and followed a one-lane road southwest to Cedonia, where the road ended at the banks of the Columbia River, some thirty miles (as the crow flies) upriver from Grand Coulee Dam. By now, the sun hung high overhead, a sweltering fireball that parched the dry plains and made the river water irresistible.

Venus shed her dumpy cotton Kay Lynn dress and plunged into the river. Song went after her, chasing her upstream until he caught her with one arm and dragged her flailing body back to shore where they lay on the riverbank, beneath the torrid sky, drinking cold beer to quench their thirst. They both knew that this was the last hour of carefree play, the last moments before terrible danger, that they were in the last days of wedded bliss as Juneau and Kay Lynn Jones.

Song rolled over and watched Venus. She lay just a few inches from him, her eyes closed, and he could hear her soft breathing. He reached tentatively, lightly touched her cheek-bone, tracing its contour, feeling his fingers tingle against her soft skin. He turned her face to his, willing her eyes open. When she blinked and focused on him, he saw his own re-flection in her eyes. Her lips parted. Song leaned in, his mouth ready. She said, "Miss Delicious is a lesbian."

Annoyed, Song said, "How in the hell do you know that?"

"Bet a hundred dollars." The Firecracker felt her head spin and realized that she was tipsy. Too much *cerveza* clouds the *cabeza*.

"You're on. Now I'd like to kiss you."

"Song…"

"Venus…" His voice was teasing, taunting, tantalizing.

"I've had too much to drink. I…I'll never even remember it."

"I'll tell you about it later."

"We have to convince Olson…."

"I know," Song answered just before the first real kiss.

They lay beneath a blazing blue sky, their bodies still damp from the river frolic, their brains half-baked by the sun, she at least half-inebriated by the beer. She should never drink alcohol, especially not out in the sun, she realized. If this lovemaking was actually to occur, she wanted to savor every moment. Now she couldn't even remember her own name.

Maybe it was heat stroke. Or maybe it was something else, some long-stifled urge about to be unleashed.

She felt his mouth against hers, then his body pressing against hers, then…a blank. Later, he would tell her all about it, and she would listen, transfixed by his vivid descriptions, wondering if he was making it all up just to scare her.

TWENTY-FOUR

In the twentieth century, salmon, a fish that had existed
in abundance for thousands of years, became a threatened and endangered species within the space of sixty
years. The sudden decline of salmon populations was
caused primarily by human encroachment on the fish's
territory, human pollution of rivers and oceans, and humankind's over fishing the stock. The anthropocentric
solution to salmon conservation was fish farms, where
imported Atlantic salmon eggs and sperm were mixed
artificially by the intervention of human hands. The
hatcheries produced millions of fingerlings, but the
farm-raised Atlantic species differed from the wild Pacific forebears, lacking the wiliness, fortitude, and even
the flavor of wild Pacific salmon. When federal and state
salmon hatchery officials realized that they had produced too many "hatchery salmon," that these fish were
intermingling with the wild salmon, thus weakening the
wild stock, the officials ordered millions of hatchery-
bred adult salmon clubbed to death. This practice of
clubbing to death tens of thousands of human-bred
salmon continues in several locations along the Columbia and Snake rivers.

THE TWO HOUSEBOATS had been floated down the Columbia,
and now were anchored in a cove twelve miles upriver from
Fort Spokane. The cove was partially obscured from the river

by a high dam constructed by the beavers of Inchelum, and
not at all intended for human exploitation. But the beavers'
dam provided a convenient curtain for the houseboats to hide
behind. Passing vessels would not be likely to look beyond
the high dam and notice the two water-worthy sheds. Even
if they were spotted, they would be nothing unusual. Some
crazy anglers making their way down the river in catamarans,
looking for salmon. No one would ever guess the houseboats
were packed with highly explosive chemicals, enough power
and might, if Gerald and Song had calculated correctly, to
blast a generous fissure in Grand Coulee Dam.

Toward evening, the blazing sun sank lower in the sky and
the hot, bone-dry air barely stirred. Song and Venus lay sleeping beneath a scrubby pine, entwined on a plaid blanket that
Kay Lynn Jones had bought on sale at the mall. As they
slept, a robust beaver climbed up onto the riverbank and observed them.

They seemed harmless enough to Ludmilla, queen of the
beavers, but she was taking no chances. Swiftly, she slid back
into the river and swam downstream to her squadron to report
the results of her reconnaissance. Every unexplained appearance of the enemy on the river had to be taken into account.
The Ludmilla beavers and the beavers of Inchelum deliberated.

Out of the quietude came a soft purring, the sound of an
outboard motor coming off the river. Venus stirred, woke
Song. They dressed and went down to the water and waited.
After a few minutes, they saw a small powerboat cruise
around a bend in the river, Gerald at the helm and Darla
seated in the bow, peering through binoculars. Song waved.

Gerald brought the boat up to the riverbank, and when he
stepped ashore, he could feel the sun-scalded earth through
his boots. No earth should feel this hot, especially not a riverbank. Darla followed Gerald up the scrubby riverbank and
the four conspirators sat on the plaid blanket beneath the pine
tree. Venus, no longer limping, walked over to the Buick and

brought back a thermos of coffee and a Tab for Gerald. Gerald rolled a joint and said, "We'll go over the routine one more time, to be sure each of you understands your responsibilities. Kay Lynn, you go first."

Venus said, "Tonight I drive the Buick into Grand Coulee. I'll arrive just as the laser light show on the dam's spillway begins. Since the public areas are closed off, with the exception of the public parking lot, I will join other tourists in the parking lot. There will be people but no cars allowed in the lot during the laser show, so I'll stash the Buick on a side street nearby. I've checked out the scene. There are plenty of side streets leading into the residential area of town. The Buick will blend right in with the tourists' vehicles. The light show lasts for just under half an hour before recycling. At the moment of recycling, there is darkness for about forty-five seconds. In that time, I will disappear down the bank. At the bottom of the bank, I will be eye-to-blades with the turbines on the east side. I'll plant explosives near the turbines and secure a timing device. By the time of the next laser show recycle, I'll reappear in the crowd, then return to the car and drive south three blocks. Just before the bridge that crosses over the river, I pick up Juneau. We continue driving south to Steamboat Rock State Park where we wait for Gerald at the trailhead near the northern entrance to the park."

Gerald turned to Song.

Song said, "At dusk on Wednesday I tow the houseboats, tied together, downriver as far as the southern tip of the Colville Reservation. Hide them in the cove where we camped that first night."

Gerald passed Song some half-smoked reefer and watched while Song inhaled. Song continued. "Thursday, just before daybreak, I'll sink them and tow them as far as the last turn before the spillway, anchor them, secure time-release devices, then head uphill to the ridge on the south side of the dam. I wait under the transformer towers until the second recycle of the laser light show, then wait fifteen more minutes. Then I plant the explosives on the tower closest to the dam and book down to the highway, where Kay Lynn picks me up at the bridge. We'll camp upriver from where I sunk the houseboats. Then Thursday morning, we'll prepare to detonate the explosives."

Darla sat lotus, massaging her stockinged feet, staring at the reservoir. Gerald didn't need to read minds to know Darla had gone into one of her funks. He leaned over and shook her. She blinked a couple times, then said, "My turn? Oh, well, here goes. On Thursday at two p.m., I'll drive into Grand Coulee, stop at a phone booth, and call in a bomb threat. Once the area is cleared of people, Juneau will detonate the underwater explosives on the upside of the dam. The blasts on both sides of the spillway will occur simultaneously and cause a fracture in the dam, enough to cause a serious leak, which will slowly build into a flood…. Of course, this all happens after everyone's off the dam. And the towns down along the river will have enough advance warning to evacuate, and I'll be the first one out of there. I guaran-damn-tee you I'll be hoofing it."

Gerald said, "After she makes that phone call, there will be a signal given. First, a single bomb will detonate. Be ready for it. When you hear that explosion, then each of you reacts. Understand?"

Venus could see that something bothered the big guy. Something about her and Juneau. Maybe he was thinking that they were different somehow. Maybe they seemed a bit softer, a bit too relaxed. Gerald stared at Venus. She looked him straight in the eye, didn't blink. He looked at Song. Song's eyebrow twitched slightly.

Gerald said, "During the past three months, while working inside the dam, I have placed explosives in strategic structural spots…."

"Honey, I never knew you worked in the—"

"Shut up."

Darla stifled a "yowser."

Gerald continued. "These will detonate last, at the proper time."

"When's that?" Song said. "The 'proper time'?"

"Never mind. It doesn't concern you. You just pay attention to your job. I'm paying you to do your job, not to question how I do mine."

Song said, "Exactly where are the explosives planted?"

"That's not your concern."

Song lit a Marlboro, blew out smoke. "It concerns all of us if anyone dies," he said. "We agreed that we'd make every effort not to cause injury or death. So I think we have a right to know that you intend to stick by our agreement. You asked me to design the overall explosives placement. Now you're telling us you acted independently."

Gerald didn't like this challenge to his leadership, to his personal plan.

"Tell you what, Jones," he said after thinking it over. "You take my cell phone. You detonate the interior explosives. You make the call." He held out his cell phone, the phone linked to the charges planted inside the dam. Song shook his head.

"Take it," demanded Gerald. Because if Juneau took the detonator, he'd know Juneau was the enemy.

"Hey, dude," Song said, "I just want your assurance that you won't blow up the interior while people are inside. We agreed that this would all happen simultaneously, after everyone's been evacuated, including the workers inside the structure. We still on the same page?"

Gerald felt queasy. Something was wrong, but he couldn't figure out what.

Song sensed Gerald's discomfort and eased off slightly. He said, "You told us when we first agreed to this plan that others are involved. Where will they be when the dam blows? What will they be doing?"

Gerald said, "You don't need to know. Anyway, I've decided to change a few things. Juneau, I'm taking you off the houseboats.''

Song could see that the big guy didn't trust him. But it was too late in the game to get rid of the Joneses. Gerald needed Juneau, and he needed Kay Lynn. He needed them more than he needed the Denny girl. Coolly, Song smoked and, through the haze, said offhandedly, "Why the change?"

But Gerald didn't reply. He was studying Venus's face. Song glanced at Venus, did a double take. One of her hazel contacts was missing again. One green eye exposed. Song winked at her, reached up and rubbed his left eye.

She instantly understood. She wanted to reach up and massage her eyeball, feel around for the contact lens, but that would be worse, caving under the big man's scrutiny.

Darla said, "Honey, is something wrong?"

Gerald blinked and said no, nothing was wrong.

How had she lost the contact lens? Was it still somewhere in her eye, or had it fallen out somewhere? When they were swimming? Making love? If they *had* made love…. Gerald was staring at her, Song rubbing his own eye, Darla carping like an old fish.

Suddenly, Song said, "Bald eagle. Up in that pine."

Darla turned to look where Song indicated by nodding his head. "Oh look, there he is. Look, honey," Darla said breathlessly. "Isn't he, like, the biggest bird you've ever seen?"

A bald eagle. Gerald had to see it. For a fleeting moment, he glanced away from Venus's face, turned to see the bird in the tree.

Frantically, Venus rolled her eyes. She dared not reach up to touch them. That motion would definitely tip off the big guy, make him more nervous. She blinked hard a few times and the lens fell back into place. When Gerald turned around to look at her, both her eyes were hazel again. She didn't flinch under his steady gaze. She smiled to divert his focus, and it worked.

Maybe the big guy decided the green eye had, after all,

been a trick of light. All along, she'd had hazel eyes. Maybe he'd been imagining it, making a green eye in his mind. Things like that happened, especially under pressure.

Darla said, "Look how he's watching us," meaning the bald eagle. "You'd think we were his prey."

Gerald said, "I've changed my mind."

"About what, hon?" Darla squinted, confused.

Gerald turned to Venus and said, "Kay Lynn, I don't trust you as far as I can throw you." He turned to Darla. "You'll carry the cell phone detonator."

Venus didn't react, just looked him straight in the eye. She couldn't read his mind, but her intuition told her he had decided to eliminate the Joneses. Maybe not now. But very soon. When they had served their purpose.

When darkness fell, they decamped. Before splitting up, Gerald said, "Remember that at all times you are being watched. You aren't the only soldiers in my army. You're being followed and watched. Is that clear?"

On the river, Song climbed into the powerboat. A bright moon illuminated the shore. From where he sat in the powerboat, Song watched Venus walk to the Buick. He heard it start up; then he saw the Buick back up, turn around, and drive away from their campsite. As soon as Venus had pulled out, Song saw the silver Lexus come out of a blind and follow Venus's car. Which meant one thing that Gerald had right.

They weren't working alone.

After Venus was gone, Gerald and Darla disappeared into the woods. Song guessed they had hidden the van in there somewhere. He watched from the river. He never actually saw them leave, but he heard their engine turn over, and through the stillness, he heard the van's tires crunching against the pine needles on the ground. Song started up the powerboat and puttered away.

When they had disappeared, the bald eagle flapped its

powerful wings and took flight. Going somewhere. Maybe to Tsagigla'al, the River Watcher.

THE PRESIDENT OF the United States is entitled to change his mind. Upon learning of Jenny Pickforth's plans to upstage his appearance at Hanford by her own appearance at Grand Coulee Dam, the president, at the suggestion of Sue Ann Denny, ordered his appearance moved from Hanford to Grand Coulee Dam. He could do that; he had the power. If Jenny Pickforth wanted to compete with him, she could find another spot along the river. This change of plans caused chaos at the White House, at Secret Service headquarters, at Dambusters headquarters in Kettle Falls, and at Grand Coulee Dam itself. But the president's orders must be honored. Meanwhile, at Jenny Pickforth's campaign headquarters, her handlers huddled. They needed a new plan, and they needed it fast. One of Pickforth's handlers knew a man named Albert Denny, a wealthy eastern Washington rancher, the local Republican party chair. Maybe Albert Denny would have a suggestion. "Call this Albert person," demanded Jenny Pickforth, and her lackey complied.

Albert was in the vintner's cottage, consulting with Jean Paul, when his cell phone rang. Albert had been hoping to hear from Darla. Sightings of the Unknown were on the rise. Albert reached over Jean Paul, groping for his cell phone. When he held it to his ear and heard the purring on the other end, Albert Denny experienced the special sensation that accompanies awe.

His heartbeat accelerated. His chest swelled. His eyes popped wide open and the pupils dilated. His breath paused in its journey to the brain. Jean Paul thought that Albert looked like a man having a religious epiphany. Then Albert began breathing again. Covering the mouthpiece, he whispered to Jean Paul, "It's Jenny Pickforth!"

Jean Paul, affecting a speck of pride by association, heaved a world-weary sigh and reached for his wineglass.

TWENTY-FIVE

I have lived! The American Continent may now sink
under the sea, for I have taken the best that it yields,
and the best was neither dollars, love, nor real estate.
—Rudyard Kipling, after fishing the Columbia River
and catching a creel-load of salmon in 1889

WHEN SEVERAL HUNDRED western Washington Dambusters
supporters traveled en masse over the Cascades and into the
scablands and coulees to bear witness to their nation's president's call for salmon rescue, the locals got nervous. Very
nervous. Across the street from the Dambusters headquarters,
Tiffie stood outside Prospector's and watched the burgeoning
crowds of salmon supporters. It was early Thursday morning,
already sweltering, and Tiffie wore a skimpy halter top over
a little pair of shorts, and a pair of high-heeled espadrilles.
Sipping latte from a Cougars mug, she watched as Fritz
Fowler greeted hordes of supporters, some carrying wide ban-
ners proclaiming salmon war, others handing out colorful leaf-
lets, a waste of good trees, in Tiffie's opinion. Tiffie rolled
her eyes at the sight of a fat man wearing a salmon outfit;
then she noticed a cute dude wearing a Dambusters T-shirt,
and she noticed that he noticed the homegrown babe across
the street. He waved.

Tiffie pretended not to notice, but she kept one eye on him
and the other peeled for fresh prey. The truth was, Tiffie had
a bad crush on Juneau Jones, and she harbored hope that he

would soon dump that scrawny wife and carry her, Tiffie, off to Tulsa or Shanghai or wherever. But she hadn't seen Juneau now for two or three days, and her libido was restless. She was scanning the crowd of Dambusters when she saw Sue Ann Denny come out of the group's headquarters and step onto a small stage erected on the public sidewalk. There was a microphone on the stage and Sue Ann grasped it and brought it perilously close to her lips. This gesture sent a small tingle through Tiffie, and then Sue Ann Denny addressed the masses.

"It's a fine day for Salmon!" Sue Ann declared.

The crowd roared approval.

"And it's a fine day for breaching the dams."

The crowd went wild.

"Let us take our struggle to the river." Sue Ann sounded every bit like the Reverend Fred Beveridge, as far as Tiffie was concerned. The crowd cheered and whistled. Sue Ann rambled on until Fritz Fowler appeared and wrestled the microphone away.

Big Fritz was at his most charismatic, Tiffie observed with mild amusement. For some reason, she had always thought of Fritz as having a secret dark side. Why, she wasn't sure. Something about the way he looked in plaid shirts. Like, unnatural. Now Fritz enthralled the crowd with his capacious address, his charismatic gestures, his charm. Bo-o-oring. Tiffie yawned and slinked inside Prospector's. She was wiping the bar when a bald man wearing some kind of uniform came in and ordered a diet Coke.

"You here for the president's visit?" Tiffie asked him out of politeness. He wasn't attractive—at least he didn't push Tiffie's buttons, but she could be civil to anyone.

"That's happening way down at Grand Coulee," said Olson.

"Well, duh," Tiffie answered defensively. "Think I don't know that? I know that. But this crowd out here is headed down there in a caravan. They're going to follow the river road all the way to Grand Coulee. Can you imagine how dumb that is? I thought maybe you were traveling with them, to enforce the law or something like that. You are a cop, aren't you?''

"Fish and Wildlife Service.'' Olson sipped his diet Coke.

"Oh, I get it,'' Tiffie joked. "You came along to protect the salmon from the salmon killers. I'm one of them, by the way.''

"What's that supposed to mean?''

"I'm a native, born and raised in eastern Washington. I'm against breaching the dams, or whatever it's called. The hell with salmon. We need water here. How are we supposed to survive without water? Anyway, there are other solutions to saving salmon.''

In the back of the saloon, Prospector, overseeing a card game, heard Tiffie talking about salmon. Shuffling his marked deck, Prospector glanced up and said, "You go, girl.'' Then he went back to the poker game. The Fish and Wildlife agent finished his diet Coke and paid.

Tiffie said, "Well then, what are you doing in K Falls?''

"We've got a beaver problem over on the reservoir,'' Olson told her. Then he left.

Tiffie went over to Prospector. "Are there beavers on the reservoir?'' she asked him.

Prospector grinned. "Hell, no,'' he said. "Hasn't been a beaver on the reservoir since back when the old salmon chief fished the falls.''

Tiffie looked at Prospector and said, "Do you believe in karma?''

"Hell no.''

"I do. I think karma is all around us. Like air, only man-made.''

Prospector looked up at Tiffie. She was standing beside him, her slim hand resting on the back of his chair. He could smell her perfume, or bath oil, or whatever it was. It smelled nice. Tiffie always smelled nice. She was a clean girl, well groomed. Good for business. And she was a local. Prospector said, "Go make your karma somewhere else."

Tiffie went back to the bar. Several Dambusters supporters came in and ordered drinks all at once. They were an unruly bunch, and, Tiffie thought, they were arrogant. They didn't tip and they didn't say "Thank you, miss," not even, "Thanks," except for one of them, another Fish and Wildlife agent—at least he wore the same uniform as the bald guy. Only this one was gorgeous. Almost as sexy as Juneau Jones. This one had a name and he told her what it was. "Sweetwater. Eric Sweetwater."

"Sweetwater," Tiffie repeated. "You must be Indian."

"Quinault," said Sweetwater. "By half."

Tiffie batted her eyes. "I'm half goddess," she said.

Sweetwater leaned across the bar. "What's the other half?"

Tiffie glanced around at the other customers. "Come back later," she said to Sweetwater, "and maybe I'll show you."

In ten minutes, Tiffie had run out of bottled water and patience. Sweetwater was long gone and no one else even partially sexy had appeared. Just riled-up river radicals demanding to be served. Finally, Tiffie lost her temper and screamed, "Take your badass attitudes and get the hell out of my saloon!"

Prospector glanced up at Tiffie and winked.

Outside the saloon, the crowds began boarding buses. The clamor annoyed Tiffie, so when the door opened, she wheeled around to snap at another Dambuster. But it wasn't one of them.

The girl was a local. Tiffie remembered that she had come in once with Juneau, and that she had overheard them talking and heard the girl say her name was Carla. But something about the girl bothered Tiffie. Tiffie was sure she had seen her before the time she came in with Juneau. Where? When?

Now the girl approached the bar, smiled faintly at Tiffie, and ordered a margarita. She took the margarita over to a table by the windows, where she sipped the drink while staring out at the chaos. Tiffie stood behind the bar, pretending to work, racking her brains for an elusive memory.

The girl took out a cell phone and placed a call. From this distance, Tiffie couldn't hear more than a few snatches of conversation. It was a short conversation, and the only phrases Tiffie could decipher were "vineyard files," and "ancient diamond." Tiffie couldn't be sure what she was talking about, but suddenly she was certain of one thing. Now she remembered where she'd seen the girl before. Of course. How could she have forgotten so soon?

Tiffie sauntered over to the table where the girl Juneau called Carla sat sucking a margarita, staring out the window. Tiffie cleared her throat and the girl looked up at her. Tiffie said, "Hey, Darla."

Darla flushed and said, "My name is Carla."

"No it's not. You're Darla Denny. We went to K Falls High together." Tiffie held out her hand, but the girl didn't want to shake it. She shrank away from Tiffie.

Tiffie said, "Tiffie Marin. The cheerleader. Remember?"

The girl shook her head and stood up. "I have to go," she said, and brushed past Tiffie.

As she fled, Tiffie called out, "You stay away from Juneau Jones…Darla."

AT 8:00 A.M., a great caravan of cars and buses and vans left Kettle Falls, heading south along the river road. The drive to Grand Coulee would take three hours. The group would pause for a rest and rally at Fort Spokane and then follow a detour to Coulee Dam National Recreation Area, where they would bivouac with more Dambusters from western Washington. By noon, they would all be gathered at the public parking lot near the spillway on Grand Coulee Dam. President Benson would arrive around 1:00 p.m., his address scheduled for 2:00 p.m. Time enough to work up a festive atmosphere.

On one of the caravan's buses, the passengers seemed more subdued than the other Dambusters when Fritz Fowler jumped aboard to rouse spirits. Fritz had a funny feeling about this busload. They claimed to be a group of anarchists from Eugene, but they were too clean-cut, too mild-mannered, and several were over thirty. They didn't want trouble, they had told the rally organizers, just wanted to support the cause by adding their numbers to the crowd. The leader's name was Dottie, and her assistant was named Sparks. They seemed nice enough, and they promised not to engage in rabble-rousing, so Fritz decided they were all right. He rejoined Sue Ann in the lead vehicle. Once Fritz had left the anarchists' bus, Olson and his assembled agents took out their weapons and loaded them.

Olson had capitulated when Paganelli presented him with evidence that the dead body that surfaced in the Priest Rapids Dam explosion was not that of the fish counter. In fact, the fish counter's body had been discovered stuffed into an oil drum and rolled over the cliff into the river. The other body belonged to an itinerant kayaker who had suffered the bad luck of riding the explosion's crest. This evidence finally convinced Olson to take a chance. Maybe Diamond and Song were right. Maybe. He'd at least provide the backup, and gleefully witness their chagrin when they realized the so-called mad bomber was nothing more than a mastermind of boastful lies. Olson was convinced he'd have the last laugh.

ON THE LEAD Dambusters bus, Sue Ann felt ecstatic. Not once during the long downriver journey did she think of Albert, or Darla, or even Gerald, for that matter. Sue Ann could think only of the salmon she was rescuing, and this heroic vision imbued her with a particular glow. As the lead vehicle drew closer to the evil concrete salmon killer, Sue Ann's soul experienced a heightened sense of spiritual correctness as a vision of her past life prophesied her present raison d'être.

She had been Kin-Ka-Now-Kla's squaw. Queen of the

salmon people. Sue Ann Denny, Queen Kin-Ka-Now-Kla re-incarnated, was destined to rescue her piscine subjects from the evil jaws of maladjusted progress.

As they pulled into Coulee National Recreation Area, Fritz noted that Sue Ann had fallen into a swoon. "You okay, Sue Ann?" Fritz asked her, patting her folded hands.

Sue Ann, her eyes closed, inhaled deeply, held her breath a couple seconds, exhaled slowly, and said, "The slug was right."

TWENTY-SIX

TIFFIE WAS REARRANGING her beehive when Mabel Fobia walked into Prospector's Saloon like she owned the place. In all the time Tiffie had worked for Prospector, she'd never seen Miss Fobia in the joint. All Tiffie really knew about Mabel Fobia was that the old coot worked behind the film-processing counter at the Hartell's in Colville that she had run the Kettle Falls Historical Society office before it burned down, that she was a spinster who lived alone in a neat little clapboard house on Harmony Lane, and that she might be related to the Shouter. That was all Tiffie knew and all she really cared to know about Mabel Fobia. The old ninny held no intrigue for Tiffie. In fact, ever since the time Tiffie first met Miss Fobia at Sunday school at the First Methodist Church, Tiffie had vowed never to become a spinster herself. All during high school, the girls of K Falls had a saying: "Be careful, or you'll end up like Fobia." So when Mabel marched into Prospector's, Tiffie might have been mildly interested in her presence, but still, her own beehive interested her more. She was trying to make the beehive into a free-fall scrungy mass like she'd seen a few hours ago on one of the Dambusters supporters, but the beehive had too much gel and stiffness and wasn't cooperating. Tiffie wasn't all that thrilled when Mabel walked straight up to the counter and demanded attention. She clipped her beehive back into place and said, "What can I do fer ya?"

"Where's that boyfriend of yours, that Juneau Jones fellow?" Mabel asked Tiffie.

"I'm sure I don't know where Juneau is," Tiffie replied, pretending that she wasn't interested in married men. "And he's not my boyfriend. He is a customer of this establishment, as far as I'm concerned. I've never even kissed him."

"I don't care if you've given him twelve blow jobs," Mabel snapped. "You tell me where I can find him. It's an emergency."

Tiffie hung her head and made doe eyes at Mabel. "Oh yeah? Well, I still don't know where he is. And I don't do blow jobs."

Mabel rapped her bony knuckles on the bar. "Get me a Canadian. Double. Straight up."

Tiffie got out the Canadian, poured Mabel's double shot. What next? she thought, watching Mabel toss back the whiskey. Mabel tapped her finger on the shot glass. "Hit me again." Tiffie did. Mabel tossed it back, threw a fistful of Sacajaweas on the bar, and left the saloon. Tiffie watched her until she had disappeared down the block; then she attacked the beehive problem. It wasn't easy being the town vixen.

Outside Prospector's, Mabel drove her Mercury away from the curb and peeled rubber up the highway, taking the turnoff to the old Elias Fobia Cabin. The cabin was boarded up, as usual. Mabel used her key to unlock a padlock on the front door. She pulled the bolt out and went inside. Through the open doorway, bright sun splashed across the cabin's single room, exposing dust and cobwebs.

Mabel sniffed the air, located some odor she didn't much care for. Was it marijuana? She thought so. She looked at the fireplace, now an empty, cold chamber where once had gathered the first white settlers on the banks of Kettle Falls, where Elias Fobia had smoked a pipe with Chief Kin-Ka-Now-Kla and then shared a First Salmon Ceremony. Mabel reached out and touched the wood mantel, where once had stood a crockery pitcher filled with fresh wildflowers and two kerosene lamps that lit up the cabin on nights when Elias

Fobia sat writing down the Indian legends as told to him by Kin-Ka-Now-Kla and others of the Kettle People. Now just look at this neglected historic treasure, she thought.

Mabel didn't see physical evidence, but she could tell that the sacred site had been defiled. She could smell the defilement; she could taste it and feel it. Something evil had invaded the Elias Fobia Cabin. Mabel got down on her hands and knees beside the hearth and pulled up a floorboard.

In spite of her arthritis, she managed to drag a heavy cardboard box up and out of a hole in the cabin floor. She started to open it, but then she remembered the Shouter. She carried the box to her car, locked up the cabin, and drove to Harmony Lane. The clock on her dashboard said 9:00 a.m., and the sun overhead agreed.

On Harmony Lane, parked outside the Shouter's cottage, Mabel placed the box beside her on the Mercury's front seat. The box's top was coated with dust, and Mabel coughed as she removed it and reached inside.

The box was stuffed with old papers, photographs, and news clips. She rummaged for several minutes, then pulled out a stack of clippings. One by one, she read them, in order of dates, beginning with the oldest clip and moving forward.

The date was July 11, twenty-three years ago. The *Kettle Falls Crier* headline read WOMAN PROTESTOR KILLED AT HANFORD NUCLEAR FACILITY. There was a picture of the woman accompanying the article. She was one of those hippie girls, with her long hair and headband and dangling earrings. The caption said her name was Moonbeam. She was smiling and holding up a picket sign that said STOP NUCLEAR POLLUTION. She was pretty, except for a slightly receding chin. Beside Moonbeam in the photo stood a young woman who reminded Mabel of the wild men of Borneo. She had crazed eyes and her hair was teased out into a white girl's imitation of an Afro. The young woman wore a buckskin jacket with fringe and looked more male than female, as far as Mabel was concerned. The newspaper identified her only as "Wild Woman," and most people never learned her real name. But Mabel knew.

On Moonbeam's other side stood a clean-cut fellow, with a neatly trimmed beard and a professional aura. That was "the Judge." Mabel remembered the Judge, and she had to snicker out loud thinking about the irony of where he was today.

Behind Moonbeam stood a third man, tall, slender. They called him "the Reverend." No one ever knew his real name. Except Mabel.

This unlikely quartet, known as the Free Spirit Congregation, according to the July 11 issue of the *Kettle Falls Crier,* had a history of traveling throughout the Pacific Northwest, causing havoc and mayhem. Ecoterrorists even before the term had been coined. But no one was listening, nothing was changing for the better, and gradually a whiff of violent protest seduced first Wild Woman, then the Reverend, and then the Judge. Only Moonbeam argued against violence, but the others threatened to kill her and her baby if she ever told.

One night as the Free Spirits fire-walked on a high-desert ridge, Moonbeam abandoned the gang, escaping through the coulees with her infant daughter. For several months, she evaded them, until that fateful encounter at an antinuclear protest at Hanford.

Moonbeam's baby was six months old when she met up with the Free Spirit Congregation among a crowd of protestors at Hanford Nuclear Facility on the Columbia River. The *Crier* news clippings followed the day-to-day activities of the protestors at Hanford. A bomb was discovered planted at Grand Coulee Dam. It had been placed in a generator station on the dam. Before it was defused, the bomb had come within seconds of blowing out a portion of the dam, of cutting the power that fed all of eastern Washington, including Hanford, perhaps causing massive flooding and destruction from Grand Coulee all the way to the ocean.

As the Free Spirits fled from the scene, Wild Woman

snatched Moonbeam's baby. Moonbeam ran after her. The Judge, the Reverend, and Wild Woman, carrying Moonbeam's baby, escaped into the coulees and were never arrested. When the federal agents ambushed her in a coulee, Moonbeam had no weapon, and no reason to run.

She came forward, her hands raised, asking for their help to recover her baby. She stood facing the armed officers, her arms wide apart, hands showing empty palms, her heart as open as it was vulnerable. She thought they had come to rescue her and her baby from the Free Spirits. But the agents shot her instead, fourteen times, and Moonbeam died in the dry coulee, her blood watering the thirsty sage. In that moment, her infant daughter became an orphan.

This much was told in the *Kettle Falls Crier*. What wasn't revealed were the true identities of the quartet. Mabel had never told what she knew. Even when the Reverend Fred Beveridge went on to receive his preacher's robes. Even when Judge Barry Benson went on to become governor, and then president of the United States, Mabel never told a soul. Even when Wild Woman took on another identity, Mabel never revealed Wild Woman's true identity. But Mabel knew who she was.

Now, Mabel clasped the news clips in one hand and brushed her cheek, with the other tears of grief and heartache falling in belated eulogy for her daughter, for the Shouter's daughter, Moonbeam, whom they had given up at birth to Mabel's sister in Spokane.

Mabel stared out the window at the Shouter's cottage. The front door was ajar and she could hear the basset hounds wailing. She didn't see the Shouter right away, but the complaining hounds told her he was in there, inside the cottage. Mabel gathered her courage, climbed out of the car, and hurried up the path to Shouter's front door.

AT 9:00 A.M., the sun, hovering on the eastern horizon, blasted record heat waves over the high desert and the air that blew into Venus's face felt parched, like sandpaper. She had lost the red hair and hazel eyes, the dumpy cotton dress, and the scraggly Kay Lynn sweater. Now she wore sleek black leather—in spite of the heat—and she had a federal agent's badge tucked inside her jacket and a gun in her waist pack. The Aston Martin, top down, sped away from Kettle Falls, Venus taking the hairpin curves in stride. When her cell phone rang, she pulled onto the shoulder and cut the engine.

The girl spoke in whispers, but she enunciated clearly when she said, "At my dad's office, in the vineyard files on my computer. My password is *swan*. Look for the diagram. And Agent Diamond? Gerald knows who you are. He's planning to kill you. And Juneau. He said he's going to kill both of you today. I have to go now." She clicked off.

Venus wheeled the Aston around and sped back towards K Falls.

BEHIND THE ASTON'S WHEEL, Venus roared into the Denny estate, sped up the curving road, and parked in front of the Denny's house. She went up and knocked on the door, then rang the bell. No answer. Crossing to the vineyard office, she encountered a gray slug heading in the opposite direction, toward the house. She stepped over the slug and headed for the vineyard. The green vines hung heavy with fruit, forming a mazelike route to the office. She ran through the maze, the vines with their grape clusters teasing her peripheral vision, suggesting danger in the deserted field. When she reached the office, the door's lock gave easily to the credit-card trick.

The vineyard's office computer responded instantly to the password *swan*. The menu offered a choice of two items: "Vineyard Accounts" and "Darla's Diary." Venus opened the "Darla's Diary" file.

The diary, nearly fifty pages long, seemed to contain a day-to-day recounting of Darla's adventures with Gerald. But time was of the essence. She scanned until she found the latest entry, a brief statement, apparently composed that same morning by Darla:

Bombs have been placed in the following locations: two houseboats now sunk in the reservoir above the dam, two (or three—I'm not certain) generator towers on the mountain west of the dam, and inside the dam structure itself. Also, one of the antipersonnel bombs, a pipe bomb, is missing. I don't know who has it. Maybe G. Maybe someone else. This pipe is loaded with shrapnel and is very deadly. I sincerely hope that none of G.'s bombs go off. I am hoping that the explosives G. planted inside the dam will be discovered, but so far, I have not had an opportunity to report them, and Gerald wouldn't tell me the exact locations where he'd planted them. All this will take place this afternoon, right after the rally on Grand Coulee Dam is evacuated. G. assured me no lives would be jeopardized, but I overheard him tell someone on his cell phone that a bomb will go off during the rally, killing the president and everybody else on the dam. G. had meant to kill Jeremy Pickforth, but when things changed, it was too late. I pray to God the plot fails. Following is a diagram of the interior of the dam. I removed it from Gerald's backpack last night, scanned it, and put it back before he discovered anything. I believe this diagram shows where the bombs are placed inside the dam. The red marks probably indicate the exact locations. But I can't make sense of it.

Venus scrolled down to the next page until the diagram appeared on the screen. Several times, she tried printing it, but the printer wasn't cooperating. She memorized the diagram and pocketed the floppy disk. She was running back through the vineyards when her cell phone rang again. This time it was Eric Sweetwater, calling from the undercover bus in the caravan.

"Olson says he still doesn't believe you have the right guy."

Nevertheless, Sweetwater told her, Olson had decided to assemble the team. They were in the caravan, undercover, armed and ready. They would stay with the caravan all the way to Grand Coulee.

Then Sweetwater delivered the bad news.

"We have a problem with your information. We can't locate any explosives inside the dam structure. Power company's searched. So has ATF's bomb squad. They scoured the dam's guts for a solid week. They couldn't find anything remotely resembling a bomb. The place is clean as a whistle. Maybe the dude is pulling your leg."

"There are bombs inside that dam." She described the diagram.

Calmly, Sweetwater said, "The place has been swept clean, Venus. The rally is going ahead as planned."

Curtly she said, "Put the chief on."

Sweetwater handed the phone to Olson. Olson listened as Venus recounted what Darla had placed in the vineyard files. When she finished, Olson said, "Pay attention. Sweetwater has just finished telling you that the dam has been swept clean. Now, we had a team on the reservoir dragging for those houseboats. Nada. We had bomb squad sweeping the power stations; we had bomb squad at the generator towers. They found nothing. This is a hoax, and we're spending taxpayer's hard-earned money on all this damn security."

"But sir—"

"Don't 'sir' me. Listen to me. Things are under control. This rally is going forward. If anything happens, we're prepared. Now, get down to Grand Coulee and meet us there. Do you understand?"

She said, "We have less than five hours to find those explosives. What the hell is wrong with those ATF guys? They should have found them by now."

"Maybe you didn't hear me."

She said, "I heard you, sir."

Olson said, "Anyway, the interior is evacuated, except for security personnel."

Olson stared out the bus window. This cock-eyed undercover plan had been a fiasco from the start. Diamond and Song would lose their jobs over this one. Maybe he would, too. He'd have to take the fall with his mutinous subordinates.

Beneath the blazing sun, the vineyards had heated up like an oven. Driving off the vineyard grounds, Venus didn't bother looking back. She had a motto about looking back: You've seen one slug, you've seen 'em all.

BEHIND THE WHEEL of his wife's silver Lexus, Albert Denny felt like the queen's chauffeur amid a cavalcade of security vehicles. In the backseat, Republican presidential hopeful Jenny Pickforth stretched her long legs and admired their contours. Jean Paul, in the front passenger seat, had twisted around to face Ms. Pickforth and they chatted amiably as Albert steered the car with one hand and held a cell phone to his ear with the other. When Albert finished his phone call, he said, "Okay, Ms. Pickforth. It's all arranged. What did I tell you?"

"Please, Albert dear, call me Jenny. And you, too, Jean Paul. I am a very relaxed sort of person."

She didn't look it in her crisp conservative suit and sensible shoes, her hair neatly bobbed and arranged, her makeup expertly drawn. Besides her Republican persona, a keen intellect, and charming southern-belle personality, Jenny Pickforth had a hunger for victory. She was everything the party needed in a presidential candidate, and Albert was prouder than ever on this momentous occasion to call himself a Republican. The party spirit so filled his soul at this moment, so enriched his sense of well-being and righteousness, he nearly drove off the road, but then he remembered his mission and drove forth determinedly.

"We're getting close, Jenny," he said as they entered the town of Grand Coulee. "The public parking lot is just a few blocks up ahead. Our local Republicans are waiting to meet you in there at exactly two p.m.'' Albert chuckled. "The president will be standing on the dam at that point, addressing the crowd. Then the news media will be tipped off to your surprise appearance and all heads will turn your way. Then you challenge Benson to a debate. Yes indeed, it's a great day for the Republican party.''

Jenny Pickforth studied her fresh manicure and smiled to herself.

OUTSIDE THE TOWN of Grand Coulee, the presidential caravan stopped. President Barry Benson instructed his wife and their three adolescent children to ride in a separate vehicle. "For security reasons, pumpkin,'' he had told Mrs. Benson. With the family ensconced in another limousine, the president settled back in his private car, and the caravan proceeded toward Grand Coulee Dam. Benson got on his cell phone and said to a security officer, "Have you located her yet?''

"Yes, sir,'' the officer replied. "Should I patch you through?''

"Go ahead.'' President Benson cleared his throat.

On the lead Dambusters bus, Sue Ann's cell phone rang inside her handbag. Deep in another era, the Squaw of Kin-Ka-Now-Kla flinched. She heard the cell phone but did not immediately comprehend its significance. What noise was this coming from the Queen of Salmon's lap? The phone rang several times before she figured out what to do. Reaching into her oversized handbag, she fished out the trilling phone, unfolded it, and said, "This is Sue Ann.''

"Sue Ann, it's Barry.''

Sue Ann Sullivan Denny, aka Squaw of Kin-Ka-Now-Kla, aka Salmon Queen, heard the old familiar voice and her heart took wing. "Barry, darling,'' she purred, having fully segued, "how lovely to hear your voice.''

Barry Benson smiled. "How have you been, sugarplum?''

"Quite well, thank you," Sue Ann said. "And how is Bitsy?"

President Benson said, "Same old hypochondriac."

"The children?"

"Rebellious brats. I can't stand them."

"Poor Barry," Sue Ann lamented.

"Sue Ann, I was wondering.... I understand that you are scheduled to introduce me at the podium, and I was wondering if you would care to join me in the presidential limousine? I could send a car for you."

"Are you alone?"

"I could be."

Sue Ann felt a nice tingle. This moment had lived in her mind for more years than she cared to count. Now Barry was back in her life. Now, finally, she was back in his. She said, "All right, then, Barry. Send the car."

When she got off the phone, Fritz looked at Sue Ann. She seemed different, almost glowing, the way she had looked that one time after she had slept with Fritz. Fritz said, "Sue Ann, what's got hold of you?"

But she didn't reply. Sue Ann Sullivan Denny, aka Wild Woman, was checking the contents of her large purse. There wasn't much inside, just some makeup and a ten-inch pipe bomb. She snapped the purse shut and smiled serenely.

TWENTY-SEVEN

Tiffie HAD THOUGHT she was done for the day with the bozos and weirdos of the world. She had only locals now. She had refreshed each one's "mother's milk" and had dished up a bowl of chili slop for Trevor Grimm, who sat alone at the counter. Tiffie tuned in her favorite daytime soap and was just beginning to relax into a Nestea when a young woman tripped over the threshold and landed in a facedown sprawl on the saloon floor. Oh God, now what?

Tiffie didn't budge or offer the strange klutz any kind of assistance; she didn't need to, because every male in the saloon had rushed to the girl's side, offering their help and their hearts. She was that gorgeous. Gorgeous enough to break up a poker game, and that's gorgeous. Even Prospector had to stare, though he didn't immediately join in the stampede to the fallen angel. As Tiffie watched, various local husbands and boyfriends committed adultery in their hearts as they transported the accident-prone tourist to a booth. Just who was this svelte invader?

Someone yelled at Tiffie to bring a damp cloth over. Tiffie did, and thought about slapping a few people around with it, but Bud Collins took the rag and wiped the girl's knee, as if it had a scrape. Tiffie couldn't see even a discoloration. She had to admit this broad was magnificent, like a movie star, and she had an aura around her that shouted, Very cool, and another aura around that shouted, Very hot, and a third aura that Tiffie couldn't read but that held a scent of exotic flowers, maybe Ylang Ylang.

She was older than Tiffie, but not by much. She had magnificent long, sleek legs and a greyhound's svelteness. She had natural blond hair, the best blue eyes Tiffie had ever envied, perfect skin, perfect everything. When she smiled at her rescuers, her face lit up the saloon. Tiffie went over and tried concentrating on the soap, but it was no use. The girl had everyone in the saloon under her spell, including Tiffie.

"I'm looking for my sister," the girl said, as she drank from a glass of mountain springwater Prospector had proffered. "Her name is Venus. Venus Diamond. She's a lepidopterist employed by the federal government. Have you seen anyone like that?"

Lepidopterist was not in the Kettle Falls vocabulary. Prospector scratched his head; the other chaps rolled the word around on their slavering tongues. Then Tiffie, smarter than the average bartender, said, "K Falls isn't exactly butterfly heaven. We don't see a lot of lepidopterists in this town. What's she look like?"

Tiffie was awfully afraid the vision would describe a twin. If there were two of these beauties, surely the Tiffies of the world faced stiff odds. But no, the enchanting girl described otherwise. "Venus is tragically short and somewhat scrawny, with unruly blond hair and obnoxiously green eyes. I mean, the shade of sun-drenched seaweed. Oh, pardon me. Was that too colorful? Sometimes my creative flow charges right on without me. Every word that spills from my mouth originates from a virtual fountain of creativity. It never stops flowing." She smiled. Tiffie could hear the locals' collective heartbeat. Each one of them had fallen in love with the stranger. Now the vision held out her pale, limp digits and Prospector took her hand and brought it to his mouth, kissed it gently as the girl said, "I am Echo. A New York poet."

New York. So that explained it. Tiffie had to admit she was more than mildly impressed. She brought the girl calling herself Echo a glass of Nestea and another damp cloth, this for her other knee, which someone pointed out, had a speck of saloon-floor grime on it. Tiffie was shocked to find herself personally wiping off the girl's insulted knee, but, hey, maybe she could learn something from this chick. Tiffie looked up and smiled into the girl's eyes. But Echo's pools of inspiration did not see Tiffie. The girl was vision. Holding her hand to her thin chest, the girl spoke:

> "Sad saloon, where have your salmon gone?
> Bad boys fished them out
> Anglers on the fly
> Care not if salmon die
> And even less
> For steelhead trout."

Every eye in the saloon misted over. The men began weeping uncontrollably. And even Tiffie felt a choking in her breast, as if some long-suppressed emotion had been regurgitated, giving her spiritual indigestion. This girl had just spoken a truth that went right to the heart of things. Maybe Tiffie was a salmon lover after all. Maybe all of them were salmon supporters. Even Prospector wept as he leaned over the girl named Echo, absorbing her truths and perfume. Then someone said, "Oh hey, I think I know your sister."

Echo said, "I knew she'd been in here. I can feel her energy."

"But she's not a blonde," said the person who had seen Echo's sister. "She's got red hair. And her eyes aren't green. They're hazel."

Echo frowned. "Then how can you possibly say that you have seen my sister?"

The person replied, "I read auras. She has the same aura as yours."

Echo glanced down at her own slim ankle and murmured, "I doubt that."

"And she doesn't call herself 'Venus Diamond.' Her name is Kay Lynn Jones."

Echo rolled her eyes. "She's probably working undercover again."

Tiffie gasped. "Juneau's wife is a cop?"

Echo, no dullard, suddenly put two and two together. "This 'Juneau'—is he by any stretch Asian?"

"Half," Tiffie answered confidently. "He told me."

Echo laughed. "Why, then, he isn't 'Juneau' at all. His name is Mr. Song. Agent Song. A very sexy chap, no?"

Tiffie nodded emphatically. "Very."

Echo stood up and smoothed her linen shift. "Take me to them," she commanded.

"But they haven't been around in days," Tiffie said. "I heard they left town for good. Pulled their trailer out of the park and split. I don't know where they went."

Echo shook her head, trying to ward off the local stupidity. "I can see that I'll have to find them by myself," she said, walking toward the door. Several pokerheads followed her, their slathering mouths pleading with the vision to stay in K Falls, never to leave. Tiffie suddenly hated this Echo person. Then, as suddenly as she had appeared, the girl was gone. Tiffie glanced out the window and saw the beguiling New Yorker drive away in a fancy sports car she couldn't identify. The girl named Echo was headed south. Maybe going to Grand Coulee Dam. She had that salmon-lover aspect.

Prospector gave Tiffie a pat on the caboose and she went back behind the bar, where he thought she belonged. The poker game picked up where it had left off.

Trevor Grimm had split without settling his bill. Tiffie scowled and made out a bill with Grimm's name on it and taped it to the cash register. Next time he came in, she'd collar him, and maybe charge him interest. You have to weed out irresponsibility early, before it becomes habitual.

The soap opera was nearing its episodic denouement, but it didn't make any sense, since she'd missed the beginning, so she switched channels. She was watching the local news coverage of President Benson's visit to Grand Coulee Dam, when a bunch of Prospector's Republican friends came in and told him they needed him down at Grand Coulee Dam. Something big was brewing. Very big. One of them whispered the name Pickforth, and Prospector instantly understood.

"Oh hell," complained Tiffie. "So I get to stay here in this ghost town while everyone else is down at the dam having a blast?"

Prospector, on his way out the door, looked back at Tiffie. She wore a forlorn expression that touched Prospector's heart. He jerked his head, and Tiffie started locking up. Stepping onto the sidewalk, Tiffie collided with Trevor Grimm.

"Gollee," complained Tiffie when she had recovered from the impact, "don't you ever watch where you're going?"

Grimm seized Tiffie's shoulders and said, "Where is he?"

Tiffie tried peeling Grimm's meaty hands off her shoulders, but they were locked on. "You owe me five dollars and forty-two cents. Not counting a tip."

"Juneau Jones. Where did he go, Tiffie?"

Grimm seemed awfully desperate to find Juneau Jones. Tiffie said, "Why is everyone so interested in Juneau Jones all of a sudden?"

"I need to know where he's hiding," Grimm said. "Come on, out with it."

Tiffie had had it up to her beehive with strangeness, but she couldn't pry Grimm's hands loose, couldn't free herself. Impulsively, she leaned forward and took a bite out of his nose.

"Yow!"

"You owe me for the chili," she shouted, and took off at a run for Prospector's car. Grimm stood on the sidewalk, holding his bleeding nose. When Tiffie and Prospector drove past, Tiffie shot him the bird. Prospector had never seen Tiffie do that, and he was mildly puzzled, though not enough to ask about it.

Grimm, recovering his wits, ran for his own car, jumped

inside, and headed down the highway after Prospector, but Prospector left Grimm behind in a cloud of eastern Washington dust and sagebrush. Grimm pulled over to the side of the road and fished out his cell phone. When Gerald answered, Grimm said, ''They're feds. One of them has a sister who just showed up in town. She sang without knowing it.'' He daubed his bleeding nose. ''They got away. I lost them.''

Gerald had parked the van in a parking lot in Grand Coulee, a quarter mile from the dam. When Grimm had finished, Gerald said, ''We don't have time to look for them. Get down there and move those houseboats.''

''What if they ambush us?''

''Don't question me! Now, move those houseboats.''

Grimm signed off and pointed his car toward Grand Coulee Dam. He hadn't gone two miles before he noticed the needle on the gas gauge had almost reached the empty mark.

SPEEDING SOUTH along the river road, Echo searched for a radio station, but nothing came in over the static. Not AM. Not FM. This lack of civilization slightly jarred the cosmopolite. She was accustomed to background stimuli, and static did not do the trick. She turned off the static. Checking her diamond-bezel timepiece, Echo put lead in her foot. She was speeding along the river road, when a car actually passed her on the left. Echo was not accustomed to being passed, so she floored the gas pedal and roared past the offending vehicle. Once again in the lead, Echo glanced into her rearview mirror and saw the car on her rear bumper, so close that she could see the driver's nice eyes and a wide grimace that showed off a mouthful of white teeth, the sort of teeth one sees a lot of in towns that flouridate their water. This, then, was no country bumpkin drag racing with her along the Columbia River. Echo slowed down just enough to study the driver's features, and now she noticed that despite his obvious agitation, he was somewhat attractive—in fact, downright handsome. She lifted her foot off the gas, slowing down enough

to let the chap pass her. As he did so, he waved, as if signaling her to pull over. So this drag race was a flirtation after
all. Echo wasn't terribly surprised, being aware of her physical attributes. She drove more leisurely now, still playing
hard to get. Up ahead, the cute driver slowed down, then
pulled over to the side of the road and stopped. She saw him
get out of his vehicle. As she passed, he held out a thumb.
Stupidly, Echo pulled over and stopped. He ambled over and
she rolled down the window.

"You headed to Grand Coulee?" the handsome chap inquired.

Echo sized him up. He had a fresh scab on the bridge of
his nose. Intuitively, she knew he had zero charisma and no
dough. Still, to Echo, he had sex appeal. She said, "Maybe."

"I'm running out of gas. There isn't a station for another
thirty miles. My car won't make it. I was hoping you might
be headed down to the rally at Grand Coulee Dam, and could
give me a lift." He smiled, showing the fluoridated teeth.

Echo checked to see that he was telling the truth. The gas
gauge in his car showed a nearly empty tank. He might be
trustworthy. Echo said, "Give me your wallet."

He gave her his wallet. She checked his identification and
counted the cash. Not enough to impress Echo, but hey....
She put the wallet in her pocket and told him to get in. They
drove off, Echo at the wheel. They didn't speak for several
minutes, but Echo was a sensitive soul and she could feel the
sparks flying. Finally, he said, "So you know my name.
What's yours?"

She told him. He said, "You remind me of a guest I had
recently."

"Oh God," she said. "Don't tell me you know my sister?"

The man said, "I run an inn. The girl resembling you
stayed overnight recently."

"So, Mr. Grimm, you are a hotelier?"

Grimm said, "Well, I run an inn...."

"And I take it you are a salmon supporter? I warn you, if you are not, I shall have to put you out."

Grimm said, "Closet. See, if you live around here, it doesn't do to support breaching dams to save salmon. But I do. I support that cause. By the way, could you drive a little faster?"

Echo raised a finely arched brow and put lead in her foot. Half an hour later, they caught up with the Dambusters caravan. But Grimm wasn't interested in joining the caravan. He told Echo to pass the caravan. When she balked, he pulled out a snub-nosed pistol and poked her ribs. Echo accelerated. Half an hour passed in frosty silence, except for the call Grimm made on his cell phone. Echo listened to his half of the conversation.

Grimm said, "You got the Shouter?" Then he laughed. "I got the slick New York gal…. What?… Oh yeah, sure. Sure, I can handle that."

When they reached the outskirts of Grand Coulee, Grimm told her to pull the car over. She did. Grimm took his wallet back and said, "I would never have thought that green-eyed girl could have such a beautiful sister."

Echo said, "Don't patronize me. I am a poet."

Grimm poked the gun at Echo's lean ribs and growled, "Turn off the ignition and get out."

Echo rolled her eyes, started to balk, but Grimm jammed the pistol harder against her, so she turned off the ignition and stepped out of the car. Grimm grabbed her arm and dragged her toward the reservoir. As they disappeared down a steep bank, Echo looked back. She could no longer see the highway or the rental car. Suddenly, she became aware of a certain quietude, a stillness in the air, and the distinct absence of other human beings. So this was wilderness. The stranger was leading her through a foreign territory, a frighteningly dull place, a place she did not understand.

Grimm said, "You blew it, cookie. You gave away the whole show. So that sister of yours is a cop?"

"Just what are you implying?" Echo demanded, irritated at the gun's barrel pressing now against her tender kidney.

"We weren't sure. You told us what we needed to know, and just in time, too."

"You are not to harm my sister," declared Echo, issuing an imperious, impotent decree.

Grimm said, "Then, too, I reckon now that you're involved, you'll have to take a one-way swim."

Echo stood beside Grimm on the edge of the reservoir. The heat had created a pulsating haze on the water's placid surface. Through the mists, she saw bare brown hills on the opposite shore. No mathematician, Echo was hard-pressed to calculate the distance, but a wild guess suggested something like half a mile. Grimm shoved her forward.

"Why don't you simply shoot me and get it over with?" she snapped irritably.

Grimm leered, then said, "A slick gal like you can figure that out. Now swim, Miss Manhattan." He prodded her with the pistol.

Echo had inherited a certain imperious gene, a gene so powerful that even the threat of death could not deter her sharp tongue and her sense of outrage. "How dare you—" she began, but Grimm dared, pushing her into the reservoir. She broke the surface in a sloppy splat, sank, returned to the surface, and gasped for air. Grimm aimed his gun.

The shot rang out. Echo sank slowly, disappearing into the haze.

VENUS WAS DRIVING THROUGH downtown Kettle Falls on the way to Grand Coulee Dam when her cell phone rang. She recognized the caller's sultry syntax, the go-to-hell cadence in a voice adored by hordes of smitten fans, mostly male, mostly virile.

Echo had made it to the opposite shore, and she now sat crouched and waterlogged beneath a single pine tree on a dusty beachhead. Her cell phone had survived the underwater swim encased in a Gore-Tex waist wallet, an ugly, unfashionable object that she wore only in the Pacific Northwest, her single concession to local style.

"They've got the Shouter," said Echo. "Whatever that means."

Behind the Aston's wheel, Venus said, "Echo, is that you?"

"Of course," snapped Echo as she swatted a pesky gnat needling her forearm. Echo felt the harsh sun attacking her delicate skin, and this vexed her. "Now, you had better proceed with your professional obligations. Don't worry about me. I'm a New Yorker, after all."

Venus steered the Aston Martin through a U-turn and headed toward Harmony Lane. When she pulled up in front of the Shouter's house, she saw a Mercury sedan parked in front. The front door to the cottage was open.

The Shouter's bullet-riddled body lay on the kitchen floor, arms outstretched, the eyes wide open. The old man's basset hounds sat mournfully beside their still master, waiting for the impossible to happen. The little cottage was filled with death, and with the stench of rotting salmon wafting from the pail on the kitchen table. On the stove, a pan of cold corned beef hash stood congealing. A coffee percolator had burned through the bottom. Venus went over and stood gazing at the Shouter. Even dead, he had personality.

Mabel had pulled up a chair beside the Shouter's body. And now she sat beside him, holding his lifeless hand in hers. In her other gnarled hand, resting in her lap, Mabel held a small pistol, which she had loaded with one bullet. That's all it would take to send Mabel off. "You came too soon," she told Venus. "I wanted you to find two corpses." She let go of the Shouter's lifeless hand, shoved the pistol into her pocket, and wept.

As the old woman wept over the Shouter's body, Venus held her in an embrace, and Mabel didn't resist the comforting gesture, for she needed consoling. She didn't even notice when the green-eyed girl slipped the pistol out of her pocket and tucked it into her own.

In the Shouter's kitchen, Mabel demonstrated just how she thought he had been murdered. The killer must have entered through the unlocked back door and waited in the kitchen until the Shouter returned home from the river. When the Shouter came in, he began preparing his usual supper of corned beef hash and black coffee. The killer fired his gun out of the shadows. Mabel showed Venus where the bullet had struck the Shouter through the back, straight through the heart. The old man had had no time to protest.

When Mabel arrived, probably less than an hour after he had been murdered, she saw both cottage doors were ajar, heard the hounds wailing. She went for help, but when she couldn't locate the only person she thought she could trust, she returned to the cottage and went inside, where she saw the Shouter's basset hounds gathered around his body, bawling over their master's still form.

Mabel thought she knew who had killed the Shouter, but she had no actual proof.

But why?

"He had seen something. Down at the reservoir." Mabel hesitated, then said, "He seemed mental, but he was sharp as you or me. He just didn't know how to communicate."

"What did he see?"

"The man my granddaughter calls 'Gerald.'"

"Who's your granddaughter?"

"Darla. Shouter had figured out the girl was our grand-daughter. He had seen her at the Elias Fobia Cabin, with the man she called 'Gerald.' Shouter recognized her as Darla Denny. Of course, we've know for years that Darla wasn't really Sue Ann Denny's daughter. She was Moonbeam's baby. Our daughter's baby. I had seen Moonbeam and the baby just before Moonbeam died. She came to see me and Shouter, to introduce us to our granddaughter. Then after Moonbeam was killed, we didn't see the baby for years. Then

Wild Woman—I mean, Sue Ann, came up here and married Albert Denny and brought Darla with her. Shouter and I, we've been following Darla's progress all these years.... And now she's mixed up with those, those..."

Mabel hugged herself. "What they do...they walk...I just can't say it. Can't put a word to it."

"Fire walking?"

Mabel nodded, tears streaking her sunken cheeks. "Shouter saw it more than once. That Gerald would build the fires near the shore, and when the coals got red-hot, he'd leap onto them. Shouter told me about it, but I didn't believe him. I thought the Shouter's senses had finally gone belly-up."

Venus said, "You think Gerald shot the Shouter just because he had witnessed Gerald fire walking?"

Mabel sniffed. "One night, Shouter told me he saw Gerald trying to force Darla to walk on the hot stones. Darla was crying. Shouter went after Gerald, almost killed him. But Gerald pulled a gun. Shouter just barely got away. But Gerald knew Shouter could identify him. That's why he had to kill Shouter."

"Let me take you home."

Mabel looked up at Venus and said, "That's really all I know." Then she leaned over the Shouter's corpse. "Old man," she said, "take me with you. Wherever the hell it is you've gone."

One of the hounds came over and licked Mabel's leg, lifting her skirt, exposing an edge of lacy black slip. Mabel reached down and petted the hound. "You stay here and watch over him," she said to the dog. "I'll be back in a little while."

Venus walked Mabel down the block to her tidy house. From there, they called the sheriff's office and the coroner. The sheriff and his deputies were all at Grand Coulee Dam, but when the coroner had arrived to keep Mabel company,

Venus borrowed the news clips from Mabel's trembling hands and said good-bye.

In parting, Mabel said, "Darla is a lot like Moonbeam was before she died."

"How's that?" Venus asked.

"All bleeding heart and compassion. All touchy-feely, and not a whiff of common sense."

"By the way," said Venus, "what did Mr. Denny send by Federal Express?"

Mabel pursed her lips and said, "Poached salmon. And I mean stolen, not cooked. To his cousin in Iowa."

Venus nodded, then left.

TWENTY-EIGHT

SHORTLY BEFORE 1:00 p.m., the Dambusters caravan arrived at Grand Coulee Dam. President Benson's supporters swarmed over the public parking lot overlooking the spillway, and soon a festive mood prevailed in spite of a dry heat that tortured Seattleites, the glaring sun a shocking sight anytime of year. Fritz wiped his brow and checked his Timex. It read 1:55 p.m. exactly. At that moment, Fritz heard a great blaring noise and then sirens. He turned, to see President Barry Benson's cavalcade cruising up the road toward the dam. Fritz hurried to join the uproarious cheering. The Dambusters were hooting louder than Sonics fans when Fritz spotted President Benson's limousine, and when it swept past, he spotted Sue Ann inside, seated beside the president.

"Wouldja look at that?" Fritz said to the fresh air. "That Sue Ann Denny sure gets around."

At the same moment, another cavalcade arrived from the opposite direction, and Fritz turned around just in time to witness Jenny Pickforth's surprise parade. "What's going on here?" Fritz remarked to no one in particular, and someone else said, "What the hell are the Republicans doing here?" A third party shouted, "Oh boy, there's Albert Denny. Let me at that redneck." Fritz sprinted to the spillway road to greet the president.

The president's caravan moved onto Grand Coulee Dam, on the road traversing the spillway's crest. President Benson beamed as he climbed out of his limousine, followed by a slightly disheveled but radiant Sue Ann Denny. Fritz, all smiles, greeted Benson. Surrounded by security forces, Benson and Sue Ann followed Fritz up a few short steps to an elaborate platform that had been constructed on the spillway road. From the platform, President Benson looked out across the river and saw a parking lot that he calculated was at least one football field length distant. He had to squint to see the faces of the crowd that had gathered there to await his arrival. He could have sent a stand-in, an imposter, Benson told himself, and the crowd would never have known the difference.

Sue Ann set her handbag down near the microphone. Turning to Fritz, she purred, "Oh, honey, I've got an awful case of stage fright. Can you do the president's introduction?"

Fritz patted Sue Ann's shoulder and agreed. As Fritz made the introduction, Sue Ann's deft foot nudged the handbag underneath the rostrum. She stepped off the platform and began walking along the spillway road. Clearing his throat, President Benson stepped up to the microphone and made his trademark victory sign. The crowd cheered wildly, but Benson heard some boos and jeers.

Benson shouted, "It's grand to be home, fellow Washingtonians," and at that simple declaration, Democrats, Greens, and Republicans found one another's throats, and the sporadic animosity escalated to surly shoving. Fisticuffs broke out. President Benson watched helplessly across the great divide as Fritz grabbed the microphone and pleaded with the crowd.

"Please, folks, please," Fritz's voice blared. "We can find a middle ground. If you salmon haters would shut up and listen to me. I said, 'Shut up,' damn it!"

A small child wearing a pink dress interrupted Fritz's pleas.

"I'm lost," said the little girl.

Fritz regarded the child with a crazed expression. How the hell had a six-year-old kid breached presidential security forces?

"How dare you bother me right now?" he shouted. "Can't you see I'm trying to prevent a riot?"

"I can't find my dad," the little girl persisted in a civilized tone. She gripped his sleeve and added, "His name is Nathan Bernstein. Dr. Bernstein. He's on the welcoming committee, but he left the stage and I can't find him. Can you help me find my dad?"

Fritz peeled the child's fingers off his sleeve. "Got to stop this brewing rumpus. Go away now, shoo. Shoo!" The Bernstein girl jostled through the chaos and was soon swallowed up in the crowd.

Sue Ann had reached the public parking lot and was minding her own business when Tiffie Terlock slammed a square fist into Sue Ann's stomach. Sue Ann doubled over and cursed. Then she went after Tiffie, who was working over another Dambuster.

The crowd mixed it up, cheering and booing. Raising his arms, President Benson pleaded through the microphone for calm. "Folks, folks," he cried out, "come on now, let's just all try to get along, can we?" Suddenly, Jenny Pickforth appeared on the rostrum beside the president. Grasping the microphone, she began vilifying Benson and his unruly constituents. Benson and Pickforth scuffled over the microphone, and soon the two candidates, both grasping the microphone, locked horns in a heated political debate vis-à-vis the salmon question.

Song, minus the Juneau Jones facial scar, had traded the cheap aviators for his favorite Revos, the very same pair he often doffed in the north elevator whenever Miss Delicious appeared. Now Song watched Gerald approach the parking lot, cell phone detonator in hand. The big guy wasn't wearing the usual wool knit cap. Freshly shaved, he wore a suit and a tie, and on his head he wore a ten-gallon hat. He blended right into the crowd. Song watched as Gerald approached Sue Ann. As they stood side by side, for the briefest moment, Song noticed Venus moving through the crowd.

Years earlier, Venus had learned to read lips, a talent that had saved her neck more than once. She watched as Sue Ann said something to Gerald. What Sue Ann had said was, "It's on the podium. Seven minutes."

Gerald nodded and walked away; then Sue Ann fished a cell phone from her pocket and Venus moved in. She was following Sue Ann through the crowds when something tugged at her leg. She looked down.

A small child in a pink dress said, "My father is Dr. Bernstein. Have you seen him?"

In that instant, the crowd swallowed up Sue Ann Denny. Venus tore the little girl's hand off her leg and plunged into the crowd.

A QUARTER MILE upriver, where the chaos could be heard but not seen, Trevor Grimm delivered the two sunken houseboats to their final resting place against the wall of the dam. From where he stood on the riverbank, Grimm let the last length of rope slip from his hands and watched as the rope sank underwater. Standing on the riverbank, cell phone detonator poised, he checked his watch, waiting for the signal. Five minutes and counting down.

THE REVEREND AND Mrs. Fred Beveridge had arrived at the dam with the Pickforth caravan, and now Reverend Beveridge joined Jenny Pickforth and President Benson at the podium on top of the dam. Reaching into his pocket, Reverend Beveridge fished out a short sermon that he had planned to deliver to the masses. Seizing the microphone from Pickforth, Reverend Beveridge began to speak, but, as was the case most every time he sermonized of late, the words flowing from his mouth were not the words he had meant to deliver. As Pickforth and Benson raged over the salmon question in the background, the increasingly odd Reverend Beveridge cried out to the masses.

"My fellow sinners," he began, much to his own shock

and dismay, "the subject of today's sermon is, 'Time and the Polyglot.' Is Nature, my fellow boomers, something of a miscreant, a freak? Or is Nature, in the Divine Order, a mere fluke, fanciful play on matter? Or is Nature, in the Divine Order—by the way, were you aware that salmon locate their spawning beds with their keen sense of smell? Did you know that the pollution of rivers and oceans caused by humankind's filthy habits has damaged the fine cilia in the salmons' nostrils, thus impairing their ability to hone in on their mating grounds? Pollution, my fellow boomers, is what kills salmon. Don't let anybody tell you otherwise. Now, as I was saying about Nature..."

ON THE BANKS of the reservoir, Grimm paced, counting down the minutes, the cell phone detonator in hand, his eager thumb poised to detonate the houseboat bombs. Where was that signal? Two minutes and counting down.

AT THE PODIUM, Reverend Beveridge continued his rant. "...Is Nature a two-headed banana slug, a flipping coin," cried the preacher, "sometimes benevolent, often brutal, occasionally compassionate, and rather frequently capricious? Did God intend to test Nature? Did Nature fall? Or, is Nature itself..."

As the preacher ranted on, the confrontation of President Benson and Jenny Pickforth deteriorated to fisticuffs. Security guards moved in, but the president threw them off. He wanted to take Pickforth out himself. But Pickforth was a strong and determined woman, no easy prey. She fought valiantly, and it was all the president could do to maintain his balance on the platform.

On the edge of the parking lot, Gerald, cell phone detonator in hand, scanned the crowd. When he saw Song coming at him, he turned to run, but Song grabbed him and pushed him to the asphalt. Song was strong, but the big guy was stronger. They struggled on the hard ground until Gerald broke free and dived into the crowd. Song chased after him.

Venus caught sight of Sue Ann Denny just as she broke from the crowds. Sue Ann had reached the highway at the edge of the parking lot and was crossing against traffic. Venus chased after Sue Ann, but Mrs. Denny was cunning, and she knew this terrain.

It was too late to stop Sue Ann's finger from pushing the button on the detonator. Venus raced back to the parking lot, commandeered a boy's bicycle, and pedaled frantically, heading for the spillway. She doubted she'd make it before the bomb went off, but she had to try.

Once across the highway, Sue Ann fled into a neat row of bungalows and disappeared somewhere among the tidy flower gardens. In the safety of a garden, Sue Ann fished out her cell phone detonator and was about to punch in the code when she noticed a slimy gray slug climbing up her ankle. Sue Ann screamed and ran.

TWENTY-NINE

A GREAT TRUMPETING SOUND filled the air. Pedaling frantically, Venus glanced up into the hot desert blue sky and there beheld the most exquisite white swan gliding overhead. The swan flew straight toward the spillway, as if guiding Venus. As she raced onto the spillway road, heading for the security blockades, the sky suddenly seemed to turn dark, ominously black, and the air grew close and thick. Then came a great thrashing sound, like a million crows all flapping their wings at once.

The terrified crowd saw the crows coming, but in the crush of humanity, people had no time to flee, no place to run and hide. So they cowered under the crow invasion, a futile gesture against the horrid sound of black wings beating, beating, beating. On the spillway, security had gone to hell. The president's bodyguards cowered like everyone else, afraid of the swooping birds, fending them off with raised arms. Venus ditched the bike, vaulted over the barricades, and headed for the podium.

Fritz, ever the organizer, tried one last time to bring order to the podium, but he soon recognized it was futile, so he turned to the more mundane task of cleaning crow droppings off his new summer suit. Someone had once told Fritz that when you envision an event strongly enough, it will make itself manifest. This was not the event Fritz had envisioned in all his years of environmental activism. Frankly, if anyone asked Fritz Fowler just now how he felt about birds and beavers and various endangered species, he would be hard-pressed to defend them. How dare the crows rain on his parade, not to mention ruin his new white suit? No, Fritz would have to revise his environmental stance. This called for a retreat. Fritz got out of there, leaving the president and all the rest of the fools to their self-made destinies. Fritz—if anyone was interested—was going fishing. For salmon.

On the chaotic stage, Venus searched for Sue Ann Denny's handbag. The minutes were ticking down now to seconds. She had to find it.

Splat. Splat. More crow guano. The president had been hit.

There it was. Underneath the platform. An oversized handbag. Venus dived.

ACROSS THE HIGHWAY, behind the neat bungalows, Sue Ann had hoofed it up the dry brown mountain that led uphill to the giant steel electricity towers. At the top of the hill, she caught her breath. She could see the armed officers emerging from the bushes, coming after her. Already her finger was poised over the cell phone detonator. Now, at her peak of glory, Wild Woman checked her Rolex, and in one defiant motion, she pushed the detonator button.

ON THE SPILLWAY ROAD, Venus flung the pipe bomb far into the reservoir on the upriver side of the dam. It exploded in a fireball, its lethal shards piercing the water's surface and scaring off the crows. Ignited during its airborne projection, the bomb had minimal force, having nothing to destroy but the air over the reservoir. Venus turned around and spotted Olson standing halfway down the spillway. She saw him make the call to evacuate the area.

GERALD RAN DOWNHILL toward the bridge. Halfway down the hill, he glanced over his shoulder and saw Bobby Beaver coming at him. Bobby edged closer, closer. Catching up to Gerald, Bob's huge teeth bit into his thigh. Gerald screamed. His leg bled profusely where Bob Beaver had gnawed. He ran pell-mell down the highway. He had to reach the bridge. Had to, before Juneau Jones caught up with him. Or was that Juneau? Gerald couldn't be positive. Anyway, the dude was closing in.

UPRIVER, GRIMM PUZZLED over events. Was that the signal bomb that had exploded? He wasn't sure. He scratched his head and his chest and occasionally picked a crow dropping off his shirt, and wondered what he should do now.

He didn't hear the agents closing in behind him. He didn't hear one of them say, "You're under arrest, Grimm," followed by the recitation of his rights. They had approached him from the rear, and being somewhat preoccupied, Grimm hadn't noticed them, but he felt the handcuffs tighten around his wrists, and when Eric Sweetwater told Sparks to shackle Grimm's ankles, Grimm could read Sweetwater's lips.

"Aw hell," Grimm said, smiling bashfully. "Guess you fellers finally caught up with me."

As they led him away, Grimm said, "I reckon I'm under arrest for fishing without a license?"

Eric Sweetwater said, "Conspiracy."

Grimm acted surprised. "What conspiracy?"

Sweetwater said, "Conspiracy to blow up Grand Coulee Dam."

Grimm made a face. "No, I never heard talk about that. All I know is, we're playing a little prank on Jenny Pickforth. Just a little fireworks."

Sweetwater said, "They don't tell patsies everything."

GERALD HAD REACHED the bottom of the hill and had one foot on the bridge spanning the river when he glanced over his shoulder and saw the Juneau look-alike bearing down on him. The big man had run out of time. When he reached the center of the bridge, directly overlooking the spillway, he climbed onto the bridge railing. Above him spread a brilliant blue sky. Below him ran the spillwaters of the throttled river.

As he climbed over the side of the bridge, the big man felt a familiar tingle between his shoulder blades.

When Song reached the bridge, it was deserted. He leaned against the railing, panting for breath. Where had Gerald gone? How had he lost him? Song bent over the rail. Had Gerald jumped into the river? If so, Song doubted that he had survived. The spillwater was shallow below the bridge, the boulders deadly. Water swirled around boulders, but Song saw no sign of the big man.

Song glanced up at the sky, empty now of avian bombers. But high above the dam, riding an updraft, sailed a lone bald eagle, its dark wings spread, its white tail and golden beak glinting in the sun.

SUE ANN CURSED the impotent cell phone detonator in her hand. Why hadn't her bomb gone off? Why hadn't the damn thing exploded? The uphill lam, combined with the illicit tryst in President Benson's limo, had sapped her energy, and the pain where Tiffie had slugged her stomach finally exhausted Sue Ann. When the officers grabbed her, she realized she was surrounded, and she felt the handcuffs and heard them click around her wrists.

When an officer took the detonator from her, Sue Ann mewled weakly, "It's just a cell phone. It belongs to Barry. I mean, President Benson. I borrowed it. To call my daughter?"

What had gone wrong with Sue Ann's plan?

Sue Ann thought it must have been Gerald. Sue Ann had always suspected that Gerald was an incompetent. No doubt in her mind, Gerald had wired the detonators incorrectly. She should have wired them herself. She knew how to make cell phone detonators. She shouldn't have depended so much on Gerald and that pinhead Grimm. Anarchists these days aren't what they were back in Sue Ann's days of rage.

But now it was too late, and as she wiped the dark rivers of mascara cascading down her cheeks, Sue Ann realized that she should be grateful for one thing: She would probably never be convicted. They could never prove she was connected to this failed bombing attempt. Eventually, the dam security forces would locate the undetonated bombs, but none of them could be traced back to Sue Ann Denny. The pipe bomb in her handbag had been planted there. Her fingerprints certainly weren't on it. Yes, she could finesse this one. That meant she could try again, once a little time had passed.

FROM THE PARKING LOT, Albert Denny watched as Sue Ann was placed in a patrol car. From where Albert stood some safe yards distant, he could see the handcuffs on his wife's wrists and he could tell that Sue Ann had been crying. Just then, Albert wished that he could recall if she was the third or the fourth wife. He thought it over, and then decided it all depended on whether or not you counted the one annulment. God, what do boomers know about commitment?

By the time all these ruminations had rambled through Albert's tortured brain, the patrol car carrying Sue Ann had driven away and Denny's churchgoing wife had been hauled off to jail like a common criminal. Ever pragmatic, Albert whipped out a clean white handkerchief and dabbed at his guano-coated shirt cuffs, idly wondering if Jenny Pickforth was unattached.

On the way to jail, Sue Ann borrowed a tissue from a federal agent named Dottie and worked halfheartedly at cleaning up her face. It wasn't so much the bird droppings as it was the black mascara. Artifice is fine, unless you manage to get caught.

A crowd drenched in bird droppings is not a happy crowd. People quickly dispersed, leaving President Benson and his competitors preaching at thin air. Benson cajoled. Beveridge preached. Pickforth postulated, glorying in the sound of her own voice. The politicians didn't hear the evacuation sirens.

Fritz had gone fishing. Albert was already driving, albeit it at a crawl, to the police station, Jean Paul in the passenger seat, thinking his private thoughts about Americans. Grimm and Sue Ann were on the way to jail. Darla had simply evaporated.

And Gerald? Where was the big guy?

THIRTY

HE HAD WORKED for the power company for five years, an exemplary employee with a spotless record and a coveted security clearance. He knew the innards of this dam better than he knew his own backside. Under the bridge, he had found the door that opened into a maintenance tunnel. His leg, badly torn by Bob Beaver's teeth, bled profusely, but he could still run. Sprinting through the tunnel, he left a thin trail of fresh blood.

Two minutes later, he entered the turbine maintenance building on the north side, ran down a well-lighted, deserted corridor to an employees' locker room. Inside, he removed his clothing, washed his leg wound. He yanked a pair of work overalls off a shelf, put these on. He worked the combination lock on his locker, opened it, fished out a pair of heavy work boots. He put these on. Racing down the deserted corridor, he stopped at a door marked INCINERATOR. He opened the door and then the incinerator chute, tossed in the bloodied cowboy clothing and boots. He raced ahead down the corridor, turning right, then left, then up a flight of metal stairs that made echoing sounds as he climbed them. At the top, he encountered some fellow security workers in one of the operations rooms. He slowed down as he passed the glass windows, nodded at them, and tipped his finger in greeting. But they hadn't even noticed him. Their eyes were on their television monitors, watching the ruckus outside. He kept walking, occasionally passing another colleague, nodding an appropriate greeting, acting as normal as possible.

A colleague said, "It's chaos out there, man," and laughed.

The big man laughed and said, "Bastards," and kept walking.

When he reached the huge glass-fronted elevator that rose up seven stories beside the spillway, he stepped inside and pressed the button for the sixth floor. The elevator door closed. He gazed through the windows as the elevator rose, watching the chaos on the spillway. He was staring out the window, but his mind was caught up in the suicide mission he had decided to carry out. Now, finally, he would soar with the eagles—hell, he'd be one. He reached into his pocket, fished out his cell phone detonator, unfolded it, and started entering the code that would detonate the bombs he had planted in the dam's guts. The bombs that would blow Grand Coulee Dam and himself to smithereens. He was still entering the code when he saw a reflection in the window glass.

She stood behind him, slightly to his right, and she had a gun pointed at him. Thinking fast, he dropped the detonator, reached up, and turned the key on the security lock. The elevator stopped between floors. Outside the windowed wall, facing the dam, a steel safety bar crossed in front of the glass. Now all he had to do was get the gun away from her and kill her right there. It would be easy.

Venus held the gun at Gerald's back and said, "Raise your hands over your head."

He raised his hands. She said, "Turn around. Slowly."

Slowly, he began to turn, then made a sudden jerking motion. She saw it coming and tried moving back to avoid a hit, but the elevator was shallow, and now she was up against the back wall. He had jerked the gun out of her hand but had dropped it, and it lay between her legs on the elevator floor.

She stood toe-to-toe with the big guy. Over his shoulder, through the window, she could see police and federal agents swarming over the spillway, clearing out the crowds. She saw the president's limousines moving out, heading for safety.

She saw a helicopter churn into view. Chaos out there. In here, deadly silence.

Gerald said, "Too bad, Kay Lynn. You made a real good fire walker."

With one foot, he shoved the gun aside and lunged at her. He held her pinned against the wall, watching her eyes, looking for vulnerability, but he saw none. All right, then, if she wanted to be tough, he'd make it tough on her. He slugged her in the gut. She doubled over, and when she did, she reached for the gun, but he struck a hard blow to the back of her neck and she fell, nearly striking the detonator.

The elevator had stopped too far above the spillway for anyone to see inside. They scuffled, but no one noticed. He threw her against the wall again and she kicked him away. But he grabbed the gun and now held it against her head. It was her own gun, and he was going to kill her with her own bullet.

She could feel his breath, his hard panting. She could feel the cold round circle at her temple, and some repetitive childhood prayer nattered in her brain. Then she saw the eagle.

A magnificent bald eagle had landed on the safety bar outside the elevator window. In its golden beak, the eagle gripped a small salmon, still wriggling, still fighting for its life.

She jutted her chin and said, "Eagle."

That startled him, just for an instant threw him off. That instant was all she needed. She wrapped her leg around his injured one, jerked hard.

He yowled and his hand lost its grip on the gun. She grabbed it. He moved in on her, pinning her back up against the rear wall. She had the gun, but she couldn't move her arms. Using the wall for leverage, she shoved him as hard as she could with one leg.

He fell backward into the elevator window, and just as it shattered, the eagle dropped its prey and took flight. The big guy fell five stories down into the spillwaters of Grand Coulee Dam. He landed near the rotating blades of a giant turbine, but he never knew that.

She knelt over the cell phone detonator. On its digital clock, the time was nine seconds before ignition.

How to turn it off?

Eight seconds. Seven. Six.

What if "off" meant "on"?

Five. Four. Three.

She pressed "off."

Nothing happened. Just ominous stillness and the distant churning of helicopter blades. The device blinked once then went off, its digital clock numerals disappeared and the screen went blank.

With two seconds to spare.

THIRTY-ONE

REVOS MAN, playboy of the Emerald City, looked up at the gray clouds. What secrets hid behind this woolly sky? Song, a native, knew, but how many strangers to this land would guess, let alone understand, the region's secret yearnings?

Deep in the native psyche bubbled secessionist schemes, secret Canadian fantasies, profound beliefs in misplaced borders. Every true native knows that Canada's natural border runs along the banks of the Columbia River. Washington State should never have been invented. It's Canada, no matter how hard it tries to be part of the United States. The Pig War had screwed up the natural boundary lines.

Standing near the office windows, Song watched Puget Sound's rippling surface segue from stark reflective gray to deep charcoal, coordinating perfectly with the changing sky. White gulls chased across the vastness, avian calligraphy spelling out imminent rainfall. Song watched as raindrops skittered down the windowpane. First it came gently, in fine, feathery drops that fell slantwise against the glass. Streetlights blinked on. The gulls screeched and flew out to welcome the storm. Song was buttoning his raincoat when the wind kicked up suddenly, rattling the windows. A nor'wester no meteorologist had predicted came in fast, furious, determinedly.

On the way out, he popped his head inside Venus's new office, the one with windows, and said, "See you at three p.m. sharp?"

"Righto."

Driving up First Avenue, the street slick with new rain,

Song entered Belltown, made a left turn on Broad, and headed for the waterfront. The rain fell harder and the wind picked up. At Western and Broad, he waited for a green go signal. The traffic-light box blew violently, horizontal, like the wind tunneling uphill from Elliott Bay. Song was first in line at the light, and when it turned green, he shot across the intersection, landing a parking spot in front of Pier 69. Struggling against the howler, he fed the meter and headed south along the waterfront to Pier 54.

She had promised to meet him here at exactly three o'clock. They were to meet at the entrance to Ye Olde Curiosity Shoppe. Song had selected the meeting place because he wanted to show her something inside the shop. He had come early, just to make sure the thing he wanted to show her was still on display. The time was now 2:40. Song ducked inside the shop's entrance. As soon as he saw her coming, he'd duck back out into the rain, fake stalwartness.

On the forty-third floor of the Bumbershoot Building, Olson sat behind his desk, counting the years, months, weeks, days, hours, minutes and...there...seconds until his retirement date. When he had absorbed the depressing results, he rose wearily and padded down the hall to inquire how the Firecracker liked her new office. It was these little things that made life worthwhile.

Olson chortled to himself.

Venus had captured the Columbia River bombers, and therefore she had earned her private office with windows. Olson had done his homework, and he had selected her new office, had even arranged for her belongings to be moved into the new space before she had returned from eastern Washington. Yes indeed, Olson was a man of his word.

Now Olson stood beside Venus at the windows in her own private office.

"Gad," she said, gazing out at the rainfall. "Just imagine what this view will be like during a sun break."

"Hmm," Olson replied noncommittally.

Something in the cadence, something slightly acidic, rode Olson's monosyllabic grunt. She didn't like how it sounded. She waited for him to say something else, and when he didn't, she said, "This is a corner office."

"Hmm."

"When you promised me an office with windows, I hardly expected one of the prime spaces. You've been most generous, sir."

He placed a hand on her shoulder. "Enjoy," he said, smirking in a decidedly nasty manner. "Enjoy." Then he went away, leaving her to enjoy alone.

At her desk, Venus opened Darla's diary file.

"Mabel Fobia told me that she is my grandmother. Grandmother Mabel also informed me that President Benson is my father, and that my real mother was named Moonbeam, and that she was a gentle creature who loved every living thing, including me. Grandmother Mabel told me the following about Sue Ann."

Venus scrolled down to the last entry, the one she had hoped to find. Darla had titled this section, "The Conspiracy."

In the early 1980's, the Reverend went back to his seminary studies. Eventually, he became pastor at Kettle Falls First Methodist. That left Sue Ann and the Judge. But soon after the Reverend left, the Judge graduated from law school and flew off to Washington, D.C., to join the establishment. He had politics in his heart and an uncle who was a senator. The Judge actually bragged to Sue Ann that one day he'd become president of the United States. And then he did just that.

Wild Woman was livid. First of all, she had always been in love with the Judge. When he and Moonbeam had their baby, Wild Woman was infuriated. Secondly, perhaps more important, Sue Ann truly believed in the cause. She was convinced that restoring the river was as easy as blowing up the dams on it. On the day Barry Benson flew off to Washington, D.C., Sue Ann Sullivan made a firewalk vow to carry out the bombings the Free Spirits had planned. Maybe the Reverend and the Judge couldn't manage to pull off a successful bombing, but Sue Ann would show them she could do it.

As a child, growing up with Sue Ann as my mom, I got to know her pretty well. I never knew about the past, never heard her mention anything about it. The plan to blow up Grand Coulee Dam wasn't an all-consuming obsession. I think the idea was more of a nattering voice that occasionally injected itself into her vintner's wife mind-set, taunting her, challenging her, reminding her that once upon a time she had been somebody, and that somebody had fire-walked to seal a pact with coconspirators. Because I remember one thing. I remember that the bottoms of Sue Ann's feet were scarred all over, and she always had trouble with her feet.

I don't know how Sue Ann and Gerald first got together. Maybe through fire walking up in the Cascades. Gerald told me there are lots of fire walkers. They meet in secrecy, in the forests, and fire-walk together. Maybe that's where they met.

I feel certain that Sue Ann sent Gerald to Astoria to use me in their scheme. After my stepdad caught her rifling the vineyard funds, he kept closer watch on the books. But Sue Ann needed money to finance her dam-bombing plans. She knew I worked in a bank. She sent Gerald to that bank to seduce me, and I inadvertently told Gerald the best time to blow out the bank wall, when the week's cash was stored in the vault.

Darla had added a postscript. "I don't know who Gerald is, or where he comes from. Maybe Sue Ann knows, but I don't think so. Gerald is an enigma that I can't solve."

VENUS SET ASIDE Darla's diary. Outside her office windows, the storm had hit hard. The view might not be much now, she told herself, but just wait. When the clouds cleared and the sun came out, this view would knock the socks off even the most jaded native. But no use in standing around waiting for the next sun break. They came when they came, and anyway, she had an appointment with the playboy. She glanced once over her shoulder at the windows, then locked up and went to the elevators.

Halfway down, on the nineteenth floor, Miss Delicious entered the cold steel box. Just the two of them, riding nineteen floors to the ground. This afternoon, Miss Delicious wore jewel tones. Formfitting jade Chanel suit, the skirt hem falling somewhere between knee and navel, closer to navel. Patterned jade stockings. You could see the garters pressing through the fabric of her skirt. Manolo Blahnik pumps in a shade of ocher. Her long raven hair was pulled up and clipped with precision carelessness at the nape of her neck, where a few hundred strings of pearls competed futilely for attention against her alabaster skin.

Just to fill the uncomfortable silence, Venus said, "How's it going?"

Miss Delicious glanced over at Venus and attempted a smile. Instead, when her eyes met Venus's, Miss Delicious went all limp and the bombshell actually blushed as she said, "Would you...would you...I mean, maybe we could, well, have a cup of coffee? There's something I have to say to you."

The elevator had touched ground. Venus followed Miss Delicious to the nearest SBC stand, treated herself and the bombshell to mocha javas. They found a couple of chairs in a corner, and after rearranging her miniskirt, Miss Delicious poured out her heart. Half an hour later, Venus glanced at her Swatch and saw the time—3:13. Holy bananas, as Darla would say.

THIRTY-TWO

SONG WAS STILL waiting, but the frown below the Revos wasn't pretty. They ducked out of the rain into Ye Olde Curiosity Shoppe. Song let her to the back of the shop, past sundry weird souvenirs. In a dark corner, where stood a dusty stuffed carcass of a two-headed calf, Song pulled her against him and kissed her hard and long.

"Why here?" she asked. "This is a curious place to be kissed."

Song explained. "When I was ten years old, I came in here one summer day to check out the weirdness. Back here, in this corner, I saw a little girl with yellow hair and green eyes. She was probably about six years old, but very small, very fragile. She was all alone back here. The same stuffed two-headed calf was here in this corner. The little girl had placed her head between the calf's two heads and was looking out at me with these green eyes. I said to myself, Boy, is this little girl geeky-freaky or what?

"Her family was all up front. She was all alone back here, and she liked it that way, just her and the two-headed calf. She was talking to the calf, first to one head, then to the other. I remember she said, 'Now you two must learn to get along.'

"I remember she had on a white shirt with ducks embroidered on the collar, and a pair of striped clam-diggers. You know, those little abbreviated Capri things? Thongs on her feet. Green, as I recall."

Venus stared at Song.

"She was weird all right," Song continued. "And I fell instantly in love with that little girl. Then she looked straight at me and said, 'Kiss me, sailor.' But before I could kiss her, her dad took her away, and I never saw her again."

Venus blinked. A synaptic stew boiled up a memory, vague, but certain. The two-headed calf suddenly looked familiar. But she mistrusted recovered memory, memory by suggestion. Song might be playing games. Changing the subject, she said, "Bet you'll never guess who just shared coffee and intimate secrets with me."

"Oh God, don't tell me. Dottie."

"Not Dottie. Try again."

Song thought about it, then said, "I've got it. Darla, the swan girl."

"Darla's still on the lam. No one has seen her since the morning of the rally."

"Think she's still alive?"

Venus said, "I honestly don't know."

"He killed her," said Song. "Had to. She knew just about everything."

"Still, I'm not sure," said Venus. "Now, your last guess, then I might tell you."

Song worked over his close shave; snapped his fingers, and said, "Aha. This time I know I've got it right. Miss Delicious."

"Correct."

Song leaned in close. "So, out with it. What's the elevator bombshell's most intimate secret?"

She said, "Miss Delicious has a terrific crush on a certain member or our team."

Song stared. "But she's not hereto, right?"

Venus shrugged. Noncommittally.

Song thought it over, then said, "This is easy. She's in love with you."

Venus scratched her collarbone. It always itched when she withheld vital information. "Bingo," she said, trusting her split-second decision to withhold the truth. Anyway, Song didn't need another lady friend. She'd tell him later. When hell froze.

Song's brash hands reached underneath her jacket and were phasing into an exploratory grope when a hard finger tapped his shoulder. Song turned around. The shopkeeper glared, jerked a thumb at the door, and snarled, "You two Lookie-Loos, scram."

On the street, Song took her hand and they walked to the pier and gazed down into murky green Elliot Bay. "Did Olson tell you the news?" Song asked casually.

"What news?"

"About the new building going up just west of the Bumbershoot?"

"Go on," she said, dreading the inevitable. "Tell me more."

Song said, "You didn't expect your water view to last forever, did you?"

"What about view-protection laws? What about height restrictions? Isn't a view sacred anymore?"

"This is Oz, sweetheart. Views come and go. Within three months, that view you just scored will be obliterated by a new high-rise building. Construction's already begun. I believe they are calling it Elliot Pointe, with an *e*."

Seething, she said, "How long has Olson known about this?"

"Eight, maybe nine months. Definitely before he gave you the view windows."

"I'm moving. Far away."

Song placed a comforting arm around her shoulders. "Sure. Like a fish could live out of water. Hell, you'll never leave Oz. You're like the wild salmon, part of the ecological balance, a true native. You couldn't survive without slugs and such. Besides, I need you, even more than I need the wild salmon."

"Speaking of which…I'm hungry," she said. "Let's hit Ivar's and order that salmon special."

"Pucker up those fish lips, cannibal."

"Fish don't have—say, by the way, I've been meaning to ask you something."

Song knew what she wanted to ask. He held up his right hand. "On my honor," he said, "nothing happened."

"We didn't…make love?"

"Nope," he said. He made a kissing sound with his lips and added, "Not yet."

LUDMILLA, queen of the beavers, waited until the laser light show on Grand Coulee Dam had ended for the night. When the people had gone away and no brighter light than the full moon fell across the Ludmilla family dam, Ludmilla made her way across the beaver dam and plopped into the reservoir. Her fur glistened silver as she swam through the moonstruck water, and when she reached the big dam, a dam bigger than any damn troop of beavers had ever dreamed of, Ludmilla scampered up an earthen bank and down the paved spillway until she reached the halfway point. There, Ludmilla shook out her fur and thumped her tail rhythmically.

It wasn't long before she heard Bob coming up the opposite bank, then skittering across the pavement in her direction. When suddenly Bob Beaver appeared before her in a cold shaft of moonlight and their eyes met, Ludmilla knew without a doubt that the territorial wars weren't over. Bob and Ludmilla would have to train their offspring well, and hope that the wild salmon returned, because without the wild salmon, nobody could live along this river, not even a beaver.

Bob led Ludmilla across the spillway. The queen did not dare look back toward her home, for now she must go with Bob and make a home with him on the other side of the river. Bob led Ludmilla down the side of the concrete spillway, past the roaring turbines, along the dam's earthen side, where the concrete met the riverbank, and here Bob paused to let Ludmilla see his workplace. Then Bob did a strange thing.

Instead of turning south toward Inchelum, Bop led Ludmilla into a hole in the earth and through a long tunnel, and when they emerged, Ludmilla saw that they were on the upper side of the big dam, very near her own home. Then Bob dived deep down into the reservoir, and Ludmilla followed, and the two beavers swam side by side below the floodwaters, down among the denizens. First, they visited the House of Coho, then the House of Pink, the Chum, Sockeye, and, finally, Chinook. In each of the salmon houses, Bob and Ludmilla saw salmon aborning, renewed by the spirit of their ancestors. Ludmilla had never seen anything like this before, and she marveled at Bob's knowledge of the river's secrets.

Bob swam farther upriver, past the Ludmilla family dam, and Ludmilla swam beside him, fascinated by the new world Bob had opened up for her. Before long, Ludmilla heard a beautiful sound, the sound of water crashing over rocks, and before her eyes appeared the most glorious waterfall. Bob climbed up out of the water, and Ludmilla followed, and they stood side by side on the crest of the waterfall and thrilled to the spray that rose and washed their faces in fine mist.

IN NEW YORK CITY, Avery Fisher Hall was sold out and there was standing room only when Echo approached center stage to wild applause. When the critics and admirers had ceased whistling and cheering, silence fell over the audience as they eagerly awaited the first public reading of this MacArthur genius's salmon poetry.

Looking as magnificent as ever, Echo arranged her clingy black gown into a dramatic ripple around her tiny feet, then lifted her voice and spewed forth her latest piscine inspiration:

"Sleek / silver / salmon
Cast your caffeinated eyes

Upon Human rods
And artificial flies
Anglers after
Your / diseased / flesh
Scale no memory
Of Your / Pink / Youth

"In that crystalline eddy
Where you hatched
Where you fed
Upon your ancestors
Flesh
House of Sockeye

Smolt
Fingerling
River Runner / Oceaneer
O Sleek / Silver
Salmon
Last Wild Salmon
Come Home...."

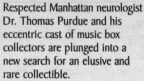

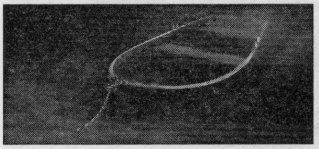

M. K. PRESTON
A CHANTALENE MYSTERY

Chantalene Morrell returns to rural
Oklahoma to answer the haunting
questions of her past. Twelve years
earlier, her father had been lynched for
a crime he didn't commit, and shortly
after, her mother disappeared without
a trace. Now Chantalene is determined
to pursue the shadow figures that haunt
her dreams—to unmask the men who
destroyed her family.

But it seems someone has already begun
pursuing vengeance for her as one by one,
the men she suspects are brutally murdered.

Unfortunately, Chantalene is
the primary suspect.

*Nominated for the
Mary Higgins Clark
Award*

PERHAPS
SHE'LL DIE

*Available
August 2002
at your favorite
retail outlet.*

W⊕RLDWIDE LIBRARY®